PRAISE FOR WILLIAM DEVERELL

Needles
"Deverell has a narrative style so lean that scenes and characters seem to explode on the page. He makes the evil of his plot breathtaking and his surprises like shattering glass." — *Philadelphia Bulletin*

High Crimes
"Deverell's lean mean style gives off sparks. A thriller of the first rank." — *Publishers Weekly*

Mecca
"Here is another world-class thriller, fresh, bright, and topical." — *Globe and Mail*

The Dance of Shiva
"The most gripping courtroom drama since *Anatomy of a Murder*." — *Globe and Mail*

Platinum Blues
"A fast, credible, and very funny novel." — *The Sunday Times*

Mindfield
"Deverell has a fine eye for evil, and a remarkable sense of place." — *Globe and Mail*

Kill All the Lawyers
"An indiscreet and entertaining mystery that will add to the author's reputation as one of Canada's finest mystery writers." — *The Gazette*

Street Legal: The Betrayal
"Deverell injects more electricity into his novels than anyone currently writing in Canada — perhaps anywhere . . . The dialogue crackles, the characters live and breathe, and the pacing positively propels."
— *London Free Press*

Trial of Passion
"A ripsnortingly good thriller." — *Regina Leader-Post*

Slander
"*Slander* is simply excellent: a story that just yanks you along."
— *Globe and Mail*

The Laughing Falcon
"*The Laughing Falcon* is, simply, a wonderful book." — *Vancouver Sun*

Mind Games
"Deverell is firing on all cylinders." — *Winnipeg Free Press*

April Fool
"A master storyteller with a wonderful sense of humour . . . one hell of a ride." — *Quill & Quire*

Whipped
"[A] smart, funny, and cleverly plotted series." — *Toronto Star*

Kill All the Judges
"Compelling. . . . For all its seemingly lighthearted humour, this is a work of great depth and complexity." — *Globe and Mail*

Snow Job
"Fine writing and tongue-in-cheek delivery with acid shots at our political circus, and so close to reality that it seems even funnier."
— *Hamilton Spectator*

ALSO BY WILLIAM DEVERELL

FICTION

Needles
High Crimes
Mecca
The Dance of Shiva
Platinum Blues
Mindfield
Kill All the Lawyers
Street Legal: The Betrayal
Trial of Passion
Slander
The Laughing Falcon
Mind Games
April Fool
Whipped
Kill All the Judges
Snow Job
I'll See You in My Dreams
Sing a Worried Song
Stung

NON-FICTION

A Life on Trial

THE LONG-SHOT TRIAL

AN ARTHUR BEAUCHAMP THRILLER

WILLIAM DEVERELL

Published by ECW Press
665 Gerrard Street East
Toronto, Ontario, Canada M4M 1Y2
416-694-3348 / info@ecwpress.com

Cover design: David A. Gee

LIBRARY AND ARCHIVES CANADA CATALOGUING IN PUBLICATION

Title: The long-shot trial / William Deverell.

Names: Deverell, William, 1937- author.

Description: Series statement: An Arthur Beauchamp thriller

Identifiers: Canadiana (print) 20230561349 | Canadiana (ebook) 20230561357

ISBN 978-1-77041-754-0 (softcover)
ISBN 978-1-77852-279-6 (ePub)
ISBN 978-1-77852-280-2 (PDF)

Subjects: LCGFT: Thrillers (Fiction) | LCGFT: Novels.

Classification: LCC PS8557.E8775 L66 2024 | DDC C813/.54—dc23

This book is funded in part by the Government of Canada. *Ce livre est financé en partie par le gouvernement du Canada.* We acknowledge the support of the Canada Council for the Arts. *Nous remercions le Conseil des arts du Canada de son soutien.* We acknowledge the funding support of the Ontario Arts Council (OAC), an agency of the Government of Ontario. We also acknowledge the support of the Government of Ontario through the Ontario Book Publishing Tax Credit, and through Ontario Creates.

Canada Council   Conseil des arts
for the Arts   du Canada

Canadä

PRINTED AND BOUND IN CANADA   PRINTING: MARQUIS   5   4   3   2   1

The Trials of
Arthur Beauchamp:
A Biography
by Wentworth Chance

Foreword to the second edition

Though some will attribute the first edition's success to the legal fireworks that followed its publication, I prefer to believe it quickly sold out because I pulled no punches. It was the frankness — the nakedness, as one reviewer put it — that drove sales. Readers found Arthur Beauchamp[1] to be warmly human when stripped down to his many quirks and failings.

Happily, this new edition afforded me a chance to amplify Chapter Three, "A Will to Die For," adding content (newly unearthed) and thickening the fog of mystery surrounding a spectacular murder trial in a remote community in the Canadian far north.

The case of Regina v. Angelina Santos *is still much debated today, and popular articles have been written about it. Regrettably, my earlier acknowledgements failed to mention a series about the trial that I found in back issues of the now-defunct magazine* Saturday Night. *Crime reporter Charles Loobie did an astounding job of reportage, and I was so transfixed upon reading it that I may have unconsciously replicated several passages. Mr. Loobie is to be*

---

1   Pronounced Beech'm, in the English way.

assured that I have revised those, as well as various other bits that suffered from coincidental phrasing.

This new addition also affords me the luxury of correcting various errors and omissions that escaped the sharp-eyed appraisal of two editors and a lawyer.

As well, I am pleased to have the opportunity of complying with BC Supreme Court Directive 10967-20. I regret having described divorce attorney Harvey Frinkell as having drunk himself to death. That was false, and the error, which appeared in the section titled "Where the Squamish River Flows," has been corrected. I apologize fulsomely to Mr. Frinkell, who is a healthy, active eighty-three-old whose lively correspondence with me proves he hasn't lost his litigious verve.

Readers will notice significant changes in the cover design: the static facial profile of Beauchamp has given way to a Star Weekly photograph from 1967, depicting my biographee barrelling angrily from the old Vancouver courthouse after a scrap with a judge. As well, I have shortened the title to simply: The Trials of Arthur Beauchamp. Too many read A Thirst for Justice as mocking him for his drinking problem. As far as I'm aware he hasn't tasted alcohol since 1987, and for that he deserves applause. Cheers, Arthur!

However, I remain saddened that the subject of this biography found fault with it and am distressed by the coolness he has shown me. I wouldn't call it a rift, but Beauchamp has blocked my emails. I sought to assure him that the section heading "Lion of the Courtroom, Lamb in the Bedroom" was intended not to be cruel (as I've heard it alleged) but tender, showing a soft yang to his fighting yin. In deference to the renowned barrister I have reworked several passages he considered "inappropriate."

The feeling that washed over me when I finished those changes was not so much relief as freedom: I was free of the great man's scowling countenance. I stopped caring what he thought of my opus. Did Boswell care what Johnson thought?

Wentworth Chance,
North Vancouver, BC

Arthur — February 2022

I 've planned a lazy Sunday, puttering in my potting shed, then enjoying a slow ramble through the cold, wintry woods with my best friend. Afterwards, I will towel him off and park him at my feet, where he generously serves as a rug, albeit furry and alive: Ulysses, the Irish wolfhound. I will then settle into my club chair with the Goldberg Variations and a good book.

Everything goes as planned except for the good book. I've just finished a gripping literary thriller partly set on these very Gulf Islands. Its sequel is on order. I'm hooked, hungry to know if the hapless hero will ever get a grip on his auditory hallucinations. I'm reluctant to begin another book before *You Talkin' to Me?* shows up at Garibaldi's post office.

I'm in my so-called private study, seeking a thin book of poetry to tide me over — one of the moderns for a change, Auden, Yeats, Belloc — when I notice a gift-wrapped, book-sized parcel on my desk, leaning against the computer screen. "To Arthur, my love," reads the heart-shaped card pinned to a gay red ribbon. Signed "M." Short for Margaret, last name Blake, i.e., my wife — or, as she prefers, in the lexicon of the woke Left, life companion.

And of course I have completely forgot that this is Valentine's Day. I'm shattered — I have nothing for Margaret. She must have sneaked the parcel into the room on returning from her invasive species workshop. I turn to respond to a soft "Ahem" — she's at my open door, eyebrows arched, faintly smiling.

"I'm embarrassed," I say. "The occasion slipped my famously absent mind. I have no gift to offer but the consuming love I shall hold for you for all eternity."

She kisses me. "You bullshitter. You won't be so sucky after you open it."

I peel off the gift wrap, and when the book is revealed I realize my mischievous wife is teasing me with a joke gift: the second edition of Wentworth Chance's unspeakably prying biography of Arthur Ramsgate Beauchamp, QC, OC, hon. LLD.

The cover of the first edition had profiled my lordly Roman nose. The publisher must have decided it scared off readers, because the restyled image is a news photo of youthful me dashing down the steps of a courthouse, black robes flying.

The title has been reworked as well. *The Trials of Arthur Beauchamp* is in a large, flashy font. The new edition is also thicker. A diagonal banner reads: *NEW MATERIAL!*

The Trials of
Arthur Beauchamp

Excerpt from Chapter Three,
"A Will to Die For" © *W. Chance*

It was 1966, he was twenty-nine, and though not much was happening in his personal life he had a thriving practice at Tragger, Inglis, Bullingham, mostly in narcotics trafficking, but also thefts, frauds, and assaults, while indulging in what his firm considered a bad habit: working pro bono for the poor.

Beauchamp was a grinder but more had been expected of him — his seniors feared he was not ready for another go at the prime-time offence of homicide. His confidence had been shattered four years earlier, when, as a supposed rising star, he was entrusted with representing a bright, rebellious Salishan accused of murdering his white mentor.[2]

He felt an overwhelming remorse and an enduring sense of shame after his young client was sentenced to a lengthy penitentiary term. Arthur's alcohol intake crept higher. He had little social life. He felt friendless, particularly as regards the opposite sex.

Still, Beauchamp carried on doggedly in the criminal courts, though with only one notable case — the successful defence of Nick "the Owl" Faloon, a diamond heist. Over the following two years he slowly regained a sense of competence,

---

2 This fascinating case is related in *I'll See You in My Dreams*, ECW Press.

besting the Federal Crown on several narcotics indictments. In 1966 he was co-counsel in a controversial conspiracy case against the d'Anglio family that entangled Vancouver's mayor and three city councillors.

By that year he had built a fair clientele of professional criminals, and — to the delight of the firm's grasping senior partners — was earning healthy fees. They were impressed enough, as of the fall of that year, to offer Beauchamp another shot at a murder.

Arthur —
February 2022

I 've tried to will my Valentine's gift into non-existence, but I'm being stalked by the ghost of my biographer. Wentworth's book keeps showing up on my bedside table or in the parlour or the toilet's reading rack: Margaret's continuing prank. I keep opening it at random, and invariably get riled at the slights and errors and exaggerations.

My extravagant return gift to Margaret is the honouring of an oft-repeated vow: to clean out an abandoned otters' den beneath our old waterfront cabin. There is nothing in nature that smells with such repellent gusto as an otters' nest, with its faeces, rotting fish tails, frog guts, and other forms of decomposing offal.

Three months ago, I contracted with the infamous island handyman Robert Stonewell, alias Stoney, to take on the task. His mantra, when reminded about his promise to jump to it, is a fervent "No problem."

To shame him, I have put the job out for tenders, with a notice in the *Island Bleat*. No one has answered. Frustrated, unaided, I now have to prove my manly worth to Margaret, who complains I leave it up to others (meaning herself, usually) to do the nasty chores.

It's raining as I stride up the beach to Blunder Point: a stunning headland, with views of the Salish Sea, east, south, and west. The cabin, perched on a low bank just above high tide, is embraced by the gracefully twisting boughs of a giant arbutus.

The cabin is twenty feet by thirty of cedar logs and shakes, with a narrow wooden staircase to a loft. It was built by hippies in the 1960s, before my time on Garibaldi. It has a sturdy woodstove but no electricity — the nearest power pole is 300 metres away — and no plumbing, though water is piped from our well. There's also an outhouse. We use the cabin mostly for storage, but hardy young guests often bunk in its bunk bed.

Ulysses romps ahead, apparently eager to help. But wolfhounds, who move with grace when on foot, were not built to crawl under a two-foot gap beneath a log cabin. So alone in my Carhartts and Wellingtons, armed with rubber gloves, a mask, a flashlight, and a metal rake, I spend two hours wiggling and squirming in and out, gagging and cursing. Even Ulysses can't stand the smell of me.

The never-ending trials of Arthur Beauchamp . . .

A treasured new addition to our cluster of structures on Blunder Bay Farm is a wood-fired sauna, and I spend an hour within it and, intermittently, under a cold outdoor shower, soaping away the otter goop.

Clothes-free, barefoot, and lobster-red, I race the fifty metres to the house, and within minutes I am supine in a robe on a couch with a mug of tea at hand, enjoying Hilaire Belloc's rousing rhymes and rhythms. I have earned this.

Then, suddenly, that damn biography by Wentworth Chance settles onto my groin, opened to Chapter Three. Margaret looks far too serious to be ribbing me, even as I respond with a carefree recital from "Tarantella": "'Do you remember an Inn, Miranda? Do you remember the fleas that tease in the High Pyrenees, and the wine that tasted of tar?'"

That elicits no laughter, not a smile.

"I just read that chapter," Margaret says sternly. "'A Will to Die For.' I'm pretty broad-minded, but . . . rollicking about with women for hire? You? The socially shy and awkward Arthur Beauchamp? My God, taking on two at a time!"

I gulp. "Is that in it?"

"If you don't demand a retraction, I'm going to believe it's true." She marches from the room.

"God help me," I mutter, a plaintive plea to the Spirit in the sky.

His/Her answer comes quickly: Tell your own version, Beauchamp. Be not afraid of the truth. Yes, Wentworth Chance has likely penned a garbled version of the Angelina Santos case by, as he put it in his foreword, *thickening the fog of mystery surrounding a spectacular murder trial in the Canadian far north.* "NEW MATERIAL!" he shouted. From what source? Who has tattled? Who retains a mind lucid enough to recall a capital murder trial in 1966, with its twists and riddles and sworn secrets?

Be not afraid of the truth. That command blossoms into something like a resolve — and to tell the truth the notion of composing a memoir of the most significant trial of my career has smouldered since my retirement from the law. Yes, I've often entertained an image of Arthur Beauchamp pecking away at a keyboard, the reclusive pipe-smoking island author, keeper of dark confidences, of privileged confessions. Aware of my initiative, barristers would shudder in gowning rooms, judges in their chambers.

And of course there is now the matter of rehabilitating my reputation — the awkward episode with the two sex workers, a preamble to *Regina v. Santos*, must be put in proper context.

I will need a writing studio, of course. Away from distractions of phone and radio and internet and the hustle and bustle of the enviropolitical pursuits of a former Member of Parliament and Green Party leader who happens to be my life companion.

I hear the cabin at Blunder Point calling: *Choose me! Choose me!*

The following day arrives crisply cold but sunny, and though we're a month away from spring, clumps of snowdrops bloom under the pear tree, along with a few bravely flowering crocuses.

I am eager to get started on my new venture — Arthur Beauchamp as true-crime author — and my first task is to attack the cabin with mops and brooms and cleaning supplies. I lug these in a wheelbarrow; there's no road access.

Ulysses accelerates, picking up either a smell or a sight of something interesting. When I push my barrow into the cabin's weedy yard I'm taken aback to see Stoney standing there, frowning in thought, a limp joint hanging from the corner of his lips, his Covid mask hanging loose from one ear.

"Something's wrong here," he says, apparently to me, as he kneels and peers under the floor beams. He shouts: "Any luck?"

"Nope." The voice of Stoney's laconic accomplice, known locally as Dog.

Stoney straightens up, a skinny, long-haired scarecrow in a beaver hat with earmuffs. He and Dog have somehow become immovable fixtures in the furniture of my life on Garibaldi, Stoney wily and lazy, Dog providing muscle and a generous spirit. Both had caught the Covid virus, both sailed through it: maybe as a result of overdosing on pot and Lucky Lager.

"For the record, boss, I am here, with Dog as my witness, pursuant to our agreement to muck out the otter's den that you been griping about like it's a planetary cat-ass-trophy. I saw your ad for help, and frankly it felt like a betrayal to your oldest friend on this island that you let some scab encroacher undercut me, thus rendering you in breach of contract. The bottom line is you owe compensation to Dog and me for the day we set aside."

Through some form of telepathy, this schemer, having divined the smelly deed had been done, decided it was safe to show up. I try to out-lawyer him.

"If there were a contract, Stoney, it would fail because of laches. That's a legal term for unreasonable delay."

Dog, who has the build of a granite boulder, squeezes out, pulls off goggles and hardhat, rises to his full five feet, three inches. Ulysses is quick to join him for some roughhousing — they love each other, Dog and dog.

"Happily, gentlemen, your day will not be wasted." I draw their attention to the wheelbarrow and its contents, and explain their intended uses. "Fair compensation will be paid."

Stoney balks. "Whoa. We're being asked to scrub and dust? I'm afraid that ain't part of my personal work ethic. Not sounding sexist, which I'm proudly not, but cleaning is generally accepted as ladies' work. Them two hotties from Mop'n'Chop, that's who you want. Only drawback is they overcharge too much."

In Stoney-speak, that's a bid to start haggling. Ultimately, agreement is reached, with a bonus for lugging my ancient oak desk up to the cabin. I carry the typewriter, an old upright Underwood that faithfully served me in decades past.

Tomorrow I shall start page one with this tentative title: *DEFENCELESS: THE TRIAL OF ANGELINA SANTOS*. The case goes back fifty-six years, but I need not command my memory to speak, to use a Nabokovian allusion, because gathering dust in the vaults of my old Vancouver law firm are its transcripts. *Defenceless* will write itself.

▶

Mysteriously, by the end of the workday, a twelve-pack of beer appears, several cans already empty. I politely reject Stoney's offer of a full one — he stubbornly refuses to believe I haven't had a drink since 1987.

Stoney and Dog pop open their cans of Lucky Lager, and we watch an orange sunset from under the boughs of the majestic arbutus. The *Arbutus menziesii* — known in the northwest States by the lovely name of madrone — is surely the temperate world's most beautiful tree, all loops and swirls, russet skin and shiny leaves and ever green.

Stoney catches me admiring it. "You wanna say sayonara to this tree, eh, before it swallows the cabin and you in it." He crushes a beer can for emphasis. A loud hiss as another is opened.

I explain to this nature illiterate that this is a magical tree, to be worshipped, a beautiful bejewelled goddess of the forest. I don't mention the tree is of deep significance: I first made love to Margaret under it. A momentous event that ended rather embarrassingly. Enough said.

Stoney persists: "You want that crookneck limb to come crashing through the shingles and crush you to death while you're only halfway through the biography of your life? — if that's your pleasure, go for it."

I make a scoffing sound, hiding the worry that he may be right — weighty arbutus limbs often break.

Stoney sizes up the hippie-crafted barrel stove, which gives off generous heat though it's a wood-gobbler. "You're gonna need another cord just to get through the winter and spring. I got a line on some dried fir and alder, plus Dog here famously wields a mighty chainsaw."

"We have plenty of fir and alder butts. I enjoy splitting wood." The truth is that I will want solitude when in the throes of creation.

"What do you say, Dog, can you see him writing a masterpiece with a twisted back?" Dog accepts that as rhetorical, merely shrugs.

"Also, maybe you wanna think about a solar panel or two — which I got a reliable source for, half-price, with a guarantee they ain't been stole — so you can avoid the fire risk of them propane lamps, and maybe run a small fridge and plug in your phone."

"After I settle in I will confer about these matters with my muse."

◆

"I hope this isn't some quixotic venture into self-discovery," Margaret says, as I prepare to leave for the cabin to embark on my late-life literary career.

"Nothing heavy, dear. My goals are merely to inform and entertain, while righting the wrongs that history wrote." It's ten a.m. I'm armed and eager. I stick a Thermos of coffee in my pack. A sandwich. A bone for Ulysses. A toilet roll for the outhouse.

"Righting what wrongs? You're sure this isn't some mission of vengeance? Wentworth was sued all over the place because of the people he maligned."

"Anyone about whom I might write harshly is gone." Chief Justice Wilbur Kroop who, at eighty-nine, was brought down by Covid-19.

"Nothing intimate about us, please. I don't want to read about how those kayakers came to shore after hearing us hollering our heads off like we were being attacked."

I was particularly loud, imploring Jesus Christ to save me. They caught us nakedly entwined under the madrone tree, orgasmically exhausted.

"And I may initiate divorce proceedings if I see any mention of Taba Jones."

An accomplished potter with whom I'd had an illicit encounter years ago. I was the seducee, though that didn't earn me a whit of forgiveness. Taba felt she was being frozen out of the Garibaldi community after Margaret came home in retirement, and rebuilt her business in Ontario.

"This isn't a full-blown memoir, darling. It's pre-us, in 1966, when I was pretending to be a city sophisticate and you were a topless teenage hippie with flowers in your hair."

She invariably rolls her eyes when I tease her about her back-to-the-land phase with Garibaldi's Earth Seed Commune. As if it's shameful, though I find it endearing.

"And the bacchanal with those two sex workers? Seriously, Arthur, can you imagine the sniggers and averted faces —"

"I'll handle it!" Too loud. I can't abide the helpless, self-pitying fool I become when quarrelling with the woman I love. I tamp it down, apologize, promise her the right to critique the final draft. We kiss and we hug and we laugh a little and we are fine again.

In the cabin, I start a fire. I adjust my chair. I roll a sheet of paper into my Underwood. I type: *Defenceless: The Trial of Angelina Santos* — that shall be my working title.

Now travel with me, dear reader, to the long ago . . .

1966 —
The Handoff

As of early fall in 1966, I had finally graduated from the fourteenth floor of our West Hastings bank building, where the toilers moiled, to a spacious office with a pair of windows on the fifteenth floor, where the barristers held court. Tragger, Inglis's associates and section heads occupied the sixteenth, partners the seventeenth. Above them was the roof, where pigeons ruled.

My windows once afforded spectacular views of Burrard Inlet and Stanley Park, until a posh new hotel noisily sprang up next door. Its upper floors and a rooftop cocktail lounge provided feeble compensation, though on a rainless day I could still make out a wedge of waterfront and a topping of North Shore mountains. The hotel, the Hastings Royal, became a favourite oasis for our solicitors, many of whom enjoyed adulterous liaisons in its rooms.

The better view was out my door, where perched my secretary, the shy and lovely Gertrude Isbister: twenty-three, sweetly smiling as she clacked away at her Selectric.

But that view was spoiled late on a Friday afternoon by the chief of the criminal division as he approached from across the secretarial pool: Alex Pappas, in his signature wear, a checked sports jacket with leather trim. Stout and short, with the wattles of an iguana.

I was expecting him for our regular week's end review of billings and disbursements. The door was open because I wanted him to see me watching him. Among the secretaries, Pappas was known as "Mister Hands." He liked to idly brush them against buttocks and breasts. I especially didn't like it when he touched Gertrude.

I went out to meet him, blocking his access to her, and directed him inside with a friendly grip on his leather-patched elbow. (The conversation that follows — indeed, all dialogue — is as best remembered.)

"A minor glitch this week," I said. "Willy Welger's cheque bounced."

"I told you, pal, get it up front."

"We're covered." I handed Pappas the $10,000 bail receipt, assigned to the firm.

"Once again you prove you're not as dumb as I assumed. What else?"

"Tony d'Anglio was pleased with how the extortion preliminary fell apart. Ten went into general for that, fifteen into trust for future services."

"He pay by cheque or cash?"

"Cash."

"Next time, you want to let me know when it's cash." In case that seemed ambiguous, he added, "It's already dirty money, they never want receipts."

Pappas had been a brazen pocketer of tax-free currency during his many years as a scrappy, loud-talking, top-earning criminal counsel. I didn't want to insult him by telling him I like to keep my hands clean. When he saw I wasn't interested in being corrupted, he just shrugged and said, "I got a nice, easy little murder for you."

I suddenly felt giddy, my heart pounding. Maybe there was an element of panic. I had yearned for a chance to redeem myself after an earlier flop, but was haunted by fear of failure, of screwing up. I was emotionally paralyzed at the thought of losing a client to the gallows and had vowed not to take another capital murder until the death penalty was rescinded. But in 1966 it was still on the books.

Yet I was weary of representing narcotics dealers and shakedown artists — there was no pride in that and little glory.

Pappas talked fast as I slid into my desk chair. "Up to you, Stretch. You got to stop kicking yourself over the Swift case. We put you in the starting lineup before you were ready. This one's almost too straightforward, a dinky little domestic shooting. As in, the domestic dropped her boss with a hunting rifle after he raped her. You want it? Otherwise, I'll give it to Shapiro."

I went briefly into Walter Mitty mode. Was this a chance to defend the honour of a housemaid in distress? That had a seductive appeal.

Pappas checked his watch. "Give me twenty minutes, and I'll see you in my office so you can look at the file. We can have a drink on it, then call it a day."

As Alex Pappas topped up my whisky glass with premium Scotch, talking non-stop, I realized I was being set up to fail. This dinky little homicide was a throwaway, a reject. Pappas had done a quick preliminary last week, decided it was a loser, and was trying to dump it off on me.

The media feasted on murders but I hadn't read anything about this case. Then it came to me that the two-day preliminary had opened September 12, the day of a provincial election. The case got buried under the return to power of the erratic right-wing Social Credit Party.

"Fort Thompson, it's up near the Yukon border. Fort Tom, they call it. Beautiful up there in the late fall. You may have to cop her out, but if you feel lucky, give manslaughter a shot, that counts as a win. Might get you associate status. I told Bullingham you're ready for the sixteenth floor."

Pappas seemed far too anxious to fob off this case. I wondered if he'd mismanaged his calendar, overbooked. Maybe he just didn't want to be stuck in Fort Tom for a week in November.

"The trial won't go for more than two, three days. Short and quick. Hell, one day if you cop a plea. Take the week off. You hunt? They got deer, elk, black bear. Cougar, you could bring home a trophy."

The transcript of the preliminary was unusually thin for a homicide. I wondered how much effort Pappas had put into it when he was not hunting for creatures to kill.

I glanced through the file summary. Four months ago, a local businessman, Frederick C. Trudd, was shot dead, with his own rifle, by his Filipina housemaid. Her claim to having been abused by him, if true, might win sympathy but would offer no defence in law.

"I won't try to kid you, pal, you got to accept Jesus as your saviour and pray Hail Mary. We have to make a pretense of trying to win, we been paid fifteen grand." A substantial sum in those days.

"A housemaid has come up with a fee that high?"

Pappas refilled my glass. "They're scrambling for more."

"Who?"

"The townspeople took up a collection."

"Could she be that popular?"

"The deceased was that unpopular. Angelina is her name. Angelina Santos. Twenty years old. Chewy little number, nice boobs, sweet disposition. Her only fault is that she took dead aim at an unarmed target from sixty feet away."

An unpopular deceased. Possibly a rapist. Would not a local jury be eager to find a reasonable doubt? "Any witnesses?"

"Nope. Just Angelina. She couldn't tell a lie."

But was the confession voluntary? I had won a few cases in which police overreached when taking statements. I took stock: why was I sitting there devising defences? Hadn't I sworn not to be a dumping ground for Pappas's losers?

Then I was hit with sudden insight: *Arthur Beauchamp, you are a craven coward. All your adult life, all through law school, you'd dreamed of being a great counsel, of taking on hope-less cases and turning them around. You were infected in high school, devouring biographies of the great counsel, Marshall Hall, Birkett, Darrow.*

Pappas topped me up as I leafed idly through the transcript. A sixteenth-floor office would be nice. So might the rank of associate, whatever that meant, other than a higher standard of living. What else might I exact from the earnest supplicant?

I looked up to see that the managing partner, Roy Bullingham, had invited himself in. The notorious skinflint was holding his accounts ledger. Bully, they called him on the seventeenth floor. On my floor, he was called Mr. Bullingham.

"Sorry to interrupt, gentlemen. Yes, I'll take a sip of that. A little soda, please, no ice." He declined the offer of a chair. He was tall and spare, a decorated officer of the Normandy invasion. (He remains a living presence as of this writing: a centenarian.)

Pappas chattered away as he attended at his slide-out bar behind the *Canadian Criminal Cases*. "Nice little bump this month, Bully, thanks in no small way to Beauchamp here. Twenty earned, fifteen more in trust."

I couldn't resist. "Numbers that are in no way commensurate with my monthly income, Mr. Bullingham."

"Yes, yes, I've been meaning to talk with you." For two years he'd been meaning to talk with me. I was earning eight hundred a month less deductions. I lived somewhat furtively in an illegal suite in Kitsilano. That wasn't sustainable — I needed to find a legal rental. My Beetle was in its death throes.

"I understand, Alex, that you now have the Macintosh homicide."

News to me. Herb Macintosh, a mining baron, was accused of stabbing his wife to death at their North Shore eyrie. The alleged weapon: a decorative Japanese sword. The West Coast was agog over it. Vancouver's pre-eminent counsel, Cyrus Smythe-Baldwin, had handled the preliminary inquiry.

"Macintosh didn't like Smythe-Baldwin," Pappas said. "Thought he had a snooty English-upper-class attitude. Wasn't getting bang for his bucks. I underbid Smitty. Not by much, but enough."

Bully checked a page of his ledger. "Yes, I noticed that. You quoted him a hundred thousand."

I was glad I was sitting, because I would have fallen. Ten times the usual rate for a projected one-week trial? (About $750,000 in today's dollars.) Could Alex Pappas possibly be worth that? Herb Macintosh was a tycoon, he didn't care, he wanted a sly lawyer not an honest one, maybe someone who wouldn't be bothered by the bribing of jurors. Macintosh was impetuous and headstrong, and I believed he'd made a mistake in dismissing Cyrus Smythe-Baldwin. Pappas was good, but not great, a headline-grabbing blowhard.

The Angelina Santos trial was set to start on November 21, the Macintosh trial two weeks later. Mystery solved: that's why Pappas was pawning Ms. Santos off on me. Having flaunted his courtroom prowess to Macintosh, he didn't dare risk taking on this doomed murder trial. In any event, Macintosh would blow his top if Pappas disappeared up north for a two-bit shooting just before his own costly defence.

"You'll need a capable junior," Bully said, as his eyes settled on me.

Pappas got the message, but stalled, taking a slow sip of whisky. Bully had a warm spot for me in his cold heart, but Pappas resented me for my string of wins. I think he felt threatened. I suspected then, and still do, that he was eager to see me wipe out in Fort Thompson. He would shed crocodile tears if Angelina Santos was sentenced to hang.

"Right," he said. "Perfect. This could work out, Stretch. You start poring through the transcripts of Macintosh's preliminary, then you can read the case law and brief the witnesses. Then you pop up to Fort Tom, look after Angelina, do what you have to do, and after she's sentenced we'll have another ten days to get ready for Macintosh's trial."

Pappas's plan worked for everyone but Angelina Santos. It wouldn't give me a lot of time to prepare for her. But playing a role in what Vancouver's excitable media called the Trial of the Century was tantalizing, irresistible. I got up, poured another, a last one. I was feeling it.

Bully frowned. "Can you handle that, Arthur? Might be confusing, two murders on the go."

What followed on my part was a slightly inebriated gut reaction. I felt challenged. Some reckless, obstinate pilot had taken over the helm, incautious about the shoals that loomed.

"I won't be your chore boy, Alex, or shine a chair. I want to do some of the key witnesses." Bully kept his eyes on me. Maybe he was sizing me up for the sixteenth floor.

Pappas shrugged. "Agreed."

"I'll have to shuffle some dates in Magistrate's Court. And move a marijuana importing that's set for December, County Court."

"I got an in with the feds," Pappas said. "I'll fix a new date for you."

"I'll need prep time for the Santos case, Alex. More than a few days."

He frowned. "It's not complex. There's no big cast of characters."

"I'm not going to plead her to murder, gentlemen. Or even manslaughter, if I see a glimmer of a chance of acquittal. If she goes down it won't be because I didn't fight for her." I can still hear my words, can see myself standing proud, in a whisky-induced state of naïve, youthful pomposity.

"That's the stuff," Pappas said. "That's what I want to hear. Guy's got balls like Sonny Liston." A pause. "Especially after a few double shots of whisky."

"Retainer's in on this Fort Thompson matter?" Bully asked, pausing on his way out.

"More juice can be squeezed," Pappas said, making a twisting gesture with his hand, as if squeezing an orange. To me: "Hang around, I'll lug over the Macintosh transcripts so your girl can make a copy."

I tottered out after Bully, and headed for the stairs with the Angelina Santos file. Angelina. What a lovely name.

1966 —
I Think I Shot Him

It was past five as I returned to my office, everyone having gone but Gertrude, in whose smiling face I exhaled alcohol fumes as I asked her to clear my calendar for two murder trials. Her eyes went large when I mentioned Herb Macintosh and told her she would be Xeroxing the files and the transcript of his preliminary inquiry. She raced off happily to share this exciting news with friends and family. Wealthy heiress slain by Samurai sword during wild party!

The Macintosh trial would be the delicious main course, after the homelier backwoods appetizer. But I fully intended to focus on the Santos case. I was pumped up with a sense of challenge that was probably enhanced, as Pappas insinuated, by the intake of high-proof spirits.

From the Santos file I pulled out several prints from an envelope of RCMP photos. Even in the mug shot Angelina looked pretty, front and side, despite her bedraggled hair. She also looked frightened, her eyes wide and bright and — to me, at least — shining with innocence.

A Kodachrome photo from 1965 showed her with a radiant smile, full-busted but slender-waisted, posing in a belted blue flower-print dress and a yellow hair ribbon. Emigrated from the Philippines two years earlier, at eighteen. Employed for almost a year by the deceased. Sent money home to her ailing mother.

The RCMP report was authored by Detectives Barnes and Biggs, Major Crimes, Prince George. The gist was this:

On Sunday, May 29, 1966, Frederick C. Trudd had just returned to his home from a business event in the Peace River region, when, after alighting from his Mercedes sedan outside the back-yard garage, he found himself looking into the barrel of his Model 700 Remington. Angelina was aiming it at him from the kitchen doorway, twenty yards away. He took a couple of steps in her direction, then turned around. At which point she shot him in the back.

According to Barnes and Biggs, the body was found face down on the lawn beside the driveway, at a forty-five-degree angle from his parked Mercedes, so it would seem the bullet's impact caused him to twist as he fell. When his body was rolled over onto a stretcher, it was observed his fly was undone, his penis exposed. The detectives therefore made the bold assumption that Angelina plugged him as he turned his back to her and relieved himself.

I found myself astonished by the presumptive nature of this report. How could Barnes and Biggs know the deceased had walked toward her, then turned away, and had a piss? That detail hadn't come from Miss Santos. There were no eyewitnesses.

I had to assume that they'd touched up the report with assumption, based on the clear fact that Trudd had been shot in the back. He'd collapsed as a 7-millimetre bullet ripped through his heart and exited through his front ribs. Shot in the back while relieving himself — I couldn't imagine a more difficult scenario for the defence.

She immediately called the police. Her words were recorded: "Please come. I think I shot Mr. Trudd and he's dead."

Two RCMP constables who were on duty half a mile away had heard a rifle shot. Dispatched to the scene, they showed up within a minute, cautioned her as to her rights, and she confessed on the spot, in tears. The officers had her speaking in accented but clear English. She was candid to a fault.

"I shot him."

"Why?"

"He raped me."

"When?"

Three days earlier, according to her, in a basement bedroom which she used when overnighting in her boss's house. As later information revealed, he'd abused her sexually before that. But she was under no apparent threat at the scene of the crime, and her employer, Trudd, a local potentate and property manager, was unarmed. He had just returned from a three-day business trip.

As to the rape, Miss Santos, either foolishly or naïvely, had cleaned her bedroom afterwards, even washed the sheets and mattress cover. She'd retained her soiled nightie and panties, however, though Pappas's report didn't indicate why.

I laid down the file as Pappas huffed into my office with a heavy cardboard box containing the Herb Macintosh transcripts, and set it on a side table.

"You going to the orgy for Boorstein tonight?" he asked.

A bachelor party at the Penthouse Cabaret. Rudy Boorstein, Mortgages and Real Estate, was getting married on the weekend. "Not sure. I have work to do. Did you look into insanity?"

"Macintosh may be nuts but he ain't insane."

"I'm talking about Angelina."

He saw her photos and the police reports arrayed on my desk. "Not a hope. I had a shrink take a go at her. Some trauma, some memory loss which she's probably faking. Had all her marbles."

"Was she badly mauled?"

Pappas shrugged. "Nah, just raped. Minor bruises. No blood, but she'd washed that man right out of her hair, spent hours in the shower. I think she just laid back and let him take his best shot." Pappas at his disgusting worst.

"Autonomous behaviour?"

"Our shrink-for-hire wasn't buying that. He'd be a bad witness, he's too honest."

"Accident?"

"She knew the rifle was loaded. Pointed it right at him. The gun was still hot when the first cops showed up. Her dabs all over it, handle, barrel, trigger. The expended bullet was found in a tree stump sixty yards back of the house. Not exactly a cold case."

"Yet people in Fort Thompson have rallied around her."

"Trudd was a shit. Grasping landlord. The whole town was under his thumb."

"Where is she?"

"Prince George Regional Corrections Centre."

"*How* is she?"

"I dunno. She's weird, seemed at peace. Prays a lot."

I looked again at her picture in that blue dress. How could this young woman be a murderer?

I sensed a presence. It was Hubbell Meyerson, in the doorway, his hands extended, outlining a woman's curvaceous shape, then miming the act of pleasuring himself. "Tonight, I'm going to get you laid," he said.

The Trials of
Arthur Beauchamp

Excerpt from Chapter Three,
"A Will to Die For" © *W. Chance*

Meyerson was Beauchamp's best friend, perhaps his only friend
in those days. They'd shared classrooms at a snobby private
secondary school that supposedly created real men. Meyerson
was as outgoing and charming as Beauchamp was shy and
inner-directed, so logic would have suggested the former would
choose the courts and the latter a desk.

But when both got articles at Tragger, Inglis such logic was
defied. Meyerson chose the solicitor side and easily mastered
drafting wills and settling complex estates. He rose faster than
Beauchamp in the hierarchy of the firm, making it to the
sixteenth floor early in 1966.

Athletic, charming, and handsome, Meyerson was totally at
ease with the women who flocked around him. Beauchamp was
not unhandsome, despite his beak-like nose, and was so slim
and tall that cronies called him Stretch. But he was shy, and
his clumsiness with women, even in the liberated sixties, almost
beggared belief.

So it seems massively out of character that the subject of
this narrative ended up, on that mid-September Friday night in
1966, at the Penthouse Cabaret with a naked stripper astride
his lap, fondling his genitals. He was almost insensate with

drink, according to my sources, yet was reciting a Shakespeare sonnet to her.

Beauchamp claimed amnesia for that evening's late hours. I would like to believe he was in denial, but he did have a history of blackouts during his ever-more-frequent blowouts. Nor has Hubbell Meyerson been helpful. At seventy-nine, he appears to be in excellent health in mind and body — he regularly rides horses at his ranch — so he was obviously joshing when he claimed to suffer a selective form of Alzheimer's.

The version I have described is supported by other contemporaries from Tragger, Inglis. Sadly, there remain few of them — sixty-hour weeks and cholesterol-laden lunches took their toll — but Rudy Boorstein, a long-time stalwart in Real Property, still in practice, clearly recalls the young stripper — she was billed as go-go dancer — doing pelvis thrusts on Beauchamp's lap to the beat of "Wild Thing" by the Troggs.

The event that brought a dozen young lawyers to the Penthouse — a nightclub owned by the Filliponi boys and favoured by celebrities, underworld figures, and prostitutes — was Boorstein's pre-wedding party.

Other versions differ slightly, which is hardly surprising given that over half a century has elapsed. Marshal Thomas, a tax lawyer with a formidable memory for a nonagenarian, backed up Boorstein and added that Beauchamp entertained the young woman with the Bard's famous Sonnet 18 ("Rough winds do shake the darling buds of May"). Russell Whiting, from Corporate, remembered not a sonnet but an exuberant rendition of the Rubaiyat ("Awake! And fill the cup . . .") All three gentlemen witnessed two underdressed ladies of the night grab their coats and lead Beauchamp out the door.

Whiting was particularly helpful, permitting me to record him over a few drinks at his golf club in Penticton. "Arthur was barely able to stand, let alone walk. So I was concerned he might get his ass rolled, and I headed after them. The girls, who were gorgeous, by the way, were laughing as they bundled Beauchamp into a taxi, and he was orating like Laurence Olivier. They took off, and I went back in and told the other guys."

"And how did they react?"

"Roars of laughter. Then Hubbell Meyerson finally confessed he'd given each of the girls fifty dollars and told them to give Stretch a good time. Mickey Filliponi came over to vouch for the two little sweeties, and promised they were clean."

Though Beauchamp remained the subject of much levity among his cronies over his rollick with the two sex workers, he also gained esteem. No longer was his virility in doubt — many colleagues expressed awe at his heroic sexual appetite.

The episode was even discussed in Jack Wasserman's column in the Sun. He didn't name names but got close: "A crackerjack young shark with a growing rep, and not just in the courtroom."

As to the secretarial staff, suffice it to say the water cooler stations buzzed like beehives and Beauchamp was getting lingering looks. One secretary, however, was in agony. Gertrude Isbister, who was secretly in love with Beauchamp, was heart-broken. (As she confided to me. She's now well retired, though serving, as she put it, as a full-time grandma.)

Why have I dwelt on that night of revelry? Certainly not with any libidinous purpose, but merely to lay to rest scuttlebutt that Beauchamp had little interest in women and that his erotic interests lay elsewhere. Even his starchy, socially conservative parents had harboured doubts about his manliness.

1966 —
The Lady on My Lap

M r. Chance, in his unauthorized biography, offers a version of events of the bachelor party so tawdry that it generated much guffawing among my compatriots of the British Columbia bar: thus I offer this truer, more restrained account.

Memories of even steely minds tend to rust over the years, like carving tools left out in the weather. So I take no great offence at Mr. Chance's confidants for having creatively filled in the blanks — one never likes to acknowledge even early senescence.

Though I can't recall the events of that mid-September Friday night in fine detail, I have a more reliable witness than those dug up by Mr. Chance. I will get to that, but first must admit to fibbing to him about having been amnesic. Being close-mouthed, I felt, would just stimulate suspicion. In hoping he would drop the matter, I underestimated his tenacity.

The truth of the matter is this:

The young lady who took to my lap was well known to me. Gina Griswold, then nineteen, whom I had defended on an information charging two counts of Vagrancy I, as it was called, or more commonly, Vag C.

In those unenlightened times, it was a crime to loiter (Vag A), to beg (Vag B), or (Vag C) to be a "common prostitute" who, found in a public place, did not, "when required, give a good account of herself." The Criminal Code listed these evil activities under the rubric of "No Apparent Means of Support."

At any rate, I had earned her an acquittal on the first count and a suspended sentence on the second. She was clearly delighted to see me at the Penthouse Cabaret. She did not fondle any genitals. Nor was she naked — she wore a G-string, and tinselled pasties on her nipples. She was clearly concerned about my state of mind and health. When I recited a favourite verse (Keats, not Shakespeare): "'I have been half in love with easeful Death,'" she told me, "You've had enough, Mr. Beauchamp."

Miss Griswold and a friend (her roommate, actually) did indeed lead me to a taxi, in which, frankly, I passed out. But these thoughtful young women not only escorted me to my little flat in Kitsilano, they even had the driver wait until they tucked me into bed.

How do I know this? Because Gina Griswold, who was a rather careless prostitute, was picked up two nights later for Vag C. In the soundproof interview room of the women's lockup, we enjoyed a good laugh over how she and her friend rescued me from that abysmal bachelor party. She assured me I had been a perfect gentleman. She also let me know that Hubbell Meyerson (*I'm going to get you laid*) had paid her to "look after" me.

On the following weekend, I putted out to Point Grey in my old VW bug to brave my monthly Sunday dinner with my stiff, bitchy, right-wing parents (whom, oddly, masochistically, I loved). Dr. Thomas Beauchamp, soon to be retired as head librarian at UBC, rarely got invited to dinner parties, because of his acid tongue and his compulsion to pounce on his tablemates for their errors in literary or historical allusions. Dr. Mavis Beauchamp, who taught the great ancient languages, was equally unpopular among UBC faculty: she was brittle in debate and to the right of Ayn Rand. She had recently written an opinion piece for the *Toronto Telegram*, decrying Canada's acceptance of immigrants from "backward countries."

I parked a telephone pole away so my rusted Beetle wouldn't shame them, and, armed with a decent five-dollar Beaujolais, found Mother in her kitchen, setting out canapés. A chicken was in the oven.

"We've invited Professor Winkle," she announced as I pecked her cheek. "He's an old friend of your father and I don't want you ignoring him. He's been very vulnerable since his wife left him."

"Ah, yes, the hypocritical Dr. Winkle, with his constant rants about the sinking morals of the student body. Such an exemplar of virtue."

A private detective, hired by his wife, had caught him with his pants down, literally, astride an associate professor of history for whom he'd lobbied for tenure.

"He'll be bringing their daughter, Madge, so please don't seek courage through drink at the prospect of having to relate to her."

"Mother, I beg you. Please stop trying to line me up with Madge Winkle." Plump and pushy, commerce grad, worked for Philip Morris in sales and advertising.

"I thought that opposites would attract. She's as bouncy and sweet-natured as you are not. Maybe a little light in the head. But she's from good stock, and she's attracted to you. But you don't seem to be attracted to any kind of woman."

(It was none of her business that I'd shared many steamy nights with a voluptuous older woman I'd fallen for. I still occasionally saw Ophelia Moore, a newly appointed magistrate, on visits to the Okanagan Valley.)

━

I reacted bravely to Mother's challenge, tucking in close to Madge at the dinner table, cordially expressing interest as she explained the health benefits of filter tip cigarettes. The disapproval on my mother's face was palpable — she believed I was faking a healthy interest in the opposite sex.

The chicken's carcass was ultimately replaced by cake, coffee, brandy, and cigarettes. Glasses were raised in celebration of the recent provincial election and the victory of Premier W.A.C. "Wacky" Bennett, who had once again kept the dreaded socialists at bay. I hadn't voted. My political leanings at the time could best be described as apatheistic.

From time to time I found myself having to repel questions about the Herb Macintosh case. It was assumed I knew the mining tycoon, that I had insights, knew secrets, proofs of guilt or innocence. I explained I knew little more than the readers of news accounts of the preliminary hearing. In any event, I had merely glanced through the file.

My concentration was on the Angelina Santos trial. I had dictated a memo to Gertrude to reserve a flight to Fort Thompson, without checking to see if it even had an airport — an Alaska Highway stopover, a Hudson's Bay trading post in times long past, that's all I knew.

I was intrigued by what I'd learned about the young immigrant. Her interviews with Alex Pappas and his unhelpful forensic psychiatrist painted a picture of a pleasant, intelligent, straightforward, and utterly sane twenty-year-old.

There was nothing remarkable about her history. Completed secondary school and a year at a vocational school, learning the hospitality business. Came to Canada as a landed immigrant in 1964, stayed with a cousin in Prince Rupert while working as a hotel maid. In early 1965, she responded to Trudd's classified ad for a full-time housekeeper, "with generous benefits."

Professor Winkle broke up my musings by rising. Father was a heroic drinker, as was I, but Winkle, who had brought champagne and brandy, outdistanced us. He made a bizarre toast to his wife, who would be getting her decree nisi in a couple of weeks.

"To Edith, my darling love whose heart I broke. And now the bond of our union is broken." He raised his glass. "A vinculum matrimonii."

"A vincula matrimonii," Father corrected. "*Vinculum* has the sense of bondage in the form of incarceration."

Mother chipped in: "Literally, from the restraints of marriage — the bonds, the chains."

"Not, however, the bonds of affection," said Father.

My parents could go on forever like that. Madge smiled at me and I at her, sharing this little interlude of academic nitpicking. Professor Winkle finally sat, but continued excoriating himself for losing "sweet Madge's loving mommy" over "a playful tryst" with a colleague.

Madge was less interested in her father's love life than her own. I felt a light tickle of fingers on my right thigh, and my reaction was fluster. I faced a dilemma: responding in kind would send a false message, but not responding might be hurtful or insulting.

I suddenly found myself on my feet, cutting Winkle off, raising my brandy snifter: "To Angelina!"

This ill-considered attempt at distraction was greeted with bafflement and cries of "Angelina?" and "What's an Angelina?" I was stuck with my impromptu change of topic, and found myself tipsily describing the particulars of the case against Miss Santos.

Nothing enhances a dinner party like a jolly conversation about murder. Mother held forth awhile on "the obvious indicia" that the shooting was a planned assassination, adding that "doubtless" the young Filipina had been improperly vetted by the Immigration Department. Father, a practical man, wanted to know why, if Angelina had been raped, she hadn't gone to the authorities.

Madge wondered if, under Philippine law, a woman was justified in killing her attacker. She was the only one among us who was sober; her craving was for the nicotine in the cigarettes she marketed. While addressing me she would twist her mouth sideways so as not to blow smoke in my face. (I rarely used tobacco in those days, except to be polite.)

Professor Winkle had recently graded a paper on historical traditions of rape-revenge — it advised that in medieval England women were entitled to detach their abusers' testicles. Father relied on Cogswell's *England in the Middle Ages* to dismiss that theory. The practice of gouging out offenders' eyeballs was, however, abided in the mid-1100s.

None of this back-and-forth was conducive to romance, but Madge sensed my resistance was broken when I drunkenly squeezed her hand. She looked at her watch, blew a spume past my left ear, and leaned into me. "I'm going to insist on driving you home."

She and her father had come in the same car, and she decided to drop him off first. En route, the chatty old boy warned me to pack long underwear for Fort Thompson. While researching eighteenth-century fur trading, he'd spent time up there. "Winter lasts ten months. It's the last frontier, redneck country, so stay out of the bars. Don't use ten-dollar words or they'll assume you're a fancy boy. You let them know you went to a posh private school, they'll pin a target on your ass."

As he got out at his West End rental, he whispered boozily into my ear: "Good to see you getting along with Madge. Your folks have been worried." He came even closer: "Not that there's anything wrong with being homo."

Madge could have dropped me off first, but now had to double back to my flat in Kitsilano. I struggled to think of a polite way not to invite her in — stupidly, I'd droned on about my charming downstairs rental with its sunroom, private patio, rose garden and . . . could I have been so bumble-headed as to have mentioned the waterbed?

I felt bad that I wasn't attracted to her. I might have shared a bed with her, if only to answer a gnawing need for release, but I was too intoxicated to risk the humiliation of being unable to perform.

"That's it," I said. "The bungalow with the side light on."

"Where's the best place to park?"

"Oh, just in front of the driveway. Yes, this is fine, right here. That was most generous of you, Madge. Were my head not spinning, I'd invite you in. My insides are roiling. Nothing to do with you." For a full minute, I carried on in this bizarre, repulsive way, digging myself in deeper.

Somehow I escaped unscathed from that vehicle, staggering as I hung on to the passenger door. Madge took a deep pull on her cigarette, and blew a smoke ring at me, a perfect zero that wobbled and broke apart.

"Fuck you," she said.

Arthur —
March 2022

I punch the period key with emphasis, then wait for the shame and remorse to kick in. That was cruel. Not to Madge personally, but to her loved ones: she died of lung cancer a few years ago. I hadn't kept in close touch with her, but sent condolences to her husband, kids, and grandkids. That scene with Madge Winkle must be buried, overtyped with x's. I dare not emulate my biographer, with his obsession over giggly secrets and raunchy speculations.

I was disrespectful elsewhere in that draft chapter. The acerbic sketches of my parents do not show their sole offspring in the warmest of light. Having set out to chronicle a bizarre, gripping trial, I've gone off track — as if still gripped by the trauma of having been raised lovelessly. And then boasting about "many steamy nights with a voluptuous older woman." A transparent effort to seem Hemingwayesque. How undignified of me to describe the late high court justice as "voluptuous." Forgive me, dear Ophelia.

I blame these gaffes and gaucheries on the sawing and hammering on the roof — the din has disrupted my focus. I loved the arbutus tree once, but I curse it now.

A sudden, eerie silence as tools are stilled. Then the sound of boots scraping down the ladder. A grunt and pull, a failed start, another grunt and pull, and Dog's chainsaw roars into life.

I give up, shroud my typewriter, pack my work-in-progress into my old leather briefcase, arouse Ulysses from his slumber, and damp down my stove. I step outside into a misty day — brightened, however, by the happy faces of daffodils in scattered clumps by the path to the outhouse. Spring is icumen in.

I retreat a few metres, up a rise, so I can check the work-in-progress of my crew. The hole in the roof, directly above the loft, is now covered with fibreglass insulation. Stacks of rough-cut shakes, split by Dog from old cedar butts, lean at the base of the offending tree, which has been punished with a severe haircut. Dog is bucking up the crookneck limb that Stoney had insisted would crush me to death.

With climate change accelerating, the March storms have become more severe every year, and a week ago a southwest gale amputated that limb. My death didn't happen, because (a) the branch merely punched a big hole in the roof, then rolled off, and (b) the storm was at night.

We were four days without power. I got back to my manuscript only today. I've been discombobulated. That shows in my typewriter's gross domestic product.

Dog shuts down, snaps open a beer. Stoney, astride a sawhorse, salutes me with his own frothy can. "I'll only say it one more time."

I steel myself for another I-told-you-so.

"I tried. I warned you, boss. It's a magical tree, you said, a goddess. It seems kinda creepy, but you were blinded by love. Maybe I'm not a big-time attorney with a wall full of degrees in Greek and Latin, but in the struggle to survive on this here island I've developed instincts about life-threatening trees."

I wait patiently until he finishes, then ask if they intend to finish the roof job today.

Stoney studies the dwindling pile of shakes. "Somehow they must've got undercounted. Not a problem, we'll split more tomorrow. Meanwhile, we're gonna need to anchor them solar panels you said you wanted for the roof."

"I did?"

"For a mini-fridge, remember? Hook up a laptop, a CD player, mood music to get your creative juices bubbling. They're available cash on delivery at a haggle-free price, except for extras, unknowables, and my commission. I also got a line on a solar technician in case you don't trust me to do the job."

In my confused state during the power outage, had I mumbled something about wanting solar power? I tell Stoney we'll talk about it when the roof is done.

"No problem," he says. It is a phrase I have learned to passionately distrust.

1966 —
Owls and Howls

Alex Pappas was unceasingly irked that I was more centred on the Santos case than the Herb Macintosh file. He regarded the latter as a trifling concern compared with the lurid spectacle of a violent murder in a mansion. His lack of interest in Angelina's defence was reflected in lines like "Can't she just say she forgot hunting season was over and mistook her boss for a moose?"

We quarrelled over how to defend Macintosh. The mining magnate wanted a brawler in his corner, and Pappas was determined to impress him, to enter the fray like a pit bull, ripping away at witnesses' throats. I urged a more cerebral approach: sway the jury through rational argument.

Pappas was forever barging into my office with some new wrinkle that had to be discussed immediately, or a new lead or a witness who had to be interviewed. I resented being unable to squeeze in enough time to prepare for Angelina's trial. But I finally stole an early October weekend and braved a flight to the distant outpost they called Fort Tom.

I was nervous about going up there — the frozen far north, redneck country. I'd be out of my element: semi-sophisticated Vancouver and its comfortable middle-class suburbs. I had little life experience that would prepare me for the rough-and-tumble of the backwoods, and in my dreams I found myself venturing like Charles Marlow into the *Heart of Darkness*.

As the ancient DC-4 banked toward a desolate airstrip, I took in a panorama of Fort Thompson, bathed yellow in the early evening sun: a sprawl of modest homes around a town centre that looked somehow decayed. The abundance of churches hinted that the townspeople had hopes for a happier afterlife.

The main artery, the Alaska Highway, bisected the town east and west, bridged a fast-flowing river, and crawled up high eastern bluffs where sat homes of the well-to-do. Beyond, to the west, were the foothills of the Rocky Mountains.

We descended over hills of logs and sawn lumber, then passed a mill, smoke spewing from its stacks. Just off the airport's access road I spotted the town's sole tourist attraction, a restored log fort built over the ruins of a North West Company fur trading post.

As the aircraft met the runway with jolting bounces, a couple of men up front cheered sardonically: loggers, from the look of them, heavy smokers, heavier drinkers. I'd had a glass or two myself, along with aspirin, seeking to deaden the discomfort of an unrelenting cold.

I was among the last of the two dozen passengers to disembark into the chill evening air, and there I was, in a remote northern outpost where in two months I had to defend twenty-year-old Angelina Santos on a charge of capital murder.

It would be too late to do anything that Saturday evening but size up the town. On Sunday, I hoped to view the crime scene before meeting Angelina, whom I'd arranged to be flown in from the women's prison in Prince George. My return flight was early Monday, so I would have a busy time of it. But today, after a look about, I hoped to retire early and enjoy a sound sleep in the town's premier hotel, the Fort.

Several minutes later, I found myself standing with my overnight bag and briefcase outside a shed-like terminal building, watching the last of three taxis disappear up the road. I was about to return inside to ask about ground transportation when a burly, full-bearded fellow in a camouflage jacket wheeled a suitcase toward me.

"Need a ride, partner?"

"I'd be most grateful." I wiped my nose, apologized for my cold, expressed the hope that the Fort Hotel would not be out of his way.

"You won't get any quality sleep in that old barn, not on a Saturday night — beer parlour's full of loud drunks, and they got a rockabilly band in there. It's a heritage building, but the owner was letting it fall apart."

"Would that be Frederick C. Trudd?"

"Fred Trudd, yeah. Lived a prick, died a prick." Sizing me up, the dark suit and tie, the long overcoat. "You Angelina's new lawyer?"

We shook hands. Buck Harris was his name. Owned a hunting lodge just out of town. I was welcome to stay. On the house.

My feeble protests were ignored — Harris went to a pay phone, told his wife to expect a guest for dinner. He then led me to a work-horse crew cab adorned with a bumper sticker promoting a Social Credit candidate in the recent election. "Better Dead than Red," said another. Two rifles were hung at the back of the cab.

The sun was dipping as we drove off, into a checkerboard of forests and clearcuts. Harris pointed out the two-storey restored fort, then we passed the Wolf River Reserve of the local South Slavey band: scattered dwellings, a log-built community hall on a hill.

Again, I thanked Harris for his hospitality.

"Don't think about it. I already gave a cheque to your partner, the Greek, what's his name . . ."

"Pappas."

"Yeah. Real hard-boiled, that guy. I kicked in three grand for your fees."

51

The $15,000 crowd funder. Money thrown away on a lost cause, I feared, though I couldn't bring myself to say that.

The town's main street — aptly called Main Street — was wide enough to permit angle parking on both sides. Centrally located was the four-storey, colonnaded Fort Hotel, which at first glance looked grand and stately, but at close range ill kept and worn. Many of the local businesses looked even more decrepit. Some were boarded up. Rustlers, a steak house, seemed the only busy eatery. "Owned by Marsha Bigelow, along with a rooming house next door. You'll want to meet her, she's Angelina's landlady."

Harris explained that most of the other businesses in town were owned by Trudd Enterprises Inc. "That's Ming's Chinese restaurant. Or was. Trudd raised rents all around by twenty percent last year, now most of his tenants are closing up. Owns the mill, too. Or his sisters do now. Couple of witches, them dames, cut of the same cloth. The fricking bloodsucker didn't have wife or kids, so they got everything. I heard it's in the courts, they're fighting over how to split it up. Hope you can get Angelina off. The whole town's counting on it."

Again came an anxiety reaction, the kind I'd felt when Pappas slyly passed the buck.

On Sunday, I awoke at a quarter to nine, after a long sleep broken occasionally by wolf howls and owl hoots. I felt somewhat restored, my nose no longer running, but clogged. Through a window of my snug log cabin, I gazed at a dazzling display of hoarfrost on trees, fences, and lawn, sunlight sifting through the mist. It seemed magical, and somehow boosted my spirits.

On arrival at Harris Hunting Lodge and Cabins, I had allowed myself to be pampered by Lorraine Harris, as bright and merry as her husband was gruff and cynical. A thick venison stew. A favourite cold remedy that "works like a damn." Immediately after dinner she sent me off to my quiet rustic cabin: clean sheets and a feather quilt and a blazing woodstove.

Showered, combed, and shaved, and in my best Sunday suit, I headed to the main lodge, arriving at the door as a small car pulled up. Out stepped a beaming, rotund fellow in priests' garb, who greeted me with a hearty handshake, announced himself as Father Etienne Larouche, and said he'd just come from morning mass. He was co-chair of the Angelina Santos support group. He was delighted to meet me, thrilled to know that Miss Santos, a devoted member of his flock, would be defended by such a famous young barrister.

I was flattered but also confused — until I learned that the local evening paper, the *Northern Daily News*, had published a wire service item about my recent courtroom exploits.

Etienne joined me and the Harrises for coffee and bacon and eggs, and carried on about Miss Santos's good works in the community — since her arrival in Fort Thompson a year ago, she'd served at church socials, at the food bank, and she was an elder-care volunteer. Yet she managed to work for Trudd six days a week, scraping enough aside to help her mother in Manila.

Angelina also helped out at the rooming house where she lived rent-free. Her landlady, Marsha Bigelow, would be dropping off my client's clothing at the RCMP lockup. I was grateful for that; Angelina would be embarrassed, ill at ease, meeting me in a prison jumpsuit.

Over breakfast I learned that Trudd, who was fifty-four, not a big man, but physically fit, had a history of abusive behaviour when in his cups. He had already been divorced twice — both marriages childless — and recently had been living with a vivacious young woman from Alaska whom he'd picked up hitchhiking. Less than half his age, she lasted eight months before running off with a prospector and several thousand dollars in cash and bearer bonds purloined from Trudd's safe. That was two months before his death, in March, and that's when he began drinking heavily.

Etienne surmised that Trudd targeted Angelina not because of unrequited lust, but with anger in his heart against his thieving ex-girlfriend — Angelina was a handy substitute victim for his fury.

Eventually, Larouche asked the blunt question about her chances of acquittal.

"I shall have to be honest, Father. They are not good. She will need all the prayers we can offer up."

"I understand. It's small consolation, but at least that son of a bitch is burning in the eternal fires."

1966 —
The Loudness of Ravens

The frost was thick on the subalpine forest that blanketed the high east bank of the town's river, the Wolf. Etienne slowed his car so I could view several substantial homes that overlooked it, the largest being the former residence of F.C. Trudd: colonial style, lapped wood siding, three storeys, a well-maintained front yard with mown lawn and caragana bushes. The house appeared to have been newly repainted: an attractive ochre. A For Sale sign at the driveway entrance.

Etienne explained that Trudd's self-indulgent sisters had gussied up the property and were trying to unload not just this house but his many business properties. They preferred the salubrious climate of the Okanagan Valley, and visited only to check on sales. An example of their uncaring: Trudd's only companions were six cats, and instead of keeping them, or giving them away, the sisters had them put down.

I had hoped to look around inside the house, but Etienne hadn't been able to reach the listing realtor. He assured me he'd keep trying.

The driveway curled around the house to the back, rising about five feet to a plateau on which stood a two-vehicle garage. It too had been freshly painted. Peeking through a window, I made out Trudd's Mercedes, a Ford 150, and a snowmobile.

Back of the garage was a rough logging road that wound steeply into scrabbly denuded hills thick with stumps. The loud calls of ravens echoed from those hills.

The rear entrance to the house led to the kitchen and was accessed by three steps leading to a narrow cedar deck. Recessed beneath the deck were a pair of basement windows. There was a servant's suite down there in which, according to Pappas's notes, Angelina had been raped.

The police report had Angelina standing at the kitchen doorway, about sixty feet away from Trudd, aiming his Remington 700 at him — presumably at an upward angle, given his slightly higher elevation. He apparently turned his back to Angelina before she pressed the trigger — the entry wound was between the shoulder blades and the exit wound was in the chest, heart-high.

The bullet was found embedded in a spruce stump up the hill, less than sixty yards from the house. I ambled up that way, spotted it easily: the forensic people had cut out a wide chunk of the wood enveloping the bullet.

Back at the house, I took the steps to the back door, looked through its window: nothing to see but a hallway and a coat rack. An outer screen door was fastened by an eye-hook. I had seen photos of an officer holding it open — it was spring-activated and would swing shut.

I mused: what if I could persuade Miss Santos to remember that the screen door closed suddenly, striking her elbow, causing the rifle to fire accidentally. I couldn't counsel her to lie, of course, but might she be open to have her memory jogged?

Fort Tom's attractive old courthouse, three storeys of rough granite stone with a faux turret, had only three courtrooms, two on the ground floor for run-of-the-mill Magistrate's Court matters and a spacious room upstairs for high court jury trials. Offices, a law library, and barristers' quarters were on the third floor.

The courthouse served a vast swath of northern BC but was no hive of activity. A lag of only three and a half months between arrest and preliminary hearing, as was the case here, would have been impossible in the cities of the south, where trials were often backed up for a year or more.

A circuit judge occasionally visited but no one had been appointed yet to preside over *Regina v. Santos*. His Lordship (there were no Ladyships in those patriarchal times) would likely have to come from the populated south, probably some junior justice from Greater Vancouver.

Next to the courthouse was the brick-walled RCMP detachment: rectangular, featureless. Etienne let me out there. "Please tell Angelina we've sent some funds to her dear mother. I'll visit her later today. I haven't been able to for the last month." As if in apology, he added, "It's a day's drive to Prince George and a day back."

The duty sergeant, a portly, amiable middle-ager named Mike Trasov, didn't care to see my Law Society card. "I know who you are, sir. And that you're helping Angelina out. We have a little coffee lounge, you'll be more comfortable than back in the cells."

The lounge offered an armchair, a small table for making notes, and a sofa for my client. A pot of hot coffee was on the maker. "Milk in the fridge," Trasov said, "and soft drinks. Crackers and cheese, if you like."

"I sense this isn't an easy case for you, Sergeant."

"No one's jumping for joy around here. Town's pretty torn up about it."

I expected to hear more than a few racist, anti-immigrant views from members of this reputedly illiberal community, but was beginning to wonder if that was a typical urban misconception.

While the officer fetched Angelina, I poured myself a cup, needing a caffeine lift — I felt enervated, weighted down by pessimism about my client's prospects. I had no clear strategy for dealing with this young woman. I would want her to relax as much as possible. Her English was supposed to be good: her second language.

But I would find it awkward relating to a client who, apparently, was incapable of telling lies. Most of my defendants hadn't suffered that handicap.

A comely, plump, tawny-skinned brunette appeared at the door wearing the same blue dress as in the police photos. Angelina's bright, wide eyes somehow suggested a state of awe or wonder. She was slightly more filled out than in the 1965 Kodachrome — the Prince George prison diet had done her no harm.

Despite those big, intense eyes she seemed to be battling a weariness. My impulse was to hug her, but I couldn't even allow myself to shake her hand. I apologized for having a cold.

"I'm sorry," she said. "I hope you'll get better quick."

She settled on the sofa with her knees together and hands clasped. Her eyes stayed fixed on a spot six inches below my chin as I carried on about her wonderful support group, about Father Etienne Larouche and my luck in meeting Buck and Lorraine Harris.

"Oh, I'm glad," she said. "They're very nice." The first smile.

I told her the community has sent some funds to her ill mother.

"I know. I feel so blessed by everyone." She added, "I hope they didn't tell her about the terrible thing I did."

"I'm sure they were discreet." I preferred not to hear guilt-acknowledging expressions like "the terrible thing I did." I warned her I was going to make a little speech. She was to listen carefully and silently.

Angelina's eyes didn't waver from that spot below my chin as I urged upon her the importance of giving a sympathetic jury something to hang on to.

I offered for her consideration a list of options. Had she been in fear for her life? Did she act in self-defence in any way? Could she have blacked out, a kind of temporary insanity? Was she in any way provoked? By his actions, by anything he said? That, I explained, could lead to a reduced charge. Or was it a pure accident? Such as the screen door swinging shut on her and the rifle accidentally discharging.

She rose. I watched, confused, as she wet a washcloth at the sink, then returned, bending to me, and wiped my suit collar. "I think it's a bit of egg. There. That's better."

"Thank you. You shouldn't have got so close, but thank you." When she sat again, her eyes, no longer hypnotized by the egg dropping, finally met mine. I felt off my game. "Miss Santos, that door is on a spring, as you know, and —"

"But —"

"Please think deeply before you say anything. This was an extremely tense time. You may not have remembered —"

"The screen door had already closed behind me. I had to open it to go in and call the police."

"I see." So truthful, so innocent, yet so guilty. "I see."

"And to wash up, wash my face, because I got sick." That was in Pappas's notes — she'd thrown up onto a flowerbed.

I blurted out some awkward, sympathetic phrase or two, and couldn't think of anything else to say. I was perplexed, and getting a headache. Something was amiss here, something about Angelina. Something I saw, or felt. As she stood close to me, I'd sensed a kind of aura, profound and warming. I studied her, the tightness of that blue dress.

"Are you pregnant, Angelina?"

A long, sad sigh. "Yes, I think I am."

"Have you told anyone?"

"I didn't want to believe it, sir."

"And the father . . . ?"

"Mr. Trudd."

1966 —
How She Rattled Me

L ong after my return to Vancouver, my brain still whirled with the impact of Angelina's revelation — I was at a loss over how to deal with the implications, unsure from whom to seek advice in the male bastion that was Tragger, Inglis.

I said nothing to Alex Pappas, of course, knowing his response would be typically tasteless. Occasionally, he caught me staring blankly out my window, trying to work through the puzzle that was Angelina Santos. He would accuse me of sitting on my butt when I should be digging up dirt about key Crown witnesses.

I was almost relieved to refocus my mind on the Herb Macintosh case. Pappas finally sent me off to meet him at his corporate offices in the Marine Building. "When you're serving the richest fucker in town, he doesn't come to you, you go to him."

I spent three hours grooming him for the courtroom. It was a struggle to mask my distaste for the self-admiring oaf — he would be called Trumpian in modern parlance. He, however, took a liking to me.

That was because he palled around with the Filliponi brothers, who'd regaled him about my revel at the Penthouse and its alleged aftermath. He seemed awed by my ability to recite from Keats with a naked hooker on my lap.

Thanksgiving arrived, as usual, on the second weekend of October. Fortunately, I was unable to answer my parents' subpoena for their traditional oppressive turkey dinner. My excuse was Angelina Santos. The trial date would be upon us in just over a month, and I had much preparation yet to do.

Gertrude Isbister, resourceful as ever, found me a return flight to Prince George on that busy weekend — it would get me there late Saturday and out late Sunday. She also phoned ahead to the women's prison to book Angelina for Sunday morning.

I had some questions to ask that I hadn't got around to the last time. Mostly about Trudd's assaults and her pregnancy — delicate questions that I wasn't sure how to frame. I also needed to delve into her mental and emotional state on that fatal day late in May.

I still had no credible strategy for a trial during which a young woman pregnant with a rapist's child would be sitting in the prisoners' dock. A devout Catholic, Angelina saw it as God's will to bring the baby to term.

All of Fort Thompson knew about her pregnancy. She had confessed it to Father Larouche — as if it were a sin. He'd counselled her to be open about it, to be unafraid — she was blessed to be with child.

Bereft of ideas about how to defend her, I could only hope to bluff my way through the trial, hoping for a miracle. I would need one, because even a sympathetic hometown jury would be strapped to come up with a doubt remotely reasonable.

The regional jail in Prince George was a short taxi hop from my airport hotel, and I was in the visiting room by half past nine on Sunday, already a busy time. The scene was depressingly typical of such facilities, with their dense population of First Nation and

Métis inmates, victims of Canada's tortured history of oppressing its original inhabitants.

A male guard led me to a table reserved for lawyers and probation officers. "Don't get too many murderers in here," he said, "especially when they're preggers." He took up a position nearby but out of earshot, and watched warily as I spread out my writing pad, notes, transcripts, and police photos.

Angelina was brought in wearing grey prison garb that was loose but didn't hide her pregnancy: she was in her fifth month.

"I am very happy to see you again," she said, taking my hand. With her radiant smile and her wide, intense eyes, she emitted a glow comme il faut for an expectant mom, but which seemed somehow incongruent under her grim circumstances. I hadn't yet found the courage to tell her that her baby would be taken away if she was convicted of homicide.

I said she was looking well. She hoped I was cured of my cold. I hoped she hadn't got it from me. She assured me she hadn't. She was healthy, as was the "beautiful miracle" she carried. A jarring phrase, given that the miracle arose from rape — yet consonant with her deeply held faith.

That pas-de-deux completed, I showed her a police photo of Trudd's R 700, and asked, "Had you ever used this rifle before?"

"No."

"Or any gun? Did you have any training in guns?"

"Only from watching. I saw Mr. Trudd shoot at deers and wolfs and once at a big dog who chased Ginger."

"Ginger?"

"A girl cat. Ginger colour. Also from Ginger Rogers. We had a Fred Astaire too." She laughed lightly. "I hope they are all with good families. I pray for them to have happy lives."

Clearly, she didn't know Trudd's sisters had put them down. I couldn't find the heart to tell her, and quickly got back to the Remington 700. "You mentioned seeing Mr. Trudd shoot at wild animals. From where?"

"Sometime right from the back door. Sometime from the stairs. Maybe fifteen times."

"What did he do with the casings?"

"I always pick them up and take them to garbage."

"And what about the bullets, the slugs?"

She shrugged. "I guess they're still there. In the trees."

"He also showed you how his rifle worked?"

"He was always worried about bad people, thiefs, when he wasn't at home. So he showed me, yes, how to load it and aim. Then he pointed it at my head and laughed."

"Were you scared?"

"Yes, because he was drinking a lot."

This episode occurred a week after Trudd's thieving Alaskan lover skipped town with her new boyfriend, in early spring. Apparently he went on a major drinking jag.

Trudd stored his three long guns — the Remington, a shotgun, and a .22 — in a rifle closet that he rarely locked. At the preliminary, officers testified that the shotgun and the .22 held live ammunition. They considered that not unusual; gun safety protocols were often breached in the north.

Angelina has admitted to a confusion about the exact flow of events in the brief time between Trudd's arrival and his death. The forensic psychiatrist hired by Pappas opined she repressed those tense twenty or thirty seconds, so as not to have to relive the trauma. Yet she remembered bits and pieces.

"Angelina, did you feel the kick of the gun when you fired it? The recoil?"

"I remember a loud noise, and falling back against the screen door, and I think I dropped the rifle. And then I am crying, and he is laying all twisted on the ground."

"So you remember that much."

"I remember the bang. And going back against the screen door. And the next I remember is opening my eyes and seeing him. And I got sick."

"Excuse me. You're saying your eyes had been closed?"

"Maybe. It is still confusing for me."

"So you weren't aiming the rifle at him. Not if your eyes were closed."

"I watched Mr. Trudd shooting deers and rabbits like this." She demonstrated, the butt of the imaginary rifle against her right shoulder, her left hand under the forestock, trigger finger cocked, eyes squinting. The guard who was watching looked displeased and a little agitated. A few inmates laughed.

"Okay, but when the gun fired, your eyes may have been closed, right?"

"Maybe. I try to do my best, Mr. Beauchamp."

"I understand. Let's just go back a little. After he got out of his car, did Mr. Trudd say something to you? A threat? Anything?"

"I don't know."

"Did *you* say anything?"

"I'm sorry, I don't know."

"You don't know or you can't remember?"

"I don't know."

"Do you remember him turning around?"

"No."

"Or urinating?"

"Urine . . . like peeing? No, I don't think so."

"Do you remember seeing his male organ exposed?"

"His . . . you mean cock?"

I confess to having been embarrassed by her use of that common vulgarism. She would have picked it up in this prison.

Pause here. It's not easy to reproduce this much younger version of Arthur Beauchamp. I am hardly overwhelmed with fond memories of him. I blush in shame over his social awkwardness, his pushy interview techniques. I was practically cross-examining my client, and offering not a thimble of empathy.

It seems bizarre, but Angelina rattled me — with her aura of serenity, her glow of pregnancy, her resolute faith, her kindness, her utter lack of cynicism. I'd been far more relaxed with heartless gangsters.

A softer approach might have teased out some hidden memory from that vital minute between the Mercedes pulling into the driveway and Trudd lying twisted on the ground. But there were serious blanks — including her act of going to the gun closet for the rifle.

"The fact is, Angelina, you can't honestly say you knew the rifle was loaded."

"No, sir, I can't honestly say, but he wanted it ready for bears or wolfs."

That was a most unsatisfactory answer, and I deserved it. But I pressed on. "This is important, Angelina — you don't remember checking to see if a bullet was in place, right?"

She nodded.

"And was the safety off?"

"I don't know. I don't know about how the safety works, I'm sorry."

"Angelina, if you didn't know the rifle was ready to fire, you obviously didn't plan or intend to kill him. I don't believe you did. I want you to think about that."

She looked confused. I didn't blame her. After all, she had told the arresting constables that she shot him because he'd raped her.

"I don't believe you are capable of murder, Angelina."

"But I shot Mr. Trudd."

I barely suppressed a groan. I did the talking for the rest of the morning, carefully explaining to her how our criminal court system works, how a jury is selected, the roles of judge and opposing counsel, entering a plea, taking an oath, testifying, the presumption of innocence, the onus of proof, reasonable doubt. She was an intelligent woman, and if she didn't grasp these concepts immediately she did so after seeking clarification.

Finally, she was called away for lunch, and I went back to my hotel, where I plotted over a soup and sandwich how to jolt her into fighting for an acquittal. I wondered if the threat of having her baby taken away might help her remember that she accidentally fired that rifle.

But when I returned to the prison for the next round, I found myself unable to extort her cooperation in that cruel way. I couldn't bear the prospect of causing more pain to a pious young woman whom God had already sorely tested.

I realized much later that my good intentions in shielding her from anguish were misplaced. My mistake was to defer a key agenda item — probing for a detailed recounting of Trudd's acts of abuse and rape and her reactions to them. I didn't have the heart, or the courage, or the skill and maturity, to properly frame intimate questions about acts of violence to her body. Bluntly, I was too inhibited, too awkward, too enslaved by the Victorian politesse drilled into me by my uptight parents.

The trial was five weeks away. Plenty of time for me to do some reading, or confer with an emotional trauma therapist. Or I could seek insights from a close female friend. If I had any close female friends. Did I dare consider Gertrude Isbister my friend as well as my secretary? I blushed just imagining asking Gertrude how she might react to a mauling from her boss.

Despite such bewilderment, I managed to spend the afternoon usefully, even managing to meet with the prison doctor, Genevieve Royce, who indeed had expertise in emotional trauma — she assured me that rape victims often repressed memories of violent sexual assaults. She had interviewed and examined Angelina only a day after her arrest, and promised to compose a medical report for me.

I then spent a couple of hours preparing my client for the witness stand, giving her lists of questions she might be asked, preparing her for the ordeal of cross-examination.

That might have been a wasted endeavour — I was not at all sure I would put her on the stand. She was too guileless, too sincere.

1966 —
Against All Odds

My temper finally erupted — not over the Macintosh case, but over Pappas's earlier, slack effort at representing Angelina. I blamed Pappas for having failed to enlist defence witnesses or follow up leads. I accused him of making light of Trudd's abusive behaviour toward her. Pappas could not be persuaded that Angelina was incapable of cold-blooded murder.

A final spat occurred when I marched into Pappas's office and laid thirty pounds of Macintosh files onto his desk, along with a list of unfinished tasks. I'd booked a flight to Fort Tom for the next day, Saturday. I said I needed time for pre-trial preparation and wouldn't be back for two weeks.

Pappas went apoplectic, fired me off the Macintosh case, and announced that up-and-comer Lev Shapiro would serve as his junior. I felt no hurt pride, indeed felt liberated. "Far more rewarding to defend an angel than an asshole," I told Pappas.

It had been a wet November, and on that rainy Saturday as I was packing for my flight north I longed for the sparkle of snowfields in the sun. I would have a week and a day in Fort Tom to patch together some kind of defence.

But I wasn't getting the breaks. Wilbur Kroop, newly raised to the bench, had just been delegated by the Chief Justice to preside over *R. v. Santos*. A disastrous choice.

This caustic crimebuster had been a highly rated Federal Crown, consistently ruthless, addicted to jailing junkies and potheads. I'd faced off against him several times, and once had nearly got him cited for contempt of court for withholding exculpatory evidence. He despised me; I detested him. I expected he would be as belli- cose a judge as he'd been a prosecutor.

I went on a night-long bender when I learned he would be sitting in the Fort Thompson assize.

To make matters worse, I was going to be outmanned. I'd fully expected to be against the senior Crown for the northern circuit, the amiable gentleman who'd prosecuted the preliminary. The Attorney General's office must have felt he wasn't up to snuff for a first-degree murder, because they borrowed a loudmouth from the Vancouver City Prosecutor's Office: Ed Santorini.

Though Eddie was seen as a top gun, that reputation was mostly self-made. He talked big but was lazy and careless, quali- ties I'd welcomed during his fumbled prosecution of Nick Faloon's diamond heist. He was also a bigot, specializing in misogyny. It seemed vaguely ironic that he would be juniored by that rarest of counsel, a woman: Clara Moncrief, newly fledged from law school.

Counsel for the defence, however, would be alone. Alex Pappas, still steaming over my chewing him out, had denied me a helpmate. I was under instructions to "keep costs from ballooning." I was scolded for paying fair rent for bed and breakfast at Harris's hunting lodge. Pappas even balked at my renting a car — I had to prove to the budget administrator's satisfaction that the resort was two miles out of town.

A comfy Ford Fairlane would be waiting for me at the airstrip that Saturday afternoon. I would have the luxury of nine days to work up a defence to the defenceless trial of Angelina Santos.

Arthur —
April 2022

I rise late to a glorious day, eat my oatmeal, do an hour of farm chores, kiss my wife adieu, and, under escort by Ulysses, tramp up the path to Blunder Point.

It's a freakishly summery day, a product of climate change. A song sparrow belts out its spring aria. Nuthatches respond with their nasal gronks. A towhee scolds. We pass through a white carpet of daisies, thence to a purple one, camas lilies wobbling in the unseasonable, balmy breezes from the ocean.

My funky seaside hideaway isn't yet in full sunshine but gets the morning's slanting rays from between the rugged trunks of mature Douglas firs. The only blemish in this picture postcard view is the tarp spread over two square metres of roof. It's been four weeks since Stoney and Dog promised to hustle back to install fresh-cut shakes. "It's Job One," Stoney announced then, a phrase repeated three weeks ago, two weeks ago, and finally, two days ago.

Never mind. I shall fling the cabin windows open. I shall let the sunshine in and breathe the warm salt air. I shall not feel guilty about taking pleasure from the warming of the planet. This lovely day will inspire me to conquer my writer's block.

Having puffed myself up as much as I can, I must now gird myself for the next chapter, about a journey whose horrors I have taken pains to suppress. I must find the strength to recall, to reveal, to relive the torment of my journey to the Northland.

My gnarled farmer's hands rise over the keyboard, and fingers descend, and words appear: as Odysseus battled against Cyclopes and Sirens, against Charybdis and Scylla, so did I with a giant, ugly, snarling Greyhound . . .

Imprisoned in the frigid waiting room of a small, filthy bus station, bodies huddled on benches and floor: it's all coming back, causing palpitations. Overnighting in the Cockroach Lodge. Stranded on the Alaska Highway, toes and fingers freezing as the driver tinkers forever with the ignition. A drunk in front of me, a crazy man behind, short tempers, a fight breaks out. Choking dust as the Greyhound grinds over long gravel stretches, babies crying, the smell of vomit . . . Will we ever reach Fort Tom, will our hero survive?

1966 —
Hush Money

It was four days before Angelina's trial was to begin and I was in a rancorous mood as I waited in the RCMP coffee lounge for her to be fetched from the cells. I was still emotionally crippled from my thirty-hour ordeal.

My Saturday flight to Fort Tom had been cancelled because of an Arctic storm front, and I'd been unwilling to wait till mid-week for the next plane. On Monday, stupidly, I took a bus, and it wasn't until late Tuesday, after a stop-and-go torment, that I finally pulled in.

Making matters worse, I'd learned on arrival that my client was still in the Prince George jail, so I spent Wednesday hovering by the ravenous woodstove of my log cabin while Arctic winds hammered at the windows. There I met with a number of respected locals — collected by Father Etienne Larouche and Angelina's landlady, Marsha Bigelow.

My plan was to bring several of these staunch citizens to the court to testify to my client's good character. A tricky strategy: if the jury accepted that the accused had a sterling reputation for honesty, would they conclude that her impromptu confession was sincere?

I took a deep breath and put on a welcoming smile as Sergeant Mike Trasov ushered Angelina Santos into the lounge. He seemed awkward in her presence, unable to look at the protrusion of her belly, and he quickly backed out, telling us to help ourselves to coffee or tea and the offerings of the fridge.

Angelina wore a light jacket over a yellow blouse and skirt, an outfit newly bought by her support team. Garb that was sunny and proclaimed innocence. Not quite maternity wear, though she was in her sixth month.

As I made tea for both of us, I offered a few lighthearted anecdotes about my travails on the long bus ride. The idea was to relax her for the tough interview to come — yet she seemed, oddly, under little strain. I joked that sitting about bus stations was like waiting at the gates of hell, and she laughed, not finding that irreverent.

She reached across our little table to squeeze my right hand, and said, "I am very sorry for your hard time." The grip of her hand was a gesture of solace, but I felt something more, something odd: an illusive transfer of energy.

We both sat back. I took a deep breath, apologized for what was to come, and said: "Miss Santos, in your interviews with Mr. Pappas and his medical expert, there is no mention of any boyfriends in your year in Fort Thompson."

"I liked a boy who gave Bible lessons . . . But I think he wanted to be a priest." She laughed lightly. "Also, I was too busy with other things."

"So you were not, um, intimate with him?"

"He kissed me once."

"All right. And did you have any other, ah, events of an intimate nature . . ." I stalled, helpless.

"Mr. Beauchamp, if you mean did I ever have consent sex with anyone, no, never. I was hundred percent virgin."

"Until Mr. Trudd . . ."

"Yes. Raped me."

I'd heard she was highly regarded by her fellow inmates for snuffing a rapist. "What date was that?"

"It was the night before he drove to Pouce Coupe. Thursday night."

The file bore only vague references to what Trudd was doing in that historic, rural village in the Peace River farmlands. Despite stunted growth, Pouce Coupe was a regional government centre back in the 1960s. According to local legend, it got its name — Cut-off Thumb, in English — from a Francophone trapper who accidentally shot his thumb off.

Trudd had attended a hearing there, held in camera. It likely related to opposition from the Wolf River Reserve's Band Council to Trudd's plans to clearcut a thousand acres of their traditional territory on the upper Wolf River. I made a mental note to call Hubbell Meyerson at Tragger, Inglis to do some sleuthing — he knew people in the province's Aboriginal Affairs branch.

It would be improper, perhaps even offensive, for me to relate the sordid details of Trudd's attack on Angelina, or the abusive events that led up to it. So I will merely summarize here the account Angelina gave me during our morning in that coffee lounge.

I have already mentioned Trudd's revolting jest of pointing his rifle at Angelina's head. She had also endured several instances of unwanted touching before the first serious event occurred in late April. That occurred while she was doing laundry — he drunkenly crept up to her from behind and ran his hands inside her work shirt and over her breasts. She screamed, two cats bolted, and Trudd stumbled over them and fell. Despite that manhandling, she helped him up and led him from the laundry room. He passed out on a couch.

Angelina felt violated, of course, but she believed God wanted her to forgive, to put the matter aside, and it was not spoken about. She continued to show up Mondays through Saturdays.

It was her routine, after a hard day's work, to shower and change into fresh clothes in a basement suite that was reserved for her use. In the late afternoon of Saturday, May 21, she stepped from behind the shower curtain to find Trudd in the bathroom doorway, inebriated again, pants down, masturbating. She didn't scream this time, or even protest, just covered herself with a towel and scooped up her clothes. He tried to grab her, but stumbled, his feet tangled in his pants. She pushed past him, ran upstairs, got dressed, and left the house, vowing never to return.

Angelina immediately related this second episode to her land-lady, Marsha Bigelow, the tough, spirited widow who owned the popular restaurant called Rustlers — she was one of the few in town not beholden financially to Trudd.

This was Marsha's rundown of her efforts to intervene: the next morning, Sunday, she found Trudd in his office at his sawmill, alone, severely hungover. As Marsha stepped in, he slammed down his phone, yelling, "Fucking bitches!"

"I had a sense the bitches referred to were Hortense and Donalda."

His unlovable sisters. I remembered Buck Harris's broadside: Couple of witches, them dames. The fricking bloodsucker didn't have wife or kids, so they got everything.

"Anyway, when I finally got him calmed down, he had the gall to tell me Angelina must have been dreaming. He said that's common with religious young women who repress their sexuality, or some such drivel like that. And then he wrote out a cheque to her for $300 and handed it to me."

He wrote "bonus" on the stub. The payment was conditional on her returning to work. That was a big sum in those days — about $2,500 in current dollars; Angelina earned less than that per month.

"I saw it as hush money so she wouldn't talk to no one else, espe-cially the cops. It was generous, but of course it was up to Angelina what to do. If it was me, I'd say sure, I'll take some easy dough to keep quiet about seeing his dirty cock. He was too hammered to do any real damage and I figured he was shit scared and he'd back right off of her from now on."

Angelina hadn't mentioned to her the previous groping assault. Had she known of it, Marsha told me, she might have left the bribe on the desk. Instead she stuck the cheque in her purse and stomped out. This information was missing from the file Pappas gave me: he'd not even interviewed Marsha Bigelow.

Angelina's mother in Manila had a heart condition, and were it not for the remittances would be living on charity. So Angelina accepted the money — she saw it as a form of apology — and on Monday, May 23, did a bank transfer to her mother's account in Manila. A bonus, according to Trudd; an apology, in Angelina's view, but Marsha Bigelow was probably dead right in calling it hush money.

Angelina didn't return to work immediately, then at mid-week Trudd's office manager contacted her, saying the boss was about to leave for three nights in Pouce Coupe, a five-hour drive south, and needed her to stay over to look after the six cats. Angelina had bonded with those pets, and Trudd trusted no one else with their care.

When she turned up for work on Thursday morning, Trudd was waiting for her by the front door. He neither looked at nor spoke to her as he brushed past to his Mercedes. He wore a business suit, and carried a briefcase and an overnight bag.

She watched him drive off toward the highway, then took her gear down to the basement suite — she had frequently stayed there when Trudd was away. She was looking forward to three nights with not much to do but tend to the six cats.

Upstairs in the kitchen, the cats thronged and purred about her ankles as she made tea and washed Trudd's breakfast dishes. The vacuuming and dusting and the ring in the bathtub would wait: she took her tea to the parlour and clicked on the big twenty-four-inch TV. *As the World Turns* would be on in a few minutes, and then *Search for Tomorrow*.

I had to glean from sources other than Angelina the events leading to the rape. She was unaware, as she watched Trudd drive off on the morning of Thursday, May 26, that he planned to spend half the day at his office before going to Pouce Coupe. According to his secretary, he spent a few hours poring over documents and making business calls. Before leaving town, he stopped at Rustlers for lunch. As it happened, its proprietor, Marsha Bigelow, was in a nearby booth with a few women friends. Trudd heard them laughing.

Marsha ruefully admitted to me that she'd regaled them about the masturbation episode and the hush money. When they noticed Trudd at the counter, their sudden silence was telling. Trudd knocked back a pair of rum and colas with his steak sandwich, then joined a few cronies over a bottle at the local bootlegger's. Throughout the afternoon his anger grew more heated over Angelina's tattling to Marsha, who was defaming him around town as a pervert.

At around eleven p.m. he staggered from the Fort Hotel's beer parlour, where he'd been intermittently sulking and raging. It was dark by then — the sun sets at 10 p.m. in late May up there — but somehow he managed to drive to his house without going off the road or being pulled over. Unluckily for Angelina Santos.

Angelina had gone to bed at half past nine, and, though weary, had to struggle for sleep. The week had taken an emotional toll. She wasn't sure how long she could abide working for this lecherous drunkard with his pawing hands. The apology money, the $300, could bind her to him, however, like a debt.

She was asleep at shortly past eleven when she became aware of a light that shouldn't be on — she'd turned everything off. Then she sensed the light was from outside, shredded through her window by the caragana bushes. When it went off, she thought she had dreamed it. Then, as she shook away the fuzz of sleep, she heard what seemed the thump of a car door swinging shut — she hadn't heard an engine, but sounds from outside were muffled in the basement.

She was sharply awake then — her first thought was of thieves, alerted that Trudd was out of town. She rose, whipping off sheet and blankets, then stalled, unsure whether to hide or head for the rifle locker. Then she heard the thudding of heavy footfalls on the basement stairs.

A light came on, glowing beneath her unlocked door. Frantic, she fumbled with the lock bolt, but it wouldn't slide shut. She tried to push a chest of drawers against the door, but couldn't find the strength.

The door swung open. Trudd stepped in, reeking of whisky, his suit rumpled, his tie loose. As she tried to flee into the bathroom, he tackled her, threw her on the bed, screaming words that Angelina unflinchingly recalled — they'd echoed in her ears throughout a sleepless night: "Marsha Bigelow! That gossipy snake! The whole fucking town is laughing!"

He tossed his jacket on a chair, unbuttoned his pants. "Doesn't matter. You're now officially the town whore, Angelina. 'Cause they're all gonna know I paid for it."

1966 —
God's Will Be Done

When I returned to Angelina on Thursday after lunch — an unhealthy burger, fries, and root beer shake at the A&W drive-in — I again pressed her to give me at least a starter kit to help construct a reasonable doubt. "Let's revisit May twenty-ninth," I said, with an air of desperation: "You didn't intend to kill Mr. Trudd, did you?"

She looked puzzled. "I don't know. I don't know what to say."

"Was he shouting or cursing as you stood there with the rifle?"

Again, her simple mantra: "I don't know." Then she added, "I can only tell my truth, as God tells me to."

I suppressed a sigh. "Do you remember what you said on the phone to the police?"

"I said, 'I shot Mr. Trudd, and I think he's dead.'"

"You actually said, "I think I shot Mr. Trudd and he's dead.' So you actually weren't sure you shot him."

She shook her head. Then, softly, "I know I did."

As a youngster in the 1940s, I had attended Sunday school (religiously) and was a firm believer in even the most fantastical tales from the Old Testament. I endured the requisite nightmares of roasting in hell, somewhat in the manner of a sizzling chicken in an oven. I pictured Satan not with horns but with the little brush moustache of Adolf Hitler. I knelt at bedtime, hands clasped, cajoling the Lord to save, in ascending order, our cat Jasper, Daddy, Mommy, and me.

Though I grew out of that, achieving by my teens a healthy level of agnostic doubt, the effects of early indoctrination and long-time habit had me sporadically attending Anglican services in Vancouver and, latterly, Garibaldi Island, where I chum with the local minister. In the course of all this, I have met some saintly people. Not many, but a few.

However, never in the course of my inconstant religious pursuits had I encountered anyone as saintly as Miss Angelina Santos. On Thursday, throughout our lengthy conversation in that long session in the RCMP coffee lounge, I didn't pick up a single angry, bitter, or even woeful note. She was grateful for the love received from her many friends in Fort Tom. She felt blessed to have a lawyer so smart and courteous and caring and who endured such a horribly long bus ride just for her.

Angelina appeared not to have felt much, if any, emotional trauma from the ugly episodes of late May, which I found extraordinary. I didn't see her as repressing her ordeal or putting on an act. Nothing about her seemed artificial.

As to the late F.C. Trudd, she spoke no ill — he was in God's hands now. As he forced himself on her, she had silently prayed. She didn't resist. It was God's will. A testing.

That is not to suggest she wasn't in fear. He raped her in anger, and her delicate skin showed bruising for days afterwards. Trudd had also threatened her against speaking out, according to Alex Pappas's interview notes. That was the chief issue Angelina and I discussed on Thursday afternoon.

Angelina confirmed that Trudd, before driving off into the night, had promised to have her deported were she to mention he'd forced himself on her. He had friends "in high places" who would see that she was sent back to Manila in disgrace as a convicted prostitute. Even her mother would reject her.

I found it hard to believe that this intelligent young woman would be intimidated by such threats. Yet, unfortunately, she hadn't followed the accepted practices for assault victims. She didn't stir from that house all weekend — she felt a duty to care for and feed the six cats, but that seemed a skimpy reason. What made even less sense is that she didn't call police, priest, doctor, neighbour, or friend, even Marsha Bigelow. What had happened was God's will, she calmly instructed me. God had a purpose unknowable by mere mortals.

Our only proof that the rape was violent — or that it had occurred at all — was that her nightie and panties were ripped, spotted with blood, and gluey with semen. Police had found these garments along with various washables in a laundry bag in the basement bedroom. She told me she'd planned to garbage the torn garments on returning to her lodgings. The remaining clothes would be washed there.

I asked why she didn't just toss them into Trudd's washer and dryer.

"Because I wash his dirty things only at his house. I am not paid to take advantage."

By that righteous rule, her sheets and bedding were "his dirty things," and they got washed. She practically wiped the house clean of evidence of crime. She took pride in her work as a housemaid. Cleaning was her duty, her responsibility.

I felt so frustrated by her innocence and decency that I went briefly into cross-examination mode: "Did you actually believe he had the power to deport you?"

A thoughtful frown. Then a shrug. "I believed when he said he had friends in government."

"Surely you didn't think Immigration would kick you out of the country because he claimed you had sex with him for money."

She considered that, then smiled. "You make it sound silly, but I do not know the laws of Canada. It would not sound silly in my country."

"He also said you would face disgrace on being sent back to your home country."

"I did not believe that, sir."

"And that your mother would reject you."

"Never." Finally, sorrow showed, her eyes dampening. "If I talk to police, he said he will phone my mother to say I am a dirty, lying whore."

This was missing from Pappas's notes. It came to me then why Angelina had made no hue and cry.

"She has two heart attacks already. If she knew what happened to me, it will kill her. I didn't want her to know. She still does not know."

Tears streamed. I passed my handkerchief to her. At the touch of her hand, she suddenly smiled through those tears and I again felt a tingling, like a current passing into me. Maybe it was illusory. Maybe a digestive issue, linked to the burger and fries.

Though Fort Tom's small RCMP detachment served a vast stretch of northern BC, its constables lacked wide experience. For major crimes, investigators usually flew up from Prince George, a mid-sized city and a hub of commerce for the underpopulated north. But it's no nearer to Fort Tom than to Vancouver, and a flight tarmac-to-tarmac took three hours by RCMP Twin Otter.

After the arresting officers heard Angelina confess — *I shot him* — they sought instructions from Prince George, and were told to make notes but not interrogate further. They were to wait for members of the Major Crimes Unit to arrive. Presumably, it was feared the lowly local constables might botch an interview and render it inadmissible.

The Prince George team — three from ID and two detectives — landed at five-thirty and were taken directly to the crime scene. The detectives tarried there awhile, wandering through the house, seeking signs of the alleged rape, but finding everything clean, neat, and tidy. Angelina's bag of dirty laundry was examined by the ID officers and ultimately passed on to the RCMP serologist for stain analysis.

It was not till after six that the two investigators sat down to talk with Angelina — only to discover that they had to do all the talking. Angelina asserted her right to silence by politely shaking her head.

She'd been in an RCMP cell during the four hours that had elapsed since her arrest, but had one visitor: Hogey Johnson, one of half a dozen local lawyers. The most senior, I was told, and the most respected. "A cracker-barrel kind of guy," said Marsha Bigelow, who had beseeched him to counsel Angelina.

I had hoped to call on him late Thursday but my head was spinning after my long session with Angelina. I felt drained: emotionally and maybe spiritually, from something that had radiated from her. Finally, I fell exhausted into a ragged sleep, struggling with an awareness that something was missing. Something critical. Essential.

Arthur —
May 2022

Midway through this merry month, I find myself lined up at the Canada Post outlet in Garibaldi's century-old General Store at Hopeless Bay. Progress has stalled because Abraham Makepeace, the store owner and postmaster, is being overly meticulous in filling out forms to be signed by island matriarch Idabel Ames.

"I'm number one," she is purported to have boasted at the funeral of her sister, Winnie Gillicuddy, who lived to 114. Idabel is only ninety-eight but carries on her sibling's tradition of blunt talk and impatience with bureaucracy.

"Take forever, why don't you?" she says. "It's going to Nanaimo, not to the end of the world."

"You want insurance or not?"

"I ain't mailing the crown jewels, it's a box of ginger cookies. Move it, man, you have people waiting." She turns to me, seeking an ally. "Can't mail a birthday card 'less it's wrapped in red tape. In the old days, you'd lick a stamp and stick it on, and you're done."

Makepeace, ever protective of the great institution that is the postal service, sullenly riffles through her incoming mail, studies the return address on a letter. "This here's from your grandson's home address, so he must've finally made parole."

She grabs her mail, turns to me. "Someday I'm gonna punch that peeping postmaster in the face." She stalks off.

Makepeace stoically reaches into the Blunder Bay slot, hauls out a thick envelope, a book-sized parcel, a cardboard box, the latest *Island Bleat*, and a couple of bills and promotions. "I was gonna toss this here card as junk mail until I saw it was an invite to you for an art show in Toronto."

I stiffen as I examine the card's display of colourful objets d'art from a potter's studio. Distinctively the works of Taba Jones, who is inviting me to her June opening at a downtown gallery. I stuff the card into a jacket pocket, hoping Makepeace hasn't noticed the artist's name or the quickie signature: "Hugs, T.J."

Fat chance. Makepeace winks conspiratorially. "Looks like she's still panting after you, Arthur." A quick glance at the lineup behind me catches omnivorous gossip Pattie Weekes straining to hear. I chuckle loudly, pretending I'm sharing in the postmaster's joke. Taba's card will be burned or garbaged — mentioning it to Margaret will only reopen old wounds.

"This here smaller parcel will be the typewriter ribbons you complained that we don't stock, and here's the book you ordered about the detective with hearing delusions."

I've often suspected Makepeace has paranormal powers. Otherwise, how could he possibly know about *You Talkin' to Me?* I sent for it online.

"Can't say I read a lot of mystery novels, but I reckon I'll read the one you're writing. Everyone's talking about it."

Everybody? Whence came the notion I was writing a mystery? I'd much rather no one knows I'm writing any kind of book. Failure would be an embarrassment. What if I succumb to a crippling writer's block? What if I can't find a publisher?

Abraham hefts the cardboard box. "This came Priority Plus from your old law office. Old trial transcripts would be my guess, smells like mice got into them. Sign here, here, and here."

I pause on my way out to glance at the *Island Bleat*. Here is the leak, in the "News Nuggets" column: *Word has it that retired mouthpiece A.R. Beauchamp has secretly lunched a new career as a famous mystery writer.* Stoney is the likely leaker of this poorly edited exclusive.

➥

I dare not take the transcripts to the house; Margaret will be appalled by their stink. So I follow a path through the forest to the cabin where "the Great Writer," to use her snarky label, toils to chronicle the past.

My absorption in the art of the written word (as opposed to the spoken, at which I was famously adept) has triggered an obsessive state that Margaret finds annoying — the Great Writer is so focused on himself, past and present, that he's neglecting his chores; his garden has become as weedy as his mind.

Not so weedy, however, to forget to immolate Taba's postcard. Into the woodstove it goes, aflame. I don't suppose any harm will be done emailing her a brief note wishing her a successful showing of her work. It would be the gentlemanly thing to do, and Margaret wouldn't need to know.

Meanwhile, I haven't found the courage to show Margaret my latest draft; I fear her sharply critical eye. She will not applaud my frank portrayal of gawky young Stretch, with his bumbling efforts to develop a rapport with his abused pregnant client. She will not admire this socially insecure oaf with his nascent drinking problem.

Why am I driven to expose in print my former self? Why am I reliving that daunting, fearsome trial from 1966? Am I merely seeking to correct the record, as sensationalized by Wentworth Chance in his revisionist history, "A Will to Die For"? Or is there a nobler, introspective purpose? A striving to acquaint myself with young Arthur, so that I may better know myself? Somehow, over the decades, I lost sight of this raw, anxious, yet ambitious twenty-nine-year-old. Only when I began to render you on the page, Stretch, did I begin to recognize you. And thus myself. This old man.

How I would love to be youthful you again. To start all over. Do it right, without the pain. Yet I am happy now. Am I not?

Enough.

The sour smell of mouse urine wafts from the box of transcripts, so I open it outside: five ring-bound volumes, legal size, double-spaced, some pages nibbled at the corners and margins, but otherwise intact.

Leafing casually through the pages, as I lay them out to air on the sunny deck, I sense memory cells reawakening, shedding light on scenes grown misty after fifty-six years. *Defenceless* will not lack for accuracy: every spoken word is in these five volumes, including my squabbles with the judge.

Also in the box, sealed in plastic, is a file folder with copies of exhibits, along with photos and various court documents and — a prize, unexpected — my own notes from 1966, my interviews and scribbled observations.

These will very quickly be put to use — young Arthur is about to get tipsy with, first, a folksy Fort Tom lawyer, and then a nervy, alluring prosecutor. I have a faded memory of the former, but will never forget the latter.

I settle into my desk chair, and roll another sheet into my typewriter. I spin back through the years to a blustery Friday in November 1966 . . .

1966 —
Just Shake Your Head

It was just before noon, Angelina's trial only three days away, and I was standing outside a storefront office at the corner of Second Avenue and Main, reading a gold-lettered window sign: *HOGARTH W. JOHNSON, BARRISTER, SOLICITOR, NOTARY PUBLIC. CONVEYANCES, MORTGAGES, CONTRACTS, CORPORATE, WILLS AND ESTATES.* A solicitor, a generalist.

His secretary, a cherubic young woman with a shy smile, greeted me and called out: "Your lunch date is here, Hogey." He hastened from an inner office: late sixties, lanky, with a Mark Twain moustache and a wide, gap-tooth grin.

"So you're the young hotshot I been reading about in the paper. Welcome to the frozen north. I have a table at Rustlers, tenderest tenderloin west of the Prairies. You care for a wee dram of something first? It's Friday."

━

Hogey literally *had* a table at Rustlers — it was by the front window, a small plaque with his name fixed to it, honouring his four decades of dedicated service to the Rotary Club. Having got to know each other in his office over a tipple of Crown Royal, we got even chummier over our grilled T-bones.

He told a few picaresque tales about this cold, northern frontier, and I entertained with vignettes from my trials. He kept calling me "young fella," making me feel I was eighteen.

"Never been comfortable with the criminal end of things," he said, pausing for a hearty belch. "I had a friend called Thomas — I'm lucky to still call him a friend — got charged with bootlegging homemade hooch out of his taxi business. Number one most popular guy in town. Thanks to me, he went down for two months plus a hundred-dollar fine. That pretty well sums up my criminal law career."

"But you did a brilliant piece of defence work last May twenty-ninth."

He nodded, distracted, absorbed in the dessert menu. "What do you say, young fella, coffee with a shot of brandy?"

"Of course."

"The chocolate sundae tempts."

"As you said, Hogey, it's Friday."

So far, Angelina Santos hadn't been much discussed, other than that Hogey knew her through Rotary-sponsored community work. He also indicated, unhappily, that a faction of townspeople — not just Trudd's cronies — had doubts that he'd raped and impregnated her. Many disputed the well-travelled rumour that he'd performed an indecent act as she was naked in the shower.

Presumably, these Trudd loyalists preferred to believe that Angelina, to use an ignoble banality, had got herself in trouble. It disturbed me that some skeptics with sexist and racist views might find their way onto the jury.

After his dessert and our drinks arrived, Hogey opened up about his brief role as Angelina's counsel. He recounted how Marsha Bigelow tore him away from his barbecue pit, causing him to abandon his spouse and their dinner guests. "I'd already had a brew or two, just to numb the shock — it was all over town: F.C. Trudd gunned down by a girl everyone thought was an angel."

At the police station, he learned Angelina had blurted out that she'd shot Trudd. "Because he'd raped her, that was the reason she gave them. This was my first inkling it wasn't accidental and could be first-degree murder. Well, young fella, that got me more than a little flummoxed."

Hogey was let into her cell, where he found her calmly reading the Bible. "I was surprised by that, you'd think she'd be in shock and fear, or bawling her eyes out. Anyway, I made her promise to button up, and if the policemen ask any more questions, I said to her, just shake your head."

As to the rape: "Well, she confirmed that, but I didn't ask about the how and the why, just told her I'd see her in the morning, and that's about it, because I had to get back to my guests. On my way out I told Sergeant Trasov she ain't gonna say anything without a lawyer present, and I guess that worked."

"Shrewdly done. And you appeared for her Monday?"

"Just to ask the magistrate to remand her a week, so Marsha and Etienne could rustle up some moolah to hire her a real lawyer."

"You mustn't denigrate yourself, Hogey. You were Johnny-on-the-spot, very professional job." I was priming his pump because I wanted more out of him. This popular practitioner had to know many tales about F.C. Trudd.

"I understand you also got a doctor to look at her right away. On a Sunday. That was quick work."

He beamed. "Did what I could. I had them take her to Jim Mulligan's clinic. Jim specializes in obstetrics and other ladies' issues."

That physician's testimony at the preliminary had been less than helpful. Though Pappas pressed him hard, Dr. Mulligan claimed "the usual physical indicia of rape" were lacking. More worrisome, he had declined my overtures to meet with him pre-trial.

The Prince George prison doctor who later examined Angelina was more congenial and had just mailed me her report. Dr. Royce had observed genital bruising and other physical trauma that were "typically suffered by victims of forceful penetration." She was also of the view that Angelina had suffered a "partial but significant amnesia" for particulars of the sexual assault.

Hogey was showing signs of being ready for an afternoon nap. When he struggled to wrestle his wallet from his pants, I got the jump on him, gave the waiter a twenty, told him to bring two more caffeinated brandies for the road, and keep the change. I wasn't through with my lanky learned friend.

"As the premier solicitor in these northlands, I would imagine you did some work for F.C. Trudd?"

He took a moment, suddenly reluctant. "Well, I guess I did odd jobs here and there for Fred — small stuff, business licences, rental agreements. Mostly, I notarized deeds from his corporate lawyers in Vancouver."

"By the way, what exactly was he doing in Pouce Coupe that weekend?"

"Some kind of screwed-up mediation thing with the Tribal Council. A land dispute. I heard tempers got pretty raw, Chief Sayaga got pissed off, and apparently Johnny Blue took a swipe at Trudd." He caught himself. "Well, I better not say what I heard, it came from a client. The Wolf River Band has a pretty good gripe, as far as I'm concerned."

"Who is Johnny Blue?"

"Ah, that would be the chief's nephew . . . Actually, all I heard was rumours."

Why the equivocation, I wondered, *why the secrecy?* Hub Meyerson had connections, and was on it. "Anyway, back to your odd jobs — did Mr. Trudd ever ask you to draft a will for him?"

Sudden silence. The pained look betrayed a struggle to come up with a credible evasion. "Well, that would normally be something his Vancouver lawyers would do." Pausing. "Now it seems to me, young fella, this gets into the, ah, tricky area of privilege."

"Of course, and I don't mean to pry, but I can't imagine that he died intestate. Not with such a substantial estate. Millions of dollars."

Hogey swirled his brandy, buying time, maybe having a problem restraining an alcohol-loosened tongue, maybe wondering how much he could trust me. I was a bit tiddled myself, and I left my brandy untouched.

"Okay, he had a will as of when his last wife divorced him. I had a hand in that. The will, I mean, not the divorce — he had the province's top divorce lawyer for that, Neil Fleishman."

"And who were the beneficiaries of that will?"

"Well, the wife, of course, his sisters and their offspring — he never had kids of his own. The local veterinarian, Dr. Muggins, was well rewarded — he'd patched together one of Fred's little gals, Fluffy, who got mangled by a fox. Also some good causes, SPCA, Ducks Unlimited, local Chamber of Commerce, Gun Club. The divorce was three years ago, and of course a divorce revokes any gifts to an ex-spouse."

I vaguely remembered that from law school. The remaining clauses of the will would survive intact, doubtless to the benefit of Trudd's sisters.

"Fred did pretty good on the alimony, on account of she deserted him. Anyway, I don't think he ever got around to updating his will, and, ah, his estate is still kind of languishing in probate. Too complicated for me, his big-time lawyers are handling it."

I apologized for my drilling, and we became chums again. He offered the facilities of his law office for phone calls and meetings. He proposed that I come over for a home-cooked dinner during the trial — his wife would love my stories about defending the mob. I said I'd get back to him on that.

I helped him into his coat and held the door to let him out into the frigid, windy day. "When I retire," he said, "it's gonna be in a cottage under the palms where the sun always shines."

I wasn't ready to brave the weather, and took my brandy — barely sipped — to the long, wooden bar, and started scribbling an aide-memoire of our conversation.

Hogey's quibbling had my antennae wiggling — it hadn't struck me till then that Trudd's will might factor into the case. Why had the jovial Rotarian been so vague about the status of Trudd's estate? I assumed he was too polite to say it was none of my business.

I was suddenly aware of a presence on my immediate right. Oddly perfumed, something herbal. Or maybe it was the cigarette she was smoking. As my eyeballs swivelled to the right, they recorded a denim jacket decorated with a peace symbol, open to a well-filled-out work shirt.

"I'll have what he's having." The contralto voice seemed oddly husky from someone so young. I turned to her, took in a profile of fuchsia lips, a thin, plumb-straight nose, and round, metal-framed John Lennon glasses hooked over an ear from which dangled a silver earring that spelled "FREE." All topped by a tousled auburn mop. Suitable for San Francisco's Haight Street or Vancouver's Fourth Avenue. In Fort Tom, it seemed an improbable fashion statement.

When she turned to me, I decided that despite her showiness she was, if not a great beauty, quite striking with her dark, wise eyes and wide, confident smile. "I don't mean to interrupt your diarizing, Arthur, but I thought we should meet."

She reached into a cluttered handbag. The card she produced read "CLARA MONCRIEF, MA, LLB., CROWN COUNSEL."

Eddie Santorini's advance guard had arrived from Vancouver.

◼▶

Clara and I got along rather well over our two rounds of Irish coffees. She was twenty-five, two years out of law school, and liberated (as one said in the sixties) from false values. I was afraid to ask her what was in her odd-smelling cigarettes — surely she wasn't brazen enough to openly smoke marijuana, an indictable offence in the 1960s. Herbal, I learned, when she apologized for the odour — she was trying to kick nicotine.

When she caught me trying to X-ray through her tight shirt, she boldly let me know she had just checked in to a corner room on the sixth floor of the Fort Hotel. "With entrancing views of downtown Fort Thompson," she added, with a deadpan look that made me smile.

She had "boned up" on me, by which I assumed she meant my track record as counsel. She recalled chuckling over Jack Wasserman's item in the *Vancouver Sun*: "A crackerjack young shark with a growing rep, and not just in the courtroom." And of course she was one of the boundless masses of West Coast lawyers who'd heard about my alleged bacchanal with two women of the night.

I had given up trying to refute this rumour mongering — why spoil everyone's fun? — and in response to Clara's teasing inquiries I merely shrugged helplessly and changed the subject to my nightmare odyssey by bus, a tale that prompted her to apologize for laughing.

In contrast, Clara's trip had been, as she put it, "a trip": a commercial flight to Prince George, then by RCMP Twin Otter to Fort Tom — along with the Crown's ID team and two detectives. They'd taken over the ten-room Alaska Highway Motel, near the airport, and she was to spend the weekend rehearsing them for their supporting roles in court. Lead counsel Eddie Santorini wouldn't be arriving until late Sunday.

I was eager to talk with their ballistics expert. Clara was fine with that as long as she was present. I would be welcome to join her and the Ident officers at the crime scene on Saturday morning at ten.

Clara confessed she'd signed on with the Crown as a short-term lark, so this feminist liberal was doubtless stewing over having to prosecute a pregnant rape victim who'd rubbed out a drunken, sexist, capitalist pig. A clever counsel would encourage such doubts, perhaps bring the doubter onside.

I was glad to be able to focus on business instead of the attractions of this upfront, unreserved woman. I was as much flustered as tempted by her implied offer to check out the views from her corner room. I had serious misgivings about the proprieties, ethics, and wisdom of a defence counsel becoming too friendly with a female Crown counsel in advance of a capital murder trial.

Also, she made me nervous. That reaction was not unusual whenever I found myself in close company of confident, attractive women. I was unsure of the rules of conduct. And Clara was especially forward, offbeat, intriguing — and therefore all the more dangerous. Especially because I was more than a little tipsy. Too often, during my young life, I had drunkenly wandered off the track into the uninhibited zone.

I walked her to the hotel, just a block away, and even stepped into the lobby for a reprieve from the cold. A busy cocktail lounge beckoned, with its roaring, log-filled fireplace, but I wasn't keen on being pulled over for impaired driving.

"Want to come up?"

"I . . . I don't think so. I mean, I would normally, but, ah, I have to sober up a bit. I'm meeting some friends to go over the jury list."

"Sure, I'll see you tomorrow at ten. Good luck with Miss Santos. Luck might not be enough. Maybe a miracle."

"Victurus te saluto."

"Means?"

"'He who is about to win salutes you.'" A boastful parting shot, which I regretted. I guess I needed to display confidence in my client's innocence.

1966 —
The Shit End of the Stick

I felt weary, and headed back to the Harrises' resort for a late afternoon nap. I had slept poorly for the last three nights, and needed
a few hours to sober up and rest the brain so I could be reasonably
sentient that evening. Buck and Lorraine had invited Etienne and
Marsha Bigelow for dinner, and we planned to review the forty-four
names of those subpoenaed for jury duty.

When I arrived, Lorraine was in the cabin, firing up the woodstove. She had also vacuumed, made my bed, and laundered my
clothes — she was like the mother I wished I'd known. I voiced
a vigorous protest against her generosity and kindness, but she
scoffed. It was no trouble. Ten members of a Montana hunting club
were arriving on the weekend: *that* was trouble.

After she left, I flopped onto the couch and drifted into a dense
zone halfway between sleeping and awake. Angelina Santos hovered
into view, gauzy, with wings, and she was laughing. At me? What
was the joke? Finally, my body and brain unwound, and I fell into a
deep oblivion.

It was almost eight o'clock when they came to get me. The knocks and calls from Etienne and Buck Harris had gone unheard, so they had to enter and shake my shoulder. They were worried I was dead. Dinner was on in five minutes.

I shambled in after a quick wash-up and change of attire, plunking down two bottles of wine, apologizing, blaming my exhaustion on having survived a very wet lunch with Hogey Johnson. That got laughs, and before I could say please pass the horseradish they were telling stories about the genial solicitor, who was notoriously absent-minded, in an undone-fly kind of way. Forgetting his wallet, losing his car keys, showing up on the wrong day.

"You gotta love the old dope," said Marsha. "He took a lot of shit from Trudd, but he kept smiling."

I heard more about this abuse as we helped ourselves to salad, potatoes, gravy, and slices of a large, roasted animal, possibly a moose. I partook of no wine or spirits; I'd sworn to keep my drinking in check.

Marsha had shared many confidences with Hogey, as well as untold coffees, beers, and chocolate sundaes, at the table the Rotary Club had labelled in his honour. He'd kept few secrets from her. I learned that Trudd owned the office building housing Hogey's storefront. Hogey paid no rent; nor did Trudd pay the lawyer's bills — an arrangement, Marsha said, that left Hogey holding "the shit end of the stick."

Trudd bullied him, put him down in public. "He called Hogey a dunce, a moron. They'd be in the pub, and Trudd would go, 'How did this fruit fly ever get outta law school?' He treated his cats better, his little princes and princesses. It wasn't that Hogey was a bootlicker, he just took it."

I asked: "Did he ever talk about Trudd's will?"

Marsha shook her head. "I think his Vancouver lawyers wrote it up."

Did she know when Trudd last consulted Hogey? She did not, and asked, "Is this important, Arthur?"

I explained I was covering all bases. I wanted to know if Hogey had provided services to Trudd in the weeks before his death. She doubted that absent-minded Hogey would remember, but his secretary, Sibyl, would have a record. "Treat her nicely, and she'll fall all over you. She's a kind of lonely hearts club type."

Hogey had offered the use of his law office, so I hoped that might include Sibyl. I remained troubled by his reluctance to share what he knew about Trudd's "screwed-up mediation thing" in Pouce Coupe. I wouldn't be surprised that Trudd — hungover, in a foul temper, unravelled by the evil act he'd done — had gone berserk, shouting foul, racist epithets.

I asked Marsha about Johnny Blue. "Well, he's okay, a bit of a rebel, a militant, but it's part of being young."

A hunch kept teasing me, hinting that Trudd's death was connected in some arcane way to that mediation hearing. The ever-helpful Père Larouche, it turned out, knew Eric Sayaga well from his many visits to the Wolf River Reserve, and he offered to set up a meeting for Sunday.

I wasn't being a good guest; I was keeping these folks focused on my murder trial when we should have been toasting Lorraine for this delicious feast — a special effort in that she had to prepare for a posse of Montana hunters arriving Saturday afternoon. We went on to talk about next year's Expo in Montreal. And how the NHL season was shaping up. And about an upcoming local bonspiel.

I helped with the dishes while names from the jury panel were called out in the adjoining guest parlour. I'd explained that for the crime of murder, the Criminal Code entitled me to weed out twenty prospects without cause from the forty-four names chosen at random from the voters' list. A dozen were from as far away as the Northwest Territories border, though most were from Fort Tom and environs.

They were doing the list alphabetically, and were now debating the qualities of Mort Grayden, a Cree from the Prairies. Buck Harris: "Senior engine mechanic at the mill. Hated Trudd for sending goons in, strike-breakers." His wife tuned in: "Pulled me out of a ditch one time, wouldn't even let me buy him a drink."

I called to them: "Mr. Grayden won't get past Edward Santorini." I explained that the prosecutor felt that Indigenous people couldn't be trusted to convict, and he would oppose them all, stand them aside.

"Anyone know Henrietta Gwendon?"

"Doesn't ring a bell."

"Retired, it says here, and she lives out by Riverbend."

"No clue."

Lorraine Harris, at my side, hollered: "She used to be the loans officer at the Nova Scotia branch."

"I remember that sourpuss," Marsha said. "Trudd kept an account there."

I told her to put an X beside her name.

Lorraine thanked me for my token service, confiscated my dish towel, and sent me off to the parlour. I settled into a soft chair, trying not to feel oppressed by the décor of many antlered heads.

Buck Harris read out the next name: "Will Klausen. From Muncho Lake. Retired army officer. Anyone?"

All faces were blank. I warned that old soldiers tended to ally themselves with the Crown. I jotted a question mark. I would take a good look at him — people of good heart often give off an aura of empathy.

"Oh, my God," Buck said, "right down at the bottom, here's Rummy Wilcox."

More exactly, Robert L. Wilcox. Widely known and well regarded. A mining engineer. Church deacon. Right-wing Conservative. Sits on Fort Tom's town council. Outspoken. Unpredictable. Had a few issues with Trudd, yet they were allied politically. The consensus was he would be hostile to the defence. He earned a fat X.

We continued in this way for nearly an hour. Meanwhile, my hunch, that undiscoverable itch, continued to gnaw at me. Out of nowhere, like a hidden clue, I recalled the echoing shouts of ravens from my visit to the property in September. Trudd's occasional potshots at trespassing wildlife must have echoed too. Did these never annoy his neighbours? Maybe not much, since their homes were on hilly, forested, five-acre lots.

My second visit would be on the morrow, Saturday, at nine. Etienne Larouche had persuaded the listing realtor to show up with the house keys. I would have an hour to look around before assistant prosecutor Clara Moncrief arrived with her RCMP team.

I stayed up awhile with Buck for a tutorial on hunting rifles, particularly the Remington model 700, a popular big game rifle and his own favourite. He showed me how its push-feed action worked: the bolt, when depressed, fed in a bullet from a three-round internal magazine. The Remington was probably "primed and cocked," as Buck put it, when Angelina retrieved it. "If not, she would have had to swing down the bolt to arm it."

But she had no memory of engaging the bolt action, or even firing the gun.

Yet her fresh prints had been raised from the rifle. The arresting officers said it smelled of recent use. Two 7-mm bullets remained in the chamber. A 7-mm Remington magnum cartridge was retrieved from the decking near the kitchen door. A 7-mm slug was found in a stump forty yards behind the body. A box of such bullets was found in the gun closet.

I asked Buck if he would join me and Father Larouche at the crime scene at nine a.m. No point in taking two vehicles, he said: he would drive me. I thanked him, then paused at the door and asked him to bring his R 700.

1966 —
I Like It Hot and Buttered

The sun cleared the southeastern horizon with a cold, piercing light as Buck Harris thrashed through the weeds and bushes and crusty snow with a metal detector. Etienne toiled beside him with a heavy magnet. They were looking for expended bullets. The RCMP had found one in a stump on May 29, and that was enough to satisfy them.

Meanwhile, Wendell Melquist, a crabby listing agent, showed me through the house, whose interior would be considered uninteresting to all but devotees of dust covers. "We remove them for serious buyers, which of course you are not." Melquist, whose thin face expressed unremitting irritation, seemed hardly an exemplar for the real estate industry, though he was probably a good fit for Trudd's similarly sour sisters.

I insisted on seeing the maid's quarters, where Angelina was raped. The space was narrow, cloistered, barely wide enough for her single bed and a dresser. The bathroom was scrubbed clean. A sickly smell of lye overladen by air freshener.

"I guess you're not finding it easy to move this property, Wendell. With its twin curses of rape and death."

"I haven't heard any proof of that rape story. Very entertaining, I'm sure, for all the local gossips who want to tear down the reputation of a hard-driving businessman."

That speech sounded hollow, rehearsed. I wondered if the vendors, the sisters, had coached him, having blinded themselves to the fact their sibling had been a rapist. I supposed they would dispute that he impregnated Angelina.

I exited by the back, tested the spring-propelled screen door. It conked Melquist as he followed me out, and I hoped my apology sounded sincere. He stood by impatiently on the stairs, watching Buck and Etienne wander around the back acre. They stopped to tie a strip of red surveyor's tape to a tree as a marker — they had found another bullet. Three markers so far.

Melquist frowned, confused, as I ran my gloved hands along the freshly painted shiplap siding, feeling for indentations.

He said, "If you don't need me anymore, I should lock up here and get along home. It's the weekend."

I followed him to ground level, ducked through the caraganas, and crouched near the basement wall: lap siding above a concrete base interrupted by three small windows. Beneath the stairs, cut into the wall, was a cat door with plastic flaps.

Melquist watched, puzzled, as I examined the basement siding. "I hope you're not looking for blemishes. We used a very reliable painting contractor."

"And who was that?"

"The Klymchuk boys."

"And when did they do this admirable paint job?"

"Early July, I believe, just before Donalda and Hortense listed it."

The sinister sisters: Donalda Wyatt and Hortense Trudd-Stephens, the former married, the latter divorced, yet still hanging on to her ex's name — by a hyphen. Both were in their middle forties, several years younger than their brother.

I followed Melquist to his car. "By the way, what happened to the cats?"

"We did the best we could. Hortense hired a cat-sitter for a while, but we couldn't sell a property overrun with cats, so measures had to be taken."

I wanted to ask what were those measures: Bullets? Poison? The river? But he was already accelerating away. Angelina still believed the cats had been re-homed with a loving family. I just couldn't find the strength to be upfront with her.

I returned to where I'd seen a slight indentation just above one of the windows. Not a blemish, but definitely a depression in the wood siding.

I waited until Melquist's car disappeared down the riverbank road before scratching off some paint with my car key. A lump of fill fell out. A click, metal-on-metal. I checked my watch — it was approaching ten.

Buck Harris, quickly summoned, used his hunting knife to pry away more paint and fill. "My best bet from here," he said, squinting, "is a thirty-calibre high-velocity. This was not fired from Trudd's 700."

We dared not tamper with evidence; we would wait for the RCMP ballistics man to dig it out. Buck retreated back to the bush with his rifle to take a sightline of the bullet's possible trajectory. Etienne stood in front of the bullet hole, and I stood where Trudd went down.

We determined that a straight line from Etienne to my chest extended roughly to a thicket of young spruce on a rise, a hundred and twenty yards away, and that's where Buck took up a position, crouching among the trees, adjusting his scope, aiming through it like a sniper. Pointing it at *me*. I can't say I wasn't having tremors: accidents happen, so do misunderstandings. I felt a need to pee. Like Trudd.

An accident almost did happen, as an RCMP van pulled up beside the house. Two plain-clothed Mounties, having quickly surveyed the scene, piled from it with handguns raised, shouting and running for ground cover. Stupidly, I raised my hands in surrender. Wisely, Buck laid down his rifle.

It took a minute for the tension to subside, but a calming explanation by our man of the cloth finally caused revolvers to be snugged back into holsters. The two men who'd raced for cover were, as I'd guessed, the homicide detectives from Prince George. Ted Biggs and Hugh Barnes. Minor players with minimal roles, like movie extras. They hid their embarrassment by being gruff, lecturing us about careless use of firearms. Proof that Buck's rifle wasn't loaded didn't mollify them.

Others who decamped from the van included the two local arresting officers and two specialists: photographer and fingerprint identifier. The ballistics man was on his way, being chauffeured by junior prosecutor Clara Moncrief.

I truly did need to pee, having overindulged in coffee that morning, and I quietly slipped behind the garage. While directing my steamy flow to the base of a telephone pole, I wasn't aware I was exposed to the road through a utility line easement. When I heard a car approach I turned about, spraying the snow like a lawn sprinkler. I peeked back to see Clara Moncrief grinning from the driver's window. She applauded my performance with four beeps: deet-da-dit-dit.

Biggs and Barnes, the detective pair, could have been twins: same height and bulky build, high-school brush cuts, sardonic smiles. They even collaborated as a tag team, backing each other up in their resolve that this was a straightforward homicide. They weren't interested in any last-minute, airy-fairy complications from a big-city shyster.

Their rhetorical weapon was sarcasm, a fusillade of it. The mystery bullet hole in the basement wall? "Yeah, that's a real big deal." "Maybe he mistook his house for a grizzly bear." The bullets in Trudd's back acreage: "Wow. They found *three* bullets out there." "What a shock. People actually hunt around here?"

Corporal Holtz, the ballistics specialist, was, by contrast, calmly professional. He dug out the bullet from the siding and bagged it.

He also collected the three 7-mm bullets that had been flagged. Measurements and photographs were taken.

At my request he also took a sightline from the bullet in the wall to the thicket of immature spruce. No cartridge had been found there, but a savvy assassin would have pocketed it.

A pair of ravens flapped and cruised overhead, loud and raucous, and once again I heard echoes from the scrubby hills. I had a sense they were talking to us, two wise birds offering counsel, urging us to do a sound check.

Corporal Holtz got the message, and loaded Buck's Remington with a couple of 7-mm shells from Buck's pickup. He cautioned us to cover our ears, but only the two detectives obeyed. The first shot was fired heavenward, and within a second or two came the loud crack of its echo, bouncing off the clearcut hills, repeating, dimming. A second shot, aimed low, sent bark splintering from a dead tree a hundred yards away. And again, the hills called back to us.

The police activity and the gunfire ought to have attracted the neighbours, but I learned that the two closest families were snow-birds, Arizona-bound in their campervans. An elderly gentleman from two properties down came by briefly, hobbling with a cane. Etienne took him in charge, accepted his offer for tea, and guided him home.

Buck Harris had to scurry home himself — the convoy of Montanans was about to pull in, after two days on the road. Clara, who had to move her Dodge Coronet for him, boldly announced we were not in a hurry and she would gladly drive me back to the lodge.

Great sweeps of windblown snow danced across our country road as Clara twiddled the radio's tuner, finally finding the regional

CBC station. "Bundle up, cozy up," said the newscaster. "Big blow coming tonight."

"Cool," Clara said. "Bundle up for the big blow." She jacked out the dashboard lighter and ignited one of her pungent herbal cigarettes. Dangling from her right ear was today's four-letter message in silver capitals: "LOVE." She was bundled in a padded jacket.

"What's with your fixation with echoes?"

"A loud echo can be easily confused with an actual gunshot. Helps me persuade a jury that more than one shot was fired." Both arresting officers, who were at a nearby accident scene, had claimed to have heard only one report from a rifle. At the preliminary, Pappas hadn't asked them about echoes. He hadn't given even a passing thought to the possibility of a sniper in the bush.

"If you think Trudd was bagged by some weirdo firing from the woods, that's impossibly coincidental. Too much of a stretch."

"That's what they call me back home. Stretch."

"As in stretch the truth? Or a stretch of the imagination?"

As in a lifetime stretch in the pen, I thought dismally. Or as in a stretched neck. I didn't confirm Clara's assumption about my second-shooter theory; I had shared too much with this lusty, genial woman — she was my opposition, for God's sake! So there was no reason for her to know I would be meeting Chief Eric Sayaga on Sunday afternoon.

A pickup the size of a small tank was crowding Clara, so she pulled over and let it pass. Three men in the cab, one of them tilting a beer. Montana plates.

"In olden days people hunted animals for food and fur," she said. "These dolts kill for pleasure."

"Or as a ritualized proof of manhood. Exercising dominance over supposedly lesser species is actually a mark of cowardice, I suspect."

Clara squinted at me through her smoke. "What I like about you, Stretch, is you're totally unaware that you're an attractive man. If I were you I'd stack that jury with women. Charm the pants off them."

"It's that easy?"

"The proof is sitting beside you." She squeezed my thigh. "Sorry, I was looking for the gearshift."

Part of me wanted to play, but I was unsure what her game was — beyond out-and-out seduction. She was appealing, in an exotic way: a counterculture Crown counsel. But I dared not become compromised by sleeping with the enemy.

She waited while another big truck passed — more Montanans — then proceeded onto the road, but soon geared down again. "This is it, isn't it?" Buck's and Lorraine's driveway. I directed her past the lodge and the several pickups and vans parked there, and she settled her Dodge beside my Ford.

I sought the right words to invite her in for a coffee or hot chocolate. *Care to take the chill off before heading back?* But she didn't wait for an offer, however gallantly phrased, and grabbed her bag and beat me to my cabin door. I couldn't blame her — a cheery light was on inside and the chimney exhaled wind-whipped smoke.

Clara looked about with approval as she shrugged off her jacket: the roaring fire, the clean kitchenette, the cozy bedroom. Somehow, Lorraine had found time to leave a light lunch: cold cutlets and a vegetable dip. Clara munched a carrot as she pondered my invitation for something hot to drink, while I struggled to avert my eyes from her tightly tucked-in blouse.

"I see a bottle of Jamaican rum," she said. "I like it hot and buttered."

She took charge, expertly, mixing spices, butter, and rum with a cinnamon stick while I was assigned the lowly task of boiling water. Even at that, I nervously fumbled about, distracted by her closeness.

She found my awkwardness either amusing or pitiable, her lips curling into a lopsided grin as we clinked mugs by the fireplace. "Don't worry, I'm not going to test your sex-ethical boundaries."

"Good, I can relax." That didn't sound right. "I mean, I'm human, I find you entirely too desirable, Clara. But ethical considerations aside, I hardly know you."

She lit one of her herbal cigarettes. "Rich bitch. McGill law degree. Master's in economics from Princeton. Dad sits in the Opposition front bench in Ottawa."

"That Moncrief?" Controversial cabinet minister under Diefenbaker.

"Right. Hugh Moncrief, scandal-ridden Conservative hack."

She asked about my master's degree. "Classical literature at Cambridge," I said. We marvelled at the coincidence that we'd each been torn between academia and the law. And that we'd both rebelled against stuffy, illiberal parents.

We shared histories into the afternoon. Eventually, looking out the window, she said, "I'd better split before I get snowed in."

At the door, she said, "I want you, Arthur. In case you hadn't noticed. But I'm willing to wait." She stubbed out her cigarette and kissed me on the mouth, her hot breath tasting of rum and cinnamon and sage and rosemary. I waved weakly as she got into her car, then stripped, showered, and stumbled off to bed.

1966 —
I'm Gonna Kill You

O ddly, I awoke rested on Sunday morning, the strain of the past few days overcome, replaced by a sense of well-being. A significant factor in this transformation was a sense of amour-propre at having acted with propriety despite the temptations of the previous afternoon. Or did I decline her approach out of fear?

What if word got out that I'd slept with Angelina's prosecutor on the weekend before the trial? Eddie Santorini would be thrilled to report me to the Law Society. A mistrial declared, a hearing before the Benchers, suspension, public humiliation.

Other feel-good factors from Saturday night: the handcrafted release of sexual tension; a deep, ten-hour sleep, and waking up without much of a hangover. For a change.

Meanwhile, the predicted storm had blown through during the night, and the Lodge's connector road was impassable. Yet my day calendar was jammed. The chief of the Wolf River Reserve expected me for an interview, as did a house painter and one of Trudd's neighbours, plus I planned one final try at persuading Angelina to help her own cause.

On Monday, before jury selection, I expected to sit down with Santorini to work out admissibility issues. Dealing with Eddie would be the most demanding of these tasks. Though only thirty-two, he had eight solid years behind him at the Vancouver City Prosecutor's Office.

We had been contemporaries at UBC Law School, but could have been planets apart: I a bookish grinder, he a crammer eking out C-level grades. He was loud and boisterous, a big man on campus, a fullback on the college team. Many freshwomen were reputed to have lost their virginity to him, putting him almost in the league of my dear friend Hubbell Meyerson, who played quarterback. Whose scheduled call I was eagerly awaiting as I stirred my first morning coffee.

I glanced out the window at the falling snow. The storm had blown itself out but my Ford Fairlane was going nowhere. My generous host had offered a solution. Last evening, while his guests were sharing tall tales over strong drinks, Buck showed me how to run a snowmobile, then parked it outside my door.

The wall phone, an extension from the lodge, rang on the dot of nine, and I was put through. Hubbell sounded as though he was calling from the moon, but I finally realized he was talking football while munching on some kind of crunchy cereal. I made out: "Scored two tickets to the Grey Cup, you game to go?"

"When is that?"

"Next Saturday, Roughies against the Riders."

"My jury may still be out."

"Oh, I forgot, you know nothing about football and care less. Let me expand on that. The lofty, patrician aesthetic of the great A.R. Beauchamp has no spare room for the rude, proletarian pastime called sports."

"The mediation in Pouce Coupe. What did you dig up?"

"You're serious about this second-shooter shit? Didn't the Warren Commission say there was no conspiracy? You going to blame it on the CIA?"

"Hub, I have a hectic day, and we're snowed in here."

"Okay, okay. So I started with the assumption that the mediation had to do with Crown land, which would involve provincial

Aboriginal Affairs. My contact there confirmed that. The hearing was planned as a quiet, private affair, like a forced marriage, presided over by a fatuous schmuck from the Peace River area, A.W. Mapple."

I'd never heard the name, but Hubbell said he was a retired country magistrate hired for odd jobs by old pals in government.

Hubbell laid out the story in masterly detail: An ancient Aboriginal burial ground had been found near the Wolf River, fifty miles upstream from Fort Thompson, in the foothills of the Rockies. It was on Crown land, a thousand acres of old-growth white spruce, and the Wolf River Reserve claimed it as their traditional lands. The province, however, had already granted cutting rights to Trudd Enterprises, which aimed to slash a logging road into the disputed area. That plan was held up while the Tribal Council sought official redress.

Mapple, the mediator, was instructed to seek a compromise: a sliver of the pie for the Natives, a heartier dish for the loggers. "Trudd had to be dragged kicking and screaming into the mediation," Hubbell said. "He wanted the whole megillah, no deals, take no prisoners. After he got whacked, everything came to a standstill."

"What about the ruckus at that hearing?"

"It was the battle of Little Bighorn, Trudd's last stand. I couldn't get all the details — Mapple's report is under seal — but they were in some kind of government boardroom. I gather Trudd showed up late on Friday, hungover, smelling like a plugged toilet in a roadhouse bar. No lawyer, just himself, facing off against four guys from the Wolf River Reserve. The mediator took pity on him, sent him off to his hotel, adjourned everything.

"When they reconvened on Saturday, Trudd was in better shape, sober, but things went downhill. After lunch, a wet one, I guess, he had a fit, hurling racist vulgarisms across the table, the usual diatribe about fucking lazy dumb Indians wanting everything handed to them on a platter. Apparently one young Native guy almost vaulted over the table at him, and it took the whole negotiating team to hold him back. That was it. Game over. Trudd announced his loggers were going in next week, and he scuttled back to his hotel in Dawson Creek for the night."

Whew. That was my reaction. Hubbell sounded smug, though he had every right to be — he'd scored a big touchdown for Team Angelina. He didn't have the names of the four tribal councillors, other than Chief Sayaga. But he did have Mapple's phone number and address in Dawson Creek, the big, thriving neighbour town to Pouce Coupe.

Had threats been made to the life or safety of F.C. Trudd? Might the recipients of his foul-mouthed wrath, already inflamed by the threatened ruin of their traditional lands, have sought bloody revenge? Hubbell's contact didn't know. I would at least try to talk to A.W. Mapple, though he was unlikely to breach any confidences from a closed-door hearing.

"Before I forget," I said, "can you double up on your efforts by ferreting out the contents of Trudd's final will?"

"Possibly."

"If you can. You've outdone yourself so far, Hub."

"Did I hear a catch in your voice? Are you holding back tears of gratitude, wondering how you can ever make it up to me?"

"We'll tear up the town after the football game."

"Sounds like a riot. Check with you later."

I feared Magistrate Mapple would not welcome a call at home on a Sunday morning. I imagined him as a cranky septuagenarian, prone to biting off the heads of callers interrupting his toasted muffins with plum jam. But nothing ventured . . .

He picked up on the second ring, with a hearty "Hello, and good morning. Mapple here." Talk radio in the background.

"And a good morning to you, sir." With duelling exuberance. "So glad I found you at home, and I truly hope I'm not disturbing you. My name is Arthur Beauchamp, I'm a fellow member of the bar, and I'm calling from the winter wonderland of Fort Thompson."

"Ah, yes, the Angelina Santos case. I was wondering when I might hear from somebody up there. Give me a moment to turn down the radio and poke the fire."

He seemed all too eager to talk to me. Might he be keen to bask in the limelight from this locally notorious trial? That seemed the case.

He became almost excessively voluble after I commended him on his illustrious career on the magistrate's bench — in truth, I lied: fame is rarely attainable to triers of traffic tickets, summary offences, and small claims. As to his mediation on the last weekend of May, he held little back, while tossing out speculative asides: "Between you and me," or "I'm only assuming," or "The good Lord knows."

Otherwise, it was a barrage: "Fred Trudd could have pared down the tribe's wish list to maybe a dozen acres, but he was the kind of guy born greedy, if you want my candid opinion. Started off in an ugly mood, shouting epithets at those four stony-faced Indians."

He wheezed a lot. I pictured him as carrying an unhealthy load of body fat. "Eighteen years as a magistrate, I figure I know how to handle Natives. Between you and me, they need a softer touch, they don't come around when they're yelled at and called dirty, lazy, cheating dumb-ass northern niggers, like Trudd, which is pretty well exactly the language he used. That's when the young guy, Johnny Blue, they called him, kind of pole-vaulted over the table at him, yelling, 'You effing slimy Nazi pervert, I'm gonna kill you.'"

1966 —
They're Tired of Being Treated Like Shit

B uck's advice was: "Go off-road until you get to the Alaska Highway Motel, then turn south to the airport road, then right when you see the sign to the reserve."

That seemed clear enough, but I was so distracted that I missed the airport road. My mind was on Mapple; I finally had an arguable defence, a credible witness. "Do you think I need a subpoena?" asked the highly respected ex-magistrate. "If you require me, of course."

As I backtracked to the airport road, I rehearsed lines for the jury: "You will remember that Mr. Trudd stayed over in Dawson Creek on Saturday. Johnny Blue, the would-be assassin, could easily have beaten him here to Fort Tom. He'd have the whole morning to set up behind that thicket of low pines, then all he had to do was wait for his target to pull into his driveway . . ."

I finally came upon a settlement of scattered homes, and soon located the Band Office in a meeting hall on a hill. A young woman, the office manager, directed me into a business-cum-lounge area, where Chief Eric Sayaga rose from a table and greeted me.

Etienne Larouche had described him as thoughtful, reserved, soft-spoken, and I found him so. A retired teacher, well into his sixties, barrel-chested, bifocals perched halfway down his nose.

"All this snow," he said. "I did not expect you so soon."

I explained I came by snowmobile.

"Those machines can be very tippy, I'm glad you took care."

A map of northern Canada dominated one wall, showing the lands of the South Slavey and other tribes of the Dene people, from the Yukon and Northwest Territories to the northern reaches of the western provinces. Elsewhere, a corkboard displayed various announcements, events, photos taken at community gatherings. A gun locker behind glass, rifles locked in place.

We talked a little about the Slavey language and its several dialects, and the struggle to keep them viable. Then about land rights. And specifically the issue that led to the contretemps in Pouce Coupe — which, Chief Sayaga enlightened me, was not named after a missing thumb but after a local band chief named Pouskapie.

I managed to steer this friendly conversation to the gun locker, asking who had access to the dozen rifles and shotguns arrayed there. "Anyone over fifteen," he said. "But our rule is they're locked up when not in use."

I asked him what prompted that rule, expecting he might blame incidents of careless handling. Or worse. "Just a safety precaution," he said. "But how can I help you?"

And that marked the end of our jolly chat. Our conversation became strained, slowly at first, accelerating as I pressed him about Trudd's abusive behaviour at the hearing. They were hardly strangers to each other, but never had he seen Trudd in such an ugly temper. The chief was uncomfortable in his recounting of the racist slurs.

He became particularly cautious when I asked if threats had been made from his side. "Too much confusion for me to remember. There was shouting back and forth. No one was in control. Magistrate Mapple was useless, he might as well not have been there."

And what about his nephew, Johnny Blue? I told him I'd heard he lunged at Trudd.

"Heard from whom?"

I hesitated, then plunged ahead. "I talked on the phone this morning with Mr. Mapple."

He raised his eyes to mine. "Didn't you find him a bit pompous?"

I had to be careful. "If he is to be believed, Johnny Blue called Trudd a Nazi pervert and said he'd kill him."

Chief Sayaga splayed his hands, and studied them for a moment. "Johnny . . . Well, he is very strong-minded. Like many in the new generation. A different generation, angrier, and they see us, their elders, as having been defeated."

"Defeated?"

"Programmed into inaction by the religious schools." A look of pain, like a wince. "Yes, I was one of them, taken from my parents, denied my heritage, my language, even my name. I was a number. I was known as Number 157."

"I'm sorry . . ."

"Excuse me, I don't accept pity, it has no value. Understand, I am proud of this new generation. These kids aren't going to allow your culture and religion and customs to be forced down their throats anymore. They're tired of sitting and waiting, Mr. Beauchamp. They're tired of being treated like shit."

I suddenly became aware I was in big trouble; I hadn't thought this out. I mounted a feeble, self-serving defence: I abhorred racist attempts to blot out Aboriginal peoples' culture and history. I'd made many friends from among Indigenous defendants whom I'd represented pro bono or on Legal Aid.

Chief Sayaga's eyes locked onto mine. "Johnny Blue is innocent of everything but an overheated remark. He had nothing to do with the death of Mr. Trudd. And yet you would make him a suspect, an easy target for a white man's jury. Once again my people are to be portrayed as savages."

I might have explained I had an ethical duty to serve the interests of my client. I might even have pressed him by asking how and when Johnny got home from Pouce Coupe, and did he or any of his close friends have access to a high-powered rifle that weekend. And if so did he have an alibi for his whereabouts on the Sunday of Trudd's murder.

But I couldn't even croak a response. My throat felt as if a cork had been stuffed down it; a lump of self-loathing blocking my larynx.

I finally asked: "Where is Johnny right now?"

Chief Sayaga walked to a window and gestured outside. Several young men and women were working with snow shovels, clearing their skating rink. Skates and pads and hockey sticks were arrayed on a bench outside a shed with a smoking chimney. I guessed Johnny Blue was the one in the blue Toronto Maple Leafs jersey. He was tall and broad-shouldered with chiselled features.

It didn't seem like a good idea to interrupt his Sunday morning shinny game. In fact I'd be better off not talking to him. I didn't want to learn he had an alibi. Nor would I need to put Chief Sayaga on the stand, given that Mapple, the mediator, was so eager to testify.

My first duty, my essential, irresistible duty, was the defence of Angelina Santos. That's what I told myself.

The chief graciously led me to the front door. He kindly resisted labelling me, in my presence, as a white liberal suckhole. I waved to the young men and women in the rink as I ski-dooed past them, but they didn't wave back, though a couple raised fists in the air.

Were his friends allies in a plot to assassinate Trudd? *They're tired of being treated like shit.*

By noon, Fort Tom's streets and avenues had been cleared, and I was better able to do my planned rounds. The Klymchuk brothers, two sturdy house painters, met me over shakes and sodas at the Malt Shoppe, and confirmed they'd applied a fresh outside coat to Trudd's home early in July.

Ryan Klymchuk had done the basement siding, where the thirty-calibre high-velocity slug was embedded. Rather than dig it out, he'd sanded off a few tiny shards of wood, added putty, and painted it over. "That's what the listing agent wanted." Was that annoying fellow, Wendell Melquist, literally covering up?

Klymchuk was reluctant to estimate how fresh was this house wound, but agreed it didn't seem weatherworn. I told him to expect a subpoena on Monday, and promised his court appearance would be brief.

Trudd's closest neighbours were all away at Sunday church services and events on May 29, but Ned Best, the elderly gentleman who'd come by as we were test-firing the Remington rifle, had been home. Etienne had walked him back there, four hundred yards up the riverbank road, and while taking tea had learned that Mr. Best "definitely" remembered hearing gunshots — plural — on the Sunday of Trudd's demise.

But, Etienne told me, this eighty-three-year-old veteran of the First World War was not as clear and quick of mind as he'd been when flying Sopwith Snipes or, later, as a bush pilot. He was regarded, however, as a local icon, a hometown hero who'd spurned pleas from his children and grandchildren to abandon frigid Fort Tom for their gentler climes.

On our way to Best's residence, Etienne bemoaned the elderly hero's loss of faith: "Sadly, he turned apostate after his wife died cruelly of cancer."

Best greeted me with a hearty handshake. He was tall, lean, fit, and wore a hearing aid. He led us into a spacious, tidy parlour, a fire going, stacks of split wood beside the hearth, family photos on the wall with his war medals. The windows looked out to the back, the echoing hills.

Ned Best was voluble: "Those rifle shots came like claps of thunder on a soft summer day. Two for sure, echoing back to me. I reckoned it was someone hunting out of season. Unless Fred Trudd was out there in the bush going after the wolf that made a meal of one of his precious kitty-cats. Then about a minute later I heard the police siren coming over the bridge and up our road, and I figured someone raised a complaint about illegal hunting, and I just went about my way until I heard the news on the radio."

I asked him where the shots came from.

"Somewhere out there among the stumps and brambles." He pointed outside. All I saw were humps of snow. Mature conifers and a greenhouse screened the view. Trudd's house and garage were not visible.

"But both shots didn't come from the same spot, did they? Wasn't one of them from closer to his house?" I was coaxing him, an ill-advised practice.

"Well, I guess it's obvious one came from there, but it was confusing with all the echoes."

Ned couldn't be sure his hearing aids were on. He usually left them inside when doing outdoor chores. Anyway, he said, the shots and sirens "would be heard by the deaf." He was "pretty sure" there were "at least" two shots. Was he outside when he heard them? Again, he was pretty sure. "In fact, on thinking about it, there'd been a lightning strike on an old pine behind my greenhouse, and I was bucking it up that Sunday."

"You were running a chainsaw?" I asked uneasily, imagining Santorini taking him apart for apparently hearing shots while chainsawing without his hearing aid.

"Took me an hour to chunk up that ugly old tree." He turned to Etienne. "You remember, Reverend, there'd been a big thunderstorm, lightning, we all lost power. One of your acts of God, eh?"

"Ned, I think that storm was in June. These shots you heard were about ten days earlier, May the twenty-ninth."

"Oh, okay. Maybe I had my dates mixed up there. I was outside, though, by the woodshed. Splitting firewood, I think."

I asked him how many rifle shots he'd heard on Saturday, when Corporal Holtz test-fired Buck's R 700.

"Well, I'd say at least four."

He was counting the echoes. Etienne took a deep breath and looked up, as if appealing to the heavens. Ned Best would be a risky witness.

"I don't understand, Mr. Beauchamp, how I can say 'not guilty,' when I believe I am guilty." Angelina spoke with a solemn certitude and a puzzled frown.

My relaxed mood of the morning had dissipated. I needed a drink. A real one. The Orange Crush in the detachment's fridge was not going to soothe my nerves. How could it be that on the eve of Angelina's trial for murder she was calmer than her lawyer? I was weary of picking up the scattered pieces that Alex Pappas had neglected or ignored. I felt rushed, out of breath, poorly prepared.

"Because you believe you are guilty doesn't mean you are guilty. That's for God and your jury to determine." She looked unconvinced by my calling on the services of the Lord. "In any event, Angelina, entering your plea is a judicial formality. It's a plea, not a denial."

Still, she seemed unsure. She had killed — would she be lying in the face of God if she claimed innocence? "I was taught never to bear false witness. From almost the day I could walk."

She was facing me, on a chair, hands clasped, smiling. I breathed slowly, sought patience, then leaned toward her, and asked, pleadingly, if she had filled in any holes in her scattershot memory of the shooting.

"I try. I hear the rifle being fired. I remember being sick. I think more is coming back, then my head aches, and I stop trying."

It was my time to tell some truth. There was no way to sugarcoat it. "Angelina, you need to understand that if you are convicted, they will take the baby away from you."

"No, they won't. God won't let them."

Arthur —
June 2022

I'm not sure how long ago I time-travelled to frigid Fort Tom — a few hours at least — but a familiar rumbling sound suddenly jolts me back to lovely, sunny Garibaldi. I recognize this sound as the groaning and chuffing of old Betsy, my Ford tractor.

It seems to be coming down the path from Potters Road, perhaps guided by some form of artificial intelligence. Or gremlins. It stops beside the cabin and the engine is cut.

The smell of burning cannabis oozes through my open door. It's the gremlins, all right. One never knows when they might attack. Their leader hollers: "Yo, Arthur, hope you don't mind we borrowed Betsy, we had to haul some shit in from the road. Have to warn you there'll be some construction noise."

Sensing trouble, Ulysses scrambles up and hightails it outside. I rise too, with a groan, dragging my creaky bones out to the deck to reconnoitre, hoping to head off whatever plans Stoney and Dog have devised today to sabotage my creativity. Hooked up to the tractor is a cart laden with tools, ladders, and solar panels. Dog is already unloading them as Stoney alights from Betsy, pinching a butt and flipping it.

"The stars are aligned in your favour, eh. I found a killer YouTube video about solar installation. Watched it twice, nailed it, man, and we're finally ready to roll."

"Hold on. What happened to the solar technician?"

"I looked at his quote and almost fell through the floor. Yeah, it's all greed in the green industry business. Not to worry, any idiot can do this install. Three hours max. You'll be boiling tea in your teapot by dinner time."

"Wait. Don't touch anything." Overcome by visions of the cabin in flames, I stumble around, fetch the transcripts, pack them in my briefcase with my manuscript.

Outside again, I fill my lungs with air so I can bellow a stop-work order, but my words are obliterated by a deafening roar, like that of a jet plane taking off.

"What's that noise?" I cry.

"Generator! No problem!"

1966 —
Guilty or Not Guilty?

It was a quarter to ten, and I was in the washroom of the gentlemen barristers' robing room, pissing away the morning's three cups of coffee while slugging down a fourth, feeling ill prepared to take on what Alex Pappas had falsely advertised as "a nice, easy little murder." In fact, the defence of Angelina Santos had ballooned into a thorny thicket of possibilities, and I was unsure how to hack through them.

As I washed my hands, I scrutinized myself in the mirror. Did I look like a master of my trade, or an impostor? I wore the uniform: white shirt, wing collar, and tabs; black trousers, waistcoat, and robe. Beside me was a brown, dog-eared leather briefcase with my files and notes and the current edition of Tremeear's *Criminal Code*.

I had given up waiting for Santorini — we were to have met at nine-thirty in the barristers' lounge, half an hour before the call to order, to talk about shortening the trial by resolving several minor issues.

The door swung open and he barrelled in, peeling off his sweater and plaid shirt at the urinal, while, with athletic prowess, he unzipped and pissed into it. A large, husky fellow, but tubbier than when he was a varsity football star. He looked hungover; a hurried shave had left patches of grizzle on cheek and jowls.

"That shithole of a hotel was supposed to give me a wake-up call. How much time?"

"Three minutes and thirteen seconds."

"I gotta pull a fucking Clark Kent." He disappeared.

On returning to the lockers, I found Santorini's transformation into Superman had stalled — he was wrestling with his detachable wing collar.

I asked, "What admissions do you want, Eddie?"

"Time and date of death. Place of death. Jurisdiction. Photos. Prints. Hey, Stretch, how'd they stick you with this bomb? You get red-carded for humping those two Penthouse pros?"

"You know what, Ed, I think I'll make you prove everything. You're getting lazy, you need the exercise." I helped him with a balky wing collar stud, snapped it into place. "You've added a couple of inches around the neck since you blew the Faloon diamond heist."

"Okay, it's hardball. Don't come sucking around asking to plead her out to manslaughter."

"Intaminatis fulget honoribus."

"Greek to me, Cicero."

"'Untarnished, she shines with honour.'"

"Not when I get through with her."

As we headed down to the criminal assize courtroom, Santorini asked what I thought of his junior, then didn't wait for an answer. "I heard you met Clara at the murder site. The set of knockers on that dame should be declared dangerous weapons. A courtroom newbie, so I'm going to have to test-drive her with some minor witnesses, see how she handles. We got adjoining suites, I'll have to cinch up my chastity belt."

Another familiar, undesired face appeared at the bottom of the stairs: reporter Charles Loobie of Vancouver's peppy, lowbrow tabloid the *Province*. Worked his way from copy boy to the law courts beat at twenty-one, soon began getting bylines — while earning a reputation as a compulsive snoop and shameless pest.

Santorini deked left to avoid him, but I was trapped against a balustrade. "A word, Artie," he said. I hated being called Artie, and I suspected he knew that. Short and pudgy, he was in his signature dress, bright tie, bright sports jacket, a Stetson hat with a Press tag stuck into the crown.

"Had a brew the other day with Alex Pappas. He gloated how he fobbed this loser off on you. He had a backup plan: if you didn't take over, he was going to cut a deal — life, no parole, to avoid the death penalty — then rush back to Vancouver. Herb Macintosh was the big show. You got the shit show. Care to confirm you got suckered?"

"What brings you to this shit show, Charles? The *Province* has zero subscribers up here — it sometimes arrives half a week late."

"Pappas reads it. He thinks you get too much good ink."

"And he urged you to come up here to get me some bad ink?"

"I came up here for a story, Artie. 'Mother of Rapist's Child Found Guilty of His Murder.' A heartbreaker."

I worked my way free and into the courtroom. It was an impressive space, grand and ornate, panelled in oak and walnut. Above the judge's bench, a young Queen Elizabeth gazed down upon her colonials. To her left was the Red Ensign, Canada's unofficial national flag until 1965, when the red maple leaf replaced it — though it was not hanging on any wall. Fort Tom seemed not in a hurry to catch up to the times.

The citizens subpoenaed for jury duty warmed the pew-like benches of the public gallery. A dozen locals sat at the back, but several chose the front row, including the stalwarts of Angelina's support group.

Sitting beside Marsha Bigelow was my garrulous new friend Hogey Johnson, who had tipped me off about the row at the mediation, when Johnny Blue took a swipe at Trudd.

I was torn about implicating Johnny, or any member of the Wolf River Band, in the violent death of F.C. Trudd. How unfair to them if my accusation was false. How unfair to the local community, creating doubt and division, feeding racist bigotry. But how could I live with myself if I failed to raise that defence and Angelina paid the ultimate price? Did I not have an ethical duty to put a theory to the jury of a secret act of calculated vengeance? Why not go whole hog and drag Chief Sayaga into it, or the whole Band?

I muzzled those thoughts and made a show of unflappability as Clara Moncrief flashed me a smile from the Crown counsel table. Bright, sexy rebel against Daddy's false values. Hippie chick in deep disguise: black robes, vest, skirt. *I'm willing to wait.*

Santorini was schmoozing with the Sheriff's Officer chaperoning the jury, seeking hints, I assumed, about who could be counted on to do their duty to the Queen. Charles Loobie and a teenaged girl representing the *Northern Daily News* were seated at a press table just to the left of me, watching me arrange files and texts.

Courtroom gabble ceased as the door to the cells opened and an officer led in Angelina. As she settled into the prisoners' dock, I thought to approach her with words of comfort, but held back on seeing her bowed in prayer.

A minute later, all rose as order was called. Justice Wilbur Kroop lazed his way from his chambers to his gaudily carved throne, upon which, after a lookabout with his cold black eyes, he lowered his bottom and waved everyone back to their seats. His wire-rim spectacles slid down the nose of his pink, glowering bumface as he focused on me — doubtless recalling how he'd resented my vigorous defences of the helpless junkies he used to prosecute.

This outspoken supporter of the Wars on Drugs and Alcohol was a puritanical teetotaller. All the more reason to portray Trudd as a drunken brute while trumpeting Angelina's abstinence from any potion stronger than a symbolic taste of the blood of Christ.

Kroop looked impatiently at the gawky young man a level below him. "Can we get going, Mr. Clerk? Shall we take the plea?" A whiny, cranky voice that would soon grate on me.

The clerk, whose name was Delbert, was obviously new at this, and nervous. He said, "Will the prisoner please stand." That sounded more of a question than a command, and seemed to confuse Angelina, who was slow to rise from the dock. But she did so gracefully, serenely, a simple silver cross suspended over a neat, white, buttoned blouse. Fawn skirt edged with pink flowers. No one in the room could possibly have ignored the plump bulge under that skirt.

Seeming more nervous than the accused, Delbert breathlessly recited the indictment for murder in the first degree, then took a deep breath, and croaked: "How do you plead, guilty or not guilty?"

All whispering and shuffling stopped as Angelina, with a slight frown, took time to ponder her answer. She didn't look at me for help, and God knows I didn't want the jury candidates seeing me coax her. An eternity seemed to pass.

Yesterday, she'd told me, "Only God will decide my guilt or innocence." I'd responded: "Then for God's sake, plead not guilty. Let the Creator decide."

The entire room let out a deep breath as Angelina found her tongue: "Not guilty" — with an emphatic nod, as if only then making up her mind.

I sagged, unable to hide my relief. My next challenge would be jury selection, a critical test of my acuity in reading strangers, a talent I'd honed in Vancouver but I feared could elude me in this hardscrabble northern town.

"Very well," said Kroop. "Let us empanel the jury."

With shaking hands, Delbert shuffled through a drum of ballot cards, pulled one out, and cleared his throat. "Number fourteen, Will Klausen."

"Nobody can hear you, Mr. Clerk," Kroop said. "Shout it out."

He did his best, and Will Klausen, retired army officer, marched reluctantly forward as if ordered to secure the beachhead at Dieppe. Mid-sixties, fit, straight of back.

"Challenge," I said. "No offence meant, sir. Thank you for your service." The ex-soldier returned to his seat, smiling with relief.

"Number twenty-two, Henrietta Gwendon."

I had an X beside the name of this retired bank employee with the sour expression. I glanced quickly at the Crown table, at Clara. *If I were you I'd stack that jury with women.* That ought not to be a blanket policy. "Challenge," I said.

"Number six, Harry Plozak."

I winced as this gentleman smiled and nodded at Angelina. A machinist at the mill, and, according to the Santos support group, no friend of his late boss. Two vigorous check marks by his name.

I tried to mask my intentions with pursed lips and a studied frown, then said, "Content."

Santorini was not dumb enough to have missed Plozak's supportive smile. "May I ask Mr. Plozak a couple of questions, Your Lordship?"

"What sort of questions?" Kroop asked.

"Possible bias, Milord."

"Do you have any basis for alleging that?"

"I might well have if I'm allowed to explore —"

"No, Mr. Santorini, you may not explore. This is Canada. We don't follow the intrusive American practice of allowing prospective jurors to be cross-examined about their opinions and beliefs."

Santorini looked aggrieved at this unexpected manifestation of fairness, and went into a stall.

"This trial is set for only three days, Mr. Prosecutor."

Santorini came out of it. "Yes, of course. I challenge Mr. Plozak."

The timid clerk squeaked out: "Number Thirty, Mort Grayden."

The engine mechanic at Trudd's mill, a Cree from Saskatchewan. *Pulled me out of a ditch one time, wouldn't even let me buy him a drink.*

I said I was content.

"Stand aside, please." And so it went.

Whenever I turned to the gallery to inspect an approaching prospect I found myself meeting the glare of two sullen women in the second row, expensively dressed, coiffed, and bejewelled. These, I assumed, were Trudd's locally unpopular sisters: Donalda Wyatt and Hortense Trudd-Stephens. In their company was realtor Wendell Melquist, who'd grumpily shown me through their empty house.

I hadn't done a terrific job husbanding my challenges, and ran out of them just before Robert L. "Rummy" Wilcox came forward — this right-wing power broker had got a failing grade from my support group. My only hope was to challenge him for cause: to make a case that he'd been allied with the deceased politically, and that they'd met socially.

But that would likely backfire: he would feel aggrieved, insulted. Others on the jury would resent me: Rummy was a popular figure in town. And anyway, Kroop was dead set against allowing counsel to question prospective jurors.

"I am most pleased to welcome Alderman Wilcox to the jury," I said with feigned conviviality. He offered me a smile that I interpreted as sardonic: Who do you think you're fooling?

Not a perfect crop, but I'd done my best. I'd managed to wrestle seven women into the jury box. Eleven white-skinned Christians and one turbaned Sikh, administrator of Fort Tom's hospital, whose wide smile had won me over and disarmed Santorini.

Kroop cautioned them not to discuss the case with anyone, apologized that he had to sequester them overnight in a hotel, then ordered a half-hour break to allow them to get settled, make their phone calls home, and choose a foreperson.

The lotto known as jury selection had used up only half the morning, but I welcomed the break: my bladder was again nagging at me. I moved smartly toward the door, weaving around people, apologizing for my jostles, then climbed two steps at a time, and quickly found myself alone in the barristers' washroom.

I was at a urinal, thirty seconds into my pour, when I heard shouts from the lockers. A familiar female voice: "Fuck that! I'm not waiting in a pee line for the public toilet." Then something from Santorini, softer, pleading. Then Clara barged into the washroom, nearly causing me to piss on my shoes, and shouted, "I'm liberating your biffy," as she slammed shut the door of a toilet cubicle.

Unheard of. Decades ago, when this courthouse was designed, female barristers were also unheard of. I called to her: "I'm all for gender equality, Clara, but please knock first."

"The ladies' robing room is a closet. No washroom. It's fucking insulting."

I zipped up, washed up, and fled.

1966 —
The Valley of the
Shadow of Death

I wasn't surprised that the jurors elected their long-time alderman as foreman, a choice that would obviously enhance Rummy Wilcox's role as influencer. I'd egregiously erred in not saving a challenge for him. He must have met with Trudd scores of times, over zoning and other municipal issues. But how close could they have been socially, given Trudd's abrasive demeanour?

I didn't like the way Wilcox studied me, suspiciously, perhaps seeing me as a slick, big-city liberal. But I'd be seen as a fool if I tried playing the hick for these folks — they would see that as phony and patronizing.

Santorini opened to the jury by baldly declaring his case to be ironclad. The Crown would prove the murder of a prominent businessman was planned, deliberate, clearly motivated, and indefensible. Yes, there was an air of tragedy surrounding the events of late May, but in no circumstances could the taking of a life of a defenceless person be condoned. If the evidence satisfies you beyond a reasonable doubt, you must judge accordingly.

Well done. Brief and emphatic. No skeptical expressions from the jury but no nods of concurrence either. Santorini had anticipated, as he had to, that my strategy would be a plea to the heart, that great organ of forgiveness.

The first witness was Errol Stankwitz, operations manager for Trudd Enterprises Inc., a loyal minion to his boss. At the preliminary hearing, Alex Pappas had tried to slug it out with him, but couldn't connect. As to Trudd's assaults and trespasses against his maid, Stankwitz either knew nothing or had wilfully blinded himself. Despite Pappas's fusillades, Fred Trudd was depicted as a generous, hard-working regular guy, much misunderstood because of his forceful manner.

Stankwitz was short, portly, and unctuous, and sported a clip-on bow tie that waggled as he described with pride Trudd's logging, milling, and real estate empire in the BC northlands. At the mention of his contributions to local charities and other good causes, someone in the gallery grunted, a scoffing sound that had the judge peering about in vain for the perpetrator.

Urged to move on to salient matters, Stankwitz chronicled Trudd's hiring of Angelina Santos and their "warm and respectful relationship during her two years of devoted service," and topped off that blather by extolling their shared love of "our four-footed feline friends."

He was "shocked, utterly shocked, on hearing suggestions that Miss Santos may have had difficulties with Fred prior to his tragic death." Spoken with such emphatic tempo that watching his bow tie was like following the bouncing ball.

Santorini, like me, seemed irked by the witness's cloying manner, and quickly switched the topic to Fred Trudd's final weekend. Stankwitz explained that an impasse "over our timber harvesting rights up the Wolf River had unfortunately chilled warm relations with our good friends on the local reserve." Thus, his boss, bravely and unaccompanied — "that was so typical of Fred, he was sometimes a one-man show" — drove down to Pouce Coupe for a weekend mediation hearing in an effort "to soothe all the bumps and bruises."

Santorini sat. "Your witness."

I bounced up. "That's not the way I heard it. Surely you're aware, Mr. Stankwitz, there was a huge fracas after Trudd showed up drunk, hurled racist epithets at members of the Tribal Council, and then walked out on them."

Astonishingly, I got all that out before Ed Santorini, caught napping, made it to his feet with an explosive *"Objection!"*

Kroop, with almost equal vigour, responded, "Upheld!"

"It's all in the mediator's report, Milord, which I learned only yesterday is in the hands of the Aboriginal Affairs ministry. I am seeking to subpoena it."

"Well, you've jumped the gun with a question that was deliberately rhetorical and lacking in factual foundation. Not an auspicious start, Mr. Beauchamp. Please proceed."

"Mr. Stankwitz, the issue between Trudd Enterprises and the Wolf River Reserve has to do with a tract of land of some thousand acres up near the headwaters of the Wolf River, am I correct?"

"Yes, the government granted us cutting rights. All signed, stamped, and approved, sir."

"The Tribal Council contends that land is their traditional territory, and as proof they have found ancient burial grounds of the Dene people. Can you agree with that?"

"That's what they claim."

"And the provincial government intervened and ordered the matter go to hearing?"

"Yes."

"Despite that, Fred Trudd bluntly refused to compromise on the issue. He had zero interest in any mediation effort. He made that clear to you. Fair to say?"

"He wasn't very happy with the situation."

"Please give me a straight and honest answer. He was not just unhappy, he was angry, and he was not going to bend, hell or high water."

"Fred could be very stubborn."

Kroop, impatient at the waffling, intervened. "I think what counsel wants to know, is did he travel to that mediation hearing with an open or closed mind."

Good for Kroop. He may not be that bad a judge after all.

"He was not going to budge, sir. He made that clear."

It was the right time to quit. "Thank you. No more questions."

━

The RCMP dispatcher, a matronly woman with a pleasant manner, had fielded Angelina's call on May 29, at twelve minutes after noon. A recording of their brief conversation had Angelina volunteering, in a low, frightened voice: "Please come. I think I shot Mr. Trudd and he's dead."

She was instructed to stay put, stay on the line, not touch anything. An ambulance was on the way. On the tape, the operator could be heard calling out Trudd's address on the police radio. When she went back on the line she heard only sobbing and what sounded like words of prayer. She didn't press Angelina for details but talked soothingly until there came the sound of a siren.

"Your witness," Santorini said.

I was stuck with that inculpatory admission, but did my best to reframe it. "'I *think* I shot Mr. Trudd.' These were her exact words?"

"Yes."

"I *think*. That suggests uncertainty, madam, would you agree?" I expected an objection, but it never came.

"I suppose so, yes."

"Clearly, Ms. Santos was distraught and confused, is that fair to say?"

"She was quite emotional, sir."

"I thought I made out, from the recording, that she was praying."

"I believe she was reciting from Psalm 23."

The psalm of David — imprinted in my mind since I was a Sunday school toddler. "'The Lord is my shepherd, I shall not want.'" That prompted a murmur from the gallery.

"Yes, sir."

"And it seems fair to say that Ms. Santos had just walked through the valley of the shadow of death . . ."

The witness smiled. "That could be."

Santorini raised a late objection, which I quickly countered. "I was merely quoting from the Good Book." There was a Bible handy, on the witness stand, and I raised it for all to see. "I hope you don't find any sin in that."

Murmurs of approval in the gallery. A few jurors smiled. The judge didn't. Instead, he sent me a warning look. A memory came, from a few years ago: Wilbur Kroop's sneering reference, during a courtroom break, to the Old Testament: "Scripted by fabulists, Beauchamp, ninety percent of it."

The next two witnesses, Constables Wilhelm Nagler and Jerry Wiesenhoff, were both young and green, Wiesenhoff just a rookie. They'd got the dispatcher's call at ten minutes past noon just as they wrapped up an encounter between a Highways Department truck and a Volvo on the Wolf River bridge, half a mile from Trudd's property. It took less than a minute for them to blare their way into Trudd's backyard.

Nagler, who was pink, freckled, and nervous, clutched the Bible as he took the witness oath, then at the final "So help me, God" raised it to his lips and gave it a smooch.

In apparent approval of that gesture, Angelina made the sign of the cross. But Kroop looked at the officer aghast. "Where did you learn to do that?"

Nagler wasn't sure what impropriety he'd committed, and stammered, "I'm sorry, sir?"

"Kissing the Bible. I can't believe police witnesses are still doing that."

Bussing the Bible had become all the rage in our lower courts, police witnesses assuming a display of holiness enhanced their credibility.

"Um, Your Honour . . . Lordship, I'm sorry, it's been the practice since I was posted here, two years ago —"

"I can't imagine a more incautious way to pass around germs."

Angelina's pursed lips signalled her disapproval of the judge's unchristian mindset. Clara gave me a deadpan eye roll, an affirmation of my advice to expect these nasty asides from Kroop: he was a bully. His clerk had already suffered verbal assaults. As a narcotics prosecutor, he'd maligned his cops in and out of the courtroom, especially after acquittals.

Ed Santorini, displeased with the dressing-down of his witness, was curt. "I'll deal with the matter, Milord. You responded to a radio call, Constable?"

"Yes. Possible homicide. It came in at twelve-ten hours."

"And where were you at that time?"

Nagler explained he and his partner were attending to a collision on the Wolf River bridge.

"And while you were busy with that, did you hear a gunshot?"

"Objection," I said. "Leading."

"I'll rephrase. Did you hear a loud noise?"

"Yes, sir. A gunshot. From a high-powered rifle, I would say."

"From?"

"The area of the eastern shoreline, approximately from Mr. Trudd's property. I have it in my notes that the shot sounded five minutes and thirty seconds before the dispatcher called." This sounded well memorized.

"And was that a single shot?"

"Yes, sir, I have no doubt about that."

"Tell us what you did at the scene."

"On pulling into the driveway, I observed a late-model Mercedes sedan parked there with its driver's door open. Near that door I observed a male individual sprawled face down who I identified as Mr. Frederick C. Trudd." Spoken with the strained syntax learned from police training manuals.

The judge wasn't through with embarrassing this young officer, and demanded to know how he identified a body sprawled face down. Nagler awkwardly explained he'd made an assumption later confirmed.

Santorini helped him out: "You were familiar with the deceased?"

"Well, pretty near everyone in town knows him . . . knew him."

"What was he wearing?"

Nagler was granted leave to check the notes he'd jotted down at the scene, then read out: "Grey slacks, grey flannel shirt, and a brown-checked sweater vest."

He knelt at the body, in a vain search for vital signs, while Wiesenhoff guarded the rifle lying at Angelina's feet. She was sitting on the steps below the kitchen door, her head bowed as if in prayer. As the two officers approached Angelina, sirens howled distantly — senior personnel and an ambulance were on their way.

"She had her hands over her face and was crying," Constable Nagler said.

Santorini halted him with a raised hand. "May the jury be excused, Your Lordship, while we embark on a voir dire."

After the jury was herded away, we went through the requisite charade of a mini-trial to determine if the accused's right to remain silent had been compromised. I saw no profit in arguing the issue, and let it play out, swivelling to appraise my client, who wore a slight frown: lost in thought, not prayer.

Bored by the voir dire, Trudd's witchy sisters wandered out to join several smokers in the corridor. Ace reporter Charles Loobie, scenting prey, followed them.

Kroop ruled that the two young officers had uttered no promises or threats and had properly recited the standard caution. The jury was quickly back in court.

"Continue, Constable," Santorini said.

"I asked her what happened, but she was very emotional and couldn't finds words at first, and then she said, 'I shot him.'"

He said, "Why?"

"He raped me."

"When?"

"Thursday, and before that too, almost."

He asked where, and she indicated downstairs, her basement bedroom.

Nagler said, "Wait." And the conversation ended there. Not, apparently, because of the din of approaching sirens but because their cruiser's radio was barking orders: Staff-Sergeant Trasov was on his way; the two constables were to suspend questioning.

Santorini asked, "And what did you do after getting those instructions?"

"Well, nothing, because Staff Trasov pulled in, with an ambulance behind him, and he and Corporal Delisle took over. I helped ribbon up the crime scene."

"Your witness." Santorini sat.

I asked, "First homicide case, Constable?"

"Yes, sir."

"Well, sounds like you followed procedure. When you checked the deceased for vital signs, did you note where the bullet penetrated the body?"

"In the middle of the back. Blood was congealing there."

"Right at the level of the heart?"

"Yes, sir."

"A bull's eye."

"I guess."

"When you say Angelina was very emotional and distressed, how did that show?"

"She was crying and . . . kind of in shock."

"And confused — you said she couldn't finds words at first."

"Well, I thought she was in mighty bad shape."

"Did she say, 'I shot him,' or 'I think I shot him'?"

"'I shot him.' I made a note of that. So did Constable Wiesenhoff. We compared notes."

"But you're aware that the dispatcher recalled her words as 'I *think* I shot Mr. Trudd.'"

"Yes, sir."

"Angelina didn't impress you as being someone with vengeance in her heart."

"Objection!" Santorini finally had enough — I'd been skirting danger.

"Sustained. It's not for the witness to say what's in anyone else's heart or mind."

I plowed ahead. "Angelina answered your questions without hesitating?"

"Except for sobbing."

"She was straightforward with you, not evasive?"

"I'd have to say yes."

"Looked at you when you spoke?"

"At me and Jerry . . . Constable Wiesenhoff."

"When you asked her when she'd been raped, she said, 'Thursday, and before that, almost.' You took that to mean she'd been sexually assaulted more than once —"

"Objection." Santorini was up. "Speculation."

I replied, "Inference is not speculation."

"I think it amounts to the same thing here," said Kroop, his round face rosily glowing with what I took to be impatience with me. "Witness, you need not answer that question."

I plowed ahead: "May I have a peek at your notes, Officer, the ones you made at the scene?"

"Certainly."

His well-used writing pad was bookmarked at May 29, and the entries were clean and legible, almost all in pencil, a few in ballpoint. Nothing in them conflicted with his testimony, but one inked afterthought caught my eye.

"Constable, you claim to have heard a rifle shot some five minutes before you were dispatched to the scene. But that seems to have been added to your notes at the end of the day." I read it out: "'Heard rifle shot from crime scene 12:04 hours when attending collision on bridge.'"

"Yes, sir, I reminded myself later to add that information."

"'Heard rifle shot,' you wrote, but you actually heard more than one shot, isn't that so?"

"No, sir."

"You must at least have heard what sounded like an echo."

"No, sir. One loud shot."

"But this was written much later. At the station, right?"

"Yes, when I had time to collect my thoughts."

"So that would have been several hours later, right? Your memory wouldn't have been as sharp."

"I checked with my partner, Jerry Wiesenhoff, and we were in accord."

This was getting me nowhere. "Thank you, Constable."

Wiesenhoff was next, but he would await his turn until after lunch break.

1966 —
Never Suck Up

I wasn't hungry and was too tense for company, so I hid in the courthouse library searching for case law about false confessions. Not the kind made under duress, but under less obvious influences. Might one falsely say, "I shot him," because of guilt in harbouring a desire for revenge? Could Angelina have felt a spiritual compulsion to share the agonies of Christ, or accepted guilt as a penalty for her sins of congress with Satan's disciple?

Nothing jumped out at me from the law reports. No other explanation for her blunt admission made sense, other than she truly believed she took Trudd's life. She'd said as much to me — yet she didn't *remember* shooting him. I preferred to assume hers was not a false confession but a false assumption.

On my exit from the library Charles Loobie again exercised his innate talent at blocking my progress, this time at the top of the staircase. "You really let that copper off the hook, Artie. He was a dumb, fat, easy target, couldn't even remember how many shots he heard. You didn't draw blood once."

I squeezed free but he joined me on the stairs. "I smoked out Trudd's sisters, literally — they were chaining fags down there. They don't believe their dear brother, with his heart of gold, would rape anyone, especially such a lower-class person. They'd heard he threatened to report her for stealing from him. Something to work with there, eh, Artie?"

I thanked him and entered the assize court. Etienne had moved to a position just behind the dock, and was communing with Angelina, maybe sharing a prayer. The sisters were back, now in the front row, next to lawyer Hogey Johnson, who looked ill at ease in their company. I had instructed Marsha Bigelow not to return — she would likely be called as a witness, and the practice was for witnesses to remain outside. She had a business to run, anyway.

The afternoon session opened with Wiesenhoff avoiding the unkissable Bible as too hot to handle. This rookie was more relaxed than his partner, more confident, but he added little new. It didn't help that he also claimed to have heard only one shot from the area of Trudd's house.

In cross, I asked: "Did you make a note about hearing gunfire?"

"No, sir, but I remember thinking someone was hunting over there, out of season."

"Was it one shot or two?"

"One for sure. I was dealing with an irate driver, so a hunting infraction wasn't a huge concern at the moment."

"That gunshot was followed by a loud echo, right?"

He pondered. "Maybe. Like I said, I was focused on our MVA."

"Okay, let's go on to the crime scene. Did you look inside the house?"

"I only slipped inside because the kitchen phone was off the hook and buzzing, and I hung it up."

"So you must have seen or heard the phone through the screen door?"

"Yes. The main door was open."

"And the screen door was spring-activated?"

"It swung shut as I returned outside."

"With some force?"

"I remember having to catch it so it wouldn't slam."

"You didn't seize the rifle?"

"I didn't touch it. I wanted to keep the scene intact until my superiors got there."

"And the body of the deceased remained exactly in place?"

"Yes, sir. And remained so until Corporal Delisle took some photographs."

Those photos had already been tendered as exhibits. They showed Trudd's body lying prone a few feet from the open driver's door, blood extruding from the entry wound in his back. His legs were splayed, both bent at the knees, a posture one might expect of a victim who'd just been urinating.

His corpse remained in that spread-eagled position until the ambulance attendants were cleared to deliver it to the morgue. It was as they turned Trudd's body face up that his penis came into view. A photo showed it resting between his legs like a white slug.

My fragile hypothesis was that he'd been shot from behind as he advanced on Angelina, and the impact spun him around. I gambled. "Constable, Mr. Trudd seemed to have fallen in an awkward position. The force of a bullet from a high-powered rifle might have sent him into a 180-degree spin?"

"It could, I suppose, but I've only seen that in cowboy movies."

Santorini missed that while whispering to Clara, and was slow to tune into the chuckling in the gallery. He started to rise, as if to object, but, having no idea what to object to, sank to his seat.

Kroop faked a sense of humour: "You were slow on the draw, Mr. Prosecutor." Followed by chortled snorts: "Hmf, hmf." Then he turned to the jury: "Ladies and gentlemen, you will have to forgive Mr. Beauchamp for his obsessive fondness for speculative questions." Then, to me: "I don't want to have to rein you in, Mr. Beauchamp."

"That makes both of us, Milord."

That was too acerbic. Kroop's glasses slid down his nose as his face tightened. "Don't test me, Counsel."

I denied him the apology he sought, and went back to work. "Constable, in your report you mentioned encountering some cats. Tell us about that."

"Well, maybe because of the loud sirens, three of Mr. Trudd's cats bolted from the cat door just below the back stairs."

Kroop rejoined the fray. "Three of them? How many cats did he have?"

"Six, sir."

Which prompted Kroop to ask: "How did you know he had six cats?"

"Well, I'd met them a few months earlier."

"What do you mean, you *met* them?"

"I was introduced to them at Mr. Trudd's house."

Kroop had the disconcerted look of one who has opened a can of worms. I jumped in. "And what was the occasion for this meeting with Mr. Trudd and his cats?"

"He'd filed a complaint about his, ah, girlfriend, you'd call her, who apparently stole some money and securities from his safe."

"And that was early in March of this year?"

"Yes, sir. I was tasked to interview Mr. Trudd at his home."

I brought it out: the conniving Alaskan hitchhiker-turned-mistress who had run off with a lover and twelve thousand dollars in cash and bearer bonds from Trudd's safe. We learned that the larceny file was still open, though the miscreant was believed to have crossed back into the States.

Kroop silently endured this — he couldn't prohibit me from exploring an episode he had introduced. Lesson learned, I hoped: do not interfere with Beauchamp's cross-examinations.

I asked Wiesenhoff about Trudd's emotional state during the interview.

"To be honest, he was in a rage so bad that I couldn't follow everything he said. A lot of profanity. He'd been drinking too, though it was early afternoon."

That helped — my game plan was to paint the victim as foul-mouthed and black-hearted. I hoped to show that Trudd took heavily to the bottle after his mistress ran off, and began drunkenly molesting Angelina.

"Was Miss Santos there, Constable?"

"Yes. We didn't interact much except she introduced me to the cats by name, and made me a grilled cheese sandwich."

◼▬

Corporal Delisle came across as calm, collected, and competent. He recorded the crime scene with photos and sketches and measurements, while keeping the two constables busy with tape measures. They found no evidence that might suggest a violent rape had occurred inside the spanking clean house, other than the ripped panties and nightie in Angelina's laundry bag. Delisle tendered those items as exhibits.

For his part, Mike Trasov escorted Angelina into the back seat of his cruiser, and offered comforting words. Constrained by a gag order from Prince George, he wasn't permitted to question her. His police radio regularly burped out commands and information: a Major Crimes unit is on its way. They'll Q and A the suspect. Don't touch anything. Do nothing.

Ultimately, the ambulance drove off with the corpse, and Trasov with the suspect. That's where Santorini ended his direct examination of this hefty, easygoing officer. I liked the fellow, he'd been kind to Angelina, accommodating to me.

I asked, "You're at the head of the RCMP detachment here?"

"Yes, sir."

"I heard locals call you the Fort Tom police chief."

"I'm nothing fancy, Mr. Beauchamp. Just head of the detachment."

"And how long have you served in the Force?"

"Some thirty years."

"All over the province, I'll bet."

"But mostly up here. I prefer it. My kind of country."

"And you've handled thousands of criminal cases."

"Don't know if I could count them."

"And you've taken statements from thousands of witnesses."

"Yes."

"And suspects."

"Until their lawyers showed up." A ripple of laughter. Not infectious enough to attract a smile from the judge. I had not been polite to Kroop, and he was still brooding.

"And despite your experience and competence, you were ordered not to take a statement from Miss Santos."

"Those were my instructions. I wasn't to talk to her. Just take prints and pictures."

"Who gave you those instructions?"

"I presume the head of Major Crimes. They were conveyed by Detectives Barnes and Biggs, who'd been dispatched to fly up here."

"And so Miss Santos was abandoned to a lonely jail cell for four hours while everyone waited for the Major Crimes team to scramble to the Prince George airport, jump into a Cessna, fly a thousand miles, and get debriefed."

That was ruled out of order, as falling into the category of "naked, unalloyed rhetoric." I asked Trasov how he felt about that delay and his gag order.

"I felt matters could have been better handled."

"In what way?"

"The accused seemed willing to talk, and that opportunity was missed."

He probably felt, as I did, that Biggs and Barnes had been undone by their smugness — they'd seen themselves as slick interrogators capable of causing the Filipina maid to gush tears of remorseful guilt.

Again, Kroop failed to control his neurotic compulsion to interrupt. "Counsel, where are you going with this?"

"I'm exploring the circumstances of my client's arrest, Milord." A weary "Proceed."

"That opportunity was missed because along came Mr. Hogey Johnson, barrister and solicitor. That's him, in the front row, the handsome man with the bushy moustache. Well-respected, civic-minded gentleman, chair of the Chamber of Commerce, main-stay of the Rotary Club — do I have that right?"

"Yes, sir. He's had me speak at their lunches. Everyone in the North seems to know Hogey."

"And late that afternoon he showed up at the detachment — after having had to abandon his barbecue and his dinner guests." I aimed that at Hogey, who bobbed his head with a tight grin. Trudd's sisters seemed confused by the attention their seatmate was getting.

I could see Kroop was antsy, and I went up a gear. "And then, Sergeant, Mr. Johnson spoke to Miss Santos in her cell for several minutes, and on his return said he'd instructed her not to answer questions from the police."

"Mr. Beauchamp, may I remind you that your task here is not to give testimony but to ask questions. What is the point you are trying to make?"

"My point, Milord, is that senior brass in Prince George, in gagging Staff-Sergeant Mike Trasov, prevented him from taking a fair and honest and full statement from Miss Santos that could have pointed to her innocence." I turned to see Angelina send me a smile, cheering me on for standing up to this infidel judge. Encouraged, I continued: "She was denied an opportunity to give a spontaneous explanation that she intended only to scare him."

That sounded like bullshit to the lawyers in the room, even to me, but a few jurors nodded, including Alderman Rummy Wilcox, who likely resented seeing his police chief treated like a simpleton. Kroop held down his bile until he'd excused the jury, then erupted, accusing me once again of the scarlet sin of speculating, topped off by a "blatant" effort to taint the jury.

"With respect, Milord, you sought to know what point I was trying to make. I answered frankly."

Kroop tried to talk over me, something about his being familiar with my tricks. I suggested that our difficulties could be avoided were I allowed to do my job. The prosecutors sat back and enjoyed the scuffle.

Kroop finally ordered a break, and stomped out, the room erupting with loud chatter as it was evacuated. Clara rewarded me with a smile and a wink.

I escaped outside for a cold breath of brain-clearing air, an effort foiled by Charles Loobie, who was in lockstep. "Is that your plan, Artie? Piss off the judge? Or is it a male domination thing, bull elks butting horns to see who owns the courtroom?"

Over post-trial whiskies, I'd been tutored on the handling of judges by my hero, M. Cyrus Smythe-Baldwin, Q.C.: *Always stand your ground if your cause is just, and never suck up.* I didn't tell Loobie this, because it would be in the *Province* the next day, misinterpreted.

He carried on: "Nice stagecraft with Angelina and the praying padre as counterpoint to the Bible-bashing judge. The assistant prosecutor with the big bazookas is giving you hungry looks, Artie. In case you hadn't noticed. Something going on there?"

I returned inside, and there she was, somehow aware I needed rescue from my tormentor. She gave me a slight squeeze as she shepherded me back to the courtroom. "What was that all about, with Justice Kroop?"

"He's hard-wired into being a prosecutor. I'm trying to break his addiction."

1966 —
The Specialist in Ladies' Issues

T he courtroom was silent as we resumed, taut with expecta-
tion, the spectators eager to know the score — who was the
winner, who the loser of the scrap between counsel and judge? They
quickly became aware that Kroop would earn neither an apology
nor an excuse for my alleged misbehaviour. He seemed at a loss
how to handle that without seeming prideful and thin-skinned. His
pinched eyes circled hawk-like, at the gallery, at Crown counsel, at
the jury — only I escaped Kroop's stern surveillance. I took that as
a victory.

Kroop faked a businesslike mien. "The day is not getting any
younger, gentlemen. I assume we're through with Sergeant Trasov?"

Santorini jumped up. "Except for one minor oversight on my
part, Milord. One more question."

"I would not want to offend Mr. Beauchamp by suggesting he
extend the traditional courtesy of allowing opposing counsel to
cure an omission." Looking at me benignly.

"My pleasure," I said, with an equal feigning of sincerity.

Santorini spoke rapidly, as if fearing he'd be cut off: "Sergeant,
prior to Mr. Trudd's death did Miss Santos complain to your detachment that she'd been raped or assaulted by Mr. Trudd?"

"No, sir, we have no record of that."

"Thank you, Sergeant Trasov," said Kroop, ignoring me, though I was standing.

"If I may be so bold, Milord, I have a few questions."

"Proceed. I thought you were through."

"Sergeant, is it fair to say that Mr. Trudd was not highly regarded by many in the community?"

"Well, the way he was raising rents — he owned most of the commercial businesses in town — he was pretty unpopular, I'd have to say."

"Had you received complaints about his behaviour?"

"He was a hard-drinking man, and I fielded a number of calls, yes."

"Drunk and disorderly, would that sum up —"

Kroop: "All right, that's enough. The deceased is not on trial."

"I propose, Milord, to show he should have been."

"Well, you won't do it with this witness. We have half an hour. Is that enough time for another? Let's not fall behind."

"I think we can squeeze Dr. Mulligan in," said Santorini.

It would be a task to squeeze this hulking fellow into an elevator, let alone a witness stand. Dr. Jim Mulligan, not a picture of health with his cantilevered midsection, sat with a rasping groan after taking the oath. The veteran physician, who had grumpily refused me audience, was clearly hostile to the defence. At the preliminary, he'd bested Pappas, who'd been too pugnacious.

Hogey Johnson had arranged for his emergency services because "Jim specializes in obstetrics and other ladies' issues." Angelina was in his clinic for only half an hour on that Sunday afternoon, with her RCMP escort guarding the door to his examination room. She was in such a numbed state that the indignity of a genital inspection was hardly felt. She remembered little: the touch of rubber gloves, swabs taken, blood drawn. The few questions that Mulligan asked were solely about her physical health.

Santorini ran through the unexceptional background of this practitioner, and qualified him to give medical opinions. He described

Angelina as a "physically healthy Filipina maid," adding, inaccurately, "with a limited English vocabulary."

"You were aware she'd claimed to have been raped three days earlier." Bluntly leading the witness.

"She didn't want to talk about that, but, yes, I'd been so informed."

"And as part of your practice, you've examined quite a few victims of sexual assault."

"A few dozen complainants, yes."

"And usually they would show physical injury, bruising, bleeding, that sort of thing?"

"Usually, but with exceptions. If several or even a few days have elapsed since the alleged assault, such indicators would be less apparent and therefore unreliable."

Jim Mulligan had obviously been down this route many times, had read the texts, learned the lines. Juror Eight, Ranjeet Singh, the administrator of the Fort Tom General Hospital, was obviously more than a casual acquaintance of the witness, and his cynical smile hinted at his low regard for him.

"I don't think we need to go into the intimate details here, Doctor, given the delicacy of the subject matter, but generally speaking were you able to make any findings one way or another —"

Kroop dived in, irritated. "You're rambling, Mr. Prosecutor." Turning to the witness. "Did you see indications the accused had been raped?"

"I observed no clear traumas, Your Lordship. I did detect a slight redness to the outer labia and the vaginal opening, either of which could be from ordinary causes of irritation, like rough sex or tight undergarments or rubbing." A couple of women in the jury stirred uneasily. "The hymen was not intact but it was difficult to locate signs of recent tearing."

Eddie was clearly out of his depth, anatomically, and he hastily wrapped up: "In conclusion, Doctor, did your examination satisfy you that she'd been recently raped?"

That was objectionable for a multitude of reasons, but I held my tongue. Eddie was digging a hole for himself by attacking Angelina's credibility — defendants fabricate, that was his assumption. This mostly hometown jury was not going to entertain the nonsensical theory that she'd had consensual sex with Trudd. They might wonder, as I did, how Eddie's knee-jerk approach would advantage the Crown.

Maybe he'd been swayed by Dr. Mulligan, who reeked of misogyny. "In my opinion," he testified, "the usual indicia of forced intercourse were not present."

A woman juror in the back row made a face.

"Your witness."

I didn't want to spend a lot of time with this charlatan. "Dr. Mulligan, you said the redness and irritation in the vaginal area were consistent with rough sex, whatever that means. So they were obviously consistent with a sexual assault, right?"

"If the alleged victim offered little or no resistance, that could be so. In my experience, there are many shades of grey in situations where consent is an issue."

I was taken aback. "In your *experience?* Dr. Mulligan, if a woman doesn't resist it's still rape, all the more aggravated if threats —"

Once again came the dreaded interruption from the judicial interventionist. "Counsel for the defence is treading on precarious ground. Dr. Mulligan is not here to debate issues of law."

I let go, thundering at Kroop. "This witness, with his 'many shades of grey,' who claims to be some kind of specialist on the nuances of rape, sits there like the Wizard of Oz voicing crazy, outdated notions, and I'm not allowed to cross-examine him? If Your Lordship persists in horning in like this my only option may be to apply for a mistrial." I took a breath. "With respect, of course."

Delbert, the timid court clerk, cowered in fear of Kroop's reaction, but the judge couldn't find words, just sat there red-faced. I didn't wait for him to find his tongue, and pushed ahead: "Doctor, did you not find bruises on Miss Santos elsewhere — her arms, legs, upper body?"

After my rant, he seemed less full of himself, more cautious. "If I saw any, they were minor. I have nothing in my notes."

"That's not quite true, because you mentioned bruising to her shoulder."

"Ah, of course, that was very fresh and purple, from ruptured capillaries in the anterior area of the right shoulder. Quite painful, I would say."

"An injury easily explained if Miss Santos suffered a severe blow from the recoil of a rifle improperly braced."

"I would have to agree."

"Obviously, a person well trained in the use of a high-powered rifle would be unlikely to incur such an injury."

"I heartily agree."

My tilt with Kroop had caused the witness a loss of bravado. I had him hooked, reeled in like a fat salmon that had stopped thrashing. Ranjeet Singh was grinning. So was Clara. Even Santorini wore a little smile. Kroop remained mutely livid.

"Dr. Mulligan, on Monday, May thirtieth, Miss Santos was remanded in custody to the women's prison in Prince George. On arrival she was examined by a prison doctor. Are you aware of that?"

"That may be so. I was not privy to that doctor's report."

Neither was the great Alex Pappas, who'd made no effort to reach out to Dr. Royce. I'd done my homework.

"You had no communication with Dr. Royce?"

"I may have had previous dealings with him. Does he have a first name?"

"Yes, Genevieve."

Snorts of poorly suppressed laughter from the gallery, chuckles from the jury, a resigned look from Santorini, as I passed around — to him, to the judge via the clerk, and to Mulligan — copies of her one-page report.

"Just a minute." Kroop was back in action. "Will this Dr. Royce be called to verify this document?"

"If the Crown raises an objection, yes, Milord."

None seemed forthcoming, probably because Eddie was embarrassed by the ineptitude of his medical witness, and was eager for this ordeal to end. So I merrily filed Dr. Royce's report as Exhibit Thirteen and went back to work. "You will note, Dr. Mulligan, that she observed contusions on Miss Santos's frontal lower left thigh and on both wrists, the coloration of which suggested them to be three to five days old."

"If that's what she saw, I have no issues. I was, of course, ah, focused elsewhere . . . Medically speaking . . ." He stalled out. Ranjeet Singh rolled his eyes.

"I hope you will agree this bruising was consistent with Miss Santos having been forcibly held down."

"I can't disagree."

"You will also note, in Dr. Royce's third paragraph, that she considered the hymen to have been recently ruptured."

"Well, that wasn't my . . . I defer to Dr. Royce, of course."

"And she also said, paragraph six, it is not uncommon for rape victims to suffer amnesia, especially if the traumatic event involves severe violence and threats."

"I can't argue with that."

"No more questions."

Mulligan heaved himself from the stand, and, looking straight ahead to avoid any eye contact, made his getaway.

Court was adjourned until ten a.m. on Tuesday.

1966 —
I'll Never, Never Do It Again

I knew Charles Loobie would be lurking outside the courtroom, but this time I eluded him, slipping out by the prisoners' door, following Angelina and a woman custodial officer down an enclosed walkway to the RCMP's lockup. I needed a few minutes with my client, to let her know the day went well and to ask if any of the testimony had jogged her memory.

She had her own questions: "Why does the judge always pick fights with you?" "What is meaning of shades of grey?" "Why do you call the doctor the Wizard of Oz?" "When do I talk?" I handled those as best I could.

Her memory continued to fire blanks. I got tongue-tied when I asked if she had seen Trudd expose his penis. She reacted oddly, I thought: a flash of disgust or fear. Then: "No, I don't remember."

Finally, I posed a scenario that sounded patently absurd to my own ears: she fired without thinking, her bullet went wayward, and Trudd was executed by an expert marksman who'd waited in the woods for Trudd to show up. She crinkled her nose with disbelief.

"Think, Angelina. Did you see anyone back there? Moving about, maybe running up into the hills?"

"The hills . . ." She frowned, then shook her head with a smile, as if trying to humour me.

"Do you know a young man on the reserve named Johnny Blue?"

"Yes, I like him. Very handsome, nice smile. We volunteered in the food bank on Sundays after church. And he liked me too. He said I was almost Indian."

I was taken aback. Hot-tempered Johnny Blue, food bank, church — that didn't quite add up. But then I didn't know Johnny Blue. Etienne's efforts to bring us together had failed, because the young man was suddenly nowhere around. If he was innocent, as his uncle insisted, why would he hide?

Angelina wasn't interested in my silly theories about lurking assassins. She insisted that I touch her belly — "to feel my beautiful baby move."

I did so, delicately, and felt the gentle jiggling of unborn life. I can't describe my emotions at that moment, aside from overwhelm.

━━

When I returned to the courthouse, only a few stragglers remained, clerks and court officers closing up shop. I took the steps two at a time, eager to change out of my court garb and respond to my stomach's griping about the skipped lunch.

I was still focused on that affecting moment with Angelina and her unborn baby, and as I barged into the barristers' lounge, I almost tripped over a human leg — it had risen from a padded chair to bar my way to the changing room.

"I loved the way you kicked that sexist quack's butt," Clara said. "It made me want to bang you on the courtroom floor."

I hastily looked about to confirm we were alone.

"Relax. Eddie split for the Fort to interview two dicks over drinks. I'm about to join them."

This free spirit seemed to revel at being unconventional in style and speech. Today's fashion statement: a mini and a denim jacket with a peace symbol patch. The leg, which I found myself holding by the ankle, was clad in blue tights. I swivelled it like a turnstile and set it back in place.

She blithely followed me into the robing room and watched me change, talking brightly, a smash review of my cross-examining skills. Then she hooked arms with me and we sailed out into the corridor, almost walking into Charles Loobie.

"When did you two become such learned friends?"

Riled, I advanced on him; he back-pedalled. "Get a life of your own, Loobie. Stop living off others. Stop haunting me." I'd ignored a rule of the profession — don't bait the media — but I didn't care.

Loobie retreated down the stairs. "Artie has a rep with ladies of easy virtue, Clara. Maybe you don't want to be on his list."

"Off the record," she said, "stick it up your ass."

Outside, in the dark, blustery cold, I boldly escorted Clara to her hotel, daring Loobie to follow — though as it turned out, he didn't. In the lounge, I ordered a double Seagram's to blunt my irritation at the snoopy newsman, then joined Clara, Eddie, and smart aleck detectives Hugh Barnes and Ted Biggs — they were on deck to testify in the morning.

The two officers were already well lubricated. I hoped they weren't driving — they were staying out of town, in the Alaska Highway Motel, run by a retired cop.

Biggs rendered a raspy version of an old hit: "'I didn't kno-o-w the gun was loaded.' That song always makes me cry."

Barnes chimed in: "'And I'll never, never do it again.'"

"It's the Andrews Sisters." Santorini got a laugh.

I ought to have to joined in the fun but was turned off by the officers' cynical bantering about a tragic event. Barnes treated me to a sloppy grin. "Maybe you can pull off a self-defence, counsellor. She thought it was a gun he was pulling from his pants." Having carelessly blurted that out, like a blown secret, he reddened with the kind of pained look of one struggling to suppress a fart.

"His cock," Barnes explained. "I bet he had a big boner on when he turned around to have a pour."

I tilted back my whisky, and rose. "I'll see you gentlemen tomorrow in court."

"I'm real scared," said Biggs. He turned his attention to the TV screen, an NHL game about to begin. "The book has the Hawks at plus one. Mikita's on a tear."

"You want a little action on that?" Santorini said. "A sawbuck on the Red Wings. Gordie Howe's still got jism."

"I'm in. Nothing to lose but my overtime pay."

I could see through the wide front window that Rustlers was crowded for dinner. But there was Hogey Johnson, warhorse of the Fort Tom Rotary Club, beckoning me to an empty chair at his reserved table.

Complicating matters, Charles Loobie was interviewing Hogey, but he rose as I entered. "Great talking to you, sir," he told Hogey. "I'll check it out."

As I hung my coat on an antler rack, Loobie loped over, approaching so close that I feared he was going to hug me. His face showed contrition and repentance: "Sorry, Artie, I was *way* out of line back there. I was taking the mickey out of you, but I can see how you misinterpreted my attempt at satire. By the way, I already called in a piece about how you eviscerated that hack MD." He hustled off to a pay phone in the vestibule.

Hogey pulled a chair over for me. He'd finished his main course, his plate scraped clean except for a set of rib bones. "This time it's on me, young fella. Get your gums on the pork ribs, it's like nuzzling your face into Gina Lollobrigida's pair of matched pillows."

I ordered the ribs. Hogey asked the waiter to put a hold on his apple pie and bring two glasses of Ne Plus Ultra, and two

Calgary Ales to wash them down. He commended me for my sterling performance, especially in "gutting it out" with the belligerent judge.

I told him I couldn't help noticing that the Trudd sisters had joined him in the front pew.

"Donalda and Hortense may not be popular with many folks around here, but they're popular with me. They pay their bills on time. Those two, they wanted to sleep in their brother's house during the trial, which would raise eyebrows, so Wendell and me balked at that — Wendell Melquist, the listing agent, he found them a nice furnished apartment in a building they didn't know they owned."

Supposedly, they were selling off entire tracts of the town's business section, as well as its main employer, the sawmill. I asked Hogey how he felt about that.

"Their problem is nobody's buying what they're selling, and that's got the two of them squabbling over whether to mark everything down at bargain basement prices. They can't give immediate title anyway, the whole shebang's still in probate."

Administration of the estate was in the hands of Russell, DuMoulin, a powerful Vancouver law firm. Hubbell Meyerson, my forensic bloodhound, had connections there — as he seemed to have everywhere.

Loobie, who'd slotted a lot of quarters into that phone, finally hung up. Stuffing his notepad into a coat pocket, he ambled over from the vestibule. "Hey, Artie, buddy, I just may have a defence for you that looks remotely plausible. But don't thank me, I'm the conduit, thank Mr. Johnson here."

Hogey winced. "Oh, fart, maybe I said too much. I told him about the Indians being on the warpath against Trudd over that land claims thing. Up the Wolf River? I think I mentioned it to you. The mediation in Pouce Coupe that went bad."

Loobie smiled proudly. "Yeah, and I tracked down the arbiter. Nice guy, garrulous, it was hard to keep up with him." He pulled out his notes. "A.W. Mapple, retired magistrate. Anyway he's driving up from Fort St. John tomorrow, all hot to trot to testify about how a young buck named Johnny Blue threatened to knock off Trudd."

Arthur —
July 2022

The work-in-progress flows gently, like sweet Afton, as I move into the crucial part of my story, the trial. That's after having rewritten and polished my early chapters, which Lisa Throckmorton, an agent-cum-editor, calls the setup.

Yes, I am working, on a trial basis, with the Lisa Throckmorton Agency, whose website describes its guiding spirit as a former senior editor at a prestigious international publisher. She emailed me from Toronto after her search engine chanced upon IslandBleat.ca, with its breaking news that I was secretly launching a new career.

"A stunning, breathtaking work," she wrote after receiving the couriered copy of my work-in-progress. "More compelling than fiction — innocence and evil, life and death, personal and real. I am so totally into it."

Having buoyed me up she let me down — is that the way agents work? The title *Defenceless* wasn't acceptable for the American market. Nor was *Defenseless*, because however spelled, the title was too gloomy, too hopeless — it shouts, "Unhappy ending!" She also worried it was about events too well chronicled, available online and in books: e.g., *The Trials of Arthur Beauchamp*.

So she wants it to be more personal, deeply so, probing the psyche of young Arthur. She also wants my opus to be more heroic, manly, the prose earthier, raunchier. That scene with the two Penthouse sex providers ends not with a bang but a whimper. Lacks credibility. No reader — including Ms. Throckmorton herself — would believe I didn't enjoy a rip-snorting threesome in my waterbed that night. My claims to innocence don't ring true.

Likewise, she has trouble swallowing my alleged nobility, my declining the advances of Clara Moncrief (better known, after her first failed marriage, as Clara Gracey). Twice, opportunities were missed for gymnastic romps with the daughter of scandal-prone front-bencher Hon. Hugh Moncrief. "Given Dr. Clara Gracey's own controversial political career, a few passionate passages would create a humongous buzz."

(*Humongous. I am so totally into it.* Those grammatical depravities make me wonder how skilled she was as an editor. Still, I am going to try her out as a lark.)

Our contacts are almost solely via email, though she once phoned me, and in a lively, deep-throated voice accused me of scissoring out a dalliance with Clara to avoid besmirching her reputation. I came across "as a wuss." She added, "It's the goddamn reader who should be jacking off, not the writer."

I was going to expunge that masturbation bit anyway. Truth be told, I'm reluctant to tell the whole truth and nothing but the truth . . .

In the meantime, I find the sedentary life of a writer encourages flab. I am out of shape. I must lengthen my walks with Ulysses. My goal is to be fit enough to celebrate British Columbia Day — two weeks away — with a trek up Mount Norbert, our highest peak. It's an annual pilgrimage, usually with a few contemporaries, though fewer of late, as age takes its toll.

Margaret has been strong-armed by the Garibaldi Historical Society into hosting a hokey garden party that long weekend, a traditional event to honour island elders. Everyone is encouraged to dress in the garb of 1871, when the province joined Canada.

I am expected to play the affable co-host. I can hardly wait.

1966 —
Inconvenient Evidence

B iggs and Barnes showed up Tuesday morning with head-banging hangovers — they'd drunk their way through three hours of hockey. Santorini was in even worse shape, ashen, faltering in speech, keeping his questions simple, like "Then what?"

In summary, the two lead investigators flew in, checked out the crime scene, worked on Angelina to no avail, wrote their reports, and flew out: that was about it. Santorini had them on the stand for barely ten minutes each.

I didn't take much longer. I had also imbibed too much that evening, with Hogey, then alone, worrying about how to handle A.W. Mapple, who would soon be landing on me after a six-hour drive from Dawson Creek. *I'll need a subpoena, of course.* Mapple hankered for the role of surprise witness, a chance at the fame he'd never found as a small-town magistrate.

I took on Hugh Barnes first: "In your report you mentioned that the deceased had just returned from, I quote, 'a business trip' to the Peace River region. Did you follow that up?"

"I heard it had to do with timber rights —"

Kroop: "You know you can't repeat what you heard."

Barnes: "I know. Sorry, Your Honour . . . Lordship."

Me: "You didn't look into the nature of that business?"

Barnes: "Not really, no."

"You also wrote that after the deceased got out of his sedan he observed Miss Santos aiming his rifle at him, that he took a few steps toward her, that he then turned his back to her, unzipped his fly, and urinated. Given that no independent witnesses recorded that scene, how could you possibly describe that chain of events?"

"That would be based on, ah, inferences and observations made at the crime scene."

"I suggest it's based on pure speculation, Officer. You have absolutely no way of knowing whether the deceased turned his back on Miss Santos, do you?"

"Other than that the entrance wound was in Mr. Trudd's back."

"Unless the fatal shot was fired from the woodland behind the Trudd property."

"In that remote possibility, okay."

I couldn't leave him with the last word. "If you'd done your homework, Detective, you'd find that possibility entirely plausible."

Ted Biggs, co-author of that report, was similarly defensive, to the extent of implying that Trudd, "like most men responding to the call of nature," would turn his back to a woman "out of decency." Foreman Rummy Wilcox nodded in solemn agreement. Ranjeet Singh looked embarrassed.

Biggs must have thought he was home free until Kroop — playing defence for a change — decided I'd let him off too lightly. "Just a minute, Detective," he said, foiling Biggs's effort to dismount the witness stand. "Mr. Beauchamp earlier raised the worrying issue that members of the local detachment, including Sergeant Trasov, an experienced veteran, were under strict orders not to question the accused. What was the sense in that? You've heard the expression, strike when the iron's hot."

"Well, Your Lordship, we felt the first members on the scene were inexperienced at homicides . . ." Biggs trailed off, looking pleadingly at Santorini for help, getting none.

Kroop persisted: "Did you not trust the estimable head of Fort Thompson RCMP to handle matters capably?"

"In, ah, retrospect, our advisement may have been, ah, ill-advised. We didn't expect the accused would seek legal advice so soon."

"As Mr. Beauchamp graphically put it, you insisted on hammering away at her despite that her advice was to remain silent."

Kroop was putting on this show in an effort to be liked by the locals, appealing to their sense of pride in their hometown cops. Having dumped on hapless Ted Biggs, Kroop smiled broadly at me. I wanted to believe I was finally winning him over. A little voice whispered: "Beware."

Yet I had to credit him with having given me a little boost — even if only not to appear one-sided. I had no questions arising from his spanking of the detectives, but I wanted them to stick around for another day. Kroop so ordered.

After the mid-morning break Santorini called some of the forensic personnel. I had little to ask the pathologist — the cause of death was undisputed: a projectile had entered Trudd's back a fraction of an inch to the left of his spinal column, ripped through his left ventricle, and exited above his fourth anterior rib. Death would have been swift if not immediate.

I asked, hopefully: "The deceased might have staggered or twisted about before oblivion came?"

"Sporadic movements could occur even as his heart stopped, especially if the victim was already moving."

"He might flail? Swirl about? Fall to his knees?"

"Possibly, but more likely the velocity of a high-powered rifle bullet entering his back would propel him forward and face down."

I had asked one question too many. At least he didn't reference cowboy movies.

The serologist, an upbeat confident woman, testified that Trudd's blood alcohol level was .04 percent, which suggested he'd either had an enormous amount to drink many hours earlier or was imbibing while driving. But no bottles, empty or otherwise, were found in his car.

Analyses of bloodstains on the panties and nightie came up positive for Blood Type B, and semen stains were shown to have been emitted from a male with Blood Type A. Such a male was F.C. Trudd. Angelina was Blood Type B. Despite Angelina's determined efforts to wash away all physical indicators of rape, the serologist also identified traces of semen from the vaginal swabs, again Blood Type A. No motile spermatozoa were found.

"It would seem, however," I suggested, "that if he impregnated her, one motile sperm did make it all the way."

"Obviously," she said, frowning, as if trying to decide if I was a moron.

Again, during lunch break, I prepped and fidgeted in the court-house library. More forensic testimony was on the afternoon bill: fingerprints, ballistics. And that would conclude the Crown's case. I was a little rattled — I hadn't fully scripted my defence. Much would have to be played by ear.

I remained in a fretful dilemma over whether to point an accusing finger at Johnny Blue, along with possible co-conspirators from the Wolf River Reserve. A.W. Mapple was on his way, eager to help me with the decision. What was I going to do about him? Potentially, he could help me raise a reasonable doubt, but how shabby would that be? *Once again my people are to be portrayed as savages.*

I had my elbows on a table, my head burrowed in my hands, as Clara Moncrief entered bearing hamburgers.

"Eddie's head has been taken over by little men with jackham-mers, so he asked me to do the rest of today's list."

"He didn't seem to be bouncing with energy."

"Woke me up at midnight, shouting from the next room, begging me to join him to, quote, 'discush stratergy over a drink.' I got up to double-check that the shared door was locked. Told him to drink lots of water, jack off, and go to sleep."

As I unwrapped my gift burger, she spread her files on the table. I thanked her for saving me from starvation.

"Always thinking of you, Stretch." She posted an air kiss. I wondered if she was enjoying her role as a double agent, betraying the state by serving the enemy. I hadn't been able to talk with her since she played footsy with me in the Fort's cocktail lounge.

She buried her nose in the fingerprint charts. I wished her bonne chance with her courtroom debut, and powered through my burger.

1966 —
The Barber of Ocean Falls

T he audience for our small-town adversarial brawl was growing
by the hour. From the staircase balcony, I could see a crowd
pressing forward as the courtroom door swung open — it would be
standing-room-only for our afternoon session.

Huddled in a corner with Charles Loobie was a white-haired,
white-bearded, rosy-cheeked Santa in civvies. This had to be the
one and only A.W. Mapple, retired magistrate, failed mediator, and
one of the last few persons on earth to have seen F.C. Trudd alive.

Mapple's pudgy right hand was already reaching out as I worked my
way through the crowd, and his left hand was poised to grab my elbow.
"Ah, the fiery young fighter for justice, Arthur Beauchamp himself.
Have I got that right, the old English way, Beech'm, not Beauchom?
Mr. Loobie here has been regaling me with your exploits." I was in
Mapple's clutches, my right hand and elbow rendered immobile.

Loobie grinned. "You sly bugger, you didn't tell me you already
did a phoner with the magistrate. I've decided you're a lot smarter
than you look, Artie. I won't blow your defence — trust me, we're
off the record, no Johnny Blue, no threat to kill no Nazi."

I ignored him, asked Mapple to meet me in the barristers'
lounge after we adjourned for the day. He looked confused. I
pointed upstairs.

He followed me toward the courtroom, his stomach bouncing as he waddled. "I hope Johnny Blue isn't around here. Between you and me, that could be awkward. You're the lawyer, but shouldn't I be served with a subpoena? So it doesn't look like I volunteered to help the defence? By the way, I'm not sure if we can properly meet in the barristers' lounge."

"Why?"

"I'm not a member of the Law Society."

"You used to be, that's good enough."

As we stopped outside the assize court, he leaned to my ear: "I don't actually have a law degree."

"You were a magistrate."

"I had to learn on the job."

It finally dawned that this old boy had been a lay magistrate. There were still several to be found in remote areas of the province, with RCMP officers prosecuting and Aboriginals being prosecuted, a pathetic form of burlesque.

"What did you do," I asked, "before you were appointed a magistrate?"

"I was the barber of Ocean Falls."

A remote coastal community. "*The* barber."

"The only one."

This wheezing barber would be scalped in cross-examination. Justice Wilbur Kroop would regard him with sneering antipathy.

He tried to follow me into court, and I had to instruct him that witnesses were excluded until called.

"Oh. I didn't know that."

"Let me buy you dinner. Where will you be tonight?"

"I have a lovely room in the Fort Hotel. I heard people call it the Fort Hovel. Sure, it's seen better times, but I say you can't deny its grandness —"

I cut his prospective ramble short, said I'd meet him in the lobby at five-thirty, then metaphorically kicked myself — the Fort Hotel's lobby was about the worst place to meet a surprise witness. But I was late, court was being called to order.

I broke free of Mapple, but not before Chief Eric Sayaga hove into view, glaring at him, then me, then marching into court. The door closed behind him.

I stood there motionless for far too long, stuck on the horns of my dilemma. *And yet you would make him a suspect, an easy target for a white man's jury.*

I hastened to the defence table, but His Lordship hadn't been waiting for me. He looked oddly content, as serene as the Queen above him.

A witness had already been sworn: the fingerprint man, Corporal DiGianni, who was pinning blow-ups onto a corkboard. Angelina, seeing my clouded expression, looked concerned. Clara, the clerk, the twelve jurors, all stared at me, wondering what calamity had befallen Beauchamp that he looked so frazzled.

Only Ed Santorini, leaning on his elbows, his head bowed, was focused elsewhere. Or nowhere, or maybe on the glass of water he held shakily.

Kroop put on a rehearsed smile. "We worried you might have fallen into a snowbank." Then his trademark wheezy laugh. "Hmf, hmf."

"Thank you for your concern, Milord." I said with a smile as ill meant as his. "I trust I haven't missed anything." I sensed my sang-froid was getting under Kroop's skin as I beckoned to Clara with an extended palm, an invitation to continue.

In fact, I had missed nothing but the routine comparing of a suspect's prints with those lifted from a weapon, in this case the Remington 700. I could have simply admitted the fingerprints matched, but wanted to see Clara in action. As she led DiGianni through the whorls, loops, and arches, I swivelled my body toward the back, feigning nonchalance as I glanced about.

There he was, Chief Sayaga, looking at me like a vengeful spirit god, his eyes steely. This was not the gentle elder statesman whom I'd interviewed on Sunday. Mapple's presence must have infuriated him, proof that I intended to run a racist defence by blaming the Indians.

I glimpsed friendlier faces, Etienne Larouche, Lorraine Harris, a few others among Angelina's friends. Hogey Johnson was still cozying up to the sour sisters, Donalda and Hortense — whose presence here seemed mainly a show of support for the dead, as they waited for probate to clear so they could dump his rundown local holdings.

Clara, who'd done a smooth, confident job with Corporal DiGianni, finally rendered him to me. Santorini, meanwhile, was so immobile as to suggest he'd fallen asleep, yet his eyelids seemed open, as if propped.

"As I understand it, Corporal, none of Miss Santos's fingerprints were found in the gun closet."

"That's right."

"None were on the 7-millimetre live bullets or on the box holding them."

"We found none."

"Several of her prints were taken from the stock and the handle of the rifle, and there was a partial on the trigger, but none on the bolt action mechanism. Agreed?"

"Correct."

"No partials. No palm prints."

"None that came up when I dusted."

"So that suggests the Remington 700 was already loaded and ready to fire, correct?"

A pause for reflection. "Let me put it this way: if it wasn't armed, she would have had to swing down the bolt to feed in a bullet."

"And if she didn't feed in a bullet, she may not have known the gun was loaded."

"I object!" Clara cried. "That's not a question, it's speculation, an inference too far."

"Oh, come, come. I merely suggested she *may* not have known the gun was loaded. She might have if she knew anything about long guns, but in the urgency of the moment, faced with an imminent threat —"

"There's been no suggestion of an imminent threat."

"Order!" Kroop was unusually tardy with his mantra about my overstepping boundaries. By the time he got around to it, I'd hammered home my point. *She didn't kno-o-w the gun was loaded.* Too bad Biggs and Barnes were not in the courtroom to sing along.

"No more questions," I said. *End each cross-examination on a high note,* advised M. Cyrus Smythe-Baldwin. *Do not dribble away your gains.*

I reminded myself to applaud Clara for her snappy, indignant response to my improprieties. Kroop, perceiving her as an ally, praised her for "standing up to Mr. Beauchamp in what I understand is your first jury trial." Essentially portraying me as a bully. He looked fondly down at Clara. "There's at least one sharp tool at the counsel table. Hmf, hmf."

Kroop seemed peeved that no one appeared to share his sense of humour. "Mr. Clerk, will you step down there and give Mr. Santorini a poke?"

That prompted soft chuckling from the gallery, barely suppressed, as poor Delbert found his feet, obviously unhappy at the prospect of approaching Santorini.

Clara tried to intercede. "If it please the court, perhaps I —"

"No, no, Delbert will do it."

Delbert stalled. "Excuse me, Your Lordship, what kind of poke?"

"Use your best judgment." Strained and impatient.

"Excuse me again, sir, but shouldn't the court officer —"

Kroop exploded: "We're undermanned here, can't you bloody see? Just wake him up!"

Jurors looked astonished. I couldn't help wonder if Kroop had finally snapped.

His poking finger extended, Delbert hovered over the lead Crown prosecutor, whose head was lolling back, his mouth open. Santorini suddenly erupted with an explosive *"What?"* — causing Delbert to stagger back a couple of steps before stumbling up to his station.

The murmuring and rustling finally quietened enough for Santorini to be heard. He apologized with a lie about a sedative his doctor had prescribed. Kroop either swallowed that or was desperate to get this whimsicality behind him. "We will proceed with the next witness after the break."

1966 —
The Sound of Music

C lara and I spent the ten-minute reprieve in the barristers' lounge pouring coffee into Santorini and plying him with aspirins. He seemed more concerned about losing a bet than winning the trial. "Fucking Crozier, let in six fucking pucks. Cost me five bucks per goal."

Our ministrations succeeded to the point that he was able to walk to the courtroom unassisted, albeit grinning foolishly. Charles Loobie was, unusually, not to be seen, and I feared he'd discovered Eric Sayaga and cornered him. But no, the chief was already seated, in the back row.

The final Crown witness was the square-shooting ballistics specialist, Corporal Ed Holtz. The jury was already aware that Clara and I had watched him test-fire the rifle in Trudd's back yard.

After Clara qualified Holtz as an expert, she had him demonstrate the workings of Exhibit One, Trudd's R 700. Following that, he used charts and maps and graphs to show distances, velocities, trajectories.

These details weren't penetrating my mind, which was again gripped by emanations I felt coming from Eric Sayaga. I wondered if he'd sent Johnny Blue into hiding. Did I dare confront the chief over his nephew's apparent disappearance? Should I keep Magistrate

Mapple handy, or tell him to jump in his car and go home? In doing so, would I be in breach of my ethical duty to my client? Would I be able to live with myself if she was convicted because I'd failed to raise a credible defence?

Too many questions. No compelling answers.

Four years ago, I had bonded with Gabriel Swift while defending him for murder. An angry, brilliant militant of the Squamish Nation, he had survived the residential schools, their horrors. His words had stayed with me: *My dad taught me never to be a good Indian. That's what they want, good Indians. Lobotomized in their religio-fascist schools.*

I had failed Gabriel Swift by persuading him to take a plea to manslaughter. His sentence of sixteen years and four months was beyond punitive. It marked the lowest point of my career. Of my life. He'd been framed by racist cops. I believed that, and my belief was later confirmed.

I'd also believed he would be put to death if convicted. A trouble-maker represented by an unseasoned advocate facing an all-white jury and a bigoted judge — it was a recipe for a hanging. (To my great relief, he escaped. The history of my courtroom flop and Gabriel's years on the run is luridly recounted in the new edition of *The Trials of Arthur Beauchamp*.)

When I broke free from my memories of 1962, Clara was making my case, saving me the effort. She brought out from Corporal Holtz that he'd dug a slug, tagged as Exhibit Eighteen, from the basement siding. He believed it to be a high-velocity bullet, likely .30-calibre.

The shot, he agreed, could have been fired from as much as 300 yards away. Improving on Buck Harris's rough assay, he'd used binoculars to take a sightline from where the slug ripped into the wall to where a volunteer stood in for the late F.C. Trudd, and beyond to the copse of young spruce.

He'd also bagged the three 7-mm bullets found in the bush by Buck and Etienne. Exhibits Nineteen to Twenty-One.

"Your witness," said Clara.

I dived right in. "Let's talk about the significance of those three bullets, Corporal. They were randomly scattered about the bush in the property's back acreage?"

"It appeared so. Two were under the snow, the third had lodged in an aspen."

"All found after a single hour of metal detecting. If we add Exhibit Four, the slug found in a stump last May, that suggests there may be many more out there."

"That seems statistically likely."

I thought: *What a fine witness.* "Sort of looks like Mr. Trudd was shooting critters from his back porch."

"All I can say is those four bullets were fired from Mr. Trudd's Remington 700."

"Just one minute." Kroop was back in action. "How can you be certain all four came from the same rifle? Am I missing something?"

Holtz explained that on the weekend he'd matched the bullets microscopically with those he'd already test-fired from Exhibit One.

Kroop still looked confused — his prosecutorial experience had been all about drugs, not guns — so Holtz explained: "All firearms are unique in the striations they inscribe on the bullet as it's propelled through the barrel."

"Think of it as a kind of ballistic fingerprinting, Milord," I said, as if to a slow student.

"I was asking for the jury, not myself." Kroop's fib was so obviously face-saving that it prompted smiles. I should have kept my mouth shut. Smythe-Baldwin: *A thin-skinned judge may forgive your insults but never your lectures.*

I resumed: "Corporal, if Miss Santos fired that rifle, its bullet could have been any one of those scattered about the deceased's lot. Is that fair to say?"

"That is possible, yes."

I flourished the four bagged slugs. "So there's no way to identify the bullet that passed through Mr. Trudd's heart, correct?"

Holtz thought about that. "True. The field could be narrowed depending on exactly where she was aiming."

"If she was aiming at all. If she was just firing a warning shot, that bullet could have fallen anywhere."

I waited for the blast from the bench, condemning me as a compulsive speculator. But Kroop, battle weary by now, seemed unwilling to engage the enemy on this dicey terrain.

"I can't disagree," Holtz said.

"Let's turn, Officer, to the slug in the shiplap, Exhibit Eighteen. The deceased was about twenty yards away when he collapsed. The straight line you measured extended another hundred and fifteen yards to a rise with a growth of young trees. A woodland copse."

"I looked around there on Saturday, yes."

"And farther back, up the hill, beyond the stumps, there appears to be an old road, a logging road maybe."

"I took note of that, yes."

"So that would provide a back access to the property."

"Presumably, but it didn't seem in use."

"The copse afforded a good view of the house and the driveway and the garage?"

"And the road out front, and the river."

"You could easily see a vehicle approaching if you hid in the growth there?"

By now, even the town dunce would know where I was going. Kroop still didn't want to tangle with me, though he cast entreating looks at the Crown table: *you're allowing him to get away with murder.* Clara didn't bite. Santorini was again not with us: staring at the wall clock, hypnotized by the sluggish movement of the minute hand.

Holtz said, "Yes, a person could hide there, but would risk exposure once he moved off."

"That exposure would be brief — there was forest and bush nearby?"

"That's true."

"Okay. Let's go on to your sound check. Tell us why you fired a couple of test shots on Saturday."

"Because you asked me to, Mr. Beauchamp."

He kept such a straight face that I had to laugh. Others joined me, a welcome break from the heaviness of this homicide trial. Angelina smiled, and looked lovely doing so. I caught the foreman, Rummy Wilcox, studying her intensely, as if seeking the murderess behind that virtuous exterior.

Holtz testified to having twice fired Buck Harris's R 700, the first shot aimed at the sky, the second splintering a stump. He agreed that the sounds reverberated loudly from the hills: once, twice, then dimming, a second apart. The initial echoes "sounded like distant claps of thunder."

"In other words, Corporal Holtz, the hills were alive with the sound of echoes." That line earned appreciative noise from the gallery, though I admit to having crafted it ahead of time: the local theatre had a billboard up for *The Sound of Music*.

My frivolity had the odd effect of bringing out the judge's inner grump. "We're nearing four-thirty, Counsel. Do you think you can finish this witness?"

"One more question." I took a breath. "What are the chances, Officer, of a young lady who has never fired a gun, let alone a high-powered rifle, scoring a deadeye shot at a moving target from sixty feet away?"

"Probably not —"

That was all he got out before Kroop interrupted: "We do not permit guesswork in a court of law."

"Thank you, Corporal, you've been very helpful." I sat.

"Mr. Prosecutor, do I understand that this was your last witness? Mr. Prosecutor?"

Santorini yanked his eyes from the wall clock, propelled himself up by gripping the table edge. "The Crown has finished its case, Milord."

"Mr. Beauchamp, are you ready to open for the defence tomorrow? We don't want the jury cooped up in their hotel for longer than justice requires."

"I am indeed, Milord." Said with a jauntiness that I hoped didn't sound as false as it felt.

"We are adjourned until ten a.m."

1966 —
Tweedledum and Tweedledee

A s I left the courthouse, Charles Loobie sprang on me like a hungry panther, stopping short of sinking his fangs into my neck. "Did you pay off that ballistics guy in cash or by cheque?"

"Sorry, Charles, I'm busy. I have places to go and people to see."

"Right. Ample Mapple, he'll be waiting for you in the Fort lobby."

He had to jog to keep up with my long strides. "Tell him I'll be late." I crossed the street to my rented Fairlane and whaled away at the windshield with a scraper.

"Maybe, Artie, you want to stop playing hard to get. I may be the best friend you've got in the whole world. You pull this off, it's a front-page banner. You'll be up there in the top ten with Smythe-Baldwin, Branca, Rankin, Sedgwick. Pappas is already looking over his shoulder."

The cold engine complained, but finally caught. I rolled down the window. "Charles, when it's all over, I'll give you the inside scoop."

"I write news, pal. History ain't news."

━━

Instead of waiting for me in the Fort's lobby, Mapple was bellying up to the bar with a rum and Coke and a bowl of salted peanuts, while boring a businessman whose sad face suggested he'd already had a hard day.

The businessman gave me a grateful smile as I led Mapple off to a quiet table in the back. I ordered another rum and Cola, a Scotch for me, and a round for the party of three at a table near the fireplace.

Biggs and Barnes were recovering from their hangover by sharing a pitcher of draft. Between gulps, they preened over Clara, who was celebrating her faultless rookie performance in court. I assumed Santorini was in his room, conked out.

"We have a few problems," I told Mapple. "For starters, there's a strong chance the judge will rule your testimony inadmissible, as hearsay." That was, frankly, a stretch, but I'd decided that putting this Santa Claus clone on the stand could be not just morally wrong but a disaster.

Yes, Mapple could testify truthfully to Johnny Blue's violent language, his death threat, his arrested attempt to leap at Trudd — but what if the Crown could reply with proof that on May 29 Johnny was leading a Scout group or playing lacrosse or was at a wedding with a hundred witnesses. Or attending services at one of Fort Tom's dozen houses of worship. Angelina: *We volunteered in the food bank on Sundays after church.*

That would lead inexorably to Angelina's conviction, and to the shameful end of my career. I imagined Barnes and Biggs cracking wise over their pitchers of beer, exploding with laughter.

Mapple looked morose, his face sagging behind the snow-white bush of beard. "Hearsay? Isn't that sort of like gossip that no one can prove was actually true? When Johnny Blue said, 'I'm gonna kill you,' it didn't sound like gossip." He snatched a handful of peanuts and jammed them into his mouth.

"It would help, Mr. Mapple, if we could put Johnny Blue on the stand. But we can't find him, and nobody is forthcoming about his whereabouts. We can't assume he's hiding out — he may have a perfect alibi. Maybe he was with friends that Sunday. You would look terrible if you pointed a finger at Johnny and it turned out he'd been at a church picnic."

Mapple shifted with discomfort, played with his drink, vacuumed up more peanuts — his bid for a brief bubble of fame was hissing air. I raised the heat: "Mr. Santorini, the prosecutor, is a shark. I've seen him rip witnesses apart. He'll accuse you of lying, of course, of making the whole thing up."

Mapple gulped his rum, had trouble getting it down. "There were other witnesses at the hearing."

"Did you have anyone taking notes?"

"No, my staff was just me, myself, and I." A sad attempt at lightness.

"Then who will back you up? Johnny's uncle, the chief? The other two negotiators? They despised Trudd."

Mapple seemed crestfallen, spoke slowly, thoughtfully. "I always got along with our Natives. I was always fair to them."

"I assume the *Province* is widely read down your way, in the Peace River." That elicited a big, unhappy shrug. "Charles Loobie has destroyed more than a few lives with his caustic pen. You don't want to come off the front page of the morning tabloid looking like a bigot."

Mapple rose. "My bowels are acting up. I forgot I don't take to peanuts very good. They don't appease my hunger either."

We arranged to meet in the dining room after he relieved his distress up in his room. I offered to buy him dinner and pick up the bills for his hotel and the gas for tomorrow's drive back home. He didn't demur. This trial was draining my skimpy financial resources.

That pitch to Mapple had emptied my forensic tank, and I was too mentally exhausted not to order a second Scotch. I needed it if I was to survive another barbed encounter with Tweedledum and Tweedledee, who were waving me over to thank me for the round.

I explained it was in celebration of Clara's first speaking part before a jury. I pulled up a chair beside her.

Biggs nudged his partner. "What say we book him for attempting to bribe us peace officers. Joking. By the way, counsellor, who was the three-hundred-pound Saint Nick?"

Barnes chimed in: "The stockings were hung by the chimney with care."

Biggs: "In hopes that St. Nicholas soon would be there with the goodies." The two detectives found that outrageously funny. "So what did the fat man stick in your sock?"

"Gifts of wisdom. He's my savant." Let them figure it out for themselves. That shouldn't be hard, even for these two lazy investigators. They would soon find out the fat man and I had a dinner date — the restaurant was open to the bar.

"These guys have a theory about Angelina Santos," Clara said brightly, messaging me with the toe of her boot: hear them out. "They want Eddie to reopen."

The detectives frowned at each other — irritated, maybe, at Clara for prompting them to divulge their theory. Biggs poured himself a full glass, blew off the foam, drained nearly half of it, wiped his lips, and said: "Your client's a fraud, she's a goody-goody bullshit artist."

"You told the judge you wanted us to stick around," Barnes said.

Biggs nodded. "So we had time to kill."

Barnes: "And we did a little digging. Turns out Santos ain't no Virgin Mary — she put out for Fred Trudd. Wasn't cheap. Cost him 300 bills."

"Current going rate for a trick in the city is a tenth of that," Biggs said. "So he figured he deserved seconds. No way, she decided, that wasn't the deal. So she shot him. Talk about a costly piece of ass, eh, counsellor?" He gave the waiter a high sign, pointed to my empty glass.

Barnes: "We didn't cover all the bases back in May, never got round to interviewing Trudd's bookkeeper. Until today. There it was, right on the ledger." He slid a Xeroxed copy toward me. *May 23, A. Santos, bonus, $300.*

Biggs: "Which Angie deposited that day in her account at the Nova Scotia branch. The next day, Tuesday, her fee-for-service showed up in a savings account in Manila. Two nights later, he closed the deal and she came across."

My refill arrived, and I saluted Biggs with it, thanking him. He leaned close to me. "Trudd's one-night stand couldn't have got her pregnant. He had no viable seed. Two marriages over three decades plus a few short-terms, and no fruit from his loins."

Barnes: "We got a tip. Santos was fooling around with a guy who gave Bible readings to her church group."

Biggs: "Unless you need us for court tomorrow, we'll try to follow that up. Informant is pretty sure they were screwing in the church basement."

Me: "I do need you for court tomorrow. I'd suggest you rehearse your lies." I knocked back my whisky and rose.

●▶

I could hardly fault Mapple for standing me up for dinner. I suspected his bowels had him on the run, so to speak. A malady probably made worse by his failed audition as a witness.

So I just sat alone in the old hotel's vast dining hall, staring bleakly at a local example of art primitif: the old fort, circa 1809, where handsome, bearded fur traders bargained with caricature Indians and Métis. A buckskinned Aboriginal on his knees before a priest, being blessed, accepting the white man's god.

That image depressed me, until I remembered it unfairly reflected on priests like Etienne Larouche. He was with Angelina that evening, tasked to unblock her memory. I'd decided not to join them — she'd be more comfortable alone with her parish priest. He would be better skilled than I, more delicate, in discussing matters such as Trudd's final flaunting of his favourite weapon.

After almost an hour and two coffee refills and no appetite, I gave up waiting for Mapple and drove off into the cold, clear, moonlit night, depressed, feeling unprepared, overwhelmed by the many loose ends of this case — they threatened to entangle me.

Arthur —
August 2022

I must now unburden myself about the debacle that occurred on August 1, BC Day. My early-morning ascent of Mount Norbert was taxing but otherwise unremarkable. The descent was an exercise in slapstick. By then it was blazing hot. I found myself talking not to Ulysses but Angelina Santos, revisiting 1966, pleading with her to remember that she'd fired just a warning shot.

Two-thirds of the way down the slope, as I was calling Justice Kroop a nincompoop and Santorini a horse's ass, I tripped over an exposed root, losing my grip on Ulysses's leash, and fell into a muddy swale thick with decomposing skunk cabbage. No sprains or major bruising, but I came up dirty and stinky from toe to chest.

Then, just off Eastshore Way, a speeder, likely late for the ferry, caused me to dart to the side, pulling Ulysses, and we stumbled into a patch of wild roses. The thick-coated dog was fine, but I came up bleeding from scratches on arms and legs. Superficial injuries, but I'm sure I looked like Chimera, the dread monster of darkness, blood mixed with mud and sweat that had soaked through shirt, shorts, and socks. I stuck to the lesser-used trails the rest of the way so as not to frighten those of weak heart.

I especially didn't want Margaret to see me in that abysmal state — there would be a fierce lecture, threats to have her addled partner's brain examined for sneaking off at dawn for a steep hike, stumbling around and nearly killing himself — after having forgotten his phone.

From Potters Road I took a path that would allow me to sneak unseen to the sauna. After using its outdoor shower and towel rack, I could present myself to my spouse in ruddy health, soaped, shampooed, and deodorized — just a few scratches, dear, scabbed over and clean.

On being unleashed, Ulysses bounded ahead, excited to be home. I stripped, kicking off my boots, bundling outerwear and underwear into a ball, depositing my muddy, bloody garb behind the sauna.

I wondered if I might have suffered heat stroke, because I was sure I could hear a ragged chorus singing "Sweet Adeline." In this befuddled way, I failed to notice that heat was pulsing from the sauna until I whipped open the door to a blast of hot, thick fog.

Stumbling about, somewhat delusional, I found myself perching upon something soft, fleshy, and sweaty, and was overcome with a sense of dread.

"Oh, poor Arthur, were you sprayed by a skunk?" That voice, next to my ear, had to be coming from the woman on whose lap I had landed. Her strong arms held me from collapsing onto the floor as they slid my torso toward the bench beside her. I made a soft landing on a towel.

There came another familiar voice: "Shower first, you bad boy. I hope Margaret knows you're here. She was freaking out. You just disappeared without your phone."

Realization finally came that I'd stumbled into the presence of the owners of the local health food store. Wellness and Wholeness, everyone called this couple, from the logos embossed on their T-shirts. These open-minded naturalists wore them everywhere — except when relaxing at the Starkers Cove nude beach.

But why were they here at Blunder Bay Farm?

Maybe I said that aloud, because Wellness answered: "We volunteered to set up."

Suddenly my aging brain snapped to attention. The garden party was today. The tea party masquerade that my wife had been coaxed into hosting, honouring island elders. It had been obliterated from my mind. I groaned. "Oh, God."

"I doubt She'll be much help," said Wholeness.

I gained my feet, wiped the steam from a porthole window. Tables were set on the lawn outside the house. Scores of people were at those tables, some in wheelchairs, others wandering about in costumery from the late nineteenth century. Parked in front of the house was the old school bus that had conveyed the disabled here, a banner decorating it: "WELCOME TO THE ANNUAL GARIBALDI HISTORICAL SOCIETY GARDEN PARTY."

I slid back down on my ass. The showers outside were in clear view of those gathered on the lawn. I was trapped in this sauna, a smelly wretch.

"Ready?" said Wellness.

"Let's do it," said Wholeness. "Join us for a health-giving ocean dip, Arthur. You'll feel and smell much better."

Wellness gripped my arm, pulled me to my feet. "Show them what you're made of, Arthur."

That advice struck home. I would pretend to the shocked masses that I'm a naturalist, that I do the nude sauna-to-sea ritual almost daily. Better to be seen as slightly eccentric and absent-minded than straight-out stupid.

Wholeness and Wellness stepped outside, their bodies steaming, and began jogging across the lawn toward the shoreline. I hesitated, then dropped the towel I was holding, and sped after them as fast as my tired old legs would go. "Last one in is a rotten tomato," I yelled.

That illustrates the disordered state of my mind that day. Margaret is still laughing.

1966 —
Contempt of Clerk

Wednesday, November 23, Day Three of *R. v. Santos*, arrived cruelly cold: minus thirty. Stupidly, I hadn't plugged in my car, and all taxis were booked till after ten. But a Montanan named Wally saved the day — he was about to do a supply run to the government liquor store. I hitched a ride in his Ford 150.

Seemingly unaware he was in a foreign land, Wally spent the fifteen-minute drive decrying Lyndon Johnson and complaining about Cuban immigrants, the Black Panther Party, and "our" failure to carpet-bomb North Vietnam. He was otherwise in good humour, having shot a bear the previous afternoon.

As we approached the Fort Hotel, I saw an ambulance and two police cruisers angle-parked outside. I was tempted to eject from Wally's pickup and make inquiries — I worried about Mapple — but carried on the extra block to the courthouse. I had only ten minutes to get gowned and into court.

I found Ed Santorini tying on his dickie, looking alarmingly hale and hearty. "Get your dukes up, Stretch, I'm back." He bobbed, weaved, threw a jab. "Slept ten straight hours, not counting piss breaks."

I asked if he knew why emergency vehicles were outside his hotel.

"Some fat old fart bought it in the middle of the night. Way I heard it, he'd asked for a wake-up at eighty-thirty, didn't respond, and they checked up on him. What's with the stricken expression?"

"He wanted to testify." Stunned, I was speaking to myself, not Santorini.

"You knew him?"

I donned my courtroom gear with shaking hands. "A.W. Mapple. Retired lay magistrate. *How* did he buy it?"

"Jim Mulligan said heart attack. Mapple wanted to testify? To what?"

"Who is Jim Mulligan?"

Santorini rattled on as we hastened down the stairs. "Local quack, remember him? — the ladies' parts expert you eviscerated. He was the on-call emergency physician, and I shared a slow elevator with him. He said the old boy's heart collapsed under the weight of his excess baggage. Why don't I know anything about this Magistrate Mapple?"

We had no time to continue that ragged conversation — it had made us late; the clerk, Delbert, was waving us toward the assize court's door. Within, the gallery was packed, the jurors seated, Clara alone at the counsel table.

As we waited for Kroop, conspiracy theories danced in my head. Dr. Mulligan — was it a coincidence he was on call last night? Was he in league with Biggs and Barnes? Did those two caustic cops, fearing Mapple might blow their cinch murder case, do a drunken dirty deed?

I felt a swell of compassion for Mapple — an amiable goofy chatterbox who presumably had a caring family, a multitude of friends. Harmless, I wanted to believe . . . but then I thought of the many innocent First Nations people he'd probably jailed.

Another conspiracy flickered and flamed, fuelled by Eric Sayaga's black looks at Mapple, the witness who would nail his combative nephew to the cross. I endured a revolting image of Johnny Blue and a comrade or two popping into the Fort pub, sneaking up the stairs . . .

The situation reeked of irony. I had warned Mapple his good name would be mud were he to testify. Had that caused him to gobble too many peanuts? Did he succumb to a lethal allergy complicated by my scaring him half to death?

Here I was blaming myself. I would be in poor form on a day when I had to be my sharpest.

What was keeping Kroop? He'd been obsessive about punching in on time. A taxi delivered him each day, sharp at nine-thirty, from a government guest accommodation a mile out of town.

Santorini and Clara were in intense conversation. The sudden death of prospective witness A.W. Mapple would be a hot topic. So would the Biggs-Barnes proposal to reopen the Crown's case so they could slime Angelina.

Charles Loobie, always seeking the crude and the rude, would delight his readers. *Rape "Victim" Paid $300 for Sex, Cops Claim.* Loobie was currently at the clerk's station, trying to buck up Delbert, who looked suicidal. I overheard: "Relax, man, it's not your fault."

The jurors looked uneasy, unsure what they were waiting for. Their leader, Rummy Wilcox, was talking low to a shrugging court officer. The alderman had been a closed book, expressionless and, worse, was avoiding eye contact with me, a powerful indication that he wasn't entertaining a reasonable doubt, and would pressure the other eleven to convict. Maybe not Ranjeet Singh, the hospital administrator, who occasionally sent encouraging smiles my way.

The Trudd sisters, realizing they were wasting time when they could be out smoking, finally hustled out, leaving Hogey Johnson to guard their seats. He looked stressed. He probably knew Magistrate Mapple, and had got word of his death.

The busiest person in the room was Angelina, sitting sideways, whispering to Etienne, with urgent hand gestures. It was as if something had come to mind. Had yesterday's session with Etienne triggered memories? I planned to spend the lunch hour with her, for a brush-up of her testimony. She would be my final witness.

Kroop arrived at twenty minutes after ten, not with the air of a sheepish student late for class but as if driven by righteous fury.

Delbert, in a fog of dismay, leaped to his feet too late with his "Order in court" — Kroop was already firmly seated, staring malevolently at his clerk, waiting for Loobie to scuttle back to the press table.

"Mr. Delbert, perhaps you could tell us what happened to my taxi."

Too frightened to face him, Delbert stared toward the back of the court. "I'm afraid they had several calls ahead of you, sir."

"Why?"

"A lot of people couldn't get their cars started."

"Did you tell the dispatchers they were holding up justice? Did you not *insist*?"

"I tried the RCMP, but all their members were out."

"Please turn around, Mr. Clerk, I can't hear you."

Delbert revolved ninety degrees. "The police were busy, sir, there'd been a sudden death in the Fort Hotel."

His Lordship was coming out of this badly, having managed to establish that Delbert had done his best. Forced into face-saving mode, he devised a flanking attack: "Mr. Clerk, what truly disturbed me on entry into these chambers was that you seemed in deep colloquy with a member of the popular press. Court staff are forbidden to talk with the media about any aspect of this case, do you understand?"

"I wasn't —"

"I don't want to hear excuses. I will be satisfied with a simple apology."

An emphatic voice from my right: "Get a spine." Clara, exhorting Delbert. Kroop, startled, glanced quickly at her, flushing with the effort to restrain anger, then returned to Delbert: "Would you like to apologize? Not to me personally, Mr. Clerk. To the Court."

"No, sir."

"What?"

"I would not like to apologize, sir."

Kroop stared at him bug-eyed. "We will take a twenty-minute recess. Counsel will join me in my chambers."

The chambers room was out of *Tales from the Crypt*: heavy curtains drawn across its window, photos of dead judges on the walls, a spinnable globe on a sturdy oak desk, eerie yellow light from a corner lamp.

Kroop welcomed us three lawyers with a smile invented for the occasion, but he barred Delbert and the Official Court Reporter. There would be no transcript of what was to transpire here.

He waited until we were seated, then braced himself against a bookcase and stabbed a finger at Clara. "Who the fuck do you think you are?"

Santorini responded for her: "I have to defend her, Judge. She kind of blurted that out."

Kroop ignored him, spoke with barely suppressed fury. "You sought to undermine my authority. Being the privileged daughter of a front-bench legislator doesn't give you licence to show me up in court. Were this not a trial for murder, I would have you removed."

Clara didn't flinch. She looked at him with more amusement than worry. "Sorry, I lost my head."

That sounded of sarcasm not apology, and a strained silence followed, Kroop's round face starting to pink as he waited for more.

She continued: "I had a professor who picked on me because I went beatnik, a traitor to my privileged class. Everyone in the class hated him. One day I told him off. They applauded."

More silence, as Kroop seemed to have trouble grappling with her barbed personal allegory. What he didn't know was that Clara Moncrief didn't want to be a lawyer anyway.

"The comment was addressed to my clerk, but was meant as an insult to me. You goaded him to defy me. My clerk! When we are back on the record, you will be asked to show cause why you should not be cited for contempt."

This wasn't my dogfight, but I had to shield my undercover agent: "Wilbur, take a deep breath, this isn't the Cuban missile crisis. Surely you can reserve the matter until after the verdict. That's the preferred practice, isn't it, in jury trials?"

That slowed Kroop from a gallop to a canter. He lost eye contact with us, a surrender signal. I was sure then that nothing would come of this. Usually, by trial's end tempers have soothed, slights are forgiven or forgotten.

Kroop made a rigorous show of writing on his memo pad, then looked up. "The court will deal with Miss Moncrief in due course. As to my mutinous clerk, I will meet with him here privately." Face having been saved, he produced a rubbery smile. "Very well, the primary reason I called you into chambers is to discuss the status of this case. How long do we have to go, Arthur? I assume you *are* calling a defence."

"You have read my mind." Strained chuckles around the room.

"Is the accused testifying?"

I returned his smile and added a shrug. "Hard to say, Judge. I'll decide after my friend's motion is dealt with."

"What motion is that?"

Santorini: "The Crown is applying to reopen its case, sir. The two chief investigators did a little extra digging just the other day, and may have come up with some nuggets."

Kroop to me: "I assume you're opposing?"

"Actually not. I'm thinking of the jury."

"Yes, yes, we can't have them sitting by idly all morning." Kroop rose. "Thank you for dropping by, gentlemen . . . and lady."

Before following us out, Clara curtsied to him. I wasn't sure if he would take that as a gesture of respect or as the equivalent of a middle finger. Delbert the clerk stood trembling outside the chambers door as we left.

The courtroom remained closed for another twenty minutes while Captain Bligh lashed his mutinous deckhand. That gave Charles Loobie too much free time to corner his victims. He went after Santorini first, then me, haranguing me about the demise of poor A.W. Mapple.

"I don't buy heart attack. Someone wanted him out of the way. Now what are you gonna do? He was your fucking secret weapon — you could've taken lazy Eddie off at the neck, he had no clue who Mapple was or why he was here."

"Until you filled him in." *I won't blow your defence — trust me, we're off the record.*

"What's it matter now? Dead men don't talk. Screws up your only winning bid: Johnny Blue, the angry, vengeful assassin." He turned to go, then paused. "Let's face it, the fact he's a redskin makes it an easier sell."

Thanks to this irritating journalist, Ed Santorini now knew that Johnny Blue blew up at Trudd. Following a guilty verdict, the word would quickly spread that Arthur Beauchamp grossly failed his client by not relying on Johnny's angry threat.

It seemed likely that Johnny Blue was hiding out, knowing those explosive words could turn the glare of suspicion on him. I might have to play it rough, and threaten Chief Sayaga with a subpoena if he can't provide proofs of his nephew's innocence.

I stood by the open courtroom door as Sayaga entered court, then followed him in. He didn't acknowledge me at first, then paused, turned. "Was Mapple on your witness list?"

"He wanted to be, but I declined his offer. That's the truth. Now I need your help."

"I don't know where Johnny is, but he is not a killer. That is also the truth."

Court was called to order not by Delbert — the rebellious sad sack had been replaced by a woman, a senior clerk with a resolute air, battle-ready.

Ever the chameleon, Kroop put on his smiley face as he explained to the jury that defence counsel had "graciously" agreed to the Crown reopening its case for "matters unforeseen."

Santorini brought Hugh Barnes in first, who marched sprightly to the stand, with a flashy smile aimed the female-majority jury. He seemed determined to make up for his earlier effort — no hearts had fluttered as Kroop excoriated him over the bungled effort to get Angelina to confess.

Santorini: "I understand you and your partner did some sleuthing yesterday at the offices of Trudd Enterprises. Tell us about that."

"Yes, sir. At thirteen-forty hours we attended at those offices, situated at 18 Mill Road on the second floor. There I met with Miss Paula Mantz, bookkeeper for Trudd's company, and she showed me and Detective Biggs a payroll ledger for this current year, which I produce here."

He displayed, like a trophy, the entire ledger, in wooden covers, with brass fasteners. A certified copy of a page dated Monday, May 23, was filed as Exhibit Twenty-Seven. *A. Santos, bonus, $300* — those were the key words. A cheque stub with similar notations was entered.

Barnes also came armed with a copy of Angelina's deposit slip at the Nova Scotia branch, along with paperwork confirming a wire transfer to her mother's account in the Metropolitan Bank in Manila. Exhibits Twenty-Nine and Thirty. The funds showed up at that bank the next day. *That night he closed the deal and she came across.*

Other scurrilous tittle-tattle could not be repeated in a courtroom: the alleged tip about Angelina being involved with a religious young Bible-reader. *Informant is pretty sure they were screwing in the church basement.*

"No more questions," Santorini said.

Kroop looked puzzled. The intimation that Trudd paid Angelina for sex was not registering. "I take it the Crown regards this bonus business as a matter of significance? Never mind, I see Mr. Beauchamp is up."

"Thank you, Milord. Detective Biggs, as you and your partner were busily gathering new evidence the other day, did you seek out any witnesses who might help explain this odd financial transaction?"

"If you mean the bookkeeper and someone from the bank, yes, sir, they're available."

"I have no need to hear from them, Detective, I'm talking about the person who prompted Mr. Trudd's effort to buy silence with $300 in hush money."

Somehow, my reference to hush money failed to send either the prosecutor or the judge rocketing from their seats, so I just sailed on: "To whom did he give that cheque?"

"To the accused, I would assume."

"In fact he gave it to her landlady, Marsha Bigelow. Do you know her?"

"I think she runs Rustlers, a steak house. I've eaten there. The sirloin is terrific."

"It was on Sunday, May twenty-two, that Trudd gave her that cheque, made out to Angelina Santos — you can't dispute that?"

"No."

"Marsha Bigelow confronted him in his office about an indecent act he'd performed while spying on Angelina as she showered. The bonus was a bid for silence."

I carried on like that, firing at will. Kroop and Santorini seemed frozen in alarm, the one waiting for the other to shout me down. I was even able to allude to Trudd's earlier sexual assault before Kroop screeched at me to desist.

Then he glared at Ed. "Mr. Santorini, may I remind you the Crown has an obligation to object when defence counsel abuses his right to cross-examine."

"Sorry, Milord, I was elsewhere."

I couldn't help myself: "Maybe he was thinking about a ten-inch sirloin at Rustlers."

That caused an explosion of laughter from the pews, some jurors struggling not to join in.

"Very funny, I'm sure. However, the jury is instructed to ignore your unseemly attempt to give testimony."

Clara sneaked a wink at me.

Ted Barnes did the same dance routine as his partner, but with an awkward misstep. When Kroop asked why he thought a $300 bonus was relevant to anything, he said, "The issue arose whether Mr. Trudd was paying her for sex."

Kroop wasn't expecting that, and sat back. I heard rumbling from the gallery, low hisses. *Your client put out for Fred Trudd.* No one in Fort Tom was going to buy that. No one on the jury. Except maybe Rummy Wilcox.

In cross, I said, "Shame on you, Detective Barnes, to have such thoughts about this pious young woman who was cruelly raped." All eyes turned to Angelina: her solemn expression as she clutched her crucifix.

1966 —
The Opening

Another lesson taught me by the great Smythe-Baldwin: Lazy counsel neglect the opening. Wise counsel exploit it. Make your opening sing.

Criminal lawyers have two opportunities to pitch the jury; the final address is better known and applauded. A good opening lays out a road map of your planned route: a short, friendly rendering of the defence's theory, embellished with reminders about reasonable doubt.

The opening also enables you to connect with the jury, to let them know you may be a lawyer but you're human, even a nice guy. You're not some ham actor; you truly believe in your client's innocence.

I began with a tribute to the Northland and its hardy inhabitants. I got smiles and sympathy with my Chaplinesque tale of my Greyhound bus ordeal.

I thanked those who aided in my hectic few days of gathering evidence — dropping names of such upstanding locals as Hogey Johnson, Father Larouche, and Marsha Bigelow, as well as Chief Eric Sayaga ("a leader of deep compassion and intelligence"), and, of course, renowned First World War fighter pilot Ned Best.

I plugged away at the second-shooter theory, reminding the jury that F.C. Trudd, the grasping landlord, had droves of enemies. The least likely assailant was a frightened, pious young woman who'd never before fired a gun.

That done, I called Marsha Bigelow to the stand. She'd been in the witness room while Barnes and Biggs performed their bits, so I had the Official Court Reporter read out their testimony. She then filled in the gaps: how she confronted Trudd over his drunken, masturbatory display in Angelina's bathroom.

"Did he explain why he made out that $300 cheque?"

"No, just handed it to me. He was all gruff and dismissive, and I wanted to tell him to stuff it, frankly, if it was to buy Angelina's silence, but the decision wasn't mine to make, and Angelina could use the money for her sick mom in Manila — she had a heart condition, and Angelina wired her money every month."

Santorini, finally: "Objection. That speech is riddled with hearsay."

I plowed ahead: "Are you personally aware she wired money to her mother?"

"Well, I did a lot of the deposits and transfers for her because she worked for Fred Trudd nine to five, six days a week."

"Okay, and Angelina accepted the $300 cheque?"

"Yeah, as an apology, that's how she interpreted it."

"She also told you about a previous assault —"

"Objection. Leading."

"Sorry. Did she also mention any previous physical incidents with Mr. Trudd?"

"She told me that a few weeks earlier while she was doing laundry he'd grabbed her from behind and groped her breasts. She let that one go because he was so plastered he conked out soon after."

Santorini: "Objection. Hearsay."

Kroop: "Too late. You were asleep at the switch again, Mr. Prosecutor."

Me: "Okay, when did she return to work?"

"Well, Fred needed her to look after the cats because he had business in Pouce Coupe for a few days. So she went back to work on Thursday."

"Did you see the deceased that day?"

"Fred stuck around town for a while, and had lunch at Rustlers. I didn't notice him there at first and he must have overheard me talking to friends about how he exposed himself to Angelina and paid her off. I should've kept my mouth shut. It went all over town, and he went on a tear and then raped that poor girl."

"Objection!"

"Sustained!"

"No more questions."

"Mr. Santorini, you're on. We have fifteen minutes before the mid-day break."

Kroop obviously wanted to see Santorini knock the stuffing out of my perky witness, but that wasn't to be. Santorini clearly sensed it would be risky to scrap with Marsha, and contented himself with portraying her as biased because of her friendship with Angelina.

In the course of that, the jury learned that Angelina got free rent for helping out at Marsha's rooming house and that they shared in community efforts: food bank, elder care. None of which helped bolster the Crown's case. Santorini looked ruffled.

Perhaps out of fealty to Biggs and Barnes, who'd both stayed in court, Santorini asked Marsha if the accused had any "close male relationships."

"Well, she's a lovely young woman, and I'm sure she had opportunities, but I don't think the right man came along." A pause. "There was a young lad active in her church she introduced to me, but he wasn't very . . ." She struggled with the desired word, possibly "masculine," then gave up. "He was headed for the priesthood."

"Okay, did she ever invite male guests to her room?"

"I don't spy on my tenants, Mr. Santorini."

Even Kroop had had enough of this. "Really, Mr. Prosecutor, is this line of questioning appropriate?"

"I'll let it go. No more questions."

"We'll resume at two o'clock."

Angelina surprised me with her skill at stagecraft: knowing the departing jurors were watching, she broke free of her escort to give me a fierce, tight hug. That caused the jurors watching to bunch up at their door. Rummy Wilcox, waiting patiently for the logjam to clear, looked our way, shook his head, dismissing our embrace as an act.

"I remember something," Angelina whispered.

Before having lunch with Angelina, I dialogued with Etienne outside the Registry — I needed a quick, candid report on his session with her yesterday. We talked softly, because Charles Loobie kept hovering into view.

"The fog is still there, Arthur, but dispersing in bits and pieces. Her belief that she shot Trudd may be slightly eroding. She has finally awakened to the truth that she won't have a baby to love if she doesn't go free. She had one moment of stark remembrance when Trudd walked toward her . . ."

I nudged him to silence — Loobie had sidled closer. We ducked into the Registry to escape him. "That moment of remembrance?"

"She remembered him showing his erect penis. She couldn't seem to talk about it, and I'm afraid it sounded like . . . let us say, a convenient memory, prompted by what she'd heard in court."

We were interrupted by a clerk who'd fielded a phone call for me. "It was a Mr. Meyerson in Vancouver."

"What did he say?"

"'Got something for you.'"

I asked the court officer to let Angelina know I'd be late. I preferred not to use the phone in the barristers' lounge and risk being overheard. Or a coin phone, with Loobie practically glued to my backside.

He was waiting for me in the corridor. "Thought I should give you a heads-up that you're doomed. Just happened to be just

outside the jury room when their sandwiches arrived, and overheard Alderman Wilcox's no-star review of your schmaltzy, staged
hug scene with Angelina."

I pretended he didn't exist as I threw on my overcoat. I headed
down to Rustlers, hoping Hogey Johnson's offer to use his law
office was still open.

1966 —
Do Not Disturb

H ogey was working on a Löwenbräu while waiting for his steak
sandwich. Seated with him was his secretary, Sibyl — they
were rescheduling appointments so he could continue sitting in on
the trial. "It's turned into a spine-tingler, young fella."

He could see I was in a hurry, and anticipated my request. He'd
be honoured if I used his law office to make my important call.
Sibyl was just heading back, and would be delighted to settle me
into a spare office. I was not to worry about long-distance charges.
He'd bought "one of them newfangled Xerox telecopier machines,"
and Sibyl could show me how to use it.

Marsha Bigelow bustled from the kitchen to intercept me as I
pulled my coat on. "How did I do?"

"A tour de force."

"You're going to get her off, aren't you?"

"I'll give it my best."

"Now don't get all modest, Arthur. You're a real, live Perry
Mason, and Perry Mason never loses."

En route to Hogey's office — across the street, half a block down — I learned that Sibyl Frick had served as his faithful mainstay for a dozen years. I wondered how she regarded the local tycoon, given he'd treated her boss like dirt. My gentle probing elicited this response: "Fred Trudd was mean and heartless. A psychopathic personality. I looked that up."

"That sounds about right, Sibyl. You have a lovely name — I expect you know it comes from ancient Greece: female prophets inspired by the gods. There's a beautiful conception of a sibyl by Michelangelo in the Sistine Chapel."

She gave me a look that seemed almost awestruck. *Treat her nicely, and she'll fall all over you.*

She escorted me inside, put some coffee on, and led me not into the spare office, but Hogey's larger one with its wall of *Western Weeklies* and *Dominion Law Reports* that I suspected he rarely consulted. A wide window looked out onto Main Street but was curtained.

"I think you'll be more comfortable here, Mr. Beauchamp. The spare office is pretty musty."

"Please just call me Arthur."

"Arthur. *Arthur.*" Getting used to it. "Hogey says you're the *best* lawyer. He says you're like a gunfighter coming to town, like Alan Ladd in *Shane.*"

She deposited me onto a high-back swivel chair behind a messy desk, and centred the phone in front of me. "You have to dial nine to get out. Here's a pen and ink and a foolscap pad." She emptied an ashtray, tidied up loose memos, notepads, and legal-sized documents, and raced off, returning seconds later with coffee, milk, and sugar.

"Here you go, Arthur. Please tell me if there's anything I can help with."

"Well, yes, there is, Sibyl, thank you. Hogey thinks Trudd's estate is still in probate, even though he may not have got around to signing a new will. Hogey seemed a little uncertain about the chain of events."

"Well, that's Hogey."

I laughed. "Hey, that's me too. My own secretary has way sharper recall than me about dates and times." I motioned to her to take a chair. She perched on the edge, as if readying herself to jump up to be of further service. I felt like a heel for manipulating this lonely hearts clubber.

"What I can't figure out, Sibyl, is whether Fred Trudd's lawyers in Vancouver are dealing with a new will or an older one."

Sibyl nodded, words gushed forth: "I know they were working on a new will last May, because I had a call from Mr. Delaire at Russell, DuMoulin about that. They were going to mail the will to us so Mr. Trudd could sign it, but it never showed up — unless it came special delivery to the post office and Hogey picked it up like he sometimes does with important contracts and stuff. But he would have given it to me to file."

"Okay, my associate is checking into whether that new will was ever prepared. If not, I guess the previous one would still be valid."

"Oh, we both signed that as witnesses. That would be in 1961, three years before Mr. Trudd's divorce. I'm sure Hogey won't mind if I copy it for you."

"That would be great." I was being treated like a visiting potentate. I couldn't imagine that Hogey would be pleased that I had the run of his private office. "Now what about Fred Trudd — did he make any office visits in May?"

"I'll check the appointment book. It's not always accurate. Sometimes he would just barge in, and otherwise we'd set a time, usually by phone. He'd come in three, four times a month, usually. Or Hogey would go to him. Or they'd talk business over drinks somewhere."

Sibyl left to copy Trudd's 1961 will and refill my coffee cup, and I flipped through Hogey's desk calendar — it showed a scribbled reminder for Monday, May 30: "FCT here 2 p.m." F.C. Trudd. Who wasn't able to show up for that appointment because his body was a day old and cold.

When I showed Sibyl the notation, she reacted with surprise. "It wasn't in the appointment book." That book did, however, reveal that Trudd and Hogey had met ten days earlier, on Friday, May 20, as well as the next day, Saturday.

Sibyl, who worked half-day on Saturdays, recalled taking a call from Trudd at mid-morning. "He said something like, Tell your useless shit of a boss, excuse the language, to get his effing ass over here right effing now."

For some reason, Trudd had begun drinking heavily on that Saturday. In the late afternoon, Angelina Santos had stepped from her shower to witness her inebriated employer pleasuring himself with his pants around his ankles.

Why had he gone on that bender? Issues with his sisters? "Fucking bitches," he'd yelled, slamming down the phone as Marsha Bigelow barged into his office.

I went back to the desk calendar. Monday, May 23: a phone number with an Okanagan prefix, and a name, Wyatt. As in Donalda Wyatt. For Wednesday, May 25, there were two interesting scribbles. The first was "Northways, arr. 1130." The phone book revealed Northways Air to be a charter outfit based in Prince George. The second read, "AHM 4 pm, no drinks." It took some pondering before I decided Hogey was warning himself to turn up sober at the Alaska Highway Motel.

I took the calendar to the copier. Sibyl just smiled. I asked her if Hogey had met with Donalda or Hortense a few days before Trudd's death. "Oh, no, Mr. Trudd didn't want him to have anything to do with his sisters. They had a pretty bad falling out."

"Over what?"

"Something about shares in his company. It's beyond me."

It was well after one o'clock when I finally got around to dialling the switchboard at Tragger, Inglis. My wily buddy Hubbell Meyerson would be getting impatient. *Got something for you.*

Reception wasn't able to connect me right away. While I waited, I flipped through the several pages of Trudd's 1961 will, skipping past the boilerplate. His Vancouver lawyer, James Delaire, was named executor.

A dozen cash bequests included a generous $80,000 to veterinarian Jonah Muggins, who'd treated Trudd's herd of cats. Lesser amounts went to the SPCA, a cat hospital in Edmonton, the local Chamber of Commerce, and various service clubs and right-wing causes. Substantial gifts of $250,000 to each of his sisters.

The residue, including his business, Trudd Enterprises, would have gone to his wife. But his 1964 divorce automatically voided that bequest, so the sinister sisters, his next of kin, would have inherited Trudd's multi-million-dollar estate.

Reception wasn't able to raise Hubbell, so I was put through to his secretary, Jackie.

"Just missed him, Stretch, he rushed out five minutes ago, late for his DND lunch."

"DND?"

"Do Not Disturb."

"And where is this DND lunch?"

"Even if I knew, I ain't at liberty to say."

"Did he leave a number?"

"Give me a break, Arthur."

"This wouldn't happen to be one of his famous quickie lunches in the Hastings Royal Hotel?" The structure that marred the view from my office window. The so-called lunch dates usually occurred in guest rooms and didn't always involve food.

"He'll be back in an hour. I promise on my death bed he'll call you."

"Goddamn, Jackie, I'm in the middle of a murder trial. He doesn't even have to pull his pants on, all he has to do is reach across the bed, pick up the room phone, and give me three minutes."

"Not on my watch, honey. I need this job."

"Miss Santos is just finishing her lunch," said Mike Trasov, as he led me into the Mounties' coffee room. This genial senior officer had become a sort of kindly, obliging uncle, sincerely concerned about the plight of my client.

I asked a favour: "The Alaska Highway Motel — where your out-of-town officers were staying — you must know who runs it."

"Sure do. The owner's a retired cop. Percy Edgursen."

I told him Donalda Wyatt and Hortense Trudd-Stephens may have taken rooms there on Wednesday, May 25, after a Northways charter flight from the Okanagan Valley. Could that be confirmed?

He returned from his office after five minutes. "The register has them each taking a room. The Northways pilot stayed over too. They flew out the next morning. You might be interested in this: Donalda was accompanied by her husband, Connor. Or Conn, as he's better known. Spelled with two n's, but C-o-n works too. As in ex-con."

I'd heard about him. A local bad boy when in his teens and twenties. "He has a sheet?"

"Went down on a weapons charge, dangerous use of a firearm, I think, or public mischief — he'd got loaded on booze and shot up a couple of road signs, barely missed a passing car full of kids. Three months and probation. Hung out with a shady crowd here, and a bunch of them got nailed for running opium and barbiturates. Conn got fifteen months, served nine. Nothing for the last ten years, since he married Donalda and they moved south. She's almost ten years older, so I guess she was getting desperate. He manages a Chev-Olds dealership in Kelowna now, he's a slick salesman, a charmer."

I pulled a bologna sandwich from my briefcase as Angelina was ushered in. She was working on dessert, dipping a little wooden paddle into a Dixie cup.

"My baby craves ice cream," she said, revealing a heretofore hidden wryness. I promised to make up for being late by spending the evening with her, preparing her for the stand. But for now I needed clarification. *I remember something.*

I gobbled my stale sandwich as she cleaned the table, trashed wrappers and containers, and washed her hands, all the while sharing small talk. She then shocked me by her recall — finally — of F.C. Trudd's last minutes.

She still couldn't bring back when, how, or why she took the Remington rifle out to the back deck. Otherwise, her "moment of remembrance," to use Etienne's words, was indeed like fog receding, as if from a sudden summer breeze.

She was sanguine with me as she described Trudd's arrival. "When he got out of his car, he shouted at me terrible words, profaning our Saviour, and he started to walk to me, and then stopped and pulled down his zipper to show me his cock, and I had a, how you call, a flashback to that night when he raped me and said he would tell my mother I was a dirty whore."

She said all that briskly, without wetness of eye or tremor of lip, which I found uncharacteristic, then followed up with "And there was a bang, bang." She crushed the Dixie cup, and lobbed it toward the waste basket. Her aim was perfect, a two-pointer.

1966 —
The Preacher, the Painter,
and the Pilot

O ur irreligious judge tried hard not to look scornful or bored as Etienne Larouche summarized his thirty years serving the Lord in northern Canadian parishes. Fort Tom's Holy Rosary Church had been his venue for the last decade, and it was at a newcomers' reception in mid-March of 1965 that he met Angelina, who had just been hired by Trudd. She immediately became a driving force in the Elder Care Society and other community efforts, devoting every Sunday, morning to night, to good works.

Etienne read into the record affidavits of praise for Angelina sworn by churchgoers and volunteers from elder care and the food bank. The Crown had consented to this procedure, but Kroop's sighs and scowls suggested he resented my clogging up the trial with what he regarded as barely admissible blather.

Foreman Rummy Wilcox, presumably a hardcore Protestant, listened to the papist's presentation with what seemed effortful indifference. Eric Sayaga was more tuned in, attentive and sombre as the plaudits continued. The Trudd sisters exchanged uneasy glances, occasionally whispering to Hogey. Sandwiched between them, he had the look of a trapped raccoon.

When Etienne finished, Santorini simply said, "No questions." He knew it was a loser's game to attack a holy man.

Ryan Klymchuk was then fetched from the witness room. Along with his brother, this hefty house painter had applied an exterior coat to Trudd's house in early July, to ready it for sale.

He had no trouble recognizing his handiwork in photos showing the embedded high-velocity slug in the basement wall. He had sanded away the splinters, plugged the hole with putty, and painted it over.

I asked, "Did you do that on your own initiative?"

"No, sir. Mr. Melquist wanted it to disappear."

"That would be Wendell Melquist, the listing agent?"

Santorini: "Objection. Hearsay."

Kroop: "Once again, Mr. Santorini, the horse has left the barn. For what it's worth, the jury will disregard the witness's last answer."

I carried on: "Did the damage you observed from the bullet's impact seem fresh?"

"Them splinters looked fairly new. Like, not faded."

"Did you show Mr. Melquist the embedded bullet?"

"Well, he was there with his clients on a site visit, so, yeah, I pointed it out, and he talked to them, and, ah, I don't know what I'm allowed to say . . ."

"Just what you saw, Ryan, not what was said, that way no one will get riled up. When you referred to Mr. Melquist's clients, do you mean those two ladies sitting over there on either side of Hogey Johnson?"

"Yes, sir. Them two ladies."

"Mr. Trudd's sisters."

"Yes, sir."

"For the record, Donalda Wyatt is on the left facing us, and Hortense Trudd-Stephens on the right."

"I'm Donalda," said the woman I misidentified as Hortense.

Scattered laughter. I apologized, set the record straight, and got back to Melquist. "Very well, he talked to them, and then what?"

"Well, he came over and talked to me."

"And that's when you agreed to make the hole in the wall disappear?"

"Yeah, I guess. I tried my best, anyway."

"Your witness."

Clara struggled to smother a grin, as Santorini rose slowly, rolling his eyes in acknowledgement that I'd stick-handled my way around the rule against hearsay. Like his hero, Gordie Howe, deking around Stan Mikita.

Despite Ed's lethargic approach to trial work, he was a capable cross-examiner, with a relaxed manner: "So the house was being fitted up for sale. Were other contractors there?"

"There was a cleaning crew inside, and I think a plumber was around."

"An ordinary workday. You weren't shocked to see a slug in a wall, were you? It must have happened before."

"Yes, sir. Buckshot too."

"Did Mrs. Wyatt or Mrs. Trudd-Stephens come by to have a look at this bullet hole?"

"No, they went off with Mr. Melquist."

"It was no big deal, just a hole in a wall, right? Under cover, protected from the elements, naturally it's going to look fresh. Could have been there for years, right?"

"I guess. I don't know. I'm just a house painter."

"But a very good one, I've heard. Thanks, that's all."

The afternoon break was brief, just long enough for me to prime my next witness, Ned Best, the retired bush pilot and First World War hero. We met in the witness room. He was neatly done up in blazer and tie, and was straight of back, looking fit, though using a cane.

I coached him as best I could, but I had to agree with Etienne: *Ned Best would be a risky witness.* The octogenarian's faculties were not razor sharp. The jury would quickly note his hearing aids. But he was a vital witness: no one else could testify to having heard two distinct shots on May 29.

As I led him down the hall, Charles Loobie pursued, quickly gaining distance. "Hey, Artie, nobody seems to want to talk about Magistrate Mapple, especially you. I heard he wrote a report about the debacle in Pouce Coupe, and it's buried somewhere in the bowels of Aboriginal Affairs."

"I wish I could help you, Charles."

"Just admit you got a certified copy and you're going to spring it on the jury. Boom! *Indian Chief's Nephew Suspected in Trudd Murder.*"

"When I decide to do that, you'll be the first to know." I feared this tiresome snoop would throw a stink bomb into the trial by digging up that report.

I ushered in Ned Best and sat him near the front. Having unglued himself from me, Loobie retreated to the press table, joining two late-arriving rivals: reporters from the *Vancouver Sun* and the CBC. A Canadian Press photographer was also lurking about, taking photos outside the courthouse; he wasn't allowed to do so within.

Also at the press table, representing the *Northern Daily News*, was eighteen-year-old rookie reporter Fannie Gibson, whose stiff, careful prose had fairly captured each day's events. Her little broadsheet was delivered to Fort Tom doorsteps around suppertime, beating out the morning *Province* by twelve hours plus the two days it took to fly a print run up there.

Fannie, in her big, owlish glasses, seemed to be editing copy or proofs, but she quickly covered up her work as Loobie plunked himself down next to her.

With jury and judge settled in, Ned Best took the stand — and we were immediately in trouble. As with all witnesses, he was instructed by the clerk thus: "Take the Bible in your right hand."

"Sorry, ma'am, I don't need a Bible to swear on. That would be a pretense on my part. I don't see how I could be a truthful person if I swore on a Bible that I don't believe in."

A quick glance at Angelina found her not aghast, as I expected, but with a slight frown of concentration, her lips moving — reciting a silent prayer? Rehearsing for her own turn on the stand? It had bothered me how, at lunch break, she had so calmly rattled off Trudd's last moments, suddenly recalled. Maybe that was a good sign. Maybe she had decided to fight. Maybe she'd finally realized that God alone would not decide her guilt or innocence, that the Lord needed a little nudge from His pregnant devotee.

Non-believer Wilbur Kroop was fine with Ned's renunciation of the Bible. "A point well made, Mr. Best. Madam Clerk, you will read to him the oath to affirm."

She did so, and he affirmed to tell the truth. A couple of the jurors looked dismayed at his rejection of the holy word. Rummy Wilcox's face was a dark cloud of disapproval. I blamed myself for this blip; I had prepared the flying ace poorly.

But the jurors who knew about his loss of faith when his wife died might forgive him. They would be proud that this holder of the Victoria Cross, who'd blasted three Fokkers and two bombers from the skies, was rooted to the North, to their hometown.

I led him briefly through his heroic CV and his decades of flying Cessnas and Beavers to remote, icy lakes, then brought him up to date: widowed five years ago, he lived alone in his house overlooking the Wolf River, two acreages down from Trudd's.

Ned was straining at the leash so I let him run free: "I was out in the yard. I'd just ate lunch, so it was around twelve-fifteen or so. Anyway, I got a woodshed out there and a greenhouse, and I was splitting wood. And that's when I heard the shots, clear as day. Two shots, I would say from a high-powered rifle."

Much better than the version he'd given me earlier — that had him chainsawing a fallen pine that had blown down in a storm ten days later.

He continued: "Normally you don't expect anyone to be shooting in the middle of spring, especially close to people's houses, though Fred Trudd would occasionally take a potshot at some pest. The Mounties came right away. I didn't think they wanted neighbours prying around while they're doing their job, so I just kept splitting wood."

I crossed my fingers and asked him if he could be more specific about where the two shots came from.

"Well, they came real close together, so it was hard to say. Back of his house, maybe, or farther away, where it's mostly stumps and shrubs. I couldn't see the house, because there's a spruce grove in the way, it obscures everything but a rooftop corner of the garage. Anyway, there was a lot of commotion over there, sirens and comings and goings, and I knew something bad had happened, but it wasn't till I turned on the radio . . ."

I had stopped listening halfway through this excursus, distracted by the courtroom door swinging open for the late entry of Chief Eric Sayaga, followed by a tall, handsome young man in a Maple Leafs jersey. Colour him Blue. I clenched my jaw to prevent it from dropping. Johnny's eyes were locked on me, dark and searing, as he joined his uncle in the back row.

"Mr. Beauchamp?" Someone was calling me. Wilbur Kroop.

"Yes, excuse me, Milord. Can we double back, Mr. Best? You said one of the rifle shots came from far out in the bush —"

Santorini was quick to his feet: "He didn't say that at all. He said *maybe* — maybe back of the house or the garage."

I tried to focus. "Okay, let's clarify. Mr. Best?"

"To be honest, that valley out there is famous for its echoes. All I know was there was at least two shots. I wouldn't be sure from where exactly."

This was not going well. Ned Best frowned and closed his eyes, as if trying to visualize, jog his memory. If he was confused, I was rattled by the untimely emergence of Johnny Blue. Loobie was staring at him hungrily, ready to pounce as soon as court recessed for the day.

As to my witness, I decided not to dig a deeper hole for myself. "Thank you, Mr. Best. No more questions."

Santorini went into full-folksy mode. "Well, sir, this is one for the memory book, a chance to enjoy a little courtroom gab with British Columbia's own Billy Bishop. I hope you can help me out here, sir, because I'm a little slow on the uptake. Those shots — at least two, you said — were they just bang-bang or a few seconds apart?"

"Two, three seconds at the most."

"And I guess those echoes came a few seconds apart too."

"I'd say maybe a second or two — sound travels fast up here."

"We had a gun expert sitting where you are, Corporal Holtz, who test-fired a Remington 700 in Mr. Trudd's backyard and he said that the first echo sounded like a clap of thunder. You'd agree with that, I assume."

"The echo is pretty loud on a clear day."

"Kind of hard to distinguish if it's an echo or the real thing, an actual rifle blast?"

"I was sure I heard two shots, but as you've noticed my hearing isn't perfect."

"I'm sure those hearing aids are a big help in here, but I don't imagine you were wearing them while wielding an axe, Mr. Best."

"Well, usually I keep them in the house when I'm out doing chores. I can hear all right except for distant voices."

"And did you hear voices from over on Mr. Trudd's property? Or anywhere?"

"No, sir."

"So you were chopping wood with an axe without your hearing aids when you heard what sounded like gunshots, do I have that right?"

I sensed that most on the jury felt bad for Ned, who laboured to answer. "I was mostly splitting with a maul and a wedge. Some of those pine butts were pretty tough and gnarly."

"I hear you. I split a ton of firewood in the back country to pay my way through law school." A feat I'd never heard about, doubtless apocryphal. "Maul and a wedge. Steel on steel. Makes quite a loud ringing noise when you hit it square."

"Even louder if you clip the edge."

Jurors were smiling, their heads nodding. I had lost my witness to Santorini, who owned him.

"Did you buck up that gnarly pine yourself, Mr. Best?"

"That tree, as I recall, came down in a storm. I had to get out my Pioneer 500."

"Oh, my gosh, I had one of those too. Real reliable chainsaw, you want my opinion. Were you using yours that day, May twenty-ninth?"

"I think I may have made a few cuts with it."

"Pretty darn loud, that saw. I hope you used ear protectors."

"Sure did. Helmet and earmuffs, safety first."

"I heard you wandered over to Mr. Trudd's property when the RCMP crew was there last weekend looking things over. What prompted that?"

"Just natural curiosity. I heard a few rifle reports."

"How many?"

"Three or four, I think."

"Would you be surprised that Corporal Holtz, in test-firing the rifle, pressed the trigger only twice?"

A pause. "I guess I got confused by the echoes."

A rare show of brilliance by Eddie Santorini. I wanted to crawl away, an injured animal.

"Thank you, Mr. Best. No more questions."

Kroop gave me a look of pity that those who didn't know him would regard as heartfelt. "We will adjourn until Thursday at ten."

I turned to see Angelina standing in the dock, her back to me, watching Johnny Blue rise to leave. He stood tall, smiled at her, clenched a fist to his heart — clearly a gesture of comradeship and support.

1966 —
The Date from Hell

It was five o'clock and I was already on my third shot of rye whiskey — from a bottle Hogey Johnson generously donated to allay my pain. He'd lent me his law office again, leaving Sibyl Frick to look after my needs while he scurried home to a wife, a rib roast, and some guests.

Sibyl had again deposited me in Hogey's private office, to await Hubbell's callback. "Your friend should be calling any minute," she said from the doorway. "I'll make sure the line is free. Can I get you anything? The Pizza Parlour delivers. You have to eat, you know."

"You've been lovely, Sibyl, thanks. Maybe we can grab something later. Actually, I should take you out."

"That would be swell." She hurried off as the phone rang, and put Hubbell through. I greeted him with a terse complaint about my inability to reach him while he was off somewhere fornicating.

"My, my, aren't we in a wintry mood. Is that dreadful judge still being mean to you?"

I refused to play, knocked back my rye, let him ramble about matters inconsequential: "The old man wants to know what's taking so long. This was supposed to last three days max, you're over budget on a cut-and-dried homicide. My issue is even more serious.

You promised to be here for the Grey Cup on Saturday. You got two days to wind this sucker up."

"I'll make that deadline easily. Ed Santorini just shot down a World War One ace by turning on the smarm full blast. The jury will be out for half an hour."

"Please don't tell me I've done all this work for nothing. Is this line safe? No chance of being overheard?"

I briefed him on how and why I was occupying the private office of Trudd's eagerly helpful local solicitor. "Shoot," I said, grabbing a pen and notepad.

"I had a very interesting session over breakfast today at the Devonshire with Jim Delaire. Senior wills and estates guy at Russell, DuMoulin. I only know him from a few Vancouver Bar events but he's an upfront person. And he's handling Trudd's estate."

A growing excitement in Hubbell's voice caused my hand to shake as I poured another shot.

"Jim has been following your trial in the morning paper. Ardently. Sympathetically, in fact — he's torn up about your Angelina Santos being raped and carrying Trudd's child, and he's intrigued by the legal consequences of that. So when I called him up yesterday he was hot to trot to tête-à-tête with me. Take a deep breath."

I sucked it in, held it, my pen hovering over my pad.

"Trudd died intestate. He voided his will when he got divorced. Delaire drafted a new one last May and mailed it, but Trudd bit the dust before executing it. The upshot? The child that your sweet angel is bearing will inherit Trudd's estate. Everything. The town of Fort Thompson. The chair you're sitting on."

I tilted my glass, and the whiskey flowed fierce and hot down my throat.

"You got a telecopier up there?"

"Yep."

"Turn it on."

I stumbled out into the blowing, black night and weaved my way down Main Street, gulping the minus-thirty-degree air, hoping it might shock me into a creditable state of sobriety. I hadn't ditched Sibyl — we'd agreed to meet later in the Fort's dining room — but I had a prior date with my client.

On entering the police station, I approached Mike Trasov with the stiff, mannered walk of one determined not to appear impaired. He wasn't fooled, and made me a tall mug of instant coffee.

He advised me that Angelina had just been seen by an obstetrics nurse. "She says your client is in excellent health. As is the tiny life she's carrying."

I responded, "Thank God," barely managing to avoid blurting out that that tiny life could one day be a local tycoon.

"Heard you had a bit of a rough day with Ned Best. He kind of missed the runway."

"My fault."

Angelina was taking dinner in her cell, so while I choked down my sham coffee, I prepared a little tutorial for her about the law relating to intestate deaths. Boiling it down, the closest relation by blood to an intestate gets the whole megillah, to use Hubbell's pet phrase. By long-standing precedent that rule applies to one not born as of the intestate's death. The Wills Act mandates that the estate be held under a trust until the girl or boy achieves adulthood.

How all of that might benefit a mother facing execution or serving a life sentence, I did not know.

Another possible snag: could it be proved to the satisfaction of a probate judge that Trudd fathered Angelina's baby? Would her avowal that she was a virgin when raped be enough? Would blood type comparisons come into play? But surely the expiration of the nine-month gestation period would tell the tale, assuming the infant arrived near the end of February. What if there was a miscarriage? Or the child died in infancy?

As I waded through these scenarios, Angelina strolled in serene as a queen, eased herself onto the sofa, looked me over critically, and rendered judgment: I looked "awful tired" from working too hard, and I should ask the judge for a day off work. I had to explain the courts don't operate that way.

During previous visits, I had avoided over-rehearsing Angelina for the witness stand — too much, and her testimony might seem scripted. I wanted her words to come out unaffectedly: how Trudd had shouted threats and obscenities as he advanced, erect penis in hand. (*Penis, please, my dear, not cock.*)

But I remained anxious about the remaining gaps in her memory — the Crown would argue that her blank moments were too convenient, too pat, and I feared the jury wouldn't believe she couldn't recall pulling that trigger. Especially problematic was why she'd retrieved and brandished a loaded rifle well before she was under threat. I had to take one final crack at filling in those amnesic holes.

But first she must know that she was bearing not just a child to love but one who would be born to unexpected riches.

Angelina's initial reaction was mute astonishment, succeeded by quizzical delight, then frowning incredulity: as if suspecting I'd made an inappropriate joke. The final stage was calm rationality, as she plied me with questions. Who chooses this trustee? Does the government appoint? Would he be like a lawyer, or like a banker or accountant? Or the sisters of Mr. Trudd? They would steal every-thing. Wouldn't they fight this in the courts? I am the mother — am I not important?

I did my best. Yes, the government must approve the trustee. The estate must be honestly managed. The sisters would have no control. They would lose in court unless they proved Trudd was not the birth father.

In the course of this to and fro, I became aware that I'd under-estimated this young immigrant maid's sharpness of mind. I had categorized her as a pious innocent, lacking insight and shrewd-ness, and had fallen afoul of that common male fault of misreading the often-baffling other sex.

When her questions were exhausted, I took my turn, urging her once again to dig into her memory cells, to bring back May 29, find the pieces missing from the puzzle.

She wandered quietly to the fridge, poured herself a glass of milk, sat again, closed her eyes, furrowed her brows. Minutes passed. Then words came, slowly, as if from one under hypnosis.

"There's a dirt road behind the house. It goes into the hills far away. But I never seen anyone on it until . . . I was washing dishes, and I heard engine noise, and looked out the kitchen window and there was a big cloud of dust, and . . . a car, a little Jeep, was coming . . . and then it went away, behind the trees." She opened her eyes wide, as if she'd shocked herself. "That's why I went to get the rifle."

The jigsaw piece fit so perfectly that I wondered if she'd made this up to please me. Yet I encouraged her: "You thought he might be a bad man, yes? A robber, or . . . worse."

"I remember I was scared. I went outside with the rifle. Waiting, watching, maybe ten minutes, maybe more. And then Mr. Trudd came home, and I was just standing there, not pointing the rifle at him. And he got out from the car, and shouted evil things, was cursing me, and showing me his . . . penis. I knew he would rape me again, and . . . I told you. Bang, bang. That's what I heard. Bang, bang."

"You didn't aim at him, did you? You just wanted to scare him off. A warning shot. Do you remember that?"

"I will try, Mr. Beauchamp. I will try harder."

I was blatantly coaching her, pushing her to create false memories. That is not what a principled barrister does. I had a sinking sense that this hitherto virtuous young lady, influenced by great expectations, was going along with me, reading from my script.

I was late for my date, and found Sibyl Frick looking forlorn in the cold, cavernous dining room of the Fort, a once-grand edifice soon to be inherited by a child of rape. For Sibyl, regrettably, the evening was as romantic as a visit to the morgue.

Blame me: I was, of course, profoundly preoccupied with the sudden, unexpected wiggles and warps of this trial by ordeal, and was flailing with the effort to sort out the implications. I couldn't help shake the worry that my client no longer felt bound by God's commandment against bearing false witness. Whisky sours and a shared bottle of wine only amplified my muddle.

Sibyl obviously felt awkward, but sat there politely. And intensely, as if wondering: *what have I got into?* She had not expected an evening out with a pre-alcoholic nervous wretch who couldn't stop cross-examining her.

"You're sure you never saw an envelope from Russell, DuMoulin."

"Arthur, I see everything that comes in the mail."

"Mr. Delaire says he sent the new will by Pacific Western Airlines courier."

"Even if Hogey picked it up at the airport, or signed it when I was on an errand, I would have filed it."

"You think the airline lost it? It should have been delivered on the Monday before Trudd died."

"It wasn't." Stubbornness showing. This had become, for her, the date from hell.

"On Saturday, the twenty-first, Trudd told you to get your boss's ass down to the mill. What was the rush?"

"Mr. Trudd did that all the time. He treated Hogey like a tyrant. Sort of like you're treating me."

That was like a hit from a hammer, and I was dazed. It suddenly dawned on me that I was drunk. I had been an utter boor, controlling and unpleasant. In grovelling apology, I reached out to touch her hand, but she jerked it away.

I said, "I'm sorry. I'm overwrought."

"Maybe you have too much on your plate."

She was right. I'd hardly touched my chicken linguini. It sat there like a giant, white turd. I wasn't feeling well. I wondered if they poisoned my food. Would they take me out of here on a stretcher, like Mapple?

Somehow we got through that meal. I topped up the bill with a six-dollar tip, then swirled and downed a hot brandy that I'd hoped would soothe my innards. I managed to walk a reasonably straight line to the door, then held it for her, but she wouldn't make eye contact.

It was snowing, and the street was slippery, and I'd have gone down if she hadn't grabbed my sleeve. I couldn't figure out a plan for the immediate future. Where do I go from here? *Why* was I here?

Nor could I figure out why Sibyl was reaching through my pockets — until she fished out my car keys. "I have a rollout. I'm just around the corner." Was that an invitation? Why was she acting so glum?

My stomach was rebelling. I felt a gust of nausea just as the Fort pub's door opened to a hot blast of beery air. I barely made it to the curb before expelling my fermenting linguini.

My last remembrance of that night was the *Northern Daily News* on Sibyl's doorstep, with its grotesque headline: "You F-ing Slimy Nazi, I'm Going to Kill You!" A photo of A.W. Mapple in happier days. A photo of Johnny Blue.

The rest is mostly blank. I refuse to speculate. I have already embellished a few scenes sketchily recalled, and don't want to be accused of writing fiction.

However, there can be no doubt that I woke up in Sibyl's bed just after seven with a massive headache. Through bleary eyes, I made her out setting down a tray with bacon, eggs, toast, coffee, and aspirin.

Arthur —
September 2022

I'm speeding through the trial of Angelina Santos on the wings of Mercury. I would like to think that my writer-whisperer, Clio, the Muse of History, is inspiring such progress, but the truth is less romantic.

It's the transcripts, the mouse-nibbled, pee-reeking uncut record of *Regina v. Santos*, that have the pages whipping from my typewriter roll, replete with cribbed courtroom dialogue. Less reliable are details of encounters in restaurants and bars, with a counterculture Crown counsel, or snide cops, or a sad Santa. As to my conversations with Angelina Santos, they are recalled with tolerable accuracy, as copied from my notepads — despite having been composed often with a shaky hand. Fortunately, for this enterprise, I have been relieved from the constraints of solicitor-client privilege, and may boldly recite her words without fear of disbarment.

Sadly, I've been at loggerheads with agent-editor Lisa Throckmorton. I declined her advice not to rely on "great gobs of trial transcript." She insisted that if I expected it to be a bestseller I would have to "creatively ad lib," adding twists and intrigue and, most of all, "passion."

She seems obsessively keen on my adding spice in the form of lurid sex scenes, suggesting scenarios that seem borrowed from mass market romances. Themes that would, for instance, have me rescuing Clara Moncrief from danger: from wolves, or a blizzard, or the lecherous senior prosecutor — then spiriting her away on a Ski-Doo to the cozy warmth of a log cabin, with a hot toddy of purplish prose, all orifices actively in play.

I had only fleetingly looked at the website for the Throckmorton Agency. On closer perusal, just today, I found I didn't recognize any of the authors mentioned there: her stable, as she puts it — none of whom have won, placed, or shown in the literary derby. The names seemed almost made up: Janice G. Unkorn, Greta Stielborn, Bertram Bookbinder, Neville H. Djankoff.

One of the links took me to a profile of Lisa Throckmorton, and, no surprise, it disclosed that the prestigious publishing house for which she served as a senior editor was Harlequin Romances. The photo is of a grinning, red-lipped redhead in big glasses who seems of indeterminate age. She has the look of an actor with her makeup all askew.

It has finally dawned that I am the butt of an elaborate joke . . .

1966 —
Confused by the Echoes

S omehow, on that Thursday morning, I managed to drag myself from Sibyl's bedroom and to my lodgings to fix myself up for what promised to be a pivotal day at the courthouse. I was fuming as I got there, mostly at myself. I had driven myself too hard, and last evening the wheels came off. Too many wild turns: the sudden emergence of Johnny Blue, the Ned Best disaster, an unborn heir to Trudd's estate, the missing, unsigned will, and, finally, Fannie Gibson's scoop in the *Northern Daily News*.

That was causing a buzz in the courthouse, citizens bent over front pages, puzzling over them, whispering, trading opinions. The teenaged reporter, a well-liked local, had got access to documents found in A.W. Mapple's hotel room. These included a copy of his report to Aboriginal Affairs about the disastrous mediation in Pouce Coupe.

Her article quoted Mapple's accounts of Trudd's drunken, obscene bullying, as well as Johnny Blue's furious response. Also under her byline was a piece about the sudden death, during the trial, of A.W. Mapple. Somehow this little broadsheet had found photos of Johnny and Mapple. On an inside page was a backgrounder on the contested claim to the thousand acres for which Trudd had cutting rights. Two columns were devoted to Ed Santorini's amiable takedown of Ned Best, under the head "I GOT CONFUSED BY THE ECHOES."

Altogether, a prize exhibition of journalese — it had been quickly picked up by the wire services.

Loobie would be convulsing with fury on this Thursday morning. He had been sitting on his interview with Mapple, maybe polishing it for the big weekend edition.

My head was clanging as I waited inside the main door for a runner to show up with an affidavit sent by telecopier to Hogey's law office. Sybil Frick, sweetly patient and profoundly forgiving, had run off copies for judge, jury, and Crown. All done without Hogey knowing — he'd rarely ventured into his office that week; the trial had him oddly rapt.

The packet finally arrived, and I checked it out: several copies of Jim Delaire's affidavit, plus certified copies of filings by Trudd Enterprises Inc. obtained from the province's corporate registry. Hubbell had done some sweaty digging for me.

I slid the papers into my briefcase, then worked my way toward the assize court door, but stalled as I heard Charles Loobie howling in the rotunda: "Whose dick did you have to suck, you sneaky bitch! You don't share? You got no journalistic ethics? They don't teach them in high school?"

I tore through the crowd like a man on fire, and found Fannie safe but frightened behind a phalanx of protectors. Loobie wiggled like a landed fish in the muscular arms of the Canadian Press photographer. The other two reporters stifled grins and made notes as Sergeant Trasov approached, clinking his handcuffs. Poor Loobie — I wondered what it was like being so thoroughly detested.

◾▶

Should our jury be made aware of a militant Aboriginal's murderous threat in a classified report whose author was dead? That, I assumed, was the conundrum Kroop was chewing over by phone with the Chief

Justice. My head kept throbbing through this long delay, despite the aspirins I was popping.

Clara Moncrief found me at the top of the stairs, where I was leaning over the railing, watching the scene below through blood-shot eyes, gulping aspirins.

"You look like you just dragged yourself out of bed. Maybe the wrong bed."

"Meaning?"

"Meaning you were seen staggering arm-in-arm down Main Street with Hogey Johnson's sex-starved secretary. It's a small town."

"Nothing happened. I vaguely remember her hosing me down in the shower. Even then, I was too repulsive to do anything more than share a bed."

"You got a booze problem, honey. You get close to pulling off a miracle, and you fucking fall apart. You're at a crisis point in this trial, so maybe you want to shape up. What's with you, anyway?"

"Shell shock. Battle fatigue. Where's Eddie?"

"Conferring with the cops about what to do about Johnny Blue."

"What's Ed's problem? He was on a roll with his Paul Bunyan act, bucking up his fake cords of wood."

"He sprained his shoulder patting himself on the back. But now he's worried the jury will hear about the melee in Pouce Coupe. Motive, opportunity, vengeance, and to top it off, jurors may buy the stereotype of a liquored-up Indian hothead as your second shooter. Eddie will try to cut you off at the pass, he's asked the judge to hear argument."

"Johnny Blue is ready for me, he has at least three witnesses."

He was down there with Eric Sayaga. The three likely witnesses included two Indigenous males and a woman, Sayaga's office manager. All here, all young, all doubtless rehearsed to back up Johnny's unassailable alibi for the mid-day hours of May 29.

"I'm not going to lay a finger on Johnny Blue, or mention Mapple's report — they'll laugh me out of court if it turns out Johnny was boating with his buddies two hundred miles down the Wolf River. Anyway, I won't play the race card. I'm going a different route."

"Like what?"

"Watch me."

The Trudd sisters were also down there, not scowling as usual, but smiling as their lawyer, the lovingly inept Hogey Johnson, appeared to be entertaining them with tall tales. He had glommed on to them fast, after their brother died. It was odd that none of them grasped that Trudd had died intestate — Hogey had expressed confusion over whether his estate was being probated, but was he that dumb?

1966 —
Surprise Witness

Court was finally called to order, with the gallery packed but the jury box empty. Kroop was armed with a folded *Northern Daily News.*

"Mr. Santorini, I understand you have concerns about the admissibility of a mediator's written report relating to a shouting match involving a Native and Mr. Trudd, as described in this newspaper. My immediate reaction is that the Mapple report is unalloyed hearsay, but of course I will hear Mr. Beauchamp."

That promise was not kept, because he took a potshot at me: "I'm curious, Counsel, were you keeping this Pouce Coupe incident in your vest pocket all this time? I'm given to understand you brought Mr. Mapple up here to play the role of surprise witness. It's regrettable, of course, that this distinguished retired magistrate met an untimely demise, so I must assume you're exploring alternate means of seeking to establish the matters alleged in this article."

"If Your Lordship would care to hear me on the matter —"

Apparently not, because he cut me off: "Frankly, Counsel, it would have helped with trial scheduling had I received the courtesy of an advance warning about this issue. Now, complex admissibility issues have to be argued, and, perhaps, additional witnesses subpoenaed. That should fill up today and Friday, so we'll have to extend into next week. Awkward for everybody. A burden on jurors eager to return to their homes and loved ones. What do you say, Mr. Santorini?"

"Burden on me too, Judge," Santorini said. "I got tickets for the Grey Cup on Saturday. I promised my dad I'd take him — he has a love thing with Ron Lancaster."

That sounded so odd that the room went eerily silent. Clara was embarrassed enough to kick his ankle. Charles Loobie, who'd been released back into society, was cocky again, grinning and scribbling.

The former college fullback recovered his fumble, and charged ahead: "Mr. Mapple is dead. Sad. We woe for him. We wish he could be here, hale and hearty, but he can't testify from the grave, he can't be cross-examined, and there's no way his report can go before the jury. If my learned friend wants to call a couple of local Indians to say they heard Mr. Blue threaten the deceased, they better be prepared, because I'm going to challenge them, and I won't be wearing kid gloves."

Kroop stopped listening to this bluster, distracted by noticing, in the back row, the Wolf River Reserve group of five. I turned to see Johnny's two pals smiling, apparently enjoying this little display of white, colonialist justice. Kroop zoomed in on Johnny, then glanced down at his front-page photo, then up at Johnny, and finally, with a puzzled frown, returned to Santorini.

"I'm sorry, Mr. Prosecutor, did you say you had concerns about the jury over this matter?"

"Yeah, I definitely do. As I understand it, in their little hotel there's a common room, and it has a TV and a radio. I know they're not supposed to tune into the news, but sometimes it can't be avoided. Or a jury member might overhear the hotel staff, or glance at the front page of the local paper."

"So what do you want me to do about it?"

"Your Lordship could firmly remind them of their oath to only rely on evidence adduced in this room."

"What's your position, Mr. Beauchamp?"

"Thank you for asking, Milord. I'm eager to move things along. I'd like to call my next witness." I was curt because my head was banging, one of the worst hangovers I could remember.

"Now?"

"Yes, before the morning wanes."

"The issue of the Mapple report — how do you respond to Mr. Santorini's objection?"

"Mr. Santorini is opposing me on a matter I'm not pursuing. If it please the court, I'd like to get on with my defence."

Kroop's mouth was open, but he couldn't quite untie his tongue. Eric Sayaga, with a puzzled frown, was conferring with his office manager. I won an encouraging smile from Angelina. She liked fighters. That's probably why she so often glanced Johnny's way. *He liked me too. He said I was almost Indian.*

Finally, Kroop called the jury in, then confused them with a rambling plea to ignore anything "emanating from news media that was accidentally seen or overheard relating to a land dispute involving the deceased." Thus quickening their interest in such an event. I would have bet the farm they had already been exposed to Fannie Gibson's scoop. I was content to leave it at that.

I rose. "I call Mr. Hogarth Johnson."

Hogey, sandwiched between the Trudd sisters, went white with surprise, and it took him several seconds to lift his gaunt frame from his pew.

As Hogey was being sworn in, he looked about for salvation: to Crown counsel, the sisters, the whispering townspeople. "I swear," he said, and cautiously lowered himself onto his chair.

"Mr. Johnson, I first want to thank you for your kindnesses toward me. You confided in me and generously allowed me the use of your office facilities."

"Of course, ah . . . you're welcome. Any time." He brightened, sensing he might not be in for a grilling.

I followed up by lauding his reputation as a well-regarded solicitor in Fort Tom, then established that he had done many services for Trudd for many decades.

"I don't care to know what advice Mr. Trudd sought or what advice you gave him. However, I am interested, as I think the jury will be, on his wills that you worked on. So let us go back to several years ago, before Mr. Trudd divorced his second wife. You helped draft a will for him that was signed and executed on December fifth, 1961. I have a copy here. You and your secretary, Sibyl Frick, witnessed it."

I put it in front of him, and he puzzled over it for a short while, then identified both signatures. "I received Fred's instructions, sir, and sent them on to his Vancouver solicitors, and they prepared this final draft and mailed it down."

"The Vancouver lawyer you dealt with was James Delaire, correct?"

"That's right. From Russell, DuMoulin. I was just the go-between. I write up lots of wills for folks around here but Fred's estate was maybe a little too complex for a country lawyer." A nervous, self-deprecating grin.

"And who were the beneficiaries of that 1961 will?"

"Well, Fred Trudd, he never had kids of his own, so most of his estate, the residue, would have gone to his wife, minus substantial gifts to each of his two sisters, and there were some good causes — SPCA, Ducks Unlimited, our Chamber of Commerce. A cat hospital, as I remember, in Edmonton, where he sometimes had his cats flown to. And there was a big sum for Jonah Muggins, who runs a vet clinic here — they were pretty close, Jonah and Fred. Active in the Gun Club. It's all there in that copy of the will you showed me."

I tendered it as Exhibit Thirty-Three without complaint from bench or Crown. Kroop had lost his zest for forensic scuffles — they could prolong the trial well beyond Friday. Santorini was silent because he clung to the hope he'd make it to the Grey Cup game. I flipped another aspirin into my mouth, washed it down.

"Mr. Trudd's marriage ended in divorce around three years ago?"

"Yep, she took off from him, and he got himself a top divorce lawyer, and the payout to her was pretty niggly, as I recall."

"And how did that impact the 1961 will?"

"As I understand the law, and I don't pretend to be any great expert, the will would still stand except the ex-wife wouldn't benefit, so the bulk of Fred's estate would go to his sisters."

"The two ladies in the front row whom you were sitting with."

"Yep. Yes, sir."

All eyes turned to them. They were as stiff as stone statues, their expressions blank.

"You've been providing legal services to them for the last several months?"

"Ever since Fred bit the . . . since his demise. He left behind a thriving forest-harvesting business and had enormous property holdings."

"We're talking about many millions of dollars in total value?"

"At least, maybe twenty million on the accounting sheets I've seen. Again, I just did the joe jobs, the Vancouver lawyers handled the big stuff."

"That big stuff seems to be in stasis, does it not? Lots of Trudd's properties are up for sale, but they're not moving. Including his own house." I was blatantly leading my own witness, but without a murmur of complaint. It felt especially strange, almost sinister, that Kroop was letting me go at it.

"Well, the properties aren't going to move if the will is still being probated. It's a complicated estate. There's some problem with administering it, I assume. I'm not privy to what's going on in the big Georgia Street boardrooms."

"Are you not aware that the 1961 will was revoked in the course of Trudd's divorce proceedings?"

Hogey struggled. "Now, I'm not sure if I ever knew that. I never had anything to do with that divorce. Like I say, I'm mostly on the outside looking in. Not seeing much, though."

"Would you be surprised to learn that Mr. Trudd did not have a valid will as of the day of his demise? That he died intestate?"

The strain was showing. I felt bad for him, but he had played loose with the canons of ethics. "He died intestate? To be honest, I don't think I knew that either. I mean, I can't say one way or another if he had a valid will. I'm guessing that you know. Because you talked to Mr. Delaire."

I went into my briefcase. "I have James Delaire's affidavit, Milord, sent by telecopier. I'm hoping we can save him a trip up here by accepting it as an admission of fact."

Kroop excused the jury, and powered through it without leaving the bench. Santorini and Clara took longer, Kroop waiting them out with toe-tapping impatience. Finally: "Mr. Delaire is well known to me as an expert in his chosen field. Indeed, he served as my tutorial instructor in wills many years ago. Frankly, I see nothing in this affidavit that could seriously be contested — it doesn't disclose anything that might be privileged."

Santorini got the message. We agreed the affidavit would be accepted as uncontested fact.

Throughout this interlude, Hogey stared into space, avoiding eye contact with Angelina, with me, with the Trudd sisters, and with the returning jurors. He jumped slightly as I resumed examining him.

"Mr. Johnson, before we deal with Mr. Delaire's affidavit, let's return to the events of last May. You regularly met with or spoke to Fred Trudd in the ten days before his death, according to your daybook."

"Well, I guess you looked at that, too, while you enjoyed the hospitality of my office." Finally, rebellion. "Yes, we had a few confabs, Fred and me."

"And they were about drafting a new will?"

Taking umbrage: "Young fella, I think we're getting into privileged conversations."

Kroop, who had had enough of Hogey's evasiveness, said, "Counsel is merely asking what subject was discussed."

"Sorry, Your Lordship. Okay, yes, a will, he wanted a new will, finally."

I carried on: "Mr. Delaire avers he received instructions from you by telephone on the morning of Friday, May twentieth, relating to a new will for the deceased. Do you see that? Numbered paragraph fourteen."

"Well, now, again you're asking me to disclose privileged —"

Kroop: "No, he's not. No one's asking you what was said. Did you talk to Mr. Delaire that day or not?"

Hogey reeled back, as if avoiding a punch. Anxious to pack it in by Friday, Kroop was letting me fire at will. I was cross-examining my own witness and testing that sacrosanct barrier known as solicitor-client privilege.

Hogey now seemed in fear of this judge. "I'm sorry, Milord. I'm not sure of the date, but we talked a couple of times. Around then. Third week of May. I was a conduit, I passed on Fred's, ah, concerns to Russell, DuMoulin. They did everything, Fred's company, his timber licences, his wills."

I put it to Hogey that on Monday, May 23, at the Fort Thompson airport, he picked up an envelope sent by Delaire via Pacific Western Air Courier.

He stumbled through his answer: "That could be, yes, I recall that now, going to the airport, and . . . I must have mislaid, or put it aside . . . Oh, maybe I took the envelope to the office, intending to go over the terms with Fred . . . I remember having trouble reaching him. That's about all I can say. I wasn't expecting to be a witness here."

I showed him a copy of his desk calendar reminder for Monday, May 30: "FCT here 2 p.m.," and asked if that might jog his memory.

"Okay, that means Frederick C. Trudd had an appointment at my office for when he got back from Pouce Coupe." Hogey frowned, the wheels of his brain cells churning. "Maybe I left the will with Fred to look over until after the weekend. That's probably why I can't find it."

"You didn't run off a copy for yourself?"

"My secretary, Sibyl, would normally do that."

"Miss Frick never saw that document, did she? You didn't want her to see it."

I had gone too far, even for time-obsessed Wilbur Kroop. "Counsel, I'm giving you lots of leeway, but you can't quarrel with your own witness, let alone pillory him. Let's move it along."

"I'll pick up the pace, Milord. Mr. Johnson, is it fair to say that a serious rift developed between the deceased and his two sisters last May?"

Fucking bitches! Trudd yelled that to his phone as Marsha Bigelow stormed into his office. That afternoon, he went on a marathon bender before invading Angelina's bathroom.

Hogey took too much time. "Answer it!" Kroop demanded.

"Sorry, Your Lordship, but I'm worried about the solicitor-client relation—"

"Your client is dead!"

"Excuse me, but I understood a lawyer has to keep his client's disclosures even past the grave."

Kroop went red, less in anger than embarrassment over his knee-jerk interruption — he knew Hogey was indisputably right. That fundamental rule would have been taught at Jim Delaire's tutorial on wills.

His Lordship tried to recover, but lamely: "The rule doesn't apply to conversations outside the solicitor-client bond. It doesn't apply to talking about the weather or the price of tea in China or whether a rift developed between the deceased and his sisters. Just answer the question."

"Okay, well, Fred had a . . . I guess you could call it a fit, over what Hortense and Donalda were up to . . . nothing illegal or wrong, they were perfectly in their rights."

That was intended for their ears — he even gave them a nod of assurance. I was in no doubt that Hogey had cuddled up to them after Trudd's death, anticipating future fat fees from these multi-millionaires-in-waiting — they would finance his retirement plan, his cottage under the palms.

"They were in their rights to do what?"

"To sell their stock in Trudd Enterprises."

I fumbled from my briefcase a certified document that Hubbell had got from the corporate registry. It showed that Hortense and Donalda each held fifty shares in Trudd Enterprises Inc. Fred had the other nine hundred. I filed it as an exhibit, passed copies around.

"Their hundred shares represented a lot of money — a couple of million, right?"

"They were Class A, freely transferable, so yeah."

I took a leap. "Who did they offer them to — MacMillan Bloedel?"

"Crown Zellerbach —" Hogey screeched to a halt. "I don't know that. I was just told."

"They were negotiating with that corporation behind their brother's back, right?"

"Objection." Ed Santorini finally remembered he had a role to play.

"Sustained. Mr. Beauchamp, I'd appreciate it if you followed the rules. You are not to cross-examine your own witness."

"Sorry, Milord, I was doing so only to speed things along. I shall refrain." To Hogey: "And has the sale of those shares been completed?"

"No, sir, because after Fred was gone Hortense and Donalda put a hold on it."

"Because they expected to inherit *all* his shares."

"Don't answer that. *Please*, Mr. Beauchamp."

"Mr. Johnson, what was the issue you wanted to discuss with Fred Trudd on his return from Pouce Coupe?" Again I skirted close to the danger zone of lawyer-client privilege.

Hogey waited for an objection that never came. Finally: "His will. The new will."

"I see. So did you actually read it? Did you open Mr. Delaire's envelope and read it?"

"Young fella, you know I can't disclose its contents. And I won't. And neither did Jim Delaire in that affidavit of yours. Lawyers get disbarred for doing that."

That assertion would backfire on Hogey. He was ill prepared for the stand, of course, but I'd had no moral duty to give him advance notice, let alone advise him to review forgotten notations on his desk calendar.

His disintegration was painful to watch. I showed him his note for Monday, May 23, with the name "Wyatt" and Donalda's phone number in Kelowna. He couldn't remember why he wrote that note. He had no reason to call Donalda Wyatt. She was not then his client.

He turned white as he stared at his scribbles for Wednesday, May 25: "Northways, arr. 1130," and "AHM 4 pm, no drinks." He had no idea what that meant, though he conceded that Northways was a charter service based in Prince George. "AHM" looked like somebody's initials. Yes, it could have stood for Alaska Highway Motel, but he wasn't sure. He could not remember showing up there at four p.m., or at any time, drunk or sober.

I asked the court officer to fetch Percy Edgursen from the witness room. When the bald, stocky retired policeman entered, I asked Hogey: "Do you recognize this gentleman?"

"Percy. Percy Edgursen."

"Owner of the Alaska Highway Motel. Retired RCMP sergeant. You know him as a fellow Rotarian, right?"

Hogey nodded. Faintly: "Yes, of course. Real good fella."

I had Edgursen produce the hotel register for May 25, showing unit nineteen taken by Hortense Trudd-Stephens, unit nine by "Mr. and Mrs. Connor Wyatt." The courtroom was as silent as a graveyard on a still winter's day as I read out those names and had two pages from the register marked as exhibits.

Those tasks done, I sent off Edgursen and returned to Hogey. "Were you aware that Mr. Edgursen was outside planting crocuses among his crabapple trees as you pulled in?"

"I'm having trouble bringing that back. It's been six months . . . I'm not sure what I was doing there . . ."

"Let me refresh your memory. You parked your Mercury sedan behind a utility shed, and you slipped around to unit nine, and were greeted by Connor Wyatt at the door to room nine. He invited you in, remember that?"

Kroop sighed audibly, a signal he was frustrated with my continuing delinquency. But he didn't box my ears, probably because he was exasperated with this witness, his faux-faulty memory, his prevarications.

I took his silence as permission to persist: "Donalda's husband, Connor. A hometown boy, born and raised in Fort Tom. Conn Wyatt, well known to the law-abiding community here."

The grunt of affirmation came not from Hogey but Rummy Wilcox, who caught the subtle allusion. He covered up by clearing his throat. Behind him, Ranjeet Singh valiantly tried to smother a smile.

"Connor's a friend," Hogey said. "He's got a good business down there in Kelowna, a car dealership." He took a deep breath and shifted course, a last chance at salvation: "Okay, it's looking bad for me here, but I got to admit that around that time, the last week of May, I was drinking like a fish. Fred was giving me a ton of grief, and I was in a kind of fog. I think I kind of repressed my memory of driving out there, for some reason . . ." He trailed off.

"Was the plan to discuss the will Mr. Delaire drafted — does that ring a bell?"

Hogey literally scratched his head, as if to rouse his memory cells.

"The will that somehow disappeared — did you give it to Donalda and Hortense?"

"I wouldn't've done that."

"You shared it with them, Hogey."

"I only remember sharing a bottle of Scotch whisky. The rest is still mighty cloudy."

"Were you so drunk on that Wednesday afternoon that you let them read the unsigned will?" No answer. "Maybe Hortense and Donalda will remember when I call them up here."

Hogey looked at them, frantic, then at Santorini, imploringly, as might a swimmer being swept away in a riptide while the lifeguard checked the baseball scores.

He finally spoke, in a trembling voice: "His sisters had been there for Fred in the old days, they'd been partners, enablers. They helped him amass his wealth, and he treated them like dirt. The least I could do was break it to them gently. Give them a heads-up so they could reach out to Fred, talk sense to him . . . I didn't see harm in that. I didn't . . ." He petered out.

"Twenty minutes ago, you said, 'Lawyers get disbarred for that.' You betrayed your oath as a solicitor, Hogey."

Kroop seemed to have given up on me. He scowled at Ed Santorini: it was *his* job to object to my leading questions and rhetoric. But Eddie's back was turned to him, as he reacted to a loud scuffling from the sisters. They worked their way to the aisle, then made like frantic, flightless chickens to the door, coats flapping, scarves trailing.

I'm not sure whether that flurried exodus caused me to snap, or my piercing headache prompted it, but I found myself thundering away: "You told them: Read it and weep, ladies, because you're about to be disinherited! Your vindictive brother is coming back on Monday to sign on the dotted line, so what are you going to do about it?"

I was in such a temper that I never heard Kroop threaten to cite me for contempt and order me removed from the room. Suddenly, I was nearly jerked off my feet by the court officer, and marched out through the prisoners' doorway.

Arthur —
October 2022

I am sitting at my laptop in my Stoney-solar-powered writing cabin (once again I have underestimated that scoundrel), when I'm alerted to an email from Lisa Throckmorton. It begins: "Despite your having cut me off like I was the Queen of Spam, I continue to toil on your behalf. Because I *believe* in you. I believe in *Defensiveness*, it's a great story, great characters, just needs a little, shall we say, *lubrication*. I can help you with that."

I don't want to encourage this impostor, so I haven't been responding to her occasional messages, but I enjoy them. I suppose her playful title *Defensiveness* is a dig at me for shunning prurient prose.

The email continues: "Based on your incomplete mss, a major publishing house is offering a six-fig advance, including rights to film and stage. They plan to enter it for all the big literary awards, *but in the fiction category.* They say no one will believe your story is actually true (especially your allegedly sexless 'affair' with Clara Gracey, nee Moncrief). However, all bets are off if you don't fabricate a happy ending."

It concludes: "Happy Thanksgiving, you ingrate!"

The address and phone number of the Throckmorton Agency appear below her signature line. I presume they're as phony as her name, but I tap in her number on my cellphone anyway. It rings a few times before a voice I recognize says, "If you're a junk caller, hang up immediately or I will kill you." I presume she then recognizes my number on her screen, because she finds her deep-throated false voice. "Sorry. Throckmorton Agency. How can I help you?"

"By not gloating over how you spoofed me. I should have known right from the start. Your search engine just *chanced* to land on *IslandBleat.ca*? I'm an idiot." And with that, we're both laughing helplessly.

I have to give Taba credit for pulling that off. I haven't waned in my affection for her, even though she caused my marriage to nearly jump the track a few times. And I respect her for not trying to stick it out on our gossipy little island after Margaret made her getaway from Ottawa.

Taba and I carried on in our lighthearted, joshing way for half an hour, making up for lost ground. Her gallery opening was a "smash," with a rave review from the *West End Phoenix*. Margaret Atwood dropped by! I regaled her with my locally infamous sauna adventure with Wholeness and Wellness. She reminisced about the party in my backwoods three years ago when locals sampled over-proof rum from the still of pioneer bootlegger Jeremiah Blunder.

"And it got dark," she recalled. "And you were wandering around in the blackness — you forgot your flashlight."

"I was stuck. There was only a glow from the fire pit."

"Tabatha Jones to the rescue. We were the only warm bodies left — those who hadn't passed out had gone home. Including your lovely wife."

I'm suddenly jittery about this turn in the conversation. I'd allowed Margaret to assume I'd packed a flashlight; there seemed little profit in confessing that Taba had led me to my front gate.

"After one of our stops, I realized I'd forgot to put my panties back on. I don't suppose they were ever found. Red with white trim?"

I stammered: "You . . . what?"

"Kidding."

1966 —
The Cat Is Out of the Bag

"Visitor!" called the guard, as he led Santorini into the men's wing of the RCMP lockup. I was in unit four, next to fat Arnie, who'd punched out the lights of his wife's lover, then kicked her down a flight of stairs. The cell opposite housed a multiple offender who ran off with the Salvation Army donations pot. He wanted to retain me.

"Welcome to La Cage aux Fools, Eddie. I kind of blew it."

"You're gonna have to suck cock, and you better hope you can bring him off. We're on lunch break, so you got time to rehearse." He sat on the cot beside me. "Way to go, Beauchamp, you hustled that poor fucker's secretary until she was creaming her pants. She gave you everything, right? Told you about Hogey's sneaky little meeting with those two dumb broads."

"Did they get to the airport okay?"

"They took the first flight out. Milk run through the Peace River to Edmonton. Didn't even pack their suitcases." A pause. "Who else have you got left? The motel guy. I'm not going to touch him, he's another fucking local everybody loves. But your Virgin Mary — I'm gonna be on her like the Normandy invasion, I'm itching to strip away that false front of pious sweetness."

"Yeah, that should impress the jury: attack an innocent rape victim who gives up her free days helping elders and feeding the poor. Enough with the bravado, Eddie. Why are you here? Are those Grey Cup tickets burning a hole in your pocket?"

. A sound that was more of a groan than a sigh. "C'mon, let's call it a wrap and blow this burg. I'll take manslaughter with a fifteen-year maximum, and let you chisel me down to twelve."

"Kroop hates me too much to rubber-stamp a plea deal. He'll give her life just to teach me a lesson."

"He's all in, pal."

"Who says?"

"He says. Bumped into him in the law library." He mimicked Kroop's cautious overture: "'Surely, Ed, you must have entertained some thoughts about how we might, ah, let us say, *abbreviate* proceedings.'"

"He can stick it up his tight ass."

Kroop watched me like a rattlesnake poised to strike as I abased myself. I was stressed out after a sleepless night. Frustrated with an evasive witness, I snapped, lost control, went off the rails. I could honestly not show cause why I should not be cited for contempt — because I had indeed misbehaved, cross-examined my witness, denounced him for dishonouring our profession.

The benches hadn't been cleared for this event, though the twelve chairs in the jury box were empty. Charles Loobie was writing vigorously, chronicling my humiliation. Clara could barely suppress a skeptical smile, convinced I was posturing, auditioning for the role of Hamlet.

"I shall not hold you in contempt," Kroop announced. "Because incarcerating you for several days — that was my initial impulse — would cause delay that would grossly inconvenience jury, counsel, court staff, and public. I will, however, ensure that your misbehaviour is reported to the discipline committee of the Law Society, so that they might consider suspending your right to practise. However . . ." A deep breath. "I may relent should counsel cooperate to ensure the case goes to the jury before the weekend, preferably by noon on Friday."

I was stunned by this extortionate proposal. I wasn't going to rush Angelina to the stand and whisk her off it without her full story being told. I had anticipated that she would be a full day, including Santorini's cross. And then there would be counsels' jury addresses. And Kroop's directions to the jury. Objections to those instructions. It would be impossible to sandwich all that into an afternoon and the next morning.

"I'll do my best," I said.

In trooped the jury. In came Hogey Johnson from the witness room, looking frazzled. I got a whiff of spirits as he passed by — it struck me then, though I should have recognized it at first meeting, that he was a full-bore alcoholic. I vowed not to end up that way, a fog-brained sot with a law degree. Yes, I would take a holiday from drink. A full month before Christmas break.

Kroop reminded Hogey he was still under oath and warned that "counsel may have a few more questions," with emphasis on *few.*

I rose. "Milord, it's my respectful submission that the witness, by revealing to others the contents of Mr. Trudd's unsigned will, has broken the bond of solicitor-client privilege. So I propose to ask Mr. Johnson, subject to your ruling, to reveal the key terms of that document."

This new, deferential version of counsel for the accused seemed to amuse Kroop, whose lips wiggled into a smile of triumph. "In the interests of justice, Mr. Johnson, I must direct you to answer counsel's question. You have already, by your admission, let the cat out of the bag."

"I don't want to sound flippant," Hogey said, "but cats were the big winners." The whiskies he'd slugged back with his lunch had soothed his rattled nerves: he was almost folksy Hogey again. "The cat hospital in Edmonton would have got a big slice, and our town vet, Dr. Muggins, even more, though the local Chamber of Commerce and our gun club were also mentioned and some kind of conservative think tank I forget the name of. Gifts of maybe a million dollars, all told. But the residue, about twenty million if it was all cashed out, was supposed to go to his cats."

I didn't get it. "His *cats?*"

"The will set up a trust to care for his cats for their lifetime." Gasps and barely stifled laughter from the gallery.

I was afraid to look at Angelina — the cats she'd loved were dead, their nine lives all snuffed out by Hortense and Donalda, but none of Angelina's confidantes, including me, had dared tell her so. I wasn't about to spring that on her in a packed courtroom, and chose my questions carefully.

"This trust fund was just for his six cats? Cats that he would likely outlive?"

"No, no, it was framed to include any cats he owned upon his demise."

"And who would administer this trust?"

"Dr. Jonah Muggins, the vet. Like I say, they got along real good. Fred didn't have anyone else he trusted. Even me."

"And did Dr. Muggins agree to take on this role?"

"I can't see why he wouldn't. That was a lot of play money, twenty million. But I never talked to him, so I assume Fred did, and got his okay. I do know that Dr. Muggins sold his practice last summer and went off to Trinidad or Tobago, or one of those islands, while he waited for the will to be probated, which never happened."

"No more questions."

"I have one," Kroop said. "Mr. Kroop's cats — where are they now?"

I had just sat, and couldn't make lift-off in time, as Hogey said, "Cat heaven, Milord."

"You mean they were put down?"

"Yes, Milord, Canada Day weekend, I believe, they were taken to the river and drowned."

A cry from behind me. Angelina. I could barely summon the strength to turn, but managed to rise, joining a court officer who was handing her tissues as the tears rolled. Dimly, I heard Hogey explain that Hortense and Donalda had instructed their realtor, Wendell Melquist, to arrange for the cats to disappear so the house could be sold more easily.

Several jurors looked distressed, and there was much snuffling in the gallery. Kroop ordered a short break. The jury was hustled out but Angelina stayed.

"I knew," she whispered. "In my heart I knew. But I couldn't believe."

Father Larouche joined us, taking her hand. "They are happy in their heaven, my dear. Believe that." And softly, to me. "But damnation awaits those two bitch sisters."

Santorini seemed unsure whether to attack Hogey or rehabilitate him. His only profitable approach would be to push back on implications that a hired assassin (or bad boy Connor Wyatt) had plugged Fred Trudd. The twenty-million-dollar motive could not be denied. Nor could the friction between sisters and brother.

Santorini lobbed a few easy questions, then got to work: "So, okay, Mr. Johnson, looks like you went off the rails last May when you had that little quickie meeting at the Alaska Highway Motel. You set it up, right?"

"No, sir, I'd have to say it was their idea. I just wanted to alert them that Fred was showing signs of a . . . maybe a mental disturbance. I felt it was my duty."

"How did this mental disturbance manifest itself?"

"Giving his fortune away to whatever cats outlived him — I thought that was a bit crazy. And of course I'd heard the reports about his terrible behaviour to Miss Santos. That wasn't the Fred I knew."

I glanced at Angelina. Her tears had not dried and her head was bowed as she made the sign of the cross.

"He needed help. I didn't know where else to go except his family."

"And so you confided in Donalda and Hortense about them getting beans-all, and his cats getting the whole shebang."

"Well, I guess I did. I had to."

"Let us make one issue abundantly clear. You sat down with them in room nine at that motel, but no one talked about doing Fred Trudd in."

"No, of course not. It was all about finding help for him."

"No one mentioned he was going away for the weekend for a mediation hearing."

A pause. "I can't remember if that came up."

"They used to be a close family here in Fort Thompson, right? A loving family."

"Born and raised here. Their parents are both gone now, but I remember Donalda and Hortense as teenagers, and them being close to their older brother."

"And as you said, when they were young women they helped Fred Trudd build his business."

"Yes, sir."

"And Donalda's husband, Connor, he was a local boy too, right? You implied he was an upright young man, well known to the law-abiding community here."

"Well, I meant that with a touch of irony. He actually ran with a rough crowd, selling dope, spent some time behind bars —"

Lazy Eddie hadn't done his homework. He was visibly rattled. "Okay, we don't need to get into that —"

I was quick to rise. "If it please the court, the witness should be allowed to finish."

Kroop: "Mr. Santorini, you opened the door, and you can't just slam it shut."

Hogey had regained some composure while not under the watchful eyes of the skedaddling sisters. "I was just going to say that Connor had a couple of run-ins with the law back in the fifties, one was for drug trafficking, but to his credit he straightened out after he married Donalda."

"Okay, let's move along. Now we all saw Mrs. Wyatt and Mrs. Trudd-Stephens leave this room in a state of upset over my friend's appalling insinuations that they were somehow connected with the murder —"

"Object!"

"Sustained."

"No more questions."

I rose. "Just a quick question in redirect. If I may, Milord."

"Arising from Mr. Santorini's cross-examination?"

"Arising from my friend's attempt to slam shut the door he'd opened. Mr. Johnson, in addition to the opium trafficking, what was Connor Wyatt's other offence for which he served jail time?"

"Don't answer that," Kroop ordered. "Mr. Wyatt is not on trial. The matter of his reputation should never have been raised, and now this trial is awash with hearsay. I blame both counsel. We'll take the afternoon break."

1966 —
One-Ton Pickup

I had a heavy heart as I watched Hogey exit centre stage: stooped, head bowed, a whipped dog. His excuse for his malpractice — that he'd met with the sisters only out of concern for their disturbed brother — might save him from disbarment but not save his good name. Lazy and forgetful: he was that, but I couldn't believe he was evil, that he plotted with Hortense, Donalda, and Connor to ensure that Fred Trudd would not live long enough to execute his will.

I remained at my table, watching as the room emptied, and caught the eye of Chief Sayaga. He brought his palms together, gently clapping, applauding my performance, and maybe honouring me for not having taken another route.

Johnny Blue also looked directly at me, smiled, gave me two thumbs up, then hugged the young woman who was the chief's office manager. His girlfriend, I gathered.

Clara Moncrief remained at the Crown table, making notes, strenuously ignoring me. She had given up on me since my blind-drunk debauch with Sibyl Frick. I didn't blame her. I too was disgusted with me. As amends to Sibyl, I had sent her a note expressing my gratitude, along with two dozen roses.

I went out to commune with the day's final witness.

Percy Edgursen strolled confidently to the witness stand. The hefty, shiny-domed sixty-eight-year-old would be comfortable there after nearly forty years of service with the BC Police and the RCMP. Like Mike Trasov, his friend and successor as senior officer at the Fort Tom detachment, he was bonded to the Great White North. His motel was a favoured stopover for those travelling the famed Alaska Highway.

I spent several minutes at my easel, painting Percy's portrait for any jurors who didn't know him, then took him to Wednesday, May 25. He'd been out fishing when his desk clerk checked in Hortense, Donalda, and Connor, but wasn't surprised to find out they'd taken rooms — they'd often stayed there during their many jaunts to Fort Thompson.

I asked Edgursen about his luck fishing. He said he'd proudly presented two fat pike to his wife, and she'd promptly returned them to him with a fillet knife. Jurors had a laugh at that.

"So after you cleaned your catch, you changed into your garden gear?"

"Yes, and I went back of the motel with some tulip bulbs. Getting them in kind of late — the crabapples were already flowering. And that's when I saw Hogey Johnson's Mercury pull into the back area, behind our laundry room, which I thought was strange — we have ample parking out front."

Hogey alighted with a briefcase and slipped around to the front, unaware that Edgursen had seen him. Edgursen heard Connor Wyatt greet Hogey and saw an arm reach out to close the Venetian blinds on the two back windows of room nine.

"You've been acquainted with Connor Wyatt for how long?"

"I had occasion to deal with him back in the late forties, when I was serving here with the BC Provincial Police."

"Deal with him in what way?"

"I arrested him for endangering lives. He was using road signs as target practice with a hunting rifle."

"What lives did he endanger?"

"A family of six was driving by in a Nash Rambler. Mom, Dad, four kids. A bullet scarred the roof."

Kroop, who'd insisted half an hour ago that "Mr. Wyatt is not on trial," jumped in with "I assume the fellow faced some serious repercussions."

"Three months incarceration and a year's probation, Your Lordship."

Pleased that the judge had done my work for me, I fast-forwarded to the events of May 25, 1966. "Did you spend any time with these guests on that Wednesday?"

"My wife and I had the Northlands pilot over to share the pike. The others didn't seek out my company. My desk clerk checked them out early in the morning, and they flew out. Except Connor. Two men came by and picked him up a little later."

"Who?"

"I couldn't say. Just caught a glimpse of two fellows in an old one-ton GMC pickup. They pulled away pretty fast."

"Thank you, Mr. Edgursen." I bowed to Santorini. "Your witness."

Eddie gave me a pissed-off look. I'd been ungrateful in rejecting his starting offer of twelve years. Two days earlier, I might have recommended it to my client. Now I was betting all my chips on a not-guilty verdict, gambling that Rummy Wilcox had a soft heart behind that crusty exterior, that he might not whip the other eleven into line.

"Watch me," I'd announced to Clara. I wondered if my fierce hangover had triggered this bout of hubris. I ought to have been focused on whether Angelina, with her sudden recall of repressed memory, would hold up in cross-examination. Santorini would attack with his weapons oiled and razor-honed: the folksy jabs, the sardonic stabs, the tricks and gibes. Yet it would be chancy not putting her on the stand.

Santorini asked, "You saw Mr. Wyatt get into that GMC truck?"

"From the window of my kitchen, which adjoins the office. Connor had gone out to the highway with his bag. He threw it into the bed of the truck and got into the cab."

"It was just an overnight bag? He didn't have a rifle?"

"No rifle."

"Connor was a son of Fort Thompson, born and raised here. Not surprising he might have wanted to stick around a few days and kick back with a few old pals?"

"Not at all. He often came up here to fish and hunt. He'd get together with Fred Trudd for a beer or a meal."

"They were friends, right?"

"It seemed that way."

"Connor never got in trouble during those visits?"

"Not that I'm aware of."

"So it's fair to say his youthful transgressions were well behind him?"

"I've no reason to doubt that."

"He's a success story, right? Runs a lucrative car dealership in Kelowna."

"That's what I've heard."

"Likewise Donalda and Hortense made lots of brief visits up here."

"Maybe not so often as Connor, but yes, they would visit their brother."

"For birthdays, Christmas, Easter, that sort of thing? Just like normal families everywhere."

"Can't argue."

Eddie sat, and Kroop addressed the jury: "We're hoping to wrap up on Friday, so the burden is on counsel to move along sprightly. If no one objects, we'll resume half an hour early tomorrow."

A rush to justice. I feared Angelina would get rattled under the prodding of this haste-making judge.

As I joined her in the coffee lounge, she was tidying up, washing glasses and cups. She seemed fidgety and anxious, was speaking rapidly. "That man Connor Wyatt, he came with his wife to visit Mr. Trudd maybe three or four times since I worked there. Good-looking man, big talker, big drinker, like Mr. Trudd."

"Did he do any hunting on these visits?"

"Maybe some ducks once . . . Should I say he liked to shoot deers?"

"It's best if you just say what you remember." Hollow advice, after all my prompting.

"I can make you coffee. Or tea? There are fig bars in the fridge." She had her back to me, drying cutlery with a tea towel.

"No, thanks. Please sit down."

She perched, rather than sat. I found it disturbing that she couldn't look me in the eye. Those fidgeting hands were twined around her necklace and its crucifix.

"Mr. Beauchamp, I told you that I saw a car coming down the road from the hills."

"I have a note that you were in the kitchen and saw a little Jeep raising dust."

"I made a mistake. Now I remember it was a truck, a big pickup."

This was pathetically untruthful. She had adapted her story to fit with Percy Edgursen's observation that Connor Wyatt was met by friends in an old GMC one-ton. I was the Svengali who had corrupted the incorruptible — I had transformed this virtuous maiden into an inelegant liar. "I will try harder," she'd promised her speech trainer.

I took a deep breath. "Angelina, I need to know what you're going to say when Mr. Santorini asks you why you fired that rifle."

She spoke rapidly: "He called me a dirty little whore, and told me to come and kiss his cock — his penis, I mean, and I was so scared, and I fired a warning shot into the air, and then a loud bang came from where the truck disappeared, and he twisted around and fell on his stomach."

When she finally made eye contact, her look was intense and pleading: *I'm trying my best. Is this what you wanted?*

Suddenly, those eyes flooded. I passed her a tissue, and she hid behind it. Her attempt at fabrication had caused her great emotional and spiritual damage. I couldn't find the will or the words to tell her she was transparently lying, and that the jury would know she falsely swore an oath on the Bible.

Santorini would quickly find an advantage, playing on her deep religious feelings, accusing her of lying in the face of God, but not before letting the jury know he came from pious Italian Catholic stock. Angelina would cave in. Angelina had never learned how to lie.

I was mindful of another dictum from the great Smythe-Baldwin: *An equivocating client is a witness best not heard.* Quite so — I dared not risk putting her on the stand, even though the jury might wonder what she was trying to hide by invoking her right to silence. Thankfully, the law forbids prosecutors and judges from making adverse comments to the jury about an accused's failure to testify.

By paring down Friday's business, I would brighten the hearts of prosecutor and judge —Eddie's chances of making it to the Grey Cup would be enhanced, and Wilbur Kroop, itching to escape the harsh northern climate, would likely be on the same flight. I couldn't bear the thought of being cooped up in a small plane with them, and had booked with Pacific Western — though I'd considered taking the bus back, a form of self-flagellation to atone for my sins.

1966 —
Murder or Nothing

I slunk down Main Street to Rustlers, alone, wanting no company but that of a thick T-bone steak, protein to fuel tomorrow's speech to the jury. Marsha set me up at Hogey's table, assuring me the wounded Rotarian would not be showing himself in public for a while. She offered to buy me a drink but I found the strength to decline.

Clara Moncrief was at the bar, all bright-eyed and hip in her peace-symbol denim jacket, sitting knees to knees with the hulking Canadian Press photographer. I was no longer on her radar. She barely acknowledged me — a glance, a look of pity at the exhausted, bedraggled lonely soul sitting uncomfortably on the throne of the old lawyer he'd flogged.

My order arrived, sizzling on a cedar plank, then Charles Loobie squeezed past the waiter, approaching me like a sniffing dog. He asked if I minded him joining me for a minute, then didn't wait for an answer, and sat, plunking down a mug of coffee.

"You got yourself another front page, pal — I just filed a colour piece about Kroop busting you for going off half-cocked. Wrote it up so it looks like you were being spontaneous instead of faking it."

"Very kind of you, Charles." I dug into my steak.

"Even kinder of me, I'm suppressing the story about how you got the dirt on Hogey by seducing his Girl Friday."

My headache was coming back. "Where did that come from?"

"Ed Santorini, via Clara Moncrief, whom you used and tossed aside. While you're fucking your way around Fort Thompson, you may want to hit on that teenybopper who writes for the local rag, she's all googly-eyed over you."

"I heard that your tantrum about her scoop made the evening news. I'm surprised you didn't get the axe."

"I'm the *Province*'s top gun, amigo. I sell a shitload of paper. One question, then I'm outta here. Nobody's talking about what it means that Trudd died intestate. His sisters are next of kin, so they get all of it, right? Unless you prove they put a hit on him — and then what, the government grabs everything?"

"The *Province* can't afford to pay for a wills expert?"

"They're working on it. Thought you'd know." He drained his mug, and stood. "Eddie wangled a government Beaver to fly him down Saturday in time for the game. He wants you to know there's a seat for you if the guilty verdict comes in by tomorrow night."

"Well, you tell him miracles can happen."

Loobie weaved his way toward the bar, toward Clara, then took a sharp left turn to the door on seeing she was flirting with the brawny cameraman who'd bear-hugged him. They were drinking hot rums. *I like it hot and buttered.*

I would have sold my ravaged soul for a glass of well-aged whisky. But I'd promised myself to hang on until a verdict was announced — an occasion for either celebration or a drowning of sorrows. Meanwhile, I needed a clear head to work on my jury speech, and that done, to wink out for a solid eight hours of sleep.

Getting up courage to brave the freezing night, I paid my tab, then stalled at the door, unsure where I'd parked my car. Probably back of the police station, my usual spot. It came to me, suddenly, that in my helpless, hungover condition, I hadn't plugged in the block heater.

"I worry, given your fucked-up state, that you don't know what you're doing." Clara slowed for an icy patch as she peered through her windshield into the starlit night. "Not giving Angelina her day in court? That's freaking crazy."

"I won't have her enduring Eddie's prodding, with his false, sleazy innuendos. She has already been raped by one prick, she doesn't have to relive the experience. And I don't want her to miscarry in the courtroom. Take the next left."

It hadn't been hard to entice her away from the photographer. He'd bored her with his career highlights, which included his award-winning coverage of Vancouver's Grey Cup riot of 1963. He'd turned her off by anticipating "an even better riot" on the coming weekend. (In fact, such a riot did occur in 1966, as a preliminary to the Grey Cup, with downtown shop windows smashed and 300 drunken hooligans arrested.)

"You got any of that Jamaican rum left?"

"Only for you, Clara. I'm levelling off."

The Harris Hunting Lodge loomed brightly in the darkness.

Again, my hosts had stoked up a welcoming fire. Clara was stretched cat-like on the couch with her hot rum. I'd brewed some Lipton's. Files, exhibits, photos, and partial transcripts were spread across the table, along with lined pages inscribed with my rough notes for the jury address.

Clara continued to disparage my strategy of muting Angelina. "She's got to swear on the Bible, to the Father, the Son, and the Holy Ghost, that she's fucking innocent. You've been banging the drum all week about an assassin in the bush. Where's your proof? A hard-of-hearing octogenarian who got confused by the echoes? Angelina is your only hope." Mimicking: "I heard a distant shot, sir, and it startled me so much that I fell against the door and the gun went off."

"She can't lie. It's not in her genes. She tried, mind you, as a kind of favour to me, and she visibly recoiled — as if she feared her God was about to smite her down."

Clara sang in a sultry off-key: "'I didn't know the gun was loaded.' Can't she just make that her refrain? Or a wayward warning shot — you've been pitching that one hard."

"Clara, I intend her to walk from that courtroom as a free woman. Your scenarios open up manslaughter, and I'm no longer interested in giving the jury that option. I won't allow her newborn to become a chattel of the social welfare system. That would destroy her. Nor am I interested in cooking up a spurious defence. I won't lose my soul to win an acquittal."

"How righteous of you. You will hold your head high as she prays for your salvation at her prison bedside."

How incongruous, I thought, how absurd — here was a state-appointed junior prosecutor denouncing counsel for the accused for failing to mount a robust defence. It seemed not to bother her that her senior remained blissfully unaware of her role as collaborator.

"Okay, Stretch, if she can't lie, what's the truth she's afraid of speaking?"

"Trudd traumatized her to the point of amnesia. I have to be honest and live with that when I address the jury."

She would not let up. "Christ, Arthur, you're gambling on murder or nothing, and putting all your chips on winning without a single, innocent word from your client. How arrogant! You think your speech will sway Rummy Wilcox? He scowls at Angelina like he's sizing her up for a noose."

"He can't help it. His face is hard-wired to look pissed off."

She frowned over the mess of paper on my table. "Gee, Stretch, you worked so hard preparing her for the stand. What a waste of effort."

My offer to help her into her coat was rejected, so I just led her to the door. I could not comprehend why she was so riled up. Was it something I said? Or did? Or didn't do?

"Maybe she wants to be heard. Have you asked her? Or do you bother consulting with your clients about such things?"

"I'll have a word with her early tomorrow. Thank you for your input. Oh, and for the ride."

The door opened to a blast of frigid air. She turned her back to me without a word or a wave.

Arthur —
November 2022

L ate November is upon us here at Blunder Bay Farm; the blustery winds off the Pacific Ocean bend the boughs of conifers and whip free the last clinging leaves of alders and maples. Boisterous, chirping juncos flit outside my writing studio: patriots, like their pals, the chickadees, refusing to desert my feeders for warmer, foreign climes.

It is also late November in Fort Thompson, though much colder. I shiver at the memory of young Arthur's frozen toes and nose.

It is fifty-six years since the Santos trial, almost to the very day. Fifty-six years since that ludicrous spat with Clara Moncrief on the eve of my jury address: a speech that would either be the crowning point of my young career or a crushing disaster. Looking back over the many decades, I see my muzzling of my client as a reckless high-stakes gamble, and (yes, Clara) arrogant. The audacity of youth prevailed over cool-headedness.

I wanted to think of myself as a noble knight, pure of heart. Yet I had coaxed Angelina to fabricate, to fill in the amnesic blanks. A shady counsel like Alex Pappas might have turned a blind eye to Angelina's suddenly souped-up memory. He would abide her perjury without compunction. Were I to follow that path, the disease of corruption would set in and I would soon be mired in the sleaze — just another cheap crook with a law degree. That's how young Prince Arthur justified his refusal to believe his client's eleventh-hour revelations.

Early on, I'd convinced myself that this case was defenceless (thus the unwieldy tentative title) but as I mined its layers I dug up nuggets of hope. Ungainly Arthur found his footing during the trial, attaining unexpected levels of forensic prowess. (I hope this doesn't sound boastful, but doubtless it does.) But had I done well enough to woo and win my audience of twelve good women and men? That final Friday of November of 1966 was my last shot, and my aim had to be unerring.

Ah, but little did I know that the trial would end in a most surprising way, and that the aftermath would offer such a bumper crop of riddles and wiggles, confounding our unsuspecting hero. Twists, they are called in the lexicon of fictional thrillers, but only rarely to be found in the table d'hôte of true crime.

Carry on, young fella . . .

1966 —
Great Speeches Flow
from the Heart

When I awoke in the morning darkness, I was shivering, still in my clothes. Around midnight, I'd plopped onto the couch to give my brain a rest before revising my speech once more.

What woke me, shortly before eight o'clock, was the roar of a plane directly above, an airliner descending.

I fed split spruce onto the embers of my fire, and as I warmed myself by the licking flames I saw last night's handwritten pages scattered over the table and on the floor. A mouse attack — I hadn't put away the cheddar and saltines I'd been nibbling.

As I towelled off I heard another aircraft pass overhead, lower, causing the Harrises' huskies to protest loudly. Who were these invading forces?

Eventually, the answer came from my bedside radio: an overexcited CBC correspondent had disembarked from a chartered DC-6 at the Fort Tom landing strip, as had her camera crew and a contingent from the Seattle NBC affiliate.

"Quite the milling crowd of media here, Brad." She went on to explain the reason for such excitement: the yet-unborn child of a young Filipina maid being tried for murder seemed destined to become a multi-millionaire.

"But here's the hitch, Brad — only if Miss Santos is found not guilty. That's according to several experts including Professor Eli Sowcher, acting dean of law at UBC. And then only if Miss Santos can prove she was impregnated by her alleged rapist. To add further intrigue, the victim appears to have met his demise just before he was to have signed a new will."

"Goodness. And when will those issues be decided, Audrey?"

"Hopefully, the case will go to the jury today. Meanwhile, a side plot is playing out, involving a scrappy young criminal lawyer and the judge who jailed him after an outburst —"

I abandoned the radio, moved into the kitchen, where my coffee was percolating. I wondered why the hell Clara had got so combative, so put out with me. Had I somehow rebuffed her? Had she expected an invitation to stay over? (Women's moods confused me back then, in my late twenties. They still do.)

I heard engine noise outside, and saw Buck Harris pull up in a snowmobile. He raised two fingers in a victory sign, left the motor running, and strolled off.

I pepped myself up with another mug of coffee, then swept the little pebbles of mouse shit from my table, sending pages of my speech flying. Cyrus Smythe-Baldwin intoned: *All great speeches flow from not the pen but the heart.* I gathered the scattered pages, and tossed them into the woodstove.

I tucked in my shirt, adjusted my tie, shrugged into my coat, jumped aboard the snowmobile, and blasted through a snow-bank, pumping myself up with a loud "Yahoo" as I headed off to town.

In the RCMP coffee lounge, as we waited for Angelina, I asked Etienne Larouche for his frank assessment of our jury. An acute observer of character, he'd watched them closely. When witnesses touched on religion, he'd told me, their expressions and body language spoke louder than words.

"I would say almost all are devout Christians. Not Ranjeet Singh, of course, but he is clearly with you. Angelina's devotion to God is an asset, but that may be outweighed by the skepticism aroused by her failure to proclaim her innocence under oath."

Etienne had not hidden his dismay at my strategy of shielding Angelina from cross-examination. He had more faith in her than I, but then he was a man of faith while I had no firm belief in either God or my client's newly enhanced powers of recall.

"Rummy Wilcox?"

"An incorrigible Baptist, head to toe. No friend of Rome, and conservative to the core. As to the political views of the rest, I doubt that any lean left. Those of the far right may feel allied with Fred Trudd's extremist views. Northerners are deeply patriotic, and believe in law and order, yet they distrust government — so in that regard they may see you as David standing up to Goliath. They dislike beatniks and draft dodgers, and are leery of outsiders, especially liberals from the big city, I regret to say. I pray you can overcome that."

Religion, conservatism, traditional values. *Know your jury*, said Smythe-Baldwin. I felt I did know this jury, thanks to my upbringing. My parents would not feel out of place here were they not such snobs.

"The local population is also heavily into sport and the outdoors, Arthur, so you may want to keep that in mind. Hunting, fishing, hockey, curling. They'll all be watching the Grey Cup tomorrow."

Angelina appeared, looking as pretty as a bouquet, wearing a flowery yellow maternity dress with a blouse of light lavender, under a dark lavender jacket. A new outfit, donated by a local dressmaker. I left her alone with Etienne for a couple of minutes so he could give her his blessing.

"Good luck," he said, tonelessly, as he departed and I entered.

Angelina offered me a mug of milky coffee, which I politely sipped, though I'd already overloaded on caffeine. She sat, looked directly at me. "Father Larouche says I am blessed to have such a lawyer like you. He says you advise me not to speak. You know what is the best plan. I am in your hands, as I am in the hands of Jesus."

I felt relief hearing that. And she seemed relieved too, at not having to testify. I could almost hear her thanking Jesus for being freed from having to profane his teachings.

I told her that the rules required me to speak first, followed by prosecutor and judge. She should not be surprised if the jury debated through the weekend and beyond before reaching a verdict. The strain of waiting, I said, can often be intense. I added, foolishly, "Remember that you are carrying another life."

"I'll try not to forget."

I deserved that one. She forgave me with a lovely, open smile. That's how I wanted the jury to see her — glowing with innocence.

There was jostling going on outside our courtroom, as a number of locals seeking entry were cordoned off to make way for the media's swollen ranks. Inside, a bank of seats near the press table was reserved for the media overflow.

Eddie Santorini was in a fine mood, enjoying the attentions of the press corps, quipping with them. In the robing room, he'd groused that I'd not given him fair notice that the accused would not be testifying. "Damn," he said. "I was gonna eat her alive." But he was obviously pleased — he might yet make it to the game on time.

Clara may have forgotten we were to start early, at nine-thirty, and she came puffing in just as the jurors were getting settled. She strode up centre aisle, looking straight ahead, ignoring everyone, especially me. I suspected she felt guilty about her sharp words from last evening.

"All rise," said the clerk as Kroop entered, putting on an air of nonchalance for the media that misfired when he slightly overshot his padded chair. He'd been thrust into stardom, this brittle newbie judge who'd jailed the scrappy criminal lawyer, and he may have been battling a sudden bout of stage fright.

I rose and announced, "The defence rests."

Kroop looked at me blankly, as if expecting me to provide additional information. Finally, still standing, I said, "May I now sum up to the jury?"

"You have no further witnesses?" He looked from me to Angelina, then to me again.

"Miss Santos has suffered enough pain," I said. "She shouldn't have to relive her ordeal in this courtroom."

Kroop reddened, perceiving rightly that my response was a calculated rebuke to his dumb question. "Are you ready then?"

"Animis opibusque parati," I said.

Kroop, lacking Latin, waited for a translation.

"Ready for anything, Milord."

I bowed, a mock show of respect that served as a brisk send-off as I turned to the jury.

"Good morning, ladies and gentlemen. I have to confess I had a speech all written out, and then I decided to toss it and just talk to you straight. Hopefully, without interruptions and spurious objections." I got some smiles from the jury when I stabbed a finger toward the prosecutors. "We had a lot of scuffles, as you may have noticed. Things can get heated when you're battling the all-powerful state, when you're fighting, as I am, for the freedom of the gentle young rape victim in the prisoners' dock. It got so bad that I talked myself into a jail cell."

I threw in the anecdote about the jailbird who'd wanted me to represent him for stealing the Sally Ann donations pot. "Things don't get bleaker than that, folks." I didn't chance a peek at Kroop, who I assume was fuming. But friendly laughter from the gallery and a few chuckles from the jurors encouraged me to desert my table and approach the jury box.

"I got so flummoxed I forgot to plug in my car last evening, and had to bum a ride out to Buck Harris's lodgings out past the reserve.

If anyone saw an odd duck in a suit, tie, and overcoat pulling into town on a Ski-Doo this morning, that was me." Reporters lapped that up. Rummy Wilcox's built-in scowl didn't break, but others of the twelve smiled generously.

With the jury warmed up, I hoped to blunt any suspicions that my client was hiding behind her statutory right to keep her mouth shut. "Let me repeat myself. Miss Santos has suffered enough pain. She is six months pregnant. Surely she should be afforded the right and the dignity not to be forced to relive her ordeal before the eyes and ears of the world." I swept an arm toward the media bank. Juror Twelve, a woman, nodded emphatically.

"Let me add this: often, there's not much reason for an accused to testify. That's the situation here, because the case against Angelina Santos is so empty, so flabby, that it would be offensive to force her to relive the traumas she has suffered — the drunken sexual assaults, the violent rape, the chilling threats of future harm. God forbid that this pious mother-to-be must endure being prodded and probed in cross-examination as she's urged to recall every gross detail of her nightmare at the hands of her employer: the groping under her blouse, the drunken ogling in her bathroom, the brutal attack and the forced penetration."

My voice was a wrathful growl. Smythe-Baldwin whispered a warning: *Don't overdo, stay in control.* I softened my tone. "Those horrific events induced bouts of amnesia that shielded her from memories of being raped, and from the perils she faced on Fred Trudd's return on Sunday. And I'm sure you folks have heard about how amnesia clouds the pain felt by survivors of severe accidents or, during wartime, the brave, wounded soldiers who fought for country and freedom."

To bring this home, I fetched Exhibit Thirteen, the medical report by the Prince George prison doctor who'd examined Angelina after she was remanded in custody. "Dr. Genevieve Royce wrote here, in paragraph six, 'It is not uncommon for rape victims to suffer amnesia, especially if the traumatic event involves severe violence and threats.' And Dr. Royce's professional opinion was that Miss Santos indeed suffered partial, significant amnesias. That's the evidence before you, folks. Uncontested by the Crown."

I sensed wariness from some jurors, doubt silently expressed. Had she not confessed? *I shot him. Why? He raped me.* I heard Rummy Wilcox asking, *How do you get around that, Mr. Hotshot Vancouver Lawyer?*

"I'm not going to quarrel with the evidence that Angelina said, 'I shot him,' to those two young constables, except to emphasize that her words to the dispatcher came earlier and were therefore more reliable: 'I think I shot Mr. Trudd.' *I think.* Means she's not sure. It may mean she was amnesic about firing that rifle. It may mean that on coming out of her blackout, seeing that Remington rifle, seeing the body, she may have simply concluded she'd shot him."

Angelina sat tall, head bowed, her hands on her belly, as if comforting the life within, as I offered the jury those several interpretations, light appetizers for them to chew on.

"'I shot him.' 'I think I shot him.'" I spread my hands and shrugged. "Either way, those aren't the words of a cold-blooded killer. A murderer would lie. Angelina Santos had every opportunity to lie. But she saw no other obvious explanation, and she spoke what she assumed was the truth."

She raised her eyes as I strolled toward her, and those eyes were damp. I dipped into a vest pocket and removed a clean, folded handkerchief, and she smiled her thanks and daubed her eyes with it. Whispers from the gallery, the sound of scribbling pencils.

"Here we have a deeply religious young lady, barely out of her teens, holding a rifle for the first time in her life, unaware it was loaded, with no idea *how* to load it, how to work the bolt action. She was so unfamiliar with handling long guns that she got a bruised shoulder from its kick. Now reflect on this image: she's sobbing uncontrollably, throwing up, in a state of shock, yet she finds the strength to do the right thing, to call the police. As she awaits them she prays. She affirms that the Lord is her shepherd.

'I shall not want. He maketh me to lie down in green pastures.'"
Lines softly voiced. A hush descended.

"When those two young constables show up, she has nothing to hide; she's open, candid — is this a woman with murder in her heart? This young woman to whom the Lord gave comfort as she walked through the valley of the shadow of death."

Kroop's face was red with wrath over what he saw as my pandering to the jury.

I worked my way back to them. "'I shot him,' she told Constable Nagler. 'Why?' he said. 'He raped me,' she said. She didn't say, '*Because* he raped me.' No, hers was a simple statement of fact, likely prompted by the fear he'd been about to attack her again. It was a response without context, because if she'd blanked out and had no memory of firing that rifle, she was cut off, denied a chance to clarify, to explain it was an accident, a wayward shot, a warning shot . . . or a startle response to a loud rifle report from the back acreage."

I gradually turned up the volume: "She was not given a chance to plead her case because those two Johnny-on-the-spot constables were shut down, ordered not to say another word to her. And when their superiors arrived, Sergeant Trasov, Corporal Delisle, they were muzzled too. Because of orders from know-it-alls who thought they were smarter than the dedicated men and women of the Fort Thompson RCMP detachment."

This was an issue intended to push Rummy Wilcox's buttons. All I got was scorn. *Who do you think you are — Gregory Peck? James Stewart? Your lawyer act stinks.* I did have fans elsewhere — from the pews came what we would call, in colloquial expression, positive vibes. Clara looked vaguely awestruck. "How arrogant!" she'd said of my plan to go it alone, without Angelina co-starring.

It was time to unpack the standard forensic weaponry, and I held forth for several minutes about the presumption of innocence, the Crown's burden of proof, its duty to clear the high hurdle of proving guilt beyond a reasonable doubt.

"The defence, however — and His Lordship will tell you this — the defence needs only to raise a reasonable doubt. And I've offered you a full platter of them. Pick and choose, folks, and after you sample those, here's the main course. Let me frame it as a question: How could any rational human being be sure that the bull's-eye shot that dispatched Fred Trudd came from the weapon of a frightened, fumbling young woman who'd never before fired a gun?" My face expressed astonishment that anyone could dare take up that challenge. "No, sir. No way. The killer was an expert marksman, an assassin driven by anger and revenge . . . or motivated by a hefty down payment on a contract to kill."

Ranjeet Singh gave me a big smile as I slowly strolled silently back to the counsel table, then paused behind Santorini. "Did you begin to sense, as I did, that the prosecutors didn't believe in their own cause? That they realized, as this trial ground on, that they'd charged the wrong person?"

I set a friendly hand on Eddie's shoulder. "We've had a few bruising battles over the years, Ed Santorini and I, and we had a good tussle here, but I can promise that after this trial is over, he and I will shake hands and share a drink. Jean Béliveau and Bobby Hull didn't hold grudges after they fought for the Stanley Cup last May. Russ Jackson and Ron Lancaster will again be friends after tomorrow's Grey Cup." I gave Ed's shoulder a brotherly squeeze.

"So I hope my learned friends don't take umbrage when I submit they hadn't reckoned on the prospect of a second, almost simultaneous rifle blast coming from the echoing hills. It came to them too late that an expert marksman had been hiding out there, an assassin who'd watched the interplay between Angelina and her rapist, and who seized an opportunity."

I had a gift bag of shiny proofs, and hauled them out one by one.

Air ace Ned Best's best effort: "'And that's when I heard the shots, clear as day. Two shots, I would say from a high-powered rifle.'"

The slug in the siding that I'd shown Melquist, the listing realtor, who'd scampered off to tell Hortense and Donalda. Days later, it was painted over. "Them splinters looked fairly new," Ryan Klymchuk testified.

The testimony of ballistics expert Corporal Holtz, who'd traced a straight line of fire from a clump of spruce directly to that slug.

I posed to the jury my favourite scenario: the sniper fired first, causing a startle response in Angelina, a jolt that caused her trigger finger to tighten convulsively.

"Ladies and gentlemen, you haven't heard a spot of proof that Fred C. Trudd turned his back to Angelina. The notion that he was so proper and modest that he would turn away from her to relieve himself beggars belief. He'd been imbibing heavily, according to the serologist, and we all know how strong drink fosters reckless behaviour and false courage. If he was afraid, if he thought she meant business, yes, he might have turned around — to run like a jackrabbit, not to take a piss." A gasp and chortle from the press section at my daring use of a garden-variety vulgarity.

"And though these shots were fired at high noon, this wasn't a cowboy movie, and it sure didn't star Gary Cooper — but in the Westerns I devoured as a teen, bodies were flying all over as six-guns blazed. So it sure doesn't take much imagination to believe that a modern, high-powered hunting rifle would send a victim spinning like a top before he sprawls face down."

The wall clock told me I'd taken up half the morning. So far, so good — I hadn't heard anyone snoring. Eddie looked antsy, waiting for his turn.

I spoke briefly about Angelina's commitment to Fort Tom, "where this young lady chose to live, and work, and generously contribute to its well-being through her good works." After I tossed in some snippets from the laudatory affidavits filed by Father Larouche, I took a slow drink from my water glass, then a deep breath. Now I had to clamber over a few credibility barriers.

I conceded that the jury might have questions about Angelina's behaviour following Trudd's drunken assault. "Why had she stayed on for another two nights? Well, when you think about it, the answer becomes clear: she could not bring herself to run off and abandon her six furry little friends whom she loved so intensely."

But why had she armed herself? Again, I said, there was a good answer. "Imagine she's in the kitchen, and through the window she distantly spots a rifleman hightailing it down that dusty old track out back. It could have been anyone, a deranged person, a sexual predator, an armed robber — and remember, she's been in a distressed state — so she grabs the R 700."

This was the weakest part of my case. Was the jury in a buying mood? Another deep breath. "But unbeknownst to Angelina, the rifleman was actually an assassin. From a high outlook, he saw Trudd's Mercedes rolling down the Wolf River Road. But he hid in the bush just as the Mercedes roared up the driveway. And her rapist stumbled out, half-drunk, shouting obscenities and threats, advancing on her, unzipping, flaunting his foul weapon, taunting her. And two shots ring out, and the echoes bounce from hill to hill, and then the only sound is the sound of weeping."

And, as if cued, came that very sound from the gallery. Then a sniffle. I turned, saw more than a few eyes glazed with mist, and I let the moment play out as I meandered once more toward the jury box.

"Who is our assassin? We may never know. But what we do know is that the deceased regarded himself as the feudal lord to the several thousand hard-working men and women of Fort Tom whom he considered beneath him. What we do know is he had scores of enemies whom he'd scorned and insulted and mistreated."

I zeroed in on the foreman. "Councillor Wilcox, you've seen how Fred Trudd left a scar on the reputation of a famously hardy and warm-hearted community. You've seen how his greed and obstruction upended so much of the civic efforts expended by you and your fellow councillors." No reaction but that signature scowl. His dislike of me seemed oddly personal. But never surrender.

"Let's face it, folks, Fred Trudd was killing this town, evicting tenants, hiking rents, forcing shops and businesses to close. This once-thriving northern capital lost its popular Chinese restaurant, Ming's, because he doubled their rent." To Juror Three, a union stalwart: "You were here, weren't you, Mr. Wentzel, when he hired strike-breakers and tried to bust the Woodworkers local?" He nodded vigorously.

"And he treated the North's first peoples like dirt." Necks and shoulders swivelled as I gestured toward the back row, at Eric Sayaga and Johnny Blue, steadfastly monitoring this contest: the Queen, the white man's monarch, versus the Filipina maid. "He threatened and shouted obscenities at the leaders of the Native community as he tried to ram through a claim to harvesting rights on an ancient burial site."

I let that hot potato drop, did a quick shift: "But if you're looking at motives, ladies and gentlemen, you may want to look no further than Trudd's estranged sisters. Two angry, acquisitive women who tried to put this entire community on the auction block. Who in a surreptitious meeting with Hogey Johnson learned their brother intended to strike them from his will. And he would have done so — had he lived through the last weekend of May. Talk about a powerful motive. A multi-million-dollar motive. I don't think I have to remind you how they scrambled from this courtroom, reeking of guilt, and took the first flight out of town."

I could not, of course, avoid mentioning Donalda's husband, Connor Wyatt, who did time for dealing narcotics and for reckless, life-endangering use of a hunting rifle. "You might wonder, ladies and gentlemen, why he didn't come forward at this trial to deny he was the shooter. The Crown could have subpoenaed him, but maybe they figured that was too chancy, especially if Connor had no alibi for where he was at high noon on the last Sunday of May."

Santorini gave me the resentful look of one who feels unfairly victimized, but I felt no pity — he could have subpoenaed Connor in rebuttal, but then he'd miss his football game.

"Okay, let me wrap this up with a few last comments. I will admit I've not been kind to the deceased. I do not rejoice in his untimely death. No fair-minded person on this planet should celebrate the loss of human life. At the same time, many won't forgive Fred Trudd for the wounds he caused to this community, to its citizens, to his employees, to this young woman in the prisoners' dock. But she forgives. Angelina Santos forgives, because she has found, through her devotion to Christ, a compassion that is deep and rare and beautiful.

"And she is with child, and that child will be born toward the end of February. And if she is convicted of either murder or the included offence of manslaughter, and if she is sentenced to prison, that baby will be taken away from her. The government will take her baby. I urge you: *do not let the state take her baby*. Give her the verdict she profoundly and richly deserves: *not guilty!* And when Angelina Santos walks in freedom from this room, you will have done an act of great justice. Thank you, ladies and gentlemen, and God bless you."

1966 —
The Stanley Cup
Runneth Over

The fifteen-minute break had me bolting for the stairs, to the barristers' lounge, fleeing a pack of seekers of quotable quotes led by apex predator Charles Loobie. "No mention of her million-dollar baby?" he yelled. "Is that nothing? The jury's not supposed to know?"

Santorini came up the middle, a fullback in black robes, plunging through the line, pounding up the stairs, shouting, "No questions, damn it, I do my talking in court."

I made it to the men's room first, to the nearest urinal, but he was only a second behind, taking the adjoining one, mocking me as our distended bladders decompressed. "Who the fuck did you think you were fooling with that Stanley Cup horseshit? Jean Béliveau? Bobby Hull? Like you ever heard of them? You wouldn't know the difference between an NHL game and the Ice Capades."

"Did a little research. Canadiens beat the Hawks four out of seven. Hell of a series."

"Your Stanley Cup runneth over, pal, and it's full of shit. And when did you suddenly become Billy Graham? Oh, the great orator is also a big fan of cowboy movies. I bet you never got beyond Roy Rogers and the Sons of the Pioneers."

Just as we shook away the last drops, Clara popped in. "Break it up, cowpokes, holster your guns."

As she disappeared into a cubicle, Eddie grabbed his speech notes and fled to the lounge. I rolled up my sleeves, soaped my hands and face, felt my body unclench, the tension loosening. I'd done my bit, the best I could — maybe a little over the top, but the passion was real. I remembered, as I assessed the jury, thinking Smythe-Baldwin would be proud of his trainee.

But I reminded myself: be wary of the gremlins of overconfidence. They can stab you in the heart.

"You were stoked, man. That was evil." Clara joined me, touching up her hair, then reaching up, taking her comb to my lank mop. "Sorry I was such a bitch. Our first fight, and we haven't even made out. I was on offer, actually."

"The mood was hardly romantic."

"I decided you were modelling yourself on those athletes who won't have sex before the big game for fear of draining their prowess on the field."

I laughed. "You're shameless. Also outrageous." I felt a swelling, a rush of desire, and hurried away.

Predictably, Ed did his folksy shtick with the jury, seeking to come off as one of the boys, rambling about his early years as a small-town joe in the Fraser Valley farmlands and how he felt right at home here in good old Fort Tom, where people don't buy the guff fed to them by city sophisticates, where folks believe that right is right and wrong is wrong, and that's what this trial is all about.

Parroting me, he made a show of casting aside his notes, but then found himself going in circles, like a wilderness hiker who'd lost his map. He returned several times to his starting point: Angelina's "blunt admission" that she'd shot Trudd because he'd raped her. "That simple response of confession and revenge motive is all you need to know, friends; the rest is just a desperate effort by the defence to obscure the truth, to paint over what actually happened."

But later on he stumbled into a trap of his own making. Maybe he'd forgotten that his two discredited detectives, Biggs and Barnes, had practically been laughed out of court when they implied that Angelina had sold her virginity for $300.

Eager to show Angelina as less than virtuous, and in fact conniving, Santorini cast doubt on the "paltry evidence of rape," questioning her failure to raise a hue and cry. As to the sole evidence of a struggle — the torn nightie and panties — he said, "They could have easily been faked . . ."

At which point his tongue wobbled to a stop, maybe in response to a loud clearing of throat from the judge's bench. To give Kroop credit, he had given us free rein during our addresses — but now Santorini threatened to go off the rails. "If Mr. Trudd didn't rape her," Kroop asked, "where's your motive?"

Eddie's effort to detour around his faux pas was impenetrable. "Exactly, Milord. Ladies and gentlemen, I'm just throwing that out as something touched on by the homicide team. For what it's worth. Which isn't much. But you can't score a run if you don't circle the bases. Let me be clear. The Crown does not ask you to find that the accused was not a victim of rape. If indeed she was raped, it was a terrible thing. Awful. But that's no justification for murder."

As to whether the homicide was planned and deliberate, he waffled, broadly hinting that the jury might settle for manslaughter as a compromise. No surprise there — he would call that a big win, would claim swaggering rights.

But a manslaughter verdict was open to him only if he could persuade the jury that no second shooter was involved, so he accused me of creating a bogeyman, a "ghoul with a phantom gun." I had devised a defence based on speculation, not reason, and without reason there could be no reasonable doubt. The arresting officers had heard only one discharge of a rifle, and that should be an end of it.

As to Ned Best: "A great hero, but a lifetime of flying airplanes doesn't exactly improve your hearing."

Santorini joined me in avoiding the issue that had caused a media frenzy: the prospect of Angelina's child being born to riches. Too unclear, too dicey, the fallout unpredictable.

He concluded with a plea and a slap: "Smart folks like you, proud, down-to-earth citizens of the great Canadian north, you're not gonna be seduced by the honeyed words of a big-city lawyer. All his smoke and mirrors can't hide these six simple words: 'I shot him.' 'He raped me.' Confession and motive. It ain't complicated. God be with you."

It was almost noon. Kroop sent off the jury for an hour-long lunch. I wasn't hungry. I waited for the room and corridors to clear, hoping to make a quick getaway up the stairs, but my path was blocked by a platoon of media led by an attractive young woman.

"Barbara Frum. I string for the *Toronto Star*. Your mother, Dr. Mavis Beauchamp, wrote an op-ed for the *Telegram* calling for tightened immigration rules. You represent a young immigrant. Do you share your mother's views?"

"Her specialty is classical Greek, so she enjoys being a Socratic provocateur. Aren't we North Americans all products of immigration? Except, of course, our Aboriginal peoples."

A quick recovery, as Chief Sayaga worked his way toward me, hand outstretched. He thanked me, but the probing microphones and notepads dissuaded him from elaborating. He knew I had pulled my punches to avoid condemning his nephew. Did that earn me forgiveness from Gabriel Swift? Was he following this trial from the penitentiary cell that was his reward for my bungled defence?

We resumed sharp at one o'clock, with Wilbur Kroop rocketing along like a junkie who'd mainlined amphetamines. Hunched over printed text, he read out the boilerplate about the jury's duties with barely a gasp for breath. He wasn't a football fan and he was spouseless, but he seemed to want to fly out of here on the wings of Mercury. Maybe his guest house was crawling with spiders and bedbugs.

To be fair, he made a good effort to be just that: fair — in the sense that he didn't coddle the Crown overmuch or dismiss my pitch as the typical poppycock to be expected from Mr. Beauchamp. For some reason he instructed the jury not to consider the defence of self-defence, though I hadn't raised it.

Oddly, too, he told them to disregard media reports "that you may have inadvertently heard or read" about a mediation hearing at which threats were allegedly made to the deceased. That either confused the jury or affirmed their suspicion that such threats had indeed been made.

Kroop also left open a finding of manslaughter, a compromise that I'd begun to dread, an easy way out for the jury. He also shied away from the issue of Angelina's pregnancy, though he warned, in general terms, that emotion and sympathy must play no role in the jury's deliberations.

He wrapped up just after two o'clock with a reminder they had to be unanimous. They would begin their task immediately, break for an hour for dinner at their hotel, and continue their "scrupulous deliberations" into the evening "and however long it will take."

Neither Santorini or I took exception to his speech. Any complaints would be niggling, and we were both exhausted.

1966 —
Entrancing Views

After nine straight days of toil, I was finally able to enjoy the luxury of a free afternoon, though was at a loss how to spend it. I was tempted, on this brittle sunny Friday, to simply take a long country walk, maybe along the river, but juries often returned to ask questions and cellphones hadn't been invented.

My plans were made for me when Clara caught up to me as I unrobed in the robing room. She stuck her hand into my pants pocket, teasingly, I thought, then I realized she'd given me her hotel room key. "Enter by the side door and take the stairs. Eddie will probably be in the lobby pontificating to the press. I'll hang around a little, complain about my sore back, then come up."

I was less worried about Eddie than about Loobie, who suspected Clara and I were friends more intimate than learned. *Defence Counsel Beds Prosecutor During Murder Trial.* Exclusive by Charles Loobie. Still, the prospect of a rollick with this irrepressible woman was tantalizing. In mitigation, I was young, wilful, reckless, and randy . . .

◗

I found my Ford Fairlane plugged in behind the police station, where I'd parked the snowmobile — Buck Harris had obviously made the exchange. Was it only two months earlier that this bushy-bearded gentleman picked up a lost wayfarer at the Fort Tom airport? Buck and Lorraine reflected the generosity I'd come to associate with this brave, caring, struggling town. *It's the last frontier, redneck country, so stay out of the bars.* Who said that? Ah, yes, Professor Winkle, the tenured historian, who scorns rural living as narrow and parochial.

The note on the windshield instructed me to pop in to retrieve the keys from Mike Trasov. As he tossed them to me he warned I'd be ticketed the next time I rode a snowmobile into town. "Traffic bylaw."

"Defence of necessity."

"Heard you had 'em weeping."

"Tears of relief because I finally shut up."

He told me Angelina was setting up a long-distance call to her mother. Etienne was with her, counselling her on how to explain matters, so I assumed the trial had made the Philippine news. Given her mom's weakened heart, the situation was delicate. I would talk to Angelina at a more appropriate time.

Main Street seemed unusually alive with tension and bustle on this sunny Friday afternoon. Passersby wanted to chat, ask questions, and I had to politely demur. The Fort Hotel was only a five-minute walk away, and had been commandeered by the press, all the rooms taken. The side door wasn't available — Loobie was outside it, sucking up to columnist Al Fotheringham. Collar up, toque almost covering my eyes, I sneaked in through the beer parlour, and thence to the lobby staircase, while cameras, starved by the courthouse ban, scarfed soporifics from Ed Santorini about our founding fathers and the jury system and how lucky we don't live in the USSR.

I was gasping for breath as, powered by a pulsing libido, I raced up six storeys to the corner room from which Clara had promised "entrancing views of downtown Fort Thompson." I kicked off my wet boots on entering, and caught my breath. The blinds were down, and my entrancing view was of her, in a loose dressing gown, in the soft light of a bedside lamp. Not a word was uttered, not a *hi* or a *hello* as we came together.

She had showered, and smelled both fresh and fragrant. As I tried to shrug from my coat, she greeted me with an extended, open-mouthed kiss. I responded awkwardly, my arms trapped in my coat sleeves, while her hands danced about like a concert pianist's. I was only dimly aware, in the fog of passion, that my trousers and shorts had pooled about my ankles — until I tried to take a step, and stumbled backwards onto the bed. Clara was clutching me, and sprawled nakedly atop me like a bellyflopping diver.

Still struggling from the bondage of my coat sleeves, my nose rammed between the pillows of her breasts, I nearly jumped from my skin as the telephone screamed from the bedside table.

"Shit!" Clara reached over, knocked the receiver from the cradle.

A woman's distant, hollow voice: "Miss Moncrief, are you there?"

"Yes, damn it!"

"The jury has reached a verdict."

Arthur —
December 2022

Dear Taba,

I felt you should know I finally acceded to your urgings (in your role as Lisa Throckmorton, raunchy literary agent) to try my hand at prurient prose. It was merely a snippet of erotica but a disaster nonetheless. It will not, of course, survive a rewrite, let alone be hinted at in the final, printable product.

Nor will the participants be identified. Suffice it to say the burlesque featured a pair of Roman gladiators named Coitus and Interruptus. One, then the other, were seen flying down Main Street to the Fort Tom courthouse.

In response to your note, yes, the manuscript is rapidly moving toward a climax (having failed to achieve one orgasmically) in the form of a speedy verdict. For a jury to reach unanimous agreement within half an hour after retiring to consider a complex murder case is practically unheard of. I recall being in dread: Was some kind of craziness afoot? Had Rummy Wilcox hypnotized dissenters? Would psychedelic drugs be found in the jury room's coffee grounds?

On a less phantasmic note, Margaret and I were pleased to get your formal invitation to your wedding in May. Mr. Duffy seems like a sterling fellow, with his six-stroke handicap, vintage Saab collection, and exquisite taste in attractive, bright, artistic women. A lawyer to boot! Margaret wants you to know she's delighted beyond measure.

As it happens, I do expect to journey to Ontario in the spring, to Kingston, to attend the graduation ceremony of Ms. Rivke Levitsky, environmental warrior and feisty former client, and to wish her a brilliant career as a trial lawyer, though that is surely preordained. It will be a quick trip, and, sadly, won't allow for a detour to Niagara Falls to celebrate your union.

And now, I must time-travel back through the decades, to the reckless days of my young life, as I hotfooted it down Fort Tom's Main Street, bootlaces undone, one sock missing, shirt mis-buttoned . . .

1966 —
Unscrupulous Deliberations

The press corps had already taken flight to the courthouse, but cameras outside captured me in an unkempt, wild-haired state. Within, a court clerk complained she'd phoned everywhere. I mumbled about having taken a brisk hike, and repeated that to others as I escaped to the robing room.

Ed Santorini's locker was empty, so he'd already gowned up and gone. I found no solution to my missing sock except to turn my pant cuffs down, then with a great pretense of calm and confidence I ambled down to court. Clara had given me a thirty-second lead, but she must have flagged a ride, because here she was, nose-to-nose with Santorini in deep discussion.

The gallery was packed, and scores more thronged the lobby. Angelina was already in the dock, and looked relieved to see that I hadn't absconded in despair. I held her hand. "Your mother is well?"

"She's praying for me. And also she gives prayers for you."

"And I for her. There's no point in praying for a just verdict. Alea iacta est. The jury has decided. Be strong."

Kroop stalked in looking aggrieved, as if he'd been treated unjustly. I supposed he felt insulted by the jury's impertinence — they'd failed to undertake the "scrupulous deliberations" he had demanded of them.

"It appears the jury has quickly reached a verdict. Do counsel have anything to say?"

"So be it, Milord," said Eddie, with a shrug. He had given up caring. He would be taking his dad to the game tomorrow, that's all that mattered.

I too would be going to that game, though only to appease Hubbell. "Let us hear from the jury, Milord."

I would know their verdict before hearing it. I would know it as soon as they walked out the door. Their body language would speak for them. Tense juries are trouble. Relaxed postures signal they have voted to acquit.

Rummy Wilcox, the first in, was unsmiling. I felt my guts clench when he looked straight at me, with an expression of triumph. I shook off my spasm of gloom, however, as the eleven others trundled in loose and easy, smiling, and I suddenly felt weightless, a helium balloon, untethered. I had read Wilcox wrong — the expression was a show of ego; he wanted me to know he'd whipped everyone into line with a blunt, no-nonsense pitch to acquit, then engineered a quick, unanimous vote.

On being asked to render the jury's verdict, Wilcox spent a few moments spinning out the drama, then trumpeted, "We find the defendant not guilty!"

The room erupted with whoops, cheers, and scattered hallelujahs. Kroop's pro forma words of gratitude to the jury could barely be heard in the din. He managed to utter a few brisk words of appreciation to counsel, but showed no interest in reviving his threats to cite agitators for contempt of court. He had little to say to Angelina except that she was free to go, but she was paying no attention to him anyway: she had locked me into a hug. Ignored, unheard, unseen, Kroop vanished from the room like a ghost in the mist.

As I escorted Angelina from the dock, she dabbed away tears, then searched out friends from among the encroaching circle of well-wishers. Bursting through that circle came Johnny Blue, and a smile lit up her face like the light of the rising sun. He whispered a few words, and she kissed his cheek.

"That was fun." Eddie enclosed me in a bear hug, dropping his voice: "When I realized you were boffing my hippie junior, I knew I was doomed." He bounded up to the gowning room.

Clara hugged me too, while stuffing something into my pocket — my lost sock, I realized. She whispered: "Congratulations. You're famous now. Top dog at twenty-nine. Unreliable lover, though."

"Eddie suspects. He won't say anything, but maybe we need to slow down."

"Slow down *what?*"

"Put a little space between us."

She rolled her eyes and walked off. I'd handled that with my usual lack of subtlety.

While I addressed a curbside media scrum — the standard homilies about the triumph of justice, plus a plea to allow Miss Santos peace and privacy — she was in the police station gathering her belongings. Father Larouche, Marsha Bigelow, and Mike Trasov then joined me in spiriting her out the back way. The media numbers had dissipated anyway, with late afternoon flights lined up on the tarmac.

Trasov drove us to the rear of Marsha's rooming house. Angelina's ground-floor suite, kept empty for the last six months, was accessed by a private entrance just off the alley, and was spotless clean. Kitchenette, bathroom with tub, single bed, a wall of snapshots.

Etienne and Marsha would stick around to see to Angelina's needs, but I had to ready myself for an early-morning flight and could stay only long enough to guarantee that her legal needs would also be met. I explained that my best friend, Hubbell Meyerson, an expert in both commercial law and wills and estates, had played a quiet role for the defence. He would lead her through the entanglements of Trudd's estate and represent her interests and those of the child she would bear.

"But I will see you again, yes? I want you to meet my baby." She studied me with a wry grin. "Little Arthur."

"I can't imagine she will enjoy being called Arthur." We all laughed, but I felt honoured.

I spent the next few hours packing up in the cabin while fielding congratulatory phone calls from the office: Alex Pappas (I could hear him grit his teeth); Roy Bullingham (promising me a sixteenth-floor office with a southern exposure), and Hubbell (he'll pick me up at the airport if he isn't too hungover after tonight's riot, which he assured me was a traditional Canadian sporting event).

I invited Buck and Lorraine for dinner at Rustlers, then made a few calls of my own, all to Clara, who was not in her room or not interested in talking to me. She saw me as unromantic, a coward, backing off. Or maybe she'd written me off as erotically hopeless: as the jury prematurely ejaculates, Stretch becomes Shrink.

As evening fell, I took a last buzz around town, turned in the rented car, and checked out the Fort's pub and lounge: no Clara. I was beginning to realize I was a little stuck on her.

I showed up at Rustlers early, and settled onto a barstool to await the Harrises. The TV set was showing, live, Vancouver's pre–Grey Cup parade — how odd, I thought, to stage a parade at night.

Before I could order, a double malt whisky appeared in front of me. "Hogey forgives you," said the bartender. And there he was, Hogey Johnson, at his regular roost, back in action, so to speak. He beckoned me over. I took a slug of my Glenmorangie for courage, then had a disquieting moment as I recognized the gentleman seated with him — jury foreman Rummy Wilcox.

Glass in hand, I worked my way slowly to their table, pausing to accept a few friendly words or handshakes from people I'd never met. I took the offered chair, observed that Hogey and Wilcox were toiling through a shared bottle of Rémy. I hadn't anticipated — though it made sense — that they might have been friends of long standing.

Hogey lightly punched my shoulder. "No hard feelings, young fella. Did what you had to do, even if you trashed the lives of a few folks on the way. I ain't going to whine. The cottage on a tropical beach was only a pipe dream anyhow. But Hortense and Donalda, maybe they deserved better than being treated like pariahs, or worse, murderous schemers."

Wilcox chimed in: "You won't see me weeping over those two dames. But they didn't top my list of suspects, because I couldn't see them, or even Connor, committing fratricide. Myself, I figured it was that Indian hothead who went after Fred Trudd, what's his name — Blue, Johnny Blue. 'I'm gonna kill you,' it was all over the radio."

Kroop's warnings had gone unheeded. No surprise. But this was a dicey conversation — what was said in the jury room stays in the jury room, under Canadian law.

"Couldn't figure why you didn't make hay with that one, counsellor, you just let it drop. Not that it mattered in the end, because someone sure as shooting plugged Fred, someone who knew what he was doing, and it wasn't some simple-minded Oriental immigrant chambermaid who wouldn't know an R 700 from a broomstick handle."

He cracked a smile, enjoying his rhetorical prowess. Until that point, I hadn't realized he was capable of smiling, though I wasn't surprised by the overlay of bigotry. I swallowed my whisky, searched for an excuse to make a quick getaway. Charles Loobie had just dragged in a suitcase, and was on the phone, calling for a taxi, I assumed — would he be my saviour?

Wilcox wasn't through with me. "By the way, counsellor, Professor Mavis Beauchamp, I heard she's your mother. The local rag ran a reprint of her opinion piece in the Toronto *Tellie* slamming our open-door immigrant policy. Good for her, and good for you for inheriting her smarts. Close the floodgates. We got enough problems with the French, let alone inviting Mau-Mau rebels and Rastafarian dope-smokers and draft-dodging longhairs."

For the first time in recorded history, I welcomed a sudden intrusion by Charles Loobie, who sidled over to us, shot glass in hand. I'd never seen the ace reporter take more than a nip, but he seemed well lubricated that evening. "Hey, pal, I'm saying sayonara to this shit town . . ." He paused, recognizing Hogey, then Wilcox, and tried to be funny: "Jeez, sorry to butt in while you're paying off your foreman and your prime witness —"

He got no further, because Wilcox clambered to his feet, grabbed Loobie by his jacket collar, pulled him forward almost nose-to-nose, and shouted, "This shit town doesn't abide shitheads. Get the fuck gone!" He sent Loobie flailing over a wooden chair, landing on his backside.

Yelling, "I was only joking," he was hustled out with his suitcase, apparently uninjured. I wanted to applaud, but contained myself, escaping to my reserved table as Buck and Lorraine Harris made a welcome appearance.

Marsha joined us for a while that evening, and we happily rehashed highlights of the trial. Flickering in the background were TV images of the predicted Vancouver riot: bottle-throwing, drunken idiots being hauled off to paddy wagons. I was inspired to remain relatively sober, though I had much to celebrate.

I was in bed by ten, awake at six, and aboard my flight by half past seven. Fort Tom's patchwork of streets, severed by the winding, frozen Wolf River, came into full view as the DC-4 banked. There was the mill, there the courthouse, there the Fort Hotel, and across the river, Trudd's empty house and the valley of the echoes.

I felt a sadness I could not account for as the town faded behind wisps of cloud and vanished from my view.

The Trials of
Arthur Beauchamp

Excerpt from Chapter Three,
"A Will to Die For" © *W. Chance*

The Santos case has been heralded as the great breakthrough trial
for young Arthur Beauchamp, emblazoning his name firmly in
the headlines. For him, it was also a triumph of grit and self-
redemption. He had been tempted to stoop low, but won honourably.

Arthur's spectacular win and the acclaim he received had a
startling repercussion. As I have pieced it together, it all began
when an investigator for Herb Macintosh's mining conglom-
erate tracked down Beauchamp during the Grey Cup game at
Vancouver's Empire Stadium. What Beauchamp was doing at
a competitive sporting event is beyond this author's comprehen-
sion — as retired BC Supreme Court Justice Ed Santorini[3] put
it — "he wouldn't know a goalpost from a lamppost."

Macintosh, who had booked a block of seats for friends and
family, met with Beauchamp at halftime, over hot dogs. The
tycoon made an offer that few sane defence counsel could refuse,
even though his murder trial was only ten days away. The figure
was reputed to be in the area of $200,000 (almost two million
in today's bucks), overtopping the hundred-thousand retainer
offered to Alex Pappas.

---

3   As portrayed in *April Fool*, and ref. *Needles*, both available in all formats.

Sources who need not be named (and who do not include the tight-lipped subject of this biography) are of the view that Pappas succumbed to a clash of egos — he'd irritated Macintosh with his cocky, slapdash manner. Nor was the demanding client pleased with Pappas's lazy shifting of pre-trial duties and brain-work to his junior, Lev Shapiro.

On Monday, Macintosh and his legal advisers met with senior partners of Tragger, Inglis. The deal was struck: Beauchamp in, Pappas out. And not just out of the trial, but out of the firm — he stormed off into the December rains to set up a private practice.

Beauchamp would not be starting from scratch, because early in the autumn he'd interviewed scores of witnesses, including the two dozen guests, plus staff, who'd been at the wild soiree in Macintosh's North Shore eyrie. He had also drafted several legal opinions on issues likely to arise at trial.

He'd already had a long, private session with Macintosh, rehearsing him for the witness stand, in the course of which a friendly rapport developed. The garrulous multi-millionaire admired Beauchamp for his flaunting of societal mores at that fabled carousal at the Penthouse Cabaret. An item in an under-ground journal had Macintosh hailing Arthur for shocking puritanical Vancouver "by dancing off with the two most luscious working broads in the Penthouse stable."

Sadly for sensation-seekers, the so-called Trial of the Century fizzled out — mostly thanks to Beauchamp's mastery of the art of fizzle. A common kitchen knife, not a Samurai sword, turned out to be the likely murder weapon. The judge granted Beauchamp's motion to disallow evidence showing the sword was smudged with Macintosh's prints.

The Santos case had honed Arthur's skill at running a whodunit defence, that is, his tactic of offering up multiple suspects. Under gruelling cross-examination, eight guests, a chef, and the senior housekeeper were shown to have harboured intense dislikes of the imperious Mrs. Macintosh. That the accused shouted in a crowded room, "Somebody free me from this damned whore," was not enough to convict him. Nor were the bloodstains on his shirt of much weight, given his proneness toward nosebleeds, as noted in his medical records.

As the trial ground on toward Christmas week, the demoralized Crown realized its case was beyond repair, and entered a stay of proceedings. The world should then have been Arthur's apple — he rose to the sixteenth floor, replaced Pappas as head of the criminal section, and savoured the not-too-distant prospect of a partnership.

But his worst enemy — his growing addiction to alcohol — still haunted. During the Christmas holidays, after the collapse of the Macintosh prosecution, he went on a binge that coincided with the announced· engagement of Clara Moncrief to rock-and-roll impresario Hugh Gracey[4]. Rumours that Beauchamp had pursued her romantically seem not without substance, but, regrettably, aren't verifiable. Unaccountably, she declined to assist in my endeavours despite my many overtures by phone, text, mail, and even going out of my way to ring the doorbell of her lovely home in Orillia.

Meanwhile, lurking in the wings was the ravishing Annabelle Maglione, who a few years hence would have Arthur enslaved to an obsession that some call love.

And then he crashed. But that's another chapter . . .[5]

---

4   Ref. *Snow Job*, as the Hon. Clara Gracey, formerly married to Hugh Gracey.
5   See: "The Skid Road Years." Ref. *The Dance of Shiva*, available in softcover and as an ebook.

Arthur —
April 2023

E *nslaved to an obsession that some call love.* What claptrap. The obsessor is Wentworth. He is infatuated with my mid-life crisis, delights in grinding his alleged hero into the dirt. He seems particularly fixated, in a masturbatory way, on my alleged three-way frolic with those "luscious working broads."

His summation of the Macintosh trial suggests it was a frolic too. A fizzle! It was damned hard work, and in no way soul-satisfying. As to Clara . . . Forget it.

Suddenly, it is spring again, a gorgeous day, sunbeams penetrating my cabin. Why am I not out hiking or fishing? Why am I grappling with Chapter Forty-Six, blindly hoping I can conquer writer's block? It came upon me suddenly, after I reached the end of the Santos trial, and had no transcripts to guide me. Yet there are post-trial gaps to be filled, so I'm plowing through the old *R. v. Santos* files, hoping to reawaken memories.

Here's a memo from early December, 1966, which Hubbell wrote after he came back from three days in Fort Tom. His role as Angelina's new counsel was well received. "I felt I got a fairly good handle on things." Here is a copy of his petition to appoint the government's public trustee to manage Trudd's estate for the benefit of Angelina's child. Hubbell got his order over the protests of the Trudd sisters. Eventually, they were paid off— Hubbell engineered a two-million-dollar settlement to avoid litigation.

The public trustee has since extended powers to Hubbell and Angelina to administer Trudd's former holdings: selling, renting, renovating real estate, maintaining the town's main industry, the sawmill. All subject to government overview. A rail line from Fort St. John that was in the works had investors planning to reopen some iron mines. All good news.

Flipping through the file marked "Aftermath," I see a stapled note, reminding me that Angelina phoned me on the morning after she gave birth. Aretha Santos, eight pounds, three ounces, arrived on the evening of February 23, 1967, nine months less six days from her impregnation.

I remember how joyful she sounded: the birth went well, and she was hardly fatigued. And she was funny. She chided me for having a name, Arthur, that didn't easily transpose into a girl's name. "Aretha" was her closest match.

I demanded photos. I told her to give my love to all. I promised I would visit. But it was not until Saturday, June 21, 1969, that I journeyed again to the Northlands. The occasion was to celebrate Angelina's wedding to Johnny Blue.

1969 —
Summer Solstice

I had chatted with Angelina, by long-distance and mail, and Hubbell had filled me in after his trips to Fort Tom, but I wasn't expecting the mother to the heir of Trudd Enterprises Inc. (renamed Northland Mills and Realty Ltd.) to be so . . . in command? So confident, so competent. So hip.

It was the longest day of the year, a golden morning in a cloudless sky. As I stepped off the plane, she ran to embrace me — in a miniskirt and a pullover. She hadn't had time to shower and dress, she explained. She'd been up late at a ladies' bachelor party, and was slightly hungover. Hungover? Angelina?

At any rate, the wedding, at the Holy Rosary Church, wasn't until mid-afternoon.

She chatted merrily as we carried on to the parking lot. "I'm so happy you could make it to our little shotgun wedding."

"Shotgun?" A colloquialism misused, I thought.

"I'm two months pregnant. So we decided to get hitched quick. That wasn't Plan One — we were going to wait. Johnny has one more year of law school."

"Just be happy you found love." That sounded plaintive. (I had found love, in Fort Tom. But love hadn't found me.)

"We fell for each other during the trial, Arthur. He sent me notes. I'll bet you didn't know that."

I didn't. But I had seen their signals to each other: the smiles, the waves, hands pressed to hearts. Their friendship, if not their romance, had bloomed during their volunteer work at the food bank. *He liked me. He said I was almost Indian.*

I had yet to meet Johnny Blue, though I had followed his career. In 1967, he was accepted at the University of Saskatchewan law school, with a bursary. His grades were impressive, and he served on both the hockey team and the debating team.

Angelina was now a Canadian citizen, and a popular figure locally, as evidenced by the waves and friendly words from those in the terminal and out in the parking lot. If Hubbell was to be believed, a lowering of Trudd's oppressive rents has encouraged talk of her running for local office.

On first glance, Angelina's sedan looked oddly out of place among the beaters and pickups in the lot. Trudd's Mercedes, I realized. "I usually use the truck, but this is a special occasion. This is my mother, Lana, and this little troublemaker is Aretha." They were in the back seat. I was invited into the front.

Lana looked to be in her mid-fifties, and seemed rather robust for one who'd been struggling with a weak heart. She was quite buoyant, expressing her delight in meeting me while bouncing two-and-a-half-year-old Aretha on her knee. The little girl looked far more Santos than Trudd: a healthy, squirming tyke with light copper skin.

I said something about beauty running through the family, and Angelina called me a smooth talker, and we headed off to town. Fort Tom seemed much unchanged, though busier, happier, enjoying the start of its short summer. "GRAND REOPEN-MING," shouted the banner above the door of Ming's Restaurant.

Scaffolding was still up at the rear of the Fort Hotel, which was being refurbished — Hubbell had wangled money from a government program to enhance historic structures. There was now a Grand

Dame look to it, the stone facade scrubbed clean, canopies over the sidewalk, the front entrance widened, with a rotating doorway.

A uniformed doorman greeted me, and a bellhop seized my bag from the trunk. "The Queen Victoria Suite," Angelina called. "He's already registered, Morgan, so take him straight up. Everything goes on my account."

The lobby had been revamped: an extended gallery, chandelier, tropical plants, plush furniture. I peeked into the cavernous restaurant. Gone was the awful mural with the fur traders and the fawning Natives. Instead, a Subarctic panorama, a mountain valley, caribou on the move.

The spacious, luxurious Queen Victoria Suite, on the sixth floor, comprised two formerly adjoining rooms. The view from the balcony window was familiar, though summery, not blanketed with snow. A king bed had replaced the double on which I'd collapsed, with Clara Moncrief sprawled atop me, smothering me between her breasts.

Johnny Blue seemed unduly shy and awkward when we finally clasped hands. We were among two dozen guests loitering on the sunlit lawn in front of the church, waiting for the ceremony. When he spotted me, he butted a cigarette, took a deep breath, adjusted his ceremonial robe, and strode over to introduce himself.

I told him he was a lucky man, in that his fiancée was lovely and warm-hearted, in addition to being a very bright woman and a wily business manager.

Angelina was on the church steps, looking on approvingly as her mother tied ribbons in Aretha's hair. "A great mom too, Mr. Beauchamp," Johnny said. Beech'm, pronounced correctly. Commendable.

I asked about his plans after graduation.

"Aboriginal rights. Criminal defence. Doing my bit to save the planet."

Even more commendable. "We have an excellent articling program at Tragger, Inglis. I can probably get you in."

He thanked me, but he would be returning to Fort Thompson to article so he could be with his wife and children. I hastily agreed that was the right decision.

This was an oddly difficult conversation — he was polite, but clearly nervous. Maybe he still felt embarrassed by the headlines three years ago about his obscene death threat at the mediation hearing. I wasn't going to raise the topic. Nor would it be proper to ask him, on his wedding day, why he hadn't reached out to me in support of Angelina at the trial.

I tried for a light tone. "Am I to believe, as Angelina insists, that you two fell in love in the courtroom?"

He reacted with what seemed a smile but could have been a wince. "That's Angie's romantic version, but . . . we were already fond of each other. We didn't date, but we were friends." He fiddled with another cigarette while measuring his words. "I think my protective instincts were triggered when that sadistic prick got boozed up and messed with her, physically groped her . . . I realized then that I really, really cared for her. And then at some point . . ." A shrug. "Call it love." He lit that cigarette.

I apologized for being so intrusive, and wished him and his bride a long and joyful life together.

Behind me, I heard, "Daddy, catch me!" and turned to see pink-frocked Aretha running toward us. Johnny quickly tamped out the cigarette, scooped her up. She pinched his nose. "No smoking, 'member?" He lifted her onto his shoulders and set off for the church.

Eric Sayaga joined me. He was in jovial spirits, urging me to turn my visit into a holiday, with a river run to the new provincial park that incorporated the old-growth forest Trudd had threatened to clearcut. The Tribal Council had developed a campsite there, near the ancient burial grounds.

I was tempted, but I'd been retained handsomely for a complex trial due soon, an alleged pyramid scheme. I especially didn't want to miss a scheduled interview with a vivacious Crown witness whose claim to have lost her shirt had prompted erotic imaginings. Her name was Annabelle Maglione, a set designer.

I blinked the dream of her away, as Etienne Larouche opened wide the church doors and summoned us to come in.

Fortunately for me, given my state of drunkenness, the reception was held in the Fort's dining hall, so I was only an elevator ride away from my bed. The last I remember, I was standing on a chair, reciting from *Twelfth Night*: "What is love? 'Tis not hereafter. Present mirth hath present laughter . . ."

The chair went over, but Mike Trasov caught me before I landed on my face. He then bundled me up to the sixth floor and into my room. Mike was retired from the Force and doing security work for the hotel. Earlier, we'd talked about Fred Trudd's murder, and as I remember he didn't seem to care if it was ever solved.

Mine wasn't the only clown act of the evening — Hogey Johnson, during a toast, lost control of his whisky-on-the-rocks and it emptied into the cleavage of a maid of honour. Hogey will somehow survive that catastrophe, as he has others — Angelina had a soft spot for him, and had hired him to attend to the routine legal needs of Northland Mills.

Sibyl Frick, his former faithful secretary, was now filling that role for Angelina, and enjoying a hefty raise in income. I still felt guilty that I took advantage of her, but she hugged me and we laughed over our gruesome dinner date. She reminded me that I'd apologized enough, by sending her two dozen roses post-trial.

In the morning, I bore my thumping hangover to Rustlers for a breakfast of flapjacks, coffee, and aspirin tablets, joining Angelina and a half-dozen of her friends, many of them sharing my morning-after pain. But we had a merry time recalling the many turns and twists from those frantic ten days of my last trip to Fort Tom.

Etienne made a courtesy visit, but soon had to hurry away for Sunday mass. I'd hoped that my few minutes with him might offer divine illumination about who did in Fred Trudd, but he said, flippantly, "God knows." He didn't seem bothered that God wasn't sharing.

I picked up the tab despite protests from Angelina and Marsha, then exchanged farewell hugs, but was foiled in my effort to call a cab for the airport. Buck Harris's big crew cab was backed up to the front door, eager to carry me away. The "Better Dead than Red" bumper sticker had survived, but another one, more upbeat, had joined it: "The Far North — the Future Is Forever."

Buck ordered me into the passenger seat, insisting that a proper closure to my visit would have him returning me to the airport in the same truck that had borne me on my first visit to Fort Tom.

I didn't feel a sense of closure. The whodunit that was *Regina v. Santos* had not ended satisfactorily. I felt a hollowness over that, a sense that it would never be solved, that its threads would dangle forever in the breeze.

That hadn't bothered Mike Trasov. I told Buck it was odd that a long-time senior cop would just shrug off cracking an infamous murder case, and allow it to grow cold.

"I'm with Mike," Buck said. "Let it be."

Arthur —
May 2023

"Let it be? That's your *ending*? A lyric from a sappy Beatles song?" That was the reaction of my acquiring editor, Ellaine, in her critique of my final draft. She tagged countless other issues in need of repair, in what she claims is a life-saving effort to rescue my memoir. She let me know her reputation as a literary sharpshooter is at risk because she'd gambled on me, signed me to a quick contract. I felt the advance was reasonable, though what did I know?

My cynical life partner thinks they signed me up fast before I could send it around. "They didn't want this fish to swim away."

Ellaine loathes the title *Defenceless*, and has devised a far better one: *Longshot*. The not-very-dynamic ending is number two on her complaint list, so I will have to give it a big kick in the pants, rouse it into life. And that is what I'm setting out to do, on this, the anniversary of the last week of May, 1966, the anniversary of Fred Trudd's death.

I defy the glorious weather, reject Ulysses's pleas to walk the beach, and sit at my computer, mute my phone, remove other distractions such as bookmarked books and magazines, and begin tapping out my denouement:

Over the decades, I continued to see Angelina and Aretha in Vancouver — occasionally for business or pleasure, but often for unhappy reasons: a crisis in their family.

—

At workday's end, I have accomplished practically nothing. Ulysses gets his way, and romps down to the shale beach, checking on me occasionally, as if wondering why I'm moping along.

An annoying vibration in my pants pocket reminds me I have not unmuted the phone. Sometimes I forget to do that for hours, occasionally days. Also annoying is the little impatient light that tells me I have voice mails. Usually these are from online thieves, but the log of unanswered calls brings up "Arthur," and a number that, sadly, I recognize. Arthur Blue is in trouble again.

Yes, Arthur Blue is Angelina's second-born. Fifty-two years old now, and his life has been a downhill slog. Raised in Fort Tom, treated like a prince, a degree in Aboriginal Studies, a lackadaisical attempt at a wilderness tour business — funded by his mother — and then he drifted down to Vancouver, hung with the wrong crowd, got hooked on street drugs.

A sad but not uncommon story. His sister, Aretha, got all the glory: the child of rape whose mom valiantly resisted an accusation of murder. Since Angelina retired, Aretha smoothly runs the show, as president and CEO of Northland Mills and Realty.

I had declined official godfather status for baby Arthur Blue — I wouldn't have time to perform the duties. He is aware of that and it doubtless adds to his many reasons for feeling rejected. Out of guilt, I've defended him for free. Once for coke, once for smack, the last one for fentanyl. Each time, he avoided jail by agreeing to enter rehab.

His last call was ten minutes ago. In the process of getting through to him, I learn he's in the Customs and Immigration lockup, just north of Blaine, Washington.

"This is my one call, Arthur, I'm being held by Immigration until the real cops show up. It's a harrowing scene, man. I was down in Seattle with some bros, someone must've slipped a packet of feelgood into my overnight bag —"

I break in. "Muzzle it. Listen to me."

"Don't slough me off on Shapiro, okay? This one needs the master."

"I *am* sloughing you off. And Lev has health issues, so he's going to slough you off to a lawyer who is still practising. He'll see that you're represented in court tomorrow for a bail hearing. The bad news is you'll be held overnight."

"Aw, God, I know better than to bug you. I just . . . your number is filed away in my brain. And I've been in a fucking frenzy since Dad called. He had some bleak news about Mom. Worse than bleak. She has inoperable brain cancer."

Arthur —
May 2023

In his seventies, Johnny Blue remains a handsome man, and he's still practising, as senior partner in the firm he founded, Blue and Associates, LLP. As a fierce champion of Indigenous rights, he has argued several appellate briefs in the Supreme Court of Canada.

He picked me up at the Fort Tom airport in his hybrid Volvo, and having updated me on his great-grandfather status — Aretha's three offspring have produced seven more so far — he seems unable to talk about Angelina out of fear of choking up, and is mostly silent.

He'd poured out words yesterday, though, when I phoned him, struggling as he relayed a neurologist's diagnosis that his wife of fifty-four years has less than sixty days to live, as a tumour races through her brain. She has been released from hospital and is resting at their home, a full-time nurse in attendance, a doctor regularly dropping by.

When I told him about his son's latest predicament, he sighed, and thanked me for getting him counsel. "We spoiled him. No, that's too easy. It was my fault. I wounded him, crippled him. I made him ashamed of me."

I'd heard it before, but Johnny never explained why he blamed himself. I'm not sure if I want to know.

Yesterday, on learning I'd booked a morning flight up here, he said, "I'm grateful, Arthur. Angelina reveres you. And also we need to talk." Then, emphatically, "*I* need to talk. It's about paternity."

And here's his chance, and he can't seem to get it out, to repeat that tricky p-word; he's focusing on the road, his hands tightly gripped on the steering wheel as we pass by the new industrial zone, the railway yards and train station.

In this silence, I spin decades back to the jury's emphatic not-guilty verdict, Angelina's radiant smile as Johnny bolted toward her. I see him whisper in her ear, and see her kiss his cheek. *We found love during the trial.* Really? Or had they shared intimacies before her arrest?

Connections begin to snap together, fitting like tiles. *You fucking slimy Nazi pervert . . .* Why would he have called Trudd a pervert unless Angelina had told him about his indecent acts? He would have been in Pouce Coupe when Marsha Bigelow spread the word about Trudd's lewd behaviour.

Biggs and Barnes: had that matching set of smarmy sleuths stumbled on the truth? My notes from 1966 have Biggs, with his beery breath, leaning to my ear: "Trudd's one-night stand couldn't have got her pregnant. He had no viable seed. Two marriages over three decades plus a few short-terms, and no fruit from his loins."

Dr. Genevieve Royce, the prison doctor, advised that Angelina's hymen had recently been ruptured. How recently? On the night of the rape, May 29? Or some days before that?

Did I ever have consent sex with anyone, no, never. I was hundred percent virgin. Had Angelina lied to me? The thought is staggering. That I'd been taken in is unthinkable.

Johnny's voice intrudes, ghost-like. "You'll see some attractive changes here." He turns off the highway into a new community park surrounding the restored trading post. He parks, and we sit in silence awhile, watching toddlers in a playground and teens playing a mixed-gender softball game.

Then: "How goes your memoir about Angelina's trial?"

He's fully aware of my literary pretensions — I've consulted with him and his spouse about several murky details. "It's done, all but some tweaking and concocting a suitable closing note. I have a new title: *Longshot*. I also have a publisher."

"Congratulations." A deep breath. "Angelina has demanded that I be open with you. Will you undertake not to mention, in words spoken or written, what I am about to relate?"

Between lawyers, an undertaking is an enduring covenant. I can find no option but to agree. And I'm intrigued.

He speaks softly but clearly as he recalls events from 1966 heretofore unspoken. "One Sunday evening in early May, I walked her home from the food bank. We sat together and talked. About little things, growing up in different worlds, living different lives. Nervous chatter from a young couple unsure about how to engage, while they tingled with desire."

I smile, remembering my similarly awkward romantic moments.

"And then I kissed her, then we necked — is that still a word? We didn't get far, mostly heavy nuzzling. I couldn't figure out how to snap open her bra." A smile, finally. "And then she drew back a little, and apologized. 'It's not you,' she said. I realized I'd sparked a flashback — a couple of weeks earlier Trudd had groped her. Came from behind, scared her out of her wits. She was afraid of him. Then she gave me a lingering kiss and I told her I loved her, and I slipped out into the alley, out of view, unseen."

The pattern continued, and it was not restricted to Sundays. Johnny would come by on odd evenings, and they would talk and kiss and touch. Eventually neither could restrain their desire. He used condoms, mostly.

I was hundred percent virgin. She'd said that in such a jaunty way.

And then, on May 21, Trudd sneaked into the basement bathroom, pie-eyed, masturbating as Angelina exited the shower, grabbing at her as she brushed by. That evening, Johnny visited her in her flat, implored her to leave Trudd's employ. But she had accepted $300 as an apology and she showed up on Thursday to care for the cats. And was raped that night.

On Saturday, Trudd stomped out of the mediation hearing, back to his hotel. Johnny returned that evening, travelling by motorcycle, and went directly to Trudd's house. "It wasn't just a whim that took me there — Trudd had shown up drunk and in a rage, and I had an awful, nagging sense that he had done something to her. I parked the bike in the bushes. Only the cats knew that I spent most of the night there."

We watch as a girl takes a mighty swing at a softball and it bounces into the parking area. Johnny scrambles from the car, throws it back, calls: "Nice try, Peggy. Foul ball by inches."

On his return, he lights a cigarette, blows smoke out his window. I finally break the silence. "You did a DNA test?"

He nods. "Some years ago. Quietly, secretly. I am Aretha's father."

Johnny and Angelina reside in a spacious bungalow on the Wolf River Reserve. It's designed with Dene Nation motifs and nestles in the pines above a cascading brook. Aretha is here, spelling off the nurse, and she clasps me in a tight hug. Still a beauty in her middle years, endowed with her mother's smile and grace. And now I see Johnny Blue in her too, and I recall, during our occasional get-togethers, my puzzlement at her apparent lack of Trudd-ness.

Johnny confided that he'd shared his DNA test results with her, and with Arthur Blue, but no one else. Angelina didn't need to see the results. She knew all along that her daughter shared the genes of Santos and Blue.

I am led to the master bedroom, and left to be alone with her. This is one of those times that I thirst for strong drink. But there is no numbing of the pain as I look into Angelina's half-lidded eyes, her face blown up slightly with steroids, her lips curled in a determined effort to smile.

An exchange of kisses. A slightly hoarse, cynical voice: "Welcome to my death, Arthur."

"I am overwhelmed with sadness. You have earned everlasting happiness in the afterlife — that is my only solace."

"I wasn't a good girl, Arthur. I'll be lucky to graduate from purgatory."

"You have always believed in a forgiving God."

"Only my God and my lover knew I had sinned. Now our children know. And finally my famous lawyer knows. My famous lawyer who believed my lies. And who is bound to silence."

That's likely true. Fifteen months ago she waived, in writing, the solicitor-client privilege that would have bowdlerized my memoir, but our agreement surely doesn't extend to deathbed confessions.

"No, I was not a virgin. Not even close. Johnny and I made love sometimes three, four times a night throughout that crazy month of May."

I gently remove a cup of fruit juice from her trembling hands, and hold it to her lips. "And so your Aretha was born out of love. My mind is spinning."

"While mine just inches along." A self-mocking laugh. "Poor Arthur. You tried so hard to hide your shock that I could carry a rapist's baby with so much hope and love and joy. You were the innocent one, and I the schemer."

Those words take an effort, and she breathes heavily for a while. *I the schemer.* And what was the scheme? To deny Trudd's sisters their legal right to inherit his lands, business, and fortune? To enhance her chances for an acquittal? To deflect any suspicion that Johnny was involved in Trudd's death?

Her voice turns weary. "There was no other way. No other way. Forgive me. Forgive Johnny." She grips my hand, then lets go and closes her eyes. "I am so tired."

I stay awhile, daubing my eyes with tissues as she sleeps. Then I'm pulled away to join Johnny and Aretha and her three teenagers out on the patio, sharing lemon tea and gluten-free pastries, striving to lift our gloom by enjoying the sun and the view and the birdsong.

I lighten the mood with some funny courtroom anecdotes, and then it's time to go, and we all hug, and I head off with Johnny in his car.

I have some lag time before catching my return flight, so Johnny suggests we take a rest stop in town. Again, we travel in silence, and again I can feel Johnny's tension, his hands taut on the steering wheel. Something other than his wife's decline is deeply troubling him.

I look out across the surging Wolf River to the high-banked valley that was once the scene of Trudd's life and death, the house levelled years ago, condominiums sprouting up. Memories return, and an ugly fantasy teases me. Was Angelina working me all along? Had I been duped by her beatific charm, by her disguise, her role-play as a naïve domestic? The alleged precarious health of her mother: a charade to gain sympathy? Raped by Trudd, finding herself pregnant, did she plot to gain control of Trudd Enterprises by cooking up an inheritance scam? Or, even more ghastly, did she do so by making a false complaint of rape?

I shake off such absurd concepts. I will not fall victim to a conspiracy theory, the pervasive evil of our time.

Downtown, a modern greystone annex thrusts from the rear of the historic courthouse. The RCMP detachment has moved; in its place is a cannabis store. Where Rustlers once stood, a modern office building hosts a Tim Hortons and a Subway. Mercifully, Marsha Bigelow passed away before having to witness this fast-food invasion.

Johnny stops at a dockside café, just above high-water mark on the twisting, surging river. The Toscana, pizza and pasta. "Funky and interesting," he says. We take an outside table near a dock where boats are tethered.

Neither of us is hungry. Johnny orders a tall vodka and soda, and I settle for a cappuccino. Johnny lights a cigarette. A soft, warm breeze swirls the smoke. He stares forlornly at a flock of green-winged teal feeding in the rushes.

"There's more to it, isn't there, Johnny? It's not just about paternity." I raise my hand, a stop sign. "Don't say anything. I'll avoid being compromised if I do the talking."

He nods. He isn't my client; he knows I could be compelled by law to repeat his words.

"Angelina importuned me to forgive you, Johnny. I would if I could, but I'm not in the forgiveness business — unlike Etienne Larouche, who was deeply invested in it during his time on earth. I believe he knew. I think Staff-Sergeant Trasov knew too. Or strongly suspected. Buck Harris as well. 'Let it be,' they said."

Johnny takes a slug of his vodka, and chains a cigarette.

"And your son knew. Because you told him. That's what crippled young Arthur. That's what made him ashamed of you. He's still at war with himself: his love for you contending with his revulsion that his father was a murderer."

Johnny can't maintain eye contact. He stares across the river, at the valley of the echoes.

"I made a snap decision not to let Angelina testify, and thank God for that. Otherwise she would have defied God and state by perjuring herself. She loved you passionately, Johnny, and she covered up for you. You spent the night with her, the night of Saturday, May twenty-eighth, and afterwards she cleaned away every fingerprint, every hair, washed and dried every sheet and towel, got rid of every speck of you."

He loses some colour, sags a little. The body language speaks for him, speaks his truth.

"In the meantime, your motorcycle was hidden deep in the bush. Except when you needed it. 'I spent *most* of the night there.'

Your words, my emphasis. There was a gap of maybe an hour for a midnight run to the reserve, to the Band Office, to access the case of hunting rifles. And you returned, and in the morning you set up a kind of hunting blind, probably in that copse of immature spruce. And you waited. And waited.

"Did Angelina know you were out there? Did she know that you were armed and prepared to kill? I hesitate here, because I can only surmise. But my best bet is that you decided not to involve her in your plan — you didn't want to risk her being a party to murder, so you didn't tell her you'd stashed a rifle, and you made an excuse to take off for a while. And when Trudd drove up, there she was with his Remington, prepared to defend herself, by herself."

I stare at the swirling eddies, the bridge, the far bank of the river, concentrating, recalling the crime scene, placing myself there as a witness. "You had to position yourself so Angelina was not in the line of fire. Trudd paused to make a vulgar, defiant show of unzipping and pissing, and then you had him square in your sights. And then, to quote Angelina's mantra: 'Bang, bang.' She fired almost simultaneously, aimlessly, an involuntary reaction. And then she took the rap for you."

Johnny tosses back the rest of his vodka, and swallows hard.

"'I think I shot Mr. Trudd,' she told the dispatcher. Then, less ambiguously, to the cops: 'I shot him.' She lied to save your ass, Johnny. She lied because she loved you."

A tense silence, which I take to be affirming. We watch the flock of teal rise from the river and beat upstream. From a willow grove comes the flutelike melody of a hermit thrush. "Beauty is truth, truth beauty," Johnny says, his voice low, gravelly. "As the poet said, that's all you need to know."

The message is clear enough. We have a pact. I will not inform on him, or repeat my accusations publicly or privately, and they shall not appear in the pages of the memoir titled *Longshot*.

Johnny looks at his watch, his hand still shaking. "We should get off to the airport." He rises, wobbly. "Do you mind driving?"

2023 —
Afterword, Afterwards

Dear Reader,

This work is the product of a dream long held: to record the history of perhaps the most fascinating trial of my early years as a barrister, a long-shot defence that inspired the bold title on the cover. (I played with a reversal: *Not by a Long Shot*. But that would risk misleading even the most perceptive and diligent of my readers.)

Though I put heart and soul into its composition, and have been comforted by the reaction of first responders, many issues remain unsettled. Indeed, the death of Fred Trudd remains shrouded in mystery. It may never be known what his intentions were as he advanced on Angelina Santos on his driveway. We may never know where the bullet went that she fired, whether through her rapist's heart or wildly into the sky. Nor can we do more than speculate that a shooter was lurking in the scrubby valley of reverberating echoes. Or who that assassin might be, and whether his motive was greed or vengeance.

To that limited extent, I regret that my memoir lacks a sense of finality, and I can only, in apology, whisper these words of wisdom: Let it be.

Author's Note

This novel is loosely based on a murder attempt trial I defended in Northern British Columbia in my early years as a criminal lawyer. It featured a young housemaid, an abusive employer, a rifle shot gone awry, and one of the most vigilant juries with whom I've ever shared a courtroom.

I am indebted to Jan Kirkby for the many hours she devoted to smoothing out the bumps in the various drafts of this novel. I'm grateful as well to Wayne R. Powell, my former law partner in Vancouver, who scoured the manuscript and tagged and corrected various blips in the laws relating to wills and estates.